THE SELECTED LETTERS OF
MASTER DAIE SOKO

With Commentary by
VENERABLE MYOKYO-NI

The Selected Letters of Master Daie Soko
With Commentary by Ven. Myokyo-ni
© 2024 Michelle Bromley

Published with the support of Hokun Trust in association
with The Buddhist Society and The Zen Trust

Funded by The Hokun Trust
Charity No: 1129031

The Hokun Trust gratefully acknowledges the generous
contribution to this book provided by Tony Brignull,
student of the late Ven. Myokyo-ni.

ISBN: 978-3-7597-2420-5
Edited by Michelle Bromley and Eifion Thomas
Designed by Sandra Hill
Publisher: BoD • Books on Demand GmbH, In de
Tarpen 42, 22848 Norderstedt
Printed by: Libri Plureos GmbH, Friedensallee 273,
22763 Hamburg
Cover image: Master Daie Soko with kind permission of
Zuiho-in, Daitoku-ji, Kyoto

Hokun Trust
58 Marlborough Place
London NW8 0PL
Email: thehokuntrust@gmail.com
www.hokun-trust.org

THE SELECTED LETTERS OF
MASTER DAIE SOKO

With Commentary by
VENERABLE MYOKYO-NI

Fragrance
of the
Dharma
Hōkun Trust

THE BUDDHIST SOCIETY TRUST

THE ZEN TRUST

The Hokun Trust is pleased to support this volume of
The Selected Letters of Master Daie Soko
with Commentary by the Venerable Myokyo-ni.

Both Song Master Daie's letters and Ven. Myokyo-ni's commentaries make the
insights of the Buddha come alive and keep the teachings relevant and meaningful
for our present time. May they continue to encourage students of the Way and
appeal to a wider public as well.

Contents

This book, *The Selected Letters of Master Daie Soko* with Commentary by the Ven. Myokyo-ni, records the correspondence of Master Daie Soko (Chin. Ta Hui 1089-1163) to his disciples, all around China. It is a Ch'an work, or Zen as it is known in Japan, and was written during the Song dynasty (960-1279). This was a period in China of both unprecedented expansion, in agricultural output, population, and technology of all kinds, including gunpowder, as well as wide commerce, both within and outside China. The Song was also a time of violent armed conflict and turbulence, as the dynasty faced the ever-increasing incursions of the Mongols from the north.

However enormous the cultural and temporal differences between China of Song times and our life here in the West today, they shrink into nonexistence, as we realise the human heart has not changed at all, our hopes, dreams, and aspirations, remain unchanged, as does the longing for calm and stability, as well as joy, hope and trust.

Venerable Myokyo-ni's vivid commentary brings alive these letters of long ago, placing them right into the here and now. Solace and help, and wise advice abound in these pages, in easy everyday language. Helpful to students of Zen as well as understandable to the merely curious; all will find much to ponder here.

We would like to thank Michelle Bromley and Eifion Thomas for their enthusiastic support of this work. Without their enthusiasm these words would have remained available only to the few.

Desmond Biddulph
President, The Buddhist Society
London, 2024

Acknowledgements

We would like to thank Nikko Odiseos President of Shambhala for permitting our use of the text from *Swampland Flowers: The Letters and Lectures of Zen Master Ta Hui*. Translated by J. Christopher Cleary. [Selections from 瞿汝稷 Qu Ruji's (1548-1610) 指月錄 *Zhiyue lu / Records of Pointing at the Moon,* Vols. 31-32.] New York: Grove Press, 1977, Shambhala Publications, 2006.

As a student instructed by Venerable Myokyo-ni, it is a joy to see this book of Zen commentaries brought to publication. In this book, based on her talks, she gives encouragement and stimulation to those on or commencing the Zen Way.

These commentaries on Master Daie's letters by Ven. Myokyo-ni provide a comprehensive presentation of what is required for serious Zen practice and deepening insights. They offer the reader – whether experienced Zen student, an inquiring beginner or simply an interested observer – a number of pointers, elucidations and guidance on the effective practice of Zen Buddhism. Myokyo-ni instilled in her students that Zen practice was for daily life, giving ourselves into what is being done at this moment. She points to Master Daie's careful warning, that not only in our talking, but also in our thinking we have to keep to the practice, to the framework and not continuously allow our own ideas, our own passions, our own weaknesses, to obstruct and rule us.

Master Daie pointing the way tells us, 'Within the wondrous mind of the original vast quiescence – pure, clear, perfect illumination – there is not a single thing that can cause obstruction.' With this book the Way becomes clear and beckons.

Eifion Thomas

This present volume brings together two special offerings – on the one hand, excerpts from the letters of Master Daie Soko (Chin. Ta-hui Tsung-kao), a 12th century Chinese Ch'an master, and on the other, the commentaries on these by Venerable Myokyo-ni (1921-2007), a modern Western Buddhist teacher. And though their dates span many centuries, their teaching is seamlessly interwoven.

Daie Soko (1089-1163) became a monk at seventeen and studied with many teachers from different Ch'an schools, before becoming a student of Engo Kokugon (Chin. Yuan-wu K'o-ch'in) and eventually his Dharma-heir. Among Ch'an communities he became a widely renowned teacher, gathering many students around him, and before long he also came to the notice of officials in high circles of government.

But historically this was a tumultuous period of political upheaval in China, and Master Daie was often caught up in the repercussions of this social and political unrest. Though at times in his life he received imperial honours and was made abbot of prestigious monasteries, at other times he was also exiled for many years before being pardoned and reinstated.

Many of the teaching methods still used in Zen training today can be traced back to him; best known are his innovations to koan study. Believing that koan practice had been reduced to a mere literary study, he created a new more rigorous method of working with the key phrase of a koan as a theme for meditation. This shaped the further development of Rinzai Zen practice up to this day. But equally important is the legacy of his letters, which were very influential and widely circulated in his own time. These are addressed mainly to lay disciples who mostly came from the scholar-official class of Chinese society and held various positions in government service. With great care and compassion, he considers the concerns of each of his correspondents and offers individual advice, guiding them through all the various situations of daily life, from the hubbub of official duties and personal difficulties to the practice of meditation. He firmly believed that insight into the Buddha's teachings could be attained by all people, regardless of their social standing and daily activities. As well as being personal instructions for his students, each of Daie's letters is also a profound discourse on many aspects of Buddhist doctrine and practice. His letters are still used today in monasteries and temples as a guide for practice and inspiration. It was during her training at Datoku-ji that Ven. Myokyo-ni was first introduced to them in the teisho given by Sesso Roshi.

Ven. Myokyo-ni (Irmgard Schlögl 1921-2007) was trained at Daitoku-ji monastery in Kyoto, Japan, where for twelve years she worked under two successive masters: Oda Sesso Roshi and Sojun Kannun Roshi. Later she was ordained by Soko Morinaga Roshi at Chithurst Forest Monastery in England and became abbess of the London Zen Centre's two training temples, Shobo-an and Fairlight. Ven. Myokyo-ni's teaching style was very traditional and in keeping with the ethos of the teachers of her lineage. Beginning with Imakita Kosen (1816-1892), whose aspiration it was to bring Zen to a wider audience outside the monastery walls, she also adapted the temple training methods and regulations to the everyday lives of her predominantly lay students, with much emphasis being placed on the Daily Life Practice. The concern Master Daie shows towards his students and the guidance and pointers he offers for their practice is very much reflected in Ven. Myokyo-ni's relationship to her own students. Her commentaries were very down-to-earth, translating the teachings into practical examples and using a variety of teaching stories from different traditions as well as anecdotes from her own training in Japan.

Both Master Daie's Letters and Ven. Myokyo-ni's commentaries make the insights of the Buddha come alive and keep the teachings relevant and meaningful for our present time. These Dharma-talks were a great inspiration to all who heard them. May they continue to encourage others on the Way.

Editorial Notes

This book is compiled from a series of talks given between 2001 and 2006. The text of Master Daie's Letters used in this book is a selection from the translation by Christopher Cleary's *Swampland Flowers: The Letters and Lectures of Zen Master Ta Hui*, reprinted here with kind permission of the publishers Shambala.

As the Cleary text uses the Wade-Giles romanisation of Chinese words, this transliteration has been kept throughout Ven. Myokyo-ni's commentaries as well. However, as her own study of these texts was originally in Japanese, many of the masters referred to are given their Japanese names, including Ta-hui Tsung-kao as Daie Soko. Where necessary for clarification the Chinese name is given in parentheses. Occasionally Ven. Myokyo-ni also changed a word in the translation, these also appear in parentheses. The numbering of the letters corresponds to the Cleary translation.

Michelle Bromley

THE LETTERS OF
MASTER DAIE SOKO

With Commentary by
VENERABLE MYOKYO-NI

LETTER 1 to LI HSIEN-CH'EN

Buddha said, if you want to know the realm of Buddhahood, you must make your mind like empty space and leave false thinking and all grasping far behind, causing your mind to be unobstructed wherever it may turn. The realm of Buddhahood is not some external world where there is a formal Buddha. It is the realm of the wisdom of self-awakening.

Once you are determined that you want to know this realm, you do not need adornment, cultivation, or realisation to attain it. You only need to clear away the stains of afflictions caused by the alien sensations that have been on your mind since beginningless time, then this mind becomes as broad and open as empty space, detached from all the clinging of the discriminating intellect, and so your false, unreal, vain thoughts too are like empty space. Then this wondrous effortless mind will be unimpeded wherever it goes.

VEN. MYOKYO-NI'S COMMENTS

We are taking as our text the letters of Master Daie Soko (Chin. Ta-hui), who was one of the great Chinese Zen masters of the Sung Dynasty. He was born in 1089 and from the earliest age, Daie showed great interest and insight into the Buddhist teachings. He became a monk at the age of seventeen and had many teachers, but became Dharma-heir of his main master, Engo (Chin Yuan-wu).

But Master Daie lived in tumultuous times and was himself swept up in them, given the highest honours, then exiled, and later called back again. A big temple was built for him in the capital, and a special retirement temple was given to him at the end of his life. He knew life in all its forms and had many disciples, among them lay people of great standing as well as ordinary people, with whom he kept in correspondence. He died aged seventy-five.

Some of his letters and talks have been collected. His record is particularly relevant for us because he is mostly addressing lay disciples. My first master, Oda Sesso Roshi, was very fond of Master Daie's Letters and I heard two series of his teisho on them. For us here in England with but one or two enrobed, Master Daie, speaking mainly to lay people, comes closer to our concerns.

The translation of this text, excerpts of Master Daie's letters, is by J. C. Cleary, which is gratefully acknowledged.

In this letter Master Daie, like all Zen masters, tells his correspondent, and us, above all to empty the heart, to clear out all notions, ideas, likes, dislikes, etc. The Japanese term for it is *mu shin*, the empty heart.

'The Buddha said that, if you want to know the realm of Buddhahood you must make your mind (heart) **clear as empty space and leave false thinking and all grasping far behind.'** In empty space there is nothing. 'Clear' is a good translation here, because very often it is also translated as 'pure'. Whenever we come across the word 'pure' in the Buddhist texts, particularly Zen texts, we must not interpret it with our idea of 'pure' in the moral sense, for it always means 'empty'. In empty space there is nothing. The technical term for it is *sunyata* – this nothing is the beginning of the insight of a Buddha. As long as there are any thoughts whirling about, they are inevitably connected with feelings and emotions and passions, and all of them are created by I. And so, 'You must make your heart as clear as empty space, and leave false thinking and all grasping far behind.'

How do I make my heart empty as space? According to the basic Buddhist teaching, 'I' am a delusion, and so 'I' only needs to get out of the way. But since I cannot do this by an act of will, there are specific methods that can help us to do this and our Daily Life Practice is a well-tested one. If I really give myself into doing something, then I give myself away and therefore I am no longer there. To 'make your heart empty as space' then, is at the same time 'to leave false thinking and all grasping behind' because if the heart is empty, there is no thinking and no thinker! Nor is it that 'I grasp' but 'I am the grasping'. Just leaving all this behind is **'causing your mind** (heart) **to be unobstructed wherever it may turn.'** Without false thinking or grasping there is no rejection, so the heart is of itself unobstructed wherever it may turn. In the midst of the multitude of things, in the midst of the hubbub, the heart remains unobstructed.

This Empty Heart is also called the Heart Mirror. Old Chinese mirrors were made of metal and so as well as having to be dusted they had to be polished to a shine or they would quickly get dull. Such a mirror will reflect exactly whatever falls into it, without adding or subtracting anything. A mirror doesn't hold on to what it has just reflected and superimpose another reflection. Yet that is just what we do with our clinging, our notions and ideas, a multi-layered jumble which makes it quite impossible for us to see clearly. Hence the cleaning, polishing and keeping that Heart Mirror always bright is what Master Daie also suggests here.

And this is not something external as Master Daie tells us, **'The realm of Buddhahood is not some external world where there is a formal Buddha, but is the realm of wisdom of the self-awakened one.'** Talking about Buddhism and of the Buddha, these are only thoughts, for there is no external Buddha to whom we can turn. The real realm of Buddhahood is the realm of wisdom, opening to one who has awakened to his own nature.

In the Mahayana tradition the Buddha on his awakening says, 'How wonderful, how miraculous, all beings are fully endowed with the Tathagata's wisdom and power. But sadly, in the case of human beings, because of their attachments, they are not aware of it.' And so in the Heart Mirror the seeing is brilliantly clear and everything is seen as it is, the way it is. But sadly because of our attachments, our heart mirror is scrambled and we cannot do so. I may believe that I don't have that many attachments, but on looking very carefully, is that really so? Although most of us, are supposed to have settled into the Daily Life Practice, we cannot help our continuous thought streams. What are those thought streams about? Are they neutral or are they mostly to do with my likes and dislikes, with my planning how to make things easier and more convenient for me, or with what I would like to do and what I want to avoid? Once again, 'I' am not doing the picking and choosing, the picking and choosing is what I am.

It is the same with the attachments; it is not that I have attachments, I am these attachments. This is a hint of what it is that stains the mirror. For the heart to be unobstructed means that the mirror has to be clear. Master Daie says that **'Once you are determined that you want to know this realm, you do not need adornment, cultivation or realisation to attain it.'** This is the first condition. We first need to be really determined. If this realm of the Buddha, the wisdom of the self-awakened one, means little to me and I do not feel deeply moved and inspired, then we need not go any further. It needs a real determination, and once so determined, 'you do not need adornment and cultivation for realisation.'

Only one thing is necessary, and Master Daie repeats it again and again, **'You must clear away the stains of affliction from alien sensations that have been on your mind** (heart) **since beginningless time,'** that is, to clear away the *klesas*, the passions. These are the alien sensations, our wanting, disliking, annoyance, the whole lot. Since beginningless time they have stained the Empty Heart, not only in this life but they also affect the karma-linkage. When easily annoyed, or greedy, or whatever it might be, the job now is to clear away the stains of these alien sensations that afflict our heart. How are we going to do that?

Once again, we come back to the Daily Life Practice of giving ourselves into the doing, giving ourselves wholly into it, until giving ourselves into it and giving ourselves away are one and the same. Then the stains slowly begin to shrink, pale and wear out and as they begin to dwindle, then the heart **'becomes as broad and open as empty space, detached from and emptied of all the clinging of the discriminating intellect.'** It is not I who have to do something or get somewhere – all that is 'my' deluded thinking. 'I' have nothing to do in this, there is only the bundle of Aggregates, the Five Skandhas: 1) a physical one (the body) and four mental ones which are 2) feelings and physical sensations, 3) perceptions and thoughts, 4) the composite formations or *samskaras*, karma-engendered and karma-producing, and lastly 5) consciousness. Nowhere in that five-strand bundle can an 'I' be found. So, the Empty Heart is as wide and open as space, unattached, free of all stains. Even the slightest stain already distorts the mirror.

But to be detached from all the clinging of the discriminating intellect is extremely difficult. It is possible, though not easy, to come to terms with greed and anger, the 'outside objects', but to detach from clinging to the discriminating intellect is desperately hard. It is said it is as difficult as cutting through a thick lotus stem, resisting even the sharpest knife. And what is discriminating? Clear seeing beholds that there is light and dark, right and wrong, Buddha and Mara. Well, is that not discriminating? We have to be careful here: the Empty Heart sees clearly what is. But by immediately making value judgments such as beneficial or worthless, great or small, beautiful or ugly, the thing/object itself can no longer be seen. Rather we see only our discriminations and so want to have or to get rid of. That is the discriminating intellect.

As an 'I' we cannot see without immediate judgement and evaluation, we cannot see neutrally – and thereby hangs the whole story. It is not that everything is the same as it is so often mistakenly understood, for nothing is the same. Although ultimately it is the same, but practically on this level of the Two Truths, there is I and you, both human beings, but as for better or worse? Master Rinzai says, 'One sits on a mountain alone, one stands in the market place bedaubed by the dust of carts and horses. Who is front (better), who is back (worse)?' The late Ananda Maitreya in Sri Lanka was actually asked this question and replied, 'It depends on motivation.'

We cling, compelled by the discriminating intellect, and we 'know', 'This is better.' But there is nothing better or worse. This 'knowing' is what the clinging is. I may say, 'Well, if there is nothing better or worse, then after all I can go out and mug somebody and steal a fortune!' This is also the discriminating intellect doing an extra clever thing and trying to have it 'my way'. But there are the Precepts and there is our humanity, and it is not decent human behaviour to club someone over the head – though considering out collective history, sadly one might be inclined to think it is!

One cannot stress it too much that most of our difficulties come from the discriminating intellect, from false and unreal thoughts. When that is seen into and cleared out then, **detached from all clinging of the discriminating intellect, all the false, unreal, vain thoughts are but like empty space** and can no longer get hold of us. They may still flutter about, but they are now seen as false, unreal and vain and they become like empty space. Without the delusion of 'I', things just are as they are. It depends on us – our motivation. An old master said, 'The heart flows with the ten thousand things. This flowing is truly mysterious.'

Master Daie ends, **'Then this wondrous, effortless mind** (heart) **will be unimpeded wherever it goes.'** 'Unimpeded, free' and I may then think that I can do what I want. But real unimpeded freedom opens only when the discriminating intellect – that is the 'I'-delusion – has really dropped off and then there is only clear seeing of what is, the way all things really are, without liking or disliking but, and that is important, with real warmth of heart. One of the qualities of an Empty Heart is human warmth and if unimpeded, the natural warmth of the heart can begin to flow freely.

With that we enter the realm of the Divine Abodes. The first one, mostly mistranslated as loving kindness, is actually the warmth of the heart, the good will, which fills the heart and flows out towards all, rather as the sun shines because shining is its nature. It does not select, it shines and it flows, and with that we begin to realise the fullness and warmth of the Buddha's Teachings.

LETTER 2 to HUNG PO-CH'ENG

The Text

> An ancient worthy had a saying: 'To look for the ox, one must seek out its tracks. To study the Path, seek out Mindlessness. Where the tracks are, so must be the ox.' The Path of Mindlessness is easy to seek out. So-called Mindlessness is not being inert and unknowing like earth, wood, tile, or stone; it means that the mind is settled and imperturbable when in contact with situations and meeting circumstances; that it does not cling to anything, but is clear in all places, without

hindrance or obstruction; without being stained, yet without dwelling in the stainlessness; viewing body and mind like dreams or illusions, yet without remaining in the perspective of dreams and illusions, empty nothingness. Only when one arrives at a realm like this can it be called the true Mindlesness. No, it's not lip-service mindlessness: if you haven't attained true Mindlessness and just go by the verbal kind, how is this different from the perverted Ch'an of silent illumination?

'Just get to the root, do not worry about the branches.' Emptying the mind is the root. Once you get the root, the fundamental, then all kinds of language and knowledge and all your daily activities as you respond to people and adapt to circumstances, through so many upsets and downfalls, whether joyous or angry, good or bad, favourable or adverse – these are all trivial matters, the branches. If you can be spontaneously aware and knowing as you are going along with circumstances, then there is neither lack nor excess.

Ven. Myokyo-ni's Comments

This letter actually says everything that needs to be known about Zen training, the rest comes down to practice – rather than trying to find out more and more, actually doing it. The old masters constantly remind and inspire us towards that decisive step of doing it ourselves.

Master Daie quotes an old master, "**To look for the ox** (bull), **one must seek its traces. To study the Path, seek out Mindlessness** (the Empty Heart). **Where the tracks are so must be the ox** (bull)." The Empty Heart reveals itself if that Path is actually walked. Master Daie continues, '**Mindlessness** (the Empty Heart) **is not being inert and**

unknowing, like earth, wood, like tile or stone, it means that the mind (heart) **is settled and imperturbable when in contact with situations and meeting circumstances.'** Do not misunderstand – if the heart is empty, swept clean, then it is not that there is nothing that can touch it. On the contrary, then it responds to circumstances as they really are, not like my deluded, misconceived responses.

This is also expressed in a Zen saying that is particularly apt for the residents in a monastery, in communal living: 'If you sleep under the same blanket, you all know where the holes are.' In other words, if you do the same training in the same place, living together, you get to know each other pretty well. You may on the surface often misinterpret things because you have got your own ideas, but underneath there is a very clear perception of what the body actually flashes. The same applies when sitting in meditation. An experienced head monk will know where each sitter is, know their frame of mind. This is why the *jikijitsu* goes around particularly when there is a long sitting like in a *sesshin*. A practised meditator walking along a row of sitters cannot help but perceive the state of each of the sitters. It is unmistakeable, in the same way, for example, that it is unmistakeable to hear how gongs are struck differently. Being a woman, I did not live in the monastery in Japan, but lived up a hill very close by. When I was late as I sometimes was, I would hear the morning interview bell going and since I knew the line the monks sat in and was familiar with the sound of how each struck the bell, I also knew how much time I had or whether I would have to really race down the hill in order not to miss the morning interviews.

A telling story about the Empty Heart concerns Rinzai's teacher, Master Obaku (Chin. Huang-po). When he had settled on Obaku Mountain after which he was named, the local deity came to pay his respects to the famous master, but however often he came, and although he looked for Obaku everywhere, he could not find him.

That is the true Empty Heart. It is not attached to anything.

Continually concerned with itself, wanting to be appreciated, frightfully embarrassed, always feeling awkward, 'I' is different from the Empty Heart. **'The Path of Mindlessness (the Empty Heart) is easy to seek out; so-called Mindlessness (Empty Heart) is not being inert and unknowing like earth, wood, fire and stone. It means that the mind (heart) is settled and imperturbable when in contact with situations and meeting circumstances.'** Remember the Buddha, sitting under the Bo-tree and Mara in all his forms could not do anything to him. That is the 'heart settled, imperturbable when in contact with situations and meeting circumstances.' When there is something really important or very unpleasant in front of us, are we just as imperturbable and settled as when everything goes 'my way'? Behind the clinging and the aversions is the delusion of being a separate 'I', the other side of which is fear. This is something which we really need to know because if we approach it a little closer, and still a little closer in our practice, we begin to be caught by that fear.

I remember the first full *sesshin* at Daitoku-ji after having been accepted by Sesso Roshi as his student. That was also when I started my *sanzen* training. Having been shown exactly what to do and being rather scared, I went for my first interview. I had heard stories about how severe it could be, but there sat a kind old gentleman who asked me whether I had got used to the daily life practice, how my breathing was in zazen and he gave me the koan I had to work on and told me how to work on it, keeping it in the heart, going at it and going at it without thinking. The interviews in a Rinzai Zen monastery are extremely short and there are three a day during a *sesshin*. Four days had thus already gone by and I was beginning to feel more confident, thinking it typical to frighten beginners and make things difficult. So expecting another morsel, I went for my next interview, but already on the threshold, I felt a bit awkward. Bowing and entering the room, feeling more and more uneasy, I did my prostration in front of him. And sitting up, there was no kind old gentleman but a mixture of a high-power generating plant, with dynamos in a row and blue sparks hissing from one to the other, and you know you'd better keep a good distance. So, it was a mixture between that and a mental X-ray set. You do not want to strip physically naked even less do you want to be stripped mentally naked, do you? And that 'thing' (it did not feel human) said to me, 'Now you know everything you need to know, now JUMP!' 'Piiing' went his little bell. I slunk out feeling as I walked along the corridor, 'Yes, yes, this is what I came for, this is what I want – but not just now, not just now!' At that last moment, it gets to you and a lot of training is needed to carry one through. That is what Master Daie is saying here. But the Empty Heart, settled and imperturbable when in contact with situations and meeting circumstances, just responds as fits the given situation, responds to the circumstances in terms of the situation, not in terms of 'I', my intention. 'I', being a smart one, feel that when just going with the situation, things can't go wrong. That is not true because there is the situation and there is the human being and there is the cat; the cat will react to a certain situation reliably like a cat reacts. But I, and this is why we have so much trouble, just react as an 'I'. Deluded by my views, likes and loathings, anger or greed, I rarely react as a true human being.

But the Empty Heart, if truly **'settled and imperturbable'** acts as a human being **'when in contact with situations and meeting circumstances. It does not cling to anything, is clear in all places without hindrance or obstruction; without being stained, yet without dwelling in the stainlessness.'** If I do not fear, if I do not feel self-conscious, then there is no problem. Thereby hangs the story, because as long as I am there, I cannot be aware of the Empty Heart and so I, feeling alone, separate and hence insecure, cannot but fear.

That fear is the other side of I, just as deep and tenacious. Therefore it is said that what needs to drop off, to be let go of, is the four-fold delusion of 'I', a person, a sentient being and a life. With that gone, the mirror is truly clear. When the mirror is clear, the heart is truly empty and remains clear under all circumstances, without clinging, 'without hindrance or obstruction, without being stained, yet without dwelling in stainlessness.' It cannot be stained anymore. It no longer belongs to the world of stains, but does not dwell in stainlessness either.

I was once with Sesso Roshi when the head monk returned from an errand. He called out, opened the door when asked to enter and sitting on his knees, absolutely correct, perfectly poised, reported about it. I did not understand much but it was obviously very funny. He was laughing freely as they were talking but he didn't lose his form even for a bit, not for a moment did he falter. That is real freedom spontaneously unfolding itself in a human being in human good form, no longer obstructed by my delusions. If a proper form is kept, it arises of itself with the full strength which I lack because of 'I' being the delusion.

So the form is most important. I do not know about today, but in my time some fifty years ago industrial diamonds could be made. A diamond is after all nothing but carbon, coal dust. Now if you load coal dust into an empty pipe and blow, the coal dust comes out the other end and settles itself over everything. But if that pipe is so strong that even very high pressure cannot burst it, then loaded with the same coal dust and real pressure applied, at the other end imperfect little diamonds come out. Power is needed for transformation. 'I' do not have it, it needs to be cultivated by practice. So it is never for 'me', but it can be cultivated. If we truly give ourselves into the practice, if we stick to our timetable, not in a way which is rigid and unfeeling but in a truly obedient way, then that power will begin to develop. This power leads to fearlessness and it is in this fearlessness that it becomes possible for 'I' to drop off. **'Only when one arrives at a realm like this can it be called true Mindlessness** (Empty Heart). **It is not lip-service, this Mindlessness** (Empty Heart).' Do not talk about it if you do not know. **'If you have not attained true Mindlessness** (Empty Heart) **and just go by the verbal kind,'** then it is no different from all kinds of perverted practice like just sitting and hoping that the sitting alone will produce something.

Master Daie again quotes an old master saying, **"'Just get to the root, do not worry about the branches.'"** It comes from Yoka Daishi (Chin. Yung Chia). Just get to the root, do not worry about the branches. My real problem is that I am my real problem and unless I work on that, the branches will just change shape; one finished, then another will sprout rather like a boil. If lanced too early, it will give rise to further boils and may lead to blood poisoning. Stick to the root! Emptying the heart is the way to the root. Without that nothing can be done. **'Once you get to the root,'** says Master Daie, **'then all kinds of language and knowledge and all your daily activities as you respond to people and adapt to circumstances are only branches.'**

We have to be careful here because getting to the root is not the end of the training, there is still much more to be done. But once the root has been reached, then as the training continues diligently and willingly, the sight begins to clear and with that, **'all kinds of language and knowledge and all your daily activities as you respond to people and adapt to circumstances'** become fitting and neutral because **'through so many upsets and downfalls, whether joyous or angry, good or bad, favourable or adverse – these are all seen as trivial matter, the branches.'** All kinds of language and knowledge, all daily activities, our response to people and circumstances, are usually acted and stiff, our ideas preconceived. With all the ups and downs in the light of the day and in the darkness of the night, when upset or when joyful, when circumstances are easy or difficult, favourable or adverse, if there is clear seeing they are all recognised as trivial matters. True, there are favourable and adverse circumstances, but they are now not judged, not taken personally but simply responded to as is proper under the circumstances. And they can be made good use of, because they are so much more opportunity for further good practice. Only when really settled is the natural response under all circumstances reliable as befits the human form. If anything contrived or intentional still lurks, then the heart is not truly empty. Therefore it is said that the first insight, that first seeing into and from the Empty Heart is relatively easy. But to then really live according to it through all the circumstances, that is very difficult indeed, and needs much more training. The *Jataka Stories*, the birth stories of the Buddha, point in that direction. Nowadays we regard them as, 'Oh well, these are just fairy stories for our children, quite unreal!' But they tell us what freely responding to all circumstances implies.

Such is the story of the Bodhisattva, not yet Buddha, who stood on a cliff and looking down, saw a starving tigress totter out from a thicket and on her heels a scrawny little cub. She was obviously on her last legs. The Bodhisattva looked at the tigress, and taking in the situation, he leaned forward and let himself fall right down, feeding her and the cub. Now what is our reaction to that?

This is a pertinent story that belongs to the Empty Heart. Ponder it. Perhaps it will give an inkling of what responding to people and adapting to circumstances through so many upsets and downfalls, whether joyful or annoying, good or bad, favourable or adverse, really requires. Do not try to hide, be open – these are all trivial matters. **'If you can be spontaneously aware and knowing while going along with circumstances, then there is neither lack nor excess.'** If you can be spontaneously aware and knowing as you go along with circumstances, in all the doing – is that not the Daily Life Practice? Not watching myself, not trying to do it, but just eating and knowing that I am eating, without watching myself, without thinking, just being aware. Sweeping and knowing there is sweeping, but not observing myself sweeping which is the wrong way. Knowing there is sweeping and the sweeping is all there is, nothing else but the sweeping – at one with it, or in *samadhi* with it. If this has become truly the natural response to circumstances, then it is not self-conscious. Is that intellectually clear? If done that way, then the activity is the only thing that exists. There is the sweeping, there is the cooking, there is the eating, there is painting, there is this or that, freely and without hindrance flowing from one into the other. When the clappers sound for mealtime, assembling in the *zendo*. And when the clappers go again, filing into the dining hall. All this flows along smoothly. Then there is neither lack nor excess. There is a beautiful saying by Layman P'ang, 'The snowflakes fall, each in its appropriate place.' We are all in the appropriate place, according to out karmic development and as our karmic lineage actually puts it. And as we go from place to place, each one is appropriate. The same Layman P'ang said, 'How wonderful, how miraculous! Carrying wood and fetching water.' If we begin to see it like this, then the heart is truly empty because in the Empty Heart are all the miracles and all the wonders and all the warmth of which I have painted pictures but have always failed to reach. But once that Empty Heart is reached, all is truly there. And what is more, not as a picture in the mind, but actually completely liveable and lived.

Please ponder that, and little by little give yourself more into the training and so come closer.

LETTER 3 to LI HSIEN-CH'EN

Since you are studying this Path, then at all times, in your encounters with people and responses to circumstances, you must not let wrong thoughts continue. If you cannot see through them, then the moment a wrong thought comes up you should quickly concentrate your mental energy to pull yourself away. If you always follow those thoughts and let them continue without a break, not only does this obstruct the Path, but it makes you out to be a man without wisdom.

In the old days Kuei Shan asked Lazy An, 'What work do you do during the twenty-four hours of the day?' An said, 'I tend an ox.' Isan said, 'How do you tend it?' An said, 'Whenever it gets into the grass, I pull it back by the nose.' Isan said, 'You really are tending the ox!' People who study the Path, in controlling wrong thoughts, should be like Lazy An tending his ox; then gradually a wholesome ripening will take place of itself.

Ven. Myokyo-ni's Comments

Master Daie is particularly helpful for us because many of his disciples were laypeople. Although these letters are more than a thousand years old, the human heart is the human heart, and they pertain just as much to us today. So we may take it that Master Daie is addressing each one of us.

'Since you are studying this Path' – what is this Path? The Zen Path, the Zen Buddhist Path, the Buddha Path, the Way the Buddha pointed out, that leads out of suffering. What kind of suffering?

What do we mostly suffer from? From feeling somehow excluded and alienated, feeling 'I only' – separated out from what is, and therefore insecure, easily frightened, alone, self-conscious. We must carefully consider here that we are really talking about two types of consciousness.

There is the consciousness which is normal awareness. And there is self-consciousness. We usually mix those two up. Normally we function only from self-consciousness and this produces our difficulties. We need to learn to come back to the straight consciousness that accurately reflects like a mirror – it does not add anything or highlight anything and when it turns to the next vista, does not drag along what was before and overlay what is.

'Since you are studying this Path,' says Master Daie, **'then at all times in your encounters with people and responses to circumstances, you must not let wrong thoughts continue.'** What are those wrong thoughts? They are the I-connected thoughts of my liking and disliking this, that or the other. 'Wrong thoughts' are not only about harming things but also thoughts that make me feel separate and alienated from what is, that take me out of life to an abstract realm, filling the head with all kinds of notions. These are the wrong thoughts.

Master Daie says, **'If you cannot see through them, then the moment a wrong thought comes up, you should quickly concentrate your mental energy to pull yourself away,'** and not let wrong thoughts continue. He does not say that you should not let them come up because that is not within our power. But once up, whether we let them continue and are carried away by them, or whether we do not let them continue, that depends on us. Those thought streams bubble along as we all know. Either they are very concentrated in planning or involved in what I want or am trying to avoid. But even when none of these thoughts preoccupy me, is the mind still without thoughts? Or does it go, 'bubble, bubble, bubble' like a constant undercurrent? Phiroz Mehta has called it the 'chattering monkey mind'. It is not quiet for a moment, has to continuously act in order to give me the feeling that after all, 'I am still here, I have not vanished.'

It carries us away from where we actually are. When that happens there is no awareness of being here now, in this place, in this chair, on that cushion, on that train. When we are in that other realm, there is nothing that can be noticed. Not being here, we cannot listen anymore, we cannot see anymore. We are truly not here but in a kind of never-never land. Then something stampedes us out again and we are back in the real-life situation, here and now.

These are the wrong thoughts. If you cannot see through them, says Master Daie, then the moment a wrong thought comes up, recognise it. And **'you should quickly concentrate your mental energy to pull yourself away.'** The moment a wrong thought comes up, be aware. The awareness is almost physical. Either it comes up with heat, the Fires, wants and dislikes, or it comes up as the bubbly stream. You notice it particularly in zazen. There you sit, alive, awake, all there. And then suddenly the hands loosen, the chin sags and away we are. Now at that moment, if there is a real sense of being with it, the moment the hands lose their grip and the chin sags, then with an energetic breath come right back into what is being done. If this is continuously practised, it will make the awareness prevail and the wrong thoughts decline. Do not try to go against them, that is quite useless. Just jump right back into the liveliness and awareness of this moment, that is where your own feet stand. The moment a wrong thought comes up, quickly concentrate your mental energy – that is what is necessary. Do not fight it. Whatever we fight against, to that we actually give power over us. Why is it so necessary to recognise wrong thoughts? Because if we always follow these thoughts and let them continue without a break, we miss the living moment. Then what happens is that we feel that life is not really what we hoped it to be, it is boring, uninteresting, unsatisfactory. This is what the Buddha called suffering.

Master Daie continues, '**If you always follow those thoughts and let them continue without a break, not only does it obstruct the Path, it makes you out to be a man without wisdom.**' A man without wisdom is somebody who falls from one difficulty into another, confronts one obstacle after another. And a man without wisdom cannot learn. He cannot learn because he cannot take in, and he cannot take in because there is no awareness. Or because he is too full. When a cup is full, you can put nothing more into it. It must first be emptied out.

Through a grid of thought streams and deep-seated opinions that we have in the head, we believe that we actually see things as they are. Do not believe it, it is not true. Although we believe we can, we are incapable because that grid obscures. The thought-streams are such a hindrance. From the earliest beginnings of the Zen school, the Sixth Patriarch already said, 'Before thinking, what is the True Face?' Our weaving of thoughts and our being cocooned in them obstructs, beclouds the mirror and so it cannot reflect clearly. Therefore 'if you always follow those thoughts and let them continue without a break, then not only does this obstruct the Path, but it makes you out to be a man without wisdom,' someone who continuously stumbles or misses the Way.

Master Daie illustrates this. '**In the old days, Kuei Shan** (Master Isan) **asked Lazy An, "What work do you do during the twenty-four hours of the day?" An said, "I tend the ox** (bull).**" Kuei Shan** (Isan) **said, "How do you tend it." An said, "Whenever it gets into the grass, I pull it back by the nose." Kuei Shan** (Isan) **said, "You are really tending the ox** (bull).**"**

The whole day long, he doesn't do this, that or the other. He just tends his bull. And how does he tend it? 'Whenever it gets into the grass, I pull it back by the nose.' That does not say that he does not feed it or does not put it to grass to feed. But whenever it gets into the grass of others, or into long thought streams, whenever it goes into lush meadows that lead it on and carry it further away, he pulls it back by the nose. It is the same with a horse. Going for a country ride, if not properly ridden and there is a nice bunch of grass, it crops it quickly or tears a branch with some new leaf. Once it has got a chomp of it, it is much harder to hold it back. Once you have let it have three or four chomps, the horse feels, 'This is my right' and from then on it will have it and it is difficult to train him out of it. So better not to let it get away from the beginning. Just the same applies to us. Once we have got into a habit, then it seems it has always been so. And there is already a complaint for when it has always been so, why should it change? Whether bull or horse or myself, whenever it gets into the grass, pull it back by the nose at once. That is, whenever the thought-streams come up, with or without Fire, pull by the nose, right back into here and now. Right back to where our feet stand. Right back into the living situation.

'Kuei Shan (Isan) **said, "You are really tending the ox** (bull).** People who study the Path, in controlling wrong thoughts, should be like Lazy An tending his ox** (bull).' 'Controlling' is perhaps not an apt translation. Rather, what is meant is when 'working with wrong thoughts', one should be like Lazy An with his bull. **'Then gradually, a wholesome ripening will take place by itself.'** But we need to be consistent and constant and just carry on and continue with it. We human beings are very adaptable Habits – good and wrong ones – can be cultivated. But we seem quick in cultivating wrong or unwholesome habits, and we are very slow in cultivating wholesome ones. Habits and my notions are what prevent me but can also spur me. We mistakenly believe that it can be done by the will alone, but the body also needs to come into it.

My will is very weak when it comes down to some emotional or habitual energy. This is where the body comes in. Anything that needs to be habituated, needs the body. If the body is not in it, it is not whole. Mind and body belong together. The Buddha himself said, 'Have I ever said, Oh monks, that there is a body without a mind and a mind without a body?' They do belong together and if we whole-heartedly put ourselves into it, again and again, gradually a wholesome ripening will take place of itself.

And so if there is really this resolute pulling back by the nose-ring, whole-heartedly, not only just 'I should, but I'm so tired….' – let it be quick and sharp! And with no option. Whatever we really whole-heartedly train in, it may not be overnight, it may take some time, but if only we continue willingly, then gradually a wholesome ripening will take place of itself. Giving ourselves whole-heartedly into what is being done, that of itself is the pulling the bull by the nose. We do not need to do anything else, but usually that does not satisfy us.

We want to *do* more, want to look round and examine ourselves, judge how we are getting on, but all those wants are already wrong thought-streams that pull us away. If we faithfully continue with what we actually need to do, then from the other side, it seems, comes the helping hand of Kannon Bodhisattva and begins to pull us back again. But if I am too self-conscious and arrogant to apply myself diligently, 'because' I have no time, 'because' I have other more important things to do, then I mess the whole thing up and the helping hand cannot come.

There is an Indian story which illustrates how even with the best intentions, things can miscarry, if they are not done whole-heartedly by giving myself into them, but are done only for my betterment. A man had been meditating in the forest and his mantra was, 'Krishna,

Krishna. When will you liberate me? Krishna, Krishna, when will you liberate me?' After some fifteen years or so Krishna felt it was about time to take him out of his misery. So he quietly walked up from behind, touched his shoulder and was about to say, 'Today' when the meditator angrily exclaimed, 'Don't you see I'm meditating? How dare you disturb me!' Krishna quietly withdrew his hand and walked away.

We had better be reverent then, and with this we enter the religious sphere. Reverently we bow the head and metaphorically we get a ring fastened into our nose with a good rope attached to help us – not by the will alone, but with a physical jerk will we throw ourselves or pull ourselves or hurl ourselves back into the here and now, into this living moment where we are anyway! We don't need to worry about not seeing or understanding, the Buddha's wisdom is inborn in any case. I do not need to watch or observe myself. Direct, immediate awareness is here anyway, provided I do not obscure it. Perhaps we can ponder that and really take it to heart.

LETTER 4 to LI HSIEN-CH'EN

THE TEXT

> 'Do not grasp another's bow, do not ride another's horse, do not meddle in another's affairs.' Though this is a commonplace saying, it can also be sustenance for entering the Path. Just examine yourself constantly: from morning to night, what do you do to help others and help yourself? If you notice even the slightest partiality or insensitivity, you must admonish yourself. Don't be careless about this!

In the old days Ch'an Master Tao Lin lived up in a tall pine tree on Ch'in Wang Mountain; people of the time called him the 'Bird's Nest Monk.' When Minister Po Chu-yi was commander of Ch'ien T'ang, he made a special trip to the mountain to visit him. Po said, 'It's very dangerous where you're sitting, Ch'an Master.' The Master said, 'My danger may be very great, Minister, but yours is even greater.' Po said, 'I am commander of Ch'ien T'ang: what danger is there?' The Master said, 'Fuel and fire are joined, consciousness and identity do not stay: how can you not be in danger?'

Po also asked, 'What is the overall meaning of the Buddha's teaching?' The Master said, 'Don't commit any evils, practise the many virtues.' Po said, 'Even a three-year-old child could say this.' The Master said, 'Though a three-year-old child can say it, an eighty-year-old man cannot carry it out.'

Now if you want to save mental power, do not be concerned with whether or not a three-year-old child can say it, or whether or not an eighty-year-old man can carry it out. Just don't do any evil and you have mastered these words. They apply whether you believe or not, so please think it over.

"'Do not grasp another's bow, do not ride another's horse, do not meddle in another's affairs.'" It's one of those very simple straightforward sayings which if only we would heed them, we would not have to do strange practices. But we love to meddle in our own affairs, even more so in others' affairs, in the world's affairs, in the affairs of our surroundings. We think we are clever, but we are not. We are like the clever tortoise who didn't want to leave footprints and so walking along, it swept them out with its tail, making its traces even more visible. That is exactly what we do. We are great meddlers. We are ready to interfere, 'Now if I were you, I would do it this way.' So Master Daie comments on 'Do not meddle in another's affairs', by saying, **'Though this is a commonplace saying, it can also be sustenance for entering the Path.'** The Chinese phrase *wu wei* is usually translated as 'non-action'. But that is not what it means. It means 'non-interference'. So Master Daie says, **'Just examine yourself constantly from morning to night, what do you do to help others and yourself?'**

Master Sesso said to me once, and I have never forgotten, 'Of course one cannot do this training for oneself alone.' To the extent that 'I' decrease, the openness and awareness and connectedness with everything else opens up. We cannot help others without helping ourselves and we must understand that in helping ourselves, we help others too. These others are not just human beings, but literally everything else which is not I.

What does this result in? That we become respectful, careful and open and therefore notice what at this moment actually is right in front of us. It is said in Torei's *Inexhaustible Lamp* that what this means is to help all things to fulfil their appropriate function. A knife is for cutting and not a screwdriver, and a needle for sewing, etc., etc. That is what their function is, and then after using them, not carelessly throwing them away or putting them down any old how. Since things have their own places, one should be respectful of their own places too and put them back in their proper places.

'If you notice even the slightest partiality or insensitivity, you must admonish yourself.' Partiality and insensitivity go together. I cannot be partial about one thing without being insensitive towards something else. Kipling's *If* expresses it, 'If all men count with you, but none too much.' If I am partial to one thing, I overlook the other. It means to be open in order to take in what is, and to respond to that, to the situation as it is, whole-heartedly, in harmony with the demands of the situation. If that is not so, if I am glued to one thing and forget, miss or don't care about the other, that is not whole-heartedness and there is no harmony with the situation.

So we need to be careful. Do we feel the slightest partiality or insensitivity? If we are totally engrossed in ourselves, we cannot notice what goes on around us. If I feel awkward when being watched, that, too, is partiality towards myself and so insensitivity to the situation. If I feel I am the hub of the universe or the person whom everyone is watching, that is simply an 'I' that has grown out of all bounds, and so is embarrassment, from which we often suffer. That is insensitivity to others and partiality to myself.

'In the old days, Ch'an Master Tao Lin lived up in a tall pine tree on Ch'in Wang Mountain.' He is often mentioned and there are many pictures depicting him, perched up there like in a nest. He was referred to as 'the Bird's Nest Monk'. One day Minister Po Chu-yi, who was also the military commander of a quite large town, came to visit him. He had heard about him and seeing him perched high up there in the tree and assessing the danger, **'Po called up, "It's very dangerous where your sitting, Ch'an Master." The master called down, "My danger may be very great, Minister, but yours is even greater." The minister said, "I am commander of Ch'ien T'ang. What danger is there?" The master answered, "Fuel and fire are joined. Consciousness and identity do not stay; how can you not be in danger?"'**

Fuel and fire are joined, there can be no fire without fuel. Wherever we are, fuel and fire are joined. The fires flare up in seconds and can consume us if we are not well-trained. They are joined in ourselves, all around, in all of us. And in all of us, consciousness and identity do not stay. Consciousness flows like a river. And identity? Identity of what? A nebulous idea of 'I' – and even if I think that I am real at least to a certain extent, is that really so?

Do I not in my heart deeply believe that I am fairly constant, not a fickle person? Do I still play the games that I liked when a child? And the toys that I played with, even my favourite toy, where is it now? Every few years, we have another set of fancies, another set of things we like, another set of games, another set of interests, another set of toys. We are ever-shifting and fluid, aren't we?

So consciousness and identity do not stay. And if it happens that one day in the attic you come across your once favourite toy, you recognise it instantly and perhaps nostalgically. But do you feel prompted to start playing with it now? Can you remember that moment when you put it down and never picked it up again?

It is a gradual process, shifting interest from one thing to the other. It is the same with our training. If it means something to us, we slowly get more and more engaged and other things pale until they finally drop off. Fuel and fire are joined, consciousness and identity do not stay. How can we not be in danger? If we want or try to stay, then we are really in danger. If at the age of sixty a woman tries to look preferably younger than her twenty-year-old granddaughter, it is both ludicrous and pitiful because she never will do so.

But how can one not be in danger? Things, habits, take over in time, if we do not let them go. Only now, our toys are our opinions. We all have notions of what we want, what we must have, what we would like to become. Joseph Campbell puts it in the right perspective when he says that we strive all our lives to get 'to the top' where we are most in danger. And he says, often somebody has spent all of their life climbing up the ladder of ambition until they have finally got to the top rung, only to realise that the ladder has been propped up against the wrong wall. Isn't it so? There is no 'happy ever after'.

'Po, the minister, then also asked, "What is the overall meaning of the Buddhist teachings?" The master said, "Don't commit any evils, practice the many virtues."' Simple, isn't it? But actually that truly is all that is necessary, nothing else. **'Po said, "Even a three-year-old child could say that." And the master retorted, "Though a three-year-old child can say it, an eighty-year-old man cannot carry it out." At that, Po bowed and departed.'**

There is another story about this same saying, 'Do not commit any evils, practise the virtues.' It is also a Zen story although the saying itself comes from the *Dhammapada*, 'Not to do anything unwholesome, to do only good, to purify the heart, this is the teaching of all the Buddhas.' In the T'ang capital of China lived a very erudite Confucian gentleman and scholar. Now, one cannot be a Confucian scholar without also being a gentleman. And he heard that somewhere down in the barbarian south a new teaching had arisen that was even more profound than that of Master K'ung (Confucius).

He felt himself in an awkward situation. He was very old and frail. He naturally wanted to find out, but he had nobody of his own level to send there. So, being a gentleman, he decided never mind whatever it entailed, he would have to travel there by himself. And so he did. The barbarian south – bandits, wild beasts, rough going, never mind. It took him months to get there. Having arrived at one of the new Zen schools, he introduced himself to the Zen master and said that he had come to find out whose teaching was the deeper. He suggested that if they each expounded their understanding, as two gentlemen, they would then easily decide whose teaching was the most profound.

This latter suggestion alone is very important. They were not trying to convince each other or vie with each other, rather as two gentlemen they could impartially settle whose insight was the deeper. Just that is the difference between clinging to 'my' deluded opinion as the better and the clarity of truly seeing what is.

Nowadays we feel we 'must win' at all cost, without thought of anything else, passionately driven, crying when we lose, beside ourselves when we win – sadly there are no gentlemen anymore.

Anyway, they agreed and the Confucian gentleman started to expound the Confucian teaching and his understanding. When it was the Zen master's turn, he merely stated, 'To do as little harm as possible, to do as much good as possible, that is the teachings of all the Buddhas.' You notice he has put in 'the teaching of all the Buddhas'?

Not surprising, the Confucian was really angry with that. A three months' dangerous journey at his time of life, having held nothing back. And they had agreed to an exchange. 'Are you mocking me?' he burst out. 'Every three-year-old child can say that.' The Zen Master said, 'No, I'm not mocking you. Please consider. It is true that a three-year-old child can repeat that jingle of the verse, but as you see, even an eighty-year-old gentleman cannot always bring it off.'

Now, the *Dhammapada* verse has 'to purify the heart' as the third line and that is missing in the other stories. Why should it be? If the practice is truly to avoid doing harm, that means not only just actual harm but being inconsiderate, not even being intentionally hurtful but just being thoughtless and saying something that might hurt. If being respectful and kind has truly become the new life, there is no need to purify the heart, for the heart of itself has become pure. Only when the heart is pure is such consistent action possible. And this is therefore the teaching of all the Buddhas.

If the heart is truly empty, not obscured by notions, feelings, wants and dislikes and thus being aware of what is thought, said, and done, with the natural warmth of the human heart liberated, we feel 'at one'. It is not possible to empty the heart by an act of will but the practice of shunning anything inconsiderate and of doing good as much as possible, will of itself effect the emptying.

When a flower begins to droop, we give it water, not too much and not too little. We soon find out, if we do it with care, how much each individual plant drinks and how much to give it. And when in summer the garden looks parched, we do not need to wonder what is wrong, just take the hose and start watering. This kind of direct response to the demands of the situation is what is meant here.

Master Daie then goes on, **'Now if you want to save mental energy, do not be concerned with whether or not a three-year-old child can say it or whether or not an eighty-year-old man can carry it out.'** That would be missing the point, and once more being carried away into one of our many thought-streams. Do not get distracted by words and thoughts. That propensity of ours is very strong and for that we have the analogy of a man who has been shot by a poisoned arrow. He says, 'I will not have that arrow removed before I know who shot it, to which tribe he belongs, from which tree that arrow was made, and what poison was used.' By the time he has found all that out, he is dead.

Therefore, do not be concerned with whether or not a three-year-old child can say it or whether or not an eighty-year-old man can carry it out. **'Just don't do any evil and you have mastered these words. They apply, whether you believe it or not, so please think it over.'** That is all there is. Try it and find out for yourself. That is the great thing about the Buddha's teaching, that you do not have to believe. You try and apply and find out for yourself. Does it work? Does it not work? If it works, then we have no further difficulty staying with it. 'They apply whether you believe it or not, so please think it over.' Ponder it carefully. Avoid doing evil, do all possible good.

The Text

If worldly people whose present conduct is without illumination would correct themselves and do good, though the goodness is not yet perfect, isn't this better than depravity and shamelessness? One who does harm on the pretext of doing good is called in the Teachings one whose causal ground is not genuine, bringing on crooked results. If with a straightforward mind and straightforward conduct you are able to see supreme enlightenment directly, this can be called the act of a real man of power. The concerns that have come down from numberless ages are only in the present. If you can understand them right now, then the concerns of numberless ages will instantly disperse like tiles being shattered or ice melting. If you don't understand right now, you'll pass through countless aeons more and it'll still be just as it is. The truth that is as it is has been continuous since before time, without ever having varied so much as a hair's breadth.

Ven. Myokyo-ni's Comments

'If worldly people whose present conduct is without illumination would correct themselves and do good' – I believe there are very few people who do not want to do good. The problem is that we cannot always do good and willy-nilly do harm; nevertheless, we can begin to correct ourselves. Do we really want to correct ourselves? Yes, as long as it is not too bothersome. And thereby hangs the real issue. Master Daie assures us that even if we are as yet without illumination, without true insight, we can correct our conduct if we do good, make an effort to be gentle, polite, good-mannered, not only in unfamiliar but in familiar surroundings. And not only with people and all sentient beings, but with everything.

Have we ever thought that we can be gentle and polite with a spoon or with a plate or a cup? It does not occur to us and yet that is what it needs to extend to. When we make an effort to do so, over a long time, it becomes habitual and it becomes natural. There is an analogy in the *Inexhaustible Lamp*: if you go for a long walk in rather thick fog, though it is not raining, when you come home your clothes will nonetheless be wet. Equally if you burn incense in a room, the room, the walls, the curtains, everything will smell of it.

The same also applies to us. We can correct ourselves little by little, not in particular things but just by being kind, considerate, respectful to everything, from the carpet to the ceiling and all that is in between. That eventually will give us a natural care for things. With the natural care and natural respect for things, something else inevitably will open. But that needs to be cultivated. It is no good saying, 'How can I do that if I have no time, am too busy?' I always have got time, if I really want to. It is remarkable how, if I really want to, even at my busiest, I nevertheless manage to have time for what I really want. I may not have time for everything I want to do but for what I really want, I do have time. I remember in my youth I was convinced I could not exist without music for any length of time. And all my life I had been a great walker. Then in Japan with things being as they were, I had to get up at four o'clock for the morning interview and with the evening sitting until half-past ten, there was little time for music. By the time I was settled into monastery life I knew I could get the evening off if I asked. So, when occasionally a friend invited me to a concert, I would be delighted. It was fine in summer but in winter, when it meant getting back in an icy tram, cold and late, to an icy room, and having to get up early next morning, I would ring up and excuse myself. And I found that I did that more and more regularly, much as I loved music. But remarkably, for my walks, summer or winter, snow or rain or shine, I always somehow managed to have time for a walk. So it was from simply looking at my own behaviour that I was forced to conclude that however much I liked music, I did not like it more than anything else, but walking I really liked because for that I found time under all circumstances and in all weather.

So it is useful to watch ourselves to find out what we really like. If, for example, we really want to do something like cultivate the habit of being polite and respectful to everything, then we'll manage to bring it off. Then even **without illumination, if worldly people can correct themselves and do good, though that goodness is not yet perfect, isn't it better than depravity and shamelessness?'** But to say that I will not do any good because I do not really know how to do good is silly, because that only brings us to the opposite. Therefore Master Daie tells us that 'though the goodness is not yet perfect, it's still better than depravity and shamelessness.' That puts it into a very crass opposition: depravity and shamelessness. Shamelessness brings us to another thing in Buddhism of which people were certainly still slightly aware in Master Daie's time; it was also said that unless we can feel shame, we cannot really come into genuine insight. Isn't that interesting? Unless we can feel shame: not embarrassment, but shame. This is why we chant the *Repentance Sutra* in the morning – 'All the harm and evil things I have committed since beginningless time.' That feeling sorry and feeling shame for having been thoughtless, for having been careless for the umpteenth time; though by now I should really not only know better, but actually be better, yet still fall into the same trap again and again. That is worthwhile pondering carefully.

But then there is another even more subtle aspect to it. I can go and wallow in the shame and guilt of having done this, or of having forgotten that; and consequently, completely forget to do the little good that I am, after all, still capable of doing. This is what Master Daie really points at. 'Though the goodness is not yet perfect' – just do it and for goodness' sake go on doing it. Slowly it will then come together and develop.

'One who does harm on the pretext of doing good.' We can do that too without realising it, by thoughtlessly trying to do good and end up doing harm. We easily recognise do-gooders and usually resent them. Do-gooders are not doing good for the sake of doing good, but out of selfishness, to make themselves feel good. In our practice we particularly have to be careful about that – I the good practiser, I do the good!

Master Rinzai warned his monks, 'Just be your natural selves and do not give yourselves airs.' If I walk about with a holy face, that is not the purpose of the exercise. **'One who does harm on the pretext of doing good is called in the Teachings one whose causal ground is not genuine, bringing on crooked results.'** 'I do it for your own good, you know.' We are familiar with that phrase and it is usually something pretty nasty, otherwise it would not be prefixed by that. So we have to be careful. What is more, doing good on purpose is usually missing or forgetting something, not seeing the whole picture and so without knowing it, hurting something or causing some kind of harm. Whereas if it is done firmly and clearly, then with the causal ground being genuine, then there will be no crooked results. Crooked results come then from the motive, from not being genuine.

Master Daie continues, **'If with a straightforward mind** (heart) **and straightforward conduct, you are able to see supreme enlightenment directly, this can be called the act of a real man of power.'** With a straightforward heart and straightforward conduct. Not blinded, not obstructed by any kind of thought-streams, not even by one single thought: that is a straightforward heart, and straightforward conduct which has no wavering, and goes straight to and is in harmony with the situation and the demands of the situation.

As we live here together over a *sesshin* you can see how often we do this wavering. Watch how people put things down, stand up or sit down. Whatever it might be, it's not possible to just do it. Each one of us has our own little habits, and it doesn't go straightforwardly. However much we want to disguise it, it still sticks out like a sore thumb.

Though we do not quite realise it, we actually share this trait not only with each other but also with our mammalian brothers. When I was young, I had a German Shepherd, who went a bit blind as he got older, but he still loved chasing things. I remember when we once went for a walk, we saw something in the distance that looked like a crow, and like a bolt he shot towards it. But when he came close enough to it, he saw that it was simply a stake of black wood standing out. Not wanting to show and admit that he had mistaken it, he started nonchalantly dancing about the moment he recognised it as if he had known all the time that it was only a stake and that he was only playing. It was absolutely fascinating. Horses do the same. And we also do the same; we do not want to make a mistake, do we? And therefore we are usually incapable of any kind of straightforward conduct. Well worthwhile pondering and considering.

'If with a straightforward heart, however, and straightforward conduct you are able to see supreme enlightenment directly'– because at this moment, here and now, a straightforward heart and straightforward conduct come together and that is where we are. This supreme enlightenment, which we always have the greatest fantasies about is the absence of I. And in the absence of I there is no difficulty. The heart is empty, the conduct therefore is straightforward, and the thing is directly here. Well, if we call it 'the thing', at that moment we have already crated a concept about it – we don't know what it is. But if this is possible without any thought about it, 'this can be called the act of a real man of power.'

'The concerns that have come down from numberless ages are only in the present.' They are nowhere else, because we cannot be anywhere else but in the present. We can only understand right now, now is the only time that we have — right now. Everything else is only imagination in the head. What was five minutes ago is only a memory, it is not real anymore. And what will be in five minutes we do not know.

'The concerns that have come down from numberless ages are only in the present.' There they are real. 'If you can understand them right now' — see through them — **'then the concerns of numberless ages will instantly disperse, like tiles being shattered or ice melting. If you don't understand right now, you'll pass through countless aeons more, and it will still be just as it is.'** This moment — the moment, now, and now — it's really all that we ever know, all that we ever can know; and it is just this moment where the actual life is. It's not in thought-streams or anything: it's in this moment, here and now. This is why we have our Daily Life Practice of giving ourselves into this moment here and now, and therefore living it. Normally we refuse to live this moment, which is the only thing that we have; and then we wonder why life is difficult or why life passes us by, or whatever it is; and we only live in thought-streams, which naturally have nothing to do with reality, and therefore are constantly disappointing and disillusioning. This means that this moment is the only thing that we ever will have. The understanding of this moment is really crucial, but we often refuse it, because we want something, or want to get rid of something. It's really the bane of our life. And that is the delusion from which I suffer, and the Buddha taught us, showed us, how to get out of it.

If in this moment we can say 'yes' to this moment, then we really live it — life wants to be lived, needs to be lived. If not, it piles up against us, all the unlived life. And that is something which all the Zen masters have tried to tell us. Stick in the present, and say 'yes' to it and live this moment.

'The concerns that have come down from numberless ages are only in the present. If you can understand them right now, then these concerns of numberless ages will instantly disperse, like tiles being shattered or ice melting. If you do not understand right now, you'll pass through countless aeons more, and it will still be just as it is.' Nothing will change. We will go on wallowing and rolling in our own thought-streams, making new ones from time to time, having a new idea and a new theory and a new illusion to cling to, and a new ideal to try to work for or fight for; and that will go on and on and on, because we will not stop in the moment.

But Master Daie tells us, **'The truth that is as it is'** – the Suchness, the Tathata – **'has been continuous since before time without ever having varied so much as a hair's breadth.'** Without ever having varied so much as a hair's breadth. It just is. And for the purpose of talking about it, he calls it truth, or the Dharma, or whatever you want to call it – it doesn't matter; because the moment it is given a name, it's only a name, and it's not the thing itself. It's not a thing either; it just is.

This truth that is as it is, the Suchness of it, has been continuous since before time. It does not need time. The Dharma, the truth, is outside of time. It is nothing to do with time. And this is why it is also not possible to catch it in words or to think about it. But it can be seen as analogous, it can be given a name. But the name is not the real one. As a useful example we can think of life, we can talk about life, but do we know it? Can we make it? And it has been continuous, not 'mine' but life, before me and will continue after I have ceased to exist. It has been continuous since before time. It has nothing to do with time. Individual forms have to do with time. They have their beginning and their end, their coming to be and ceasing to be. But life and its laws – Dharma, the Truth, 'has been continuous since before time without ever having varied so much as a hair's breadth.'

LETTER 4 to LI HSIEN-CH'EN (continued)

The Text

> Matters of worldly anxieties are like the links of a chain joining together continuously without a break. If you can do away with them, do away with them immediately. Because you have become habituated to them since beginningless time to the point where they have become totally familiar, if you do not exert yourself to struggle with them, then as time goes on and on, with you unknowing and unawares, they will have entered deeply into you and finally on the last day of your life you won't be able to do anything about it. If you want to be able to avoid going wrong when you face the end of your life, then from now on, whenever you do anything, don't let yourself slip. If you go wrong in your present doings, it will be impossible not to go wrong when you are facing death.

Ven. Myokyo-ni's Comments

'Matters of worldly anxieties are like the links in a chain, joining together endlessly without a break.' 'Matters of worldly anxieties' – our problems, our difficulties, are made by ourselves, by our likes and dislikes. They 'are like the links in a chain.' If it is not this, then it is that. If I do not want this, then I want that, if I have just stopped disliking this, suddenly I start disliking that. Like the links of a chain that 'join together continuously without a break.' There is the joke about a woman restlessly worrying, not quite knowing what it is that is worrying her. 'Our final mortgage is paid off. The children have had good reports from school. For my birthday today, my husband gave me lovely flowers, he really loves me.' Looking round frantically, 'I have nothing to worry about!' We do like our worries, they shield us from seeing the real cause of our restlessness.

'If you can do away with them, do away with them immediately.' If we really ponder our anxieties, then as long as 'I' live, I must want. That does not mean as long as the body lives, it is only as long as the delusion of 'I' exists in my mind. As long as 'I' and thought continue, I cannot cease to want, and whatever I want becomes bigger and more urgent. Whatever I fear and refuse gains power over me. The same also applies to our troubles and dilemmas. Do not fear them, let them be. Drop them.

But Master Daie also tells us why we cannot do away with them immediately – that means, cannot do away with 'I' immediately. **'Because you have become habituated to them'** – to the anxieties, to the I-thinking – **'since beginningless time, to the point where they have become totally familiar, if you do not exert yourself to struggle with them, then as time goes on and on, with you unknowing and unaware, they will have entered deeply into you.'** And that is exactly what happens. Whatever we give into, and habitually give into, and habitually continue giving into – that begins to truly take us over.

But there is another side to it too, and that is the good news. Any cultivation that we habitually, continuously, give ourselves into, on which we continuously, habitually work – that also begins to have its effect. We human beings are remarkably adaptable. That's why we make up such a large number, having grown under all circumstances; and why we are also so aggressive, because we are very adaptable. We can adapt ourselves to most circumstances but only if we have to. We adapt ourselves naturally to circumstances which are better. We do not naturally adapt ourselves to circumstances which are not so good, unless we have no option. 'But if you do not exert yourself to struggle with them, then as time goes on and on, with you unknowing and unaware,' and this is the dangerous thing, 'they will have entered deeply into you.'

What is 'unknowing and unaware'? 'Oh, just this once does not really matter. Just this once; at the moment, I'm really so tired,' or whatever it might be. 'Just this once, only just this time,' but then it becomes more frequent, and so quite unknowing and unaware, it overtakes me. Having started with 'only just this once' as an exception, three weeks later with a perfectly straight face, I will say, 'But I have always done this!' and make a permanence out of it.

An example from riding school is when you are trying to get the horse to go exactly into the corners of the track. If both you and the horse are tired at the end of an hour and the instructor may be looking in another direction, the horse tries to cut the corner. So you let it go, just this once. But now it does not want to go into the next corner either. With real effort and with the teacher looking on as well, you manage to get it into the corner. The next corner brings hardly any resistance, is quite smooth. But then it comes to that corner where it had its will and ha! It just won't! And it is a real struggle. It is in all of us mammals. So 'just this once' is dangerous. It is not the big things, it is the little ones that trip us up. And one of the most important and dangerous is 'just this once'.

'If you do not exert yourself to struggle with them (the worldly afflictions), then as time goes on and on, unknowing and unaware, they will have entered deeply into you.' To avoid this, the form, *sila* practice, deportment, is strongly emphasised, because if that holds, not too much can go wrong. In all religions there are detailed instructions how a monk has to walk, move, bow, the whole lot. And not only monks, in the army, too, the stress is on uniformity. And 'I' dread, 'I' dislike uniformity because it cancels me out. I do not like it. Same dress, same behaviour, not sticking out a bit. It takes quite some time to forge that 'way of doing it.' But once it is forged, it goes into the body and then the body can contain an eruption of the emotions in quite a different and much easier way. Hence the importance of the form. Able to keep the form makes it possible in all situations to behave in a decent human way. But if such habituation is not there, if always given into, always 'just this once', 'unknowing and unaware they will have entered deeply into you **and finally on the last day of your life you won't be able to do anything about it.'** It will be the same old thing, the worldly anxieties.

In the Southern Teachings there is the story of the Three Messengers. A young man dies. He had been well off and lived quite heedlessly. Now he stands in front of Yama, Lord of the Dead, and complains bitterly. 'I have not done anything yet, I have hardly seen life! Why must I be called to you at such an early time? It is not fair, it is not right. It is not just.' Yama has pity with the confused man, 'All right, I will let you go. But take care you spend your life decently, to good purpose and do not waste it as you have done so far.' 'No, I certainly will not!' Yama then promised, 'Next time there will be no more haggling, because before I call you again, I will send you three messengers who will warn you.' 'Oh, thank you,' said the young man and off he went. And he spent the next forty years of his life exactly as he had done the first twenty – learned nothing, did nothing, did not bestir himself, but went on as always 'from beginningless time to the point where it has become totally familiar.'

Again he found himself in front of Yama and not having learned anything, he started complaining as of old, 'It is too early for me. And you promised me three messengers and I have not seen one.' Yama said, 'But I have sent you three messengers. It is only that in your heedless behaviour you have not seen them! Have you then never seen a man or woman of eighty or ninety, toothless, crooked, tottering along, leaning on a staff?' 'Oh, plenty about,' said the man. 'Well, that was the first messenger,' said Yama. 'And have you never seen a crippled, grievously sick man or woman, rolling in the dust with pain?' 'Lots of them about,' said the man. 'That was the second messenger. And have you never seen a corpse?' 'Oh yes, I see some every morning.' 'Didn't you think that this might be the third messenger?' said Yama. And that was that.

We, too, have these messengers of old age, sickness and death all round us. We do not see somebody rolling in the dust with pain but we have got a surfeit of opportunities nowadays to see pictures and read about those messengers and be heedful.

But then on the last day of your life, you won't be able to do anything about it. **'If you want to be able to avoid going wrong when you face the end of your life'** – do we? Or do we feel, 'that's quite a long way off yet'? It may be quite a long time ahead but the cultivation of an attitude takes time. And therefore, **'then from now on, whenever you do anything, do not let yourself slip.'**

When it really comes down to it, we human beings know jolly well what we should do, how we should behave, how we should be – and not only do we know it, but in our very heart we actually really want to do so and to be so. We do not need to be told 'how to be' because we know that. What we need to know is how to bring it off. It is worth pondering why, in spite of wanting to, we just cannot manage to be or do what in our very heart we want to do. The Buddha showed us the way to bring it off. And that is, by not clinging, by not attaching, by not spinning thoughts nor making mental images out of them and then believing in them.

Whatever our opinions are, they have somehow had a beginning. Once we have caught hold of them, they wax stronger and stronger so that we believe them to be the final knowledge and we would die for them. Yet they are nothing but veils, threads in the head.

Though I have no natural inclination towards the practice of visualisations, I have always been interested from the psychological side. I once had the opportunity to ask the late Lama Anagarika Govinda about it. He told me visualisations had to start with the various divinities and deities. There is always a positive and a negative one, a beneficial and a wrathful one, each pair with increasing impact and power. The practice is to start with the smallest beneficial one and to visualise it with all the attributes and then to make that picture three-dimensional and finally to concretise it until it lives. Then you bow and say, 'Mind has made it, mind can dismantle it,' and start the reverse process, dismantling it until it is completely gone. After that you start with the dark one in the same way. And that continuous through all the deities. It is a twenty-year process.

But by the time you have gone through the whole process, you have found all your anxieties, all your particular hang-ups, all your archetypes – including the terrible ones – and you know that it is all inside you. The Indian saying, that all the gods and all the demons are inside you, is the short description of it. It is inside us and nowhere else, does not need to be looked for outside. In us it can be found and in us it can be sorted out and in us it can come to an end.

Therefore warns Master Daie, **'Do not let yourselves slip. If you go wrong in your present doings, it will be impossible not to go wrong when you are facing death.'** That is not a threat, but a simple statement. Remember that man with the three messengers. He always complained if something did not go his way and he never took any steps to pull himself together. We can only pull ourselves together in the present, there is no other time that we have. We cannot pull ourselves together yesterday, can we? Or tomorrow, though we think we can tomorrow, but it does not necessarily happen because tomorrow may be something quite different. 'It will be impossible not to go wrong when you are facing death.' And that is what we take with us. The material form perishes, the mental aggregates (*skandhas*) remain. All forms come to be and cease be, and the aggregates too, are impermanent. But that mental bundle, also changing, goes on and according to what is taken in during the life of the physical form, according to that it will find its next rebirth.

If you do not want to or cannot believe it, since there is nothing that we have to believe outright in Buddhism, then the Wheel of Life can be seen as a helpful framework, whether you call it rebirth or whether you call it genetics or whatever you want to call it. So it is useful to consider that and perhaps it may give us an extra bit of strength when next time that 'Oh just this once' arises. That is where the beginning is and that is where the end is. It is just 'this once', nowhere else, no great resolutions, no great things to be done, just 'this once'.

But we can also use 'this once' in a conducive way. I may feel I have always given in, but at this point, I just cannot any more. I simply cannot. Then you can take up 'Just this once' and go through with it. It is the same old 'Just this once', but made good use of. These things are freely given to make use of. As we are told in Buddhism, there is action in a skilful and in an unskilful way. Things are as they are but how we use them, how we confront them, how we react to them, may be in a skilful or in an unskilful way. And with 'Just this once' when it comes to a real limit, a breakthrough can be made which is far-reaching.

Just as we build things up until they become or seem to have become real, so we can also dismantle them. Again, an example from riding: if you take out a fresh horse in the morning, it likes to play up. It trots along and it likes to play, like every mammal including ourselves. It may see a bit of paper or a leaf rolling in the wind and it begins to play frightened. If you are at one with it and not somewhere else, you go along with it but you know that there comes a point where suddenly, always suddenly, the playing jumps over into real panic and the horse bolts. If you get it just at that point before it bolts, before the play becomes real and pull it back, all goes cheerfully along again. But if you miss that point and the horse has bolted, you can pull on the reins, but in its fright it does not feel it. A real panic has got it.

The same applies to us too. We do get ourselves to that turning point, and then we get into trouble when we go on with it. But we can turn the other way round. Instead of building up something silly, we can also work and build up something truly supportive that will not allow us any of the usual subterfuges, projections, emotive and totally irrational judgements and convictions. This will make us aware of the moment and trigger an appropriate response to the situation as it is. We are never outside the situation, we do not hang in a vacuum. And it is within the situation that I either react in response to my prompting, my liking and disliking, or being aware of the situation as it is, willingly respond to it in terms of the situation. That is the difference.

If the response is in terms of the situation, then there is inevitably a natural feeling of joy and partaking, and from that also comes the realisation that we are all closely inter-connected. Only concerned with ourselves and with what 'I notice' cuts me off. But simply being aware, then when somebody is in an unhappy state, we are prompted to help. That is where the good will comes in and the warmth of the heart, which is the human heart, the seat of compassion. These are the first two of the Four Brahma Viharas, the Divine Abodes, divine because they go beyond what 'I' can do. And these we cultivate when we walk the Buddha's Path.

It does not matter about becoming a living Buddha in this life, though we are all supposed to become one sooner or later, in the aeons to come. But even if we only come to the state where we are always friendly and joyful in our workplace and amongst our family and nearest and dearest, that alone, considering what the world is nowadays, is already a good enough way of showing that life can be lived not entirely depending on 'I' and my likes, but that it can be lived truly for the sake of all of us. Because it cannot be lived for 'I' only, nor only for the sake of others, it can only be lived for the sake of all of us. And this 'for all of us' is what fulfils the heart's longing.

LETTER 4 to LI HSIEN-CH'EN (continued)

The Text

> There is a sort of person who reads the scriptures, recites the Buddha-name and repents in the morning but then in the evening runs off with the mouth gossiping. The next day he does homage to the Buddha and repents as before. All through the years till the end of his life he takes this as daily ritual. This is extreme folly. Such people are far from realising that the Sanskrit word *kshama* means to repent faults. This is called 'cutting off the continuing thought-stream.' Once you have cut it off, never continue it again. Once you have repented, do not commit wrong-doings again. This is the meaning of Repentance according to our Buddha which good people who study the Path should not fail to know.

The mind, discriminating intellect and consciousness of students of the Path should be quiet and still, twenty-four hours a day. When you have nothing to do, you should sit quietly and keep the mind from slackening and the body from wavering. If you practise to perfection over a long, long time, naturally body and mind will come to rest at ease and you will have some direction in the Path. The perfection of quiescence and stillness indeed settles the scattered and confused false consciousness of human beings. But if you cling to quiescent stillness and consider it the ultimate, then you are in the grip of perverted silent illumination Ch'an.

Ven. Myokyo-ni's Comments

This couldn't be better advice and so we will ponder carefully what Master Daie suggests. **'There is a sort of person who reads the scriptures, recites the Buddha-name and repents in the morning.'** I do not know how many of you do so at home, but here in the temple we start the morning chant with the *Repentance Sutra*. How many do at least that as a daily practice at home? That is the first thing to look at. But then when that is done, or when in the evening we go home or gather together, we start our usual talking and gossiping. Next morning we start again with chanting the *Repentance Sutra*, and in the evening we relax again – we have forgotten it.

'There is a sort of person who reads the scriptures, recites the Buddha's name and repents in the morning, but' continues Master Daie, **'then in the evening runs off with the mouth gossiping.'** Coming together at the annual Summer School is a good example. We start the morning with meditation and then we have talks on the Buddha-dharma but the moment we are out of the meditation or lecture room, everybody starts chattering like children when school is dismissed. Having been confined for a time, we explode because the confinement has practically exceeded our bearing tolerance of being silent. And so the strength of being silent, being contained, needs to be practised. If we just continue heedlessly all through the years, at the end of life what will we do?

In the Southern Scriptures there is a passage where the Buddha returns to the meditation hall from outside. He hears his monks talking and entering, asks, 'What have you been talking about?' They tell him they have been talking about the Dharma. The Buddha nods and says, 'If you talk about the Dharma and inquire about the Dharma, that is right, otherwise it is better to be silent.' We, in our ordinary daily life, do we talk about the Dharma? Or do we talk ceaselessly about ourselves, our opinions and convictions, or just gossip and chat. And then we are surprised that whatever strength we have collected, we cannot contain and it is released, 'let fly' or it explodes of itself.

I came to experience that personally on my very first *sesshin* in Daitoku-ji. I decided that I would not open my mail for that week. Coming home at the end of the *sesshin* a bit earlier than usual, I thought, 'Now I'll have a little celebration by looking at my mail.' As I did so, suddenly it was as if the spring in a watch had snapped – BRRRRRRRRRR it went inside me, and all the collectedness accumulated during the *sesshin* discharged itself, was gone. What a waste!

'The next day he does homage to the Buddha and repents as before. All through the years till the end of his life he takes this as daily ritual. This is extreme folly.' Without knowing it, we continuously do the same. Depending on our inner strength (collectedness), when that reaches our bearing tolerance, we 'let off steam'. This is what all the old masters refer to as the 'running off at the mouth' and it does not need to be just the mouth. It is one's own self, that continuous thought-stream that we allow ourselves to be carried away by. Master Daie calls this 'extreme folly', extreme silliness. **'Such people are far from realising that the Sanskrit word *kshama* means to repent faults.'**

To repent faults? Do we even think that we need to repent faults nowadays? What we mistake for repentance is wallowing, 'Oh my fault, oh my great fault, oh what have I done!' But repentance is not the wallowing but getting clear about what I have done so that it will not happen again. To realise that is to repent faults. It usually comes down to not transgressing the precepts.

'This is then called cutting off the continuing thought-stream.' Once you have cut it off, well, in order to be able to cut off the thought-stream, it is necessary to be aware of it. In order to be able to work with our inadequacies, difficulties, etc., we must be clearly aware of them. Usually we aren't, because we have a habit of covering them over, calling them something else, not wanting, not daring, not willing to confront them directly.

However, if the faults are properly repented, then I need not think about them anymore. I know it is my own silliness. If not looking, I stumble on the doorstep, lose my balance, fall and graze my knee and it hurts, am I then like a little child, hitting the step and saying, 'Naughty step! Naughty step!' or do I say, 'Well, serves you right, you fool,' and perhaps next time just look. And actually, if it is taken to heart like this and learned in the body, then we naturally look out a little more carefully, become a bit more aware. But if we do not take it to heart, then it will happen again and again and we will not learn from it.

In the Buddha-dharma there is nothing that cannot be used as grist to the mill. Even the transgressions, if they are properly looked at and repented, are helpful in preventing it happening again and in cutting off the continuing thought-streams.

This is why in the monastery the new monks are not told the rules of the monastery. They are expected to find out quickly by themselves. If they are unobservant and do not conform, then there is a bloodcurdling yell that really cuts through so that the next time when thoughtlessly the same is about to happen, the body remembers. That body-remembrance is the important thing. If only told, 'Now you'd better not do that,' it cuts no ice. But if it really cuts through the body, as with the sudden shout, then this is cutting off the continuous thought-stream. Once it is cut off, do not fall back into the old habit, stick to the new. The body remembers that I repent the fault.

It is the same with the energy that has been pulled together. In our training, we learn to cultivate that energy which is the agent for transformation. Never let it discharge, rather with that additional strength continue the same old round once more, and still once more. Without this 'once more' we are right back again on the good old track and have learnt nothing. So, having cut off the thought-stream, we do need the strength to avoid falling back into the old habit. That is really all. Once you have repented, cut off, felt what you did, do not commit the transgression again. This is the meaning of repentance according to our Buddha. It is not wallowing in, 'Oh, it's all my fault, oh, I am hopeless, oh, my fault' and five minutes later doing exactly the same again.

Master Daie continues, **'Once repented, not to commit wrong-doings again. This is the meaning of repentance according to our Buddha, which good people who study the Path should not fail to know.'** This is also the reason why 'good form' is stressed so much – that is, being well-mannered, quick but not rushed, and a good clear voice with which the monk speaks (no mumbling). With friends at home, do we talk with that kind of voice? Do we? Why not? We mumble out of laziness or fearing that if we might say something wrong, it will not be immediately spotted and we can quickly excuse it with, 'this is not what I said.'

And with that comes another fact – that really, underneath all our beliefs that we want to go the Buddha's Way, we are quite determined to keep our own dear ways going. But my way and the Buddha's Way often cross, and it is then the question, of whether it is my way or the Buddha's Way that wins? That is also what repentance means. But I, being a very mixed-up person, want to have my way, but I also want to do it the Buddha's Way. And so I have problems.

All those things come under the meaning of repentance. We need to be aware of them, so as not to fall into one or the other excuses. Master Daie then continues, **'The Mind (heart), discriminating intellect and consciousness of students of the Path, should be quiet and still twenty-four hours a day.'** There is the heart, there is the discriminating intellect that evaluates and judges and there is consciousness, awareness itself, the pure 'choiceless awareness' as Krishnamurti calls it. So the heart, the discriminating intellect which is the self-consciousness, and the choiceless awareness of students of the path, all, 'should be quiet and still twenty-four hours a day.'

That is what I want, not to be upset by anything anymore, not to be annoyed anymore, just really cool. So I work towards it, repressing any feelings. I might as well be in the grave then, all cool. Or the other way, I am jolly well not going to be upset by anything. And if you are in the process of upsetting me, you must be removed! Either one or the other. Because discriminating consciousness, the self-consciousness, can see things only from the point of 'I', only from 'my' point of view. I may flatter myself on being 'objective' but I cannot be so!

However, my point of view is far, far too short-sighted and it is also far too partial. To see the whole situation as it is, for that the choiceless awareness of taking in what actually is there, is necessary. But because 'I' obstruct that, we self-consciously make all the howlers, the mistakes, the silly things, the tragedies, the fights and everything that we have always done and make ourselves and others thoroughly unhappy in the process.

But if the thought-stream is 'quiet and still twenty-four hours a day' – 'Well, how can it be quiet and still twenty-four hours a day', I immediately say, 'when in the midst of a real hubbub of city life?' Most of us nowadays can drive a car. If you are in a car in heavy traffic, say in London around Hyde Park Corner or Marble Arch, can you allow yourself to go into a state of panic or anxiety, 'I have to be careful now! Be careful now!' Can you? Or do you just have to be quiet and calm, be open and attentive to the situation and go with it?

That is what is meant by 'should be quiet and calm', not 'I do not feel anything, I must be above it, I must be beyond it' which is simply silly. But fully given into the situation, flowing with the situation, at that moment there is also quiet calmness. The heart is calm, the discriminating intellect can no longer function because I am not there. But awareness is there to go with it. This is why an old master said, 'The heart flows with the ten thousand things, this flowing is truly mysterious.' It does not get rigid, it is not caught up in anything, it does not stick to anything; it flows freely with the changing situations and itself is quiet and still without getting carried away by emotions.

Therefore **'When you have nothing to do, you should sit quietly and keep the mind** (heart) **from slackening and the body from wavering.'** 'When you have nothing to do' – that is the crucial sentence, isn't it? We can even, and often do, misuse zazen for something to do. Hopefully no longer, but for example during a *sesshin*, people wait to the last minute before going into the zendo, fidgeting about outside – a continuous restlessness while waiting, and then when it is time to start the zazen period all feel relieved and surge in, 'Ah, now there is something to do, now I have to do zazen.' But that is misusing zazen, is not what zazen is. Zazen is to be still and quiet. And therefore I have suggested to quite a few to try – for half an hour only, when there is nothing special to do at home – to sit yourself down in your most comfortable armchair and there remain sitting for half an hour, quiet and still without letting thought-streams carry you away, without fidgeting, just quiet and still, giving yourself over. Anybody tried it? What happened? Try it, it is a real test. Within ten minutes you'll find you've got the itches, even if you didn't start with any – 'must do something, telephone, telly, make a cup of tea.' But 'to sit quietly and keep the heart from slackening and the body from wavering' that is what zazen means – to sit quietly and keep the heart still and the body from fidgeting.

'If you practise to perfection,' says Master Daie, **'over a long, long time, naturally body and mind** (heart) **will come to rest at ease, and you will have some direction in the Path.'** Body and heart will come to rest at ease if there are no distractions, no thought-streams to pull you about. If these are gone and it has become really quiet and you are now used to it, then 'the heart will come to rest at ease and you will have some direction in the Path.' That is what the Sixth Patriarch emphasised when he said, 'Before thinking' or 'without thinking.' In that 'without thinking' or 'before thinking' is the 'the wisdom and power of the Tathagata' that the Buddha discovered on his awakening. That is all that the heart needs. Then it can come to rest at ease. While it is continuously blown about by the storms of passions like the sea in a hurricane, this coming to ease is not possible. And then there can be no direction of the Path.

I start to practise believing that I should come to that state of 'without thought', not knowing that this is impossible because I am the thought. And therefore, what being 'without thought' really comes down to is that the thought of 'I' has dropped off and this is what I am terrified of – that I might suddenly vanish and no longer be.

You scratch the surface a little and underneath you find fear of losing control, fear of losing myself. Fear is the other side of I and basically it is lack of strength. Yet underneath is also the whole 'wisdom and power of the Tathagata'. If its power is pushed up by my partiality, it discharges itself in volcanic eruptions called the *klesas*, the afflicting passions. It is said in the Mahayana teachings, 'The passions are the Buddha-nature and the Buddha-nature is the passions.' That does not mean that I can go and have a violent row with you and then say that I have only been showing my Buddha-nature! It rather happens that, I being there and picking and choosing, the energy, that by itself is the Buddha-nature, is forced up ready to discharge itself as anger, etc. But it is the same energy. As long as I am there desperately wanting or rejecting, as long as thoughts are there, it will erupt as the passions. When I am no longer there, there are no more thoughts, and so the heart rests at ease.

'The perfection of quiet calmness and stillness indeed settles the scattered and confused false consciousness of human beings.' What is that false consciousness? That is the self-consciousness which is scattered and confused. There is consciousness, and there is self-consciousness. There is consciousness per se – the pure awareness that is the clear seeing of things as they actually are, which the Buddha said is inherent in all of us – that clear seeing from which the appropriate action comes as a natural response. And then there is the self-consciousness: the one that makes me feel embarrassed; the one that is ambitious; the one that wants; the one that dislikes; the one that strives for something – all this, that is the false consciousness. It is important to always be clear which of the consciousnesses is acting. Because we are totally unaware that we have two consciousnesses, and we continuously – if we read things like this – mix them up, because we do not know the difference.

But actually it is a very simple difference. Pinch yourself in the soft part of the arm. Do you need to make a conscious effort to realise what it is? And what is the reaction if the pinch is a little bit strong? Ow!

'But if you cling to quiet calmness and consider it the ultimate, then you are in the grip of perverted silent illumination Ch'an.' So 'if you cling to quiescent stillness and consider it the ultimate' – which it isn't – 'then you are in the grip of the perverted silent illumination Ch'an' – where you just sit, and quietly sit, and go on quietly sitting. You might as well be in the grave then, for the use that you are; and at the same time frightened of getting involved in an ordinary daily life as an ordinary mature human being.

Rather than being gripped by the 'perverted silent illumination Ch'an', to just sit quietly with nothing to perturb us anymore, then we can gratefully remember the Buddha – after all, it is his footsteps that we follow. Did he, after his enlightenment, just settle down, never open his mouth, have nothing to do with anything, just not letting himself be perturbed by anything? Or did he spend the rest of his life walking about all over north-eastern India, talking to people, helping people, showing them the way out of suffering, full of compassion?

If we have no more feelings, we cannot feel compassion either, instead we could not care less. Or we feel a maudlin sentimentality which is the opposite of compassion. Compassion is on the other side of thinking, when there is no more 'I', just clear seeing of what this moment requires. Sometimes it might be a pat on the shoulder and sometimes it may be a push. We learn more by physical impact than by mental intake, and so Zen training has always been full of kicks and shouts. The one thing that all the texts warn against is grandmotherly kindness. When molly-coddled all along, then when something suddenly happens, we cannot react accordingly. Real grandmotherly kindness slaps at a weak moment and thus it supports. And that is what Zen training believes in, and why it is said that the old masters had ways of making men.

So do not forget the physical side. Nowadays we are so convinced that everything can be worked out in the head, by the mind – do not believe it, it is not possible. Even as simple an act as lifting your arm, can you lift it by mind only, without throwing yourself into the act? Can you stand up by an act of mind alone? And yet you do it, fifty, a hundred times a day. Something else is necessary, that keeps the heart alive and enables the wholeness of the swing to go into the action of standing up This is what makes things alive and what slowly over the years produces the entrance to what the Buddha called the 'wisdom and power of the Tathagata', where there is no need to hold back. There is no hesitating over this or that, and there is no deliberation. Master Rinzai says, and this can be taken as a gauge, to freely open and show stomach, spleen, liver and gall!

LETTER 4 to LI HSIEN-CH'EN (continued)

The Text

The Sanskrit word *prajna* means wisdom. Those who lack clear *prajna* and are greedy, wrathful, stupid and lustful, those who do not have clear *prajna* and harm sentient beings, those who do such things as these, they are running away from *prajna*. How can this be called wisdom?

By keeping aware of the matter of birth and death, your mental awareness, mental attitude, is already correct. Once the mental attitude is correct, then you won't need to use effort to empty your mind, as you respond to circumstances in your daily activities. When you do not actively try to clear out your mind, then you won't go wrong. And since you do not go wrong, correct mindfulness stands out alone. When correct mindfulness stands out alone, inner truth adapts to phenomena. When inner truth adapts to events and things, events and things come to fuse in inner truth. When the phenomena fuse with the inner truth, you save power. When you feel the saving, this is the empowerment of studying the Path. In gaining power, you save ultimate unlimited power. In saving power, you gain unlimited power.

Ven. Myokyo-ni's Comments

'The Sanskrit word *prajna* means wisdom' and is the last of the *paramitas*. It is the Wisdom of the Tathagata – not what we call wisdom, the worldly wisdom which always splits into this and that. And **'those who lack clear *prajna* and are greedy, wrathful, stupid and lustful'** – in other words those who lack the clear *prajna* are therefore subject to and inflamed by the Fires. We know these as stupidity/delusion, greed/desire and hatred and they give rise to wrath, anger, lust, notions and opinions. Those who lack clear *prajna* are subject to the Fires. We can look at ourselves and ask whether we are subject to the Fires or whether we are on a way where *prajna* becomes more and more steadfast?

Those who are subject to the Fires do not have clear *prajna* and that has consequences, for those who do not have clear *prajna* harm sentient beings. **'And those who do such things as these are running away from *prajna*.'** Why should it be that without clear *prajna* sentient beings are harmed? And not only sentient beings, all things, sentient and inanimate. A cup plonked down with a clank, a chair scraped over the floor, that also is harming things. If we really bear that in mind, it cultivates an attitude of care and consideration for everything. And that is precisely what takes us out of ourselves and towards clear *prajna*.

This hurting or harming of things, not just intentionally but by not taking care, not being considerate, is the consequence of being involved in only I, in my ideas and notions and so not noticing, therefore lacking consideration for anything, not just sentient beings. But if that consideration is there, then suddenly a relationship is found with everything.

Nowadays there is much talk about loneliness and old age, but if one's relationship with everything is realised, how can there be anything in the shape of loneliness or even fear? Buddhism teaches this interconnectedness but much practice in our ordinary daily life is needed to bring it about. It means to be fully within the situation, to be careful and considerate, aware of what is there, and gentle instead of blundering blindly through circumstances and objects. That is what we can practise continuously, every minute of our daily life. If we do that, then things begin to change. If we find that things are not changing very much, then we also know that we lack the willingness and consideration of being there, being present in our circumstances, respecting them.

If we do not respect things, we will not be considerate. If we do not respect things, we will never be able to respect ourselves and therefore will never acquire inner strength. As Master Daie tells us, **'Those who do such things are running away from *prajna*. How can this be called wisdom?'** And he suggests a particular line of approach. **'By keeping mindful** (aware) **of the matter of birth and death, your mental attitude is already correct.'** Keeping aware of the matter of birth and death is the Great Matter of coming to be and ceasing to be, as the Buddha taught it. Everything comes to be and ceases to be, nothing is without change. Everything changes, whether we like it or not. If we are clearly aware of this matter of birth and death, then we are also willing to do something about it. For the Buddhist this is not just about death, but a question of being reborn, not only from life to life but also from hour to hour. To be reborn in one of the three dark states of the Wheel of Becoming is a calamity indeed, because once reborn in them it is not possible to easily reach human birth again; and it is only from the human state that deliverance is possible.

Through much effort and great good karma we now have been born human. Are we going to waste this great opportunity, to be reborn perhaps as a slug that gets squashed? And how long will it then take until human birth is attained again? Hundreds of rebirths, all of them unpleasant. I may think, 'rebirth is an Eastern idea and I do not really believe in it.' What do I believe in then? Do I fear death? 'No,' say I, because it is not right in front of me now, but I might feel slightly different when it is right there.

So perhaps we begin to understand what the Buddha is pointing at with this ever-changing round of birth and death. When the body breaks down, what happens with the other four skandha-strands? They go on, continuously twisting and changing, rather like in a telephone switchboard; they will go into forms that fit them. Having had no consideration for anything else but Me, what do you think that fourfold bundle is naturally going to be attracted to – a glorious human birth? So perhaps that matter of birth and death is not quite so simple and might be considered very seriously and to good purpose.

'By keeping aware of that matter of birth and death, your mental attitude is already correct,' because being aware – and keeping aware – such a mental attitude is not totally ego-orientated, and being aware will keep us considerate, taking in the surroundings and responding properly. **'Once the mental attitude is correct,'** says Master Daie, **'then you will not need to use effort to empty your mind** (heart)**, as you respond to circumstances in your daily activities.'** When the mental attitude is correct, you need not use effort to empty the heart, to let go of all judging, picking and choosing, wanting and refusing, all 'my' notions and fancies and ingrained convictions. The 'correct attitude' is emptying the heart. If I am being careful and attentive to that matter of birth and death, then the mental attitude will naturally be responsive, no longer an I-orientated attitude of 'couldn't care less' or 'this I want/must have'. An I-orientated attitude gives rise to the Three Fires, and this will only increase suffering. But if the mental attitude is correct, then there is no need to use effort to empty the heart because it happens of itself.

This correct response to circumstances in daily activities is our Daily Life Practice. To begin with, it tends very much to split into 'my' ordinary daily life and 'my' practice. But where is the practice except in my ordinary daily life? That is the life I live. I often hear from people, 'I have been so busy, I really could not get round to do any practice.' What an absolutely foolish thing to say! The busier I am, the more chance there is to give myself into it. But I will not see that the one is the other. I will keep things separate. On the one hand, 'my practice' (which I often only think of as zazen and see it as apart from my daily life), and on the other, my job and my home life. And then I want a bit of leisure for 'me' too. So, there seems no time for practice under such circumstances. But if Daily Life Practice is daily life from the moment the eyes open in the morning, till the eyes close in the evening, then in responding to circumstances in our daily activities, that is our practice – getting up, washing the face, brushing the teeth, getting dressed, cooking, eating breakfast.

Master Daie says that to empty the heart you have to respond to circumstances in your daily lives. **'When you don't actively try to clear out the mind** (heart), **then you won't go wrong'** – not actively trying to empty the heart, just going smoothly along, responding to the daily circumstances, obeying them freely, willingly, just as they are. And not taking them 'personally' either! For responding to the circumstances, whether at home or at work, if it is always with a great 'Yes', then with that comes a willingness to see what is all around us and not offending.

'When you do not actively try to empty your heart, then you will not go wrong. **And since you do not go wrong, the correct mindfulness** (attitude) **stands out alone. And when correct mindfulness** (attitude) **stands out alone, inner truth adapts to phenomena.'** Everything has a structure, and everything is connected. And if you adapt yourself to the circumstances in daily activities and smoothly flow with them, it is almost like playing. You need not take them personally because there is nothing personal about them. Sometimes the play goes this way and sometimes it goes that way. If you just take it as a play, you do not need to feel upset by it. That is just how it goes – sometimes you win and sometimes you lose, quite naturally. Then only the correct attitude stands out, and you won't go wrong in daily activities. A sense of play is important because the moment it becomes playful, it becomes not mine alone but it is mutual and in that mutuality there is always a sense of partaking and therefore also a sense of joy. So 'when correct attitude stands out alone,' as Master Daie says, then 'the inner truth adapts to phenomena.' When the correct attitude stands out alone, there is no picking and choosing 'I' about, and so 'inner truth adapts to phenomena.'

And when phenomena are truly seen into, and the **'inner truth adapts to events and things, then events and things come to fuse in inner truth.'** Then it all comes together. In this kind of coming together, just like in any structure, everything is in its place of minimum energy, and then there are few, if any, obstacles and it goes smoothly. This is the sense of playing and when that is the case, the individual unique object and the truth of what is, become one. An analogy we can think of – and it is only an analogy – is to look at a tree. For example, a chestnut tree. Full of leaves as it is, yet there is not one leaf that is exactly the same as the others. But each leaf in its uniqueness is indubitably a chestnut leaf, and in its uniqueness expresses that chestnut-ness of this tree and of all chestnut trees. If we can possibly look at that, it will help us.

We read in the *Analects of Confucius* about the cultivation of the human being: 'At fifteen, I set my heart upon learning. At thirty, I had planted my feet firmly on the ground. At forty, I no longer suffered from perplexities. At fifty, I knew what were the biddings of heaven. At sixty, I heard them with a docile heart and with a docile ear. And at seventy, I could follow the dictates of my own heart, for what I desired no longer overstepped the boundaries of right and heaven.' That is when it has really come together. In the Buddhist training, we need not wait until we are seventy, but we really need to put ourselves into it. When it has been fully cultivated, 'gentled', then there is the natural human being, acting not because he should do this that or the other, but because he cannot overstep anymore. He does not *have to be good*, because *he is good*.

In that oneness is the complete unity with everything. So, **'when phenomena fuse with their inner truth, you save power'** because there is no effort necessary. Then it is play, a dance, and there is no more rigid or brittle 'I' but a smooth and easy going, or being at one with the circumstances, like water running. Of all drops which make up the water, none of them goes against it, they all flow with it. Layman P'ang says, 'The snowflakes fall, each in its appropriate place.' They do not choose and fight with each other where they want to be. Each in its appropriate place. 'When phenomena fuse with their inner truth, you save power.'

And **'when you feel the saving, this is the empowerment of studying the Path.'** As long as we are subject to the Fires, we lack this empowerment, because the power is in the Fires. Yet it is inherent

– as the Buddha saw on his own awakening, that all beings are fully endowed with the Wisdom and Power of the Tathagata. But from his deep insight he also added that sadly human beings, because of their attachments, are not aware of it. So 'I', being the clever one, want to get rid of my attachments, spending maybe lifetimes on it, without realising that there is only one attachment, the cardinal one, and that is 'I'. When that has fallen off, all the other attachments have gone too. And therefore, 'when phenomena fuse with their inner truth, then you save power' and there is no more picking and choosing but a quiet standing on one's own two feet. Circumstances are as they are and you go with them.

A hurricane can blow over even the strongest tree, just because it is rigid. But a bamboo or a willow can never be blown over, because they bend – and when the storm is over, they stand up again. We say somewhat derogatorily that someone who 'bends with the wind' has no real point of view, is weak. But what can be blown away by the wind are dried leaves already fallen off. A willow just bends with the wind, is not blown away, yet does not fight against being blown away. And when it is over, it stands upright again. If we are rigidly standing against it, circumstances certainly have the power to blow us over. Being rigid is not real strength. So 'when phenomena fuse with inner truth, you save power.' And 'when you feel the saving, this is the empowerment of studying the Path,' where we can peacefully say 'Yes' or can just say, 'I don't know.' Then we do not have to feel embarrassed nor to strut about, we no longer need to put up a ham actor show because of the lack of power. If there is the true power of the Path, all this is quite unnecessary.

Knowing that one is no-thing, then nothing can possibly upset one anymore, or if one feels one must be something, then it is best to feel like a great fool. Soko Roshi once said laughing, 'All that Zen does is to turn people into fools because only a fool can take all that happens and still laugh.' Can we? Or do we still judge and evaluate? Can we bear to be scolded, even for something that we have done? And if accused of something which we have not done, ooh, then we are really up, aren't we? That is not empowerment, because if you are really in balance, what somebody else says or accuses us of, is their business, not ours. We do not need to take it off them. But if not squarely standing on our own feet, if we wobble or need the continuous propping up by others to feel that we are, and can continue to exist, then ours is a pretty poor, sad life. Oh, what a waste. So we'd better heed the Buddha's Path. For **'in gaining power you save unlimited power; in saving power, you gain unlimited power.'** It is a double thing. The less of 'I', the more of the Buddha-nature.

When we consider the Buddha's life, historically we know nothing, but the legends in all traditions make it absolutely clear what is necessary along that Path. All the temptations of Mara came at him: the responsibility to his family, lust for Mara's alluring daughters, fear from Mara's demons. He did not fight these temptations, he did not react to them, he just sat, unconcerned, and so they had no power over him. If in our daily lives, with their natural ups and downs, we can remain unconcerned and can admit, 'Yes, that was a foolish thing to do, I'll not do that anymore,' then we become more careful with everything around. And we will find that there is no 'I-willfulness, but only a great 'Yes' to circumstances and a going along with them, almost dancing with them. That then is a daily life which is smooth, which is joyful, which does not waste any power. That is where the saving of power starts and also where it comes to an end, with the unlimited power, which is inherent anyway and freely available for everything that is necessary. And with that, and that is the incredible thing about it, not only is the individual affected, but like ripples in a pond, it touches and strengthens what is around it, whether animate or inanimate. So instead of feeling like an 'I', thoroughly alone somewhere, there is suddenly an interconnectedness with everything and a participation in what actually is, and that is where the power and the strength is unlimited. In a human being it is also the warmth of heart which then wells up and extends to all beings; and with the heart fulfilled it participates naturally in what is.

LETTER 4 to LI HSIEN-CH'EN (CONTINUED)

THE TEXT

This matter may be taken up by brilliant, quick-witted folks, but if you depend on your brilliance and your quick wits, you won't be able to bear up. It is easy for keen and bright people to enter but hard for them to persevere. That is because generally their entry is not very deep and the power is meagre. With the intelligent and quick-witted, as soon as they hear a spiritual friend mention this matter, their eyes stir immediately and they are already trying to gain understanding through their mind's discriminating intellect. People like this are creating their own hindrances and will never have a moment of awakening. 'When devils from outside wreak calamity, it can still be remedied.' But this (reliance on intellectual discrimination) amounts to, 'when one's own family creates disaster, it cannot be averted.' This is what Yung Chia meant when he said 'the loss of the wealth of the Dharma and the demise of Virtue all stem from the mind's discriminating intellect.'

This might be specially written for us, too. A friend told me that while travelling in India, he went to an assembly where the Guru spoke in English. He happened to sit next to a young American. The talk was about the long time the training takes to attain to genuine insight. The young man got fidgety and whispered, 'All this long, long time! Bet when we get hold of it, we'll do it in three months!' Just this is our trouble because, first of all we are convinced that if things are truly explained to us, we can understand them. And then we are further convinced that we are capable of understanding everything. And finally, we are convinced that if we do understand everything, then we will be at peace and there's nothing further to wish for. And that just shows how hopelessly we are running contrary to what is.

But there is also another version of the brilliant, quick-witted understanding – our own opinionated ideas, our own fancies that come to us, whether in the small hours of the night or in our daydreaming, when we believe in the dreams that we produce. Then I firmly believe I understand what you are thinking and intuitively 'know' what she at this moment is mulling over in her mind, or what is best for you to do. Thus convinced, I foolishly advise accordingly and then am surprised that my advice does not work and that everyone is getting a bit annoyed with me. That is being swallowed by one's own emotional household. We do not realise it and truly believe that I am right. That is the difficulty that we face.

Although this seems particularly pertinent to us today, it has actually always been so. As human beings we are split and so Master Daie says, **'This matter may be taken up by brilliant, quick-witted folks, but if you depend on your brilliance and quick wits, you won't be able to bear up.'** Intellectually this is easy to understand, but then to actually really live it is quite a different thing. It is easy to understand how to swim. It is easy to understand how to ride a bicycle. You can even accurately describe it, but that does not mean that you can actually jump into deep water and swim or get on a bicycle and ride away on it.

The more quick-witted we are, the more we can deceive ourselves. Here is an analogy, perhaps a little obsolete because we do not wear fur coats anymore. But take it as some forty years ago. It is hot summer now, but it will soon be autumn and winter not far behind. My old winter coat is getting a little shabby, I must do something about it. I sit at home, pondering the problem of the winter coat. Although only summer, I deem it sufficiently urgent to make me ignore with good conscience that there is a little bit of washing to be done which I do not particularly fancy doing. So I become restless, the urgency of the winter coat has faded but I do not admit to myself that I do not want to do that washing. Suddenly my eyes hit on a letter on my desk, 'Goodness me, it has sat there for a week, I really must answer it.' I sit myself down with a will, feeling rather virtuous, and since I also happen to have a stamp, I go right out to post it this very minute so that it goes off tomorrow with the first mail.

On my way home where my washing is still waiting, but needing to screen it from myself, it occurs to me, 'My old neighbour, she is a lonely, old woman and so enjoys my visits.' Feeling even more virtuous, I look in on her and we two girls have a good evening until it's quite late and I realise I must run home because tomorrow is a busy day in the office. So, the washing is conveniently forgotten.

Next morning in the office it is not nearly so busy and that coat comes into my mind again. All my life I have wanted a mink coat. But how could I afford such an expensive coat? Yet a mink coat is not easily worn out, I am only forty, it would last me for the rest of my life. So actually, it would be an investment, wouldn't it? It will take at least three other coats to make up for the life of a mink coat. But I cannot afford one. And then comes an inspiration – I could try and find an extra job, an evening job, so that I could make enough money. And then with a little bit of help, hire purchase or something, I might manage to buy that mink coat after all.

And so this evening I do not go home where my little bundle of washing is waiting, but look for an extra evening job. And having found one I go home, highly elated, knowing that the mink coat is on line, so to speak. Already seeing myself wearing it, I go to bed still dreaming, while my bundle of washing is still waiting. Next morning with new vigour I go to the office, and from there straight to my evening job, coming home late, the washing completely forgotten. As the money accumulates and autumn draws in, I am beginning to worry. After all, I know nothing about fur coats and things being what they are, the salesman will soon spot that and might cheat me.

So in the little spare time that I still have, I begin to learn about mink coats, how to recognise good fur. My washing, still there, just cannot be thought of, I am far too busy. As I become truly familiar with the quality of mink coats, I am now also wondering, if I now have the mink coat, then come next summer with moths and all that, how to preserve that coat? After all, it is to last me for the rest of my life. And so on top of all other studies, I am beginning to study preservation of fur coats which keeps me even more busy. The washing, I do not even think of it anymore, have cleanly forgotten it.

All my studies – mink, furs, quality of, preservation of, etc. – lead me to get interested now in minks themselves – how best to rear them in order to get the perfect coat? Not just any mink coat but the perfect one. That leads me to the study of the breeding and feeding of minks. I have now a full schedule and am beginning to be known as an expert on minks. Learned societies ask me to give talks on minks. That goes on for some time, an excellent cover up. But that bundle of washing is still there and a little uneasiness urges again, prompting a new excuse. Somehow I am beginning to get worried, times are difficult, uncertain, what can be done about it, what will be the fate of humanity? One reads about asteroids that are coming, and so I begin to study along those lines. My bundle is still waiting.

And now we can stop and carefully look at this escalating sequence. Is that bit of washing, a few pants and a shirt, is that really so little that continuing to ignore it, in the end not even the fate of humanity and of the universe can cover up, that it is still there?

And so in our training we stick to our bundle and do not allow ourselves any evasions. By thus sticking to our bundle we cultivate strength to continue. That strength is crucial.

When I first came to Japan, full of enthusiasm and interest in Zen, I asked people connected with Zen what had brought them to it. They all said, 'Strength.' I felt disappointed, poor Zen, has it come down to that, just the bully, brute power! I knew nothing of that inner strength that is forged by training and can stand on its own feet, does not budge and has no need to budge. The Buddhist term for this strength is 'virtue', that strength which is inherent in all sentient beings. By training we become aware of this inherent power. Without it we are enslaved by our fancies, our wants and dislikes, the whole lot. The more quick-witted we are, the more our fancies get hold of us and carry us far away from the Buddha's Ancient Path.

Master Daie continues, '**It is easy for keen and bright people to enter, but hard for them to persevere. That is because generally their entry is not very deep and the power is meagre.**' Quick-witted people think they know at the first glimpse but lack the power and will to penetrate further. If the power is meagre, things soon fall down like a house of cards. It all runs smoothly as long as things are fine, but the moment things become difficult, one way or another, it all breaks down. So '**with the intelligent and quick-witted, as soon as they hear a spiritual friend mention this matter,**' this Great Matter of Birth and Death, this Great Matter of Genuine Insight, the

Great Dharma, **'their eyes stir immediately and they are trying to understand through their mind's discriminating intellect.'**

'With the intelligent and quick-witted, as soon as they hear a spiritual friend mention this matter' they want it. But whatever we mistakenly want from outside, the heart has only one want, to again become aware of and be at one with that inborn wisdom, to come back to itself, to what it really is and what we really are. The delusion of 'I' feels split off from that. But the heart that is in all of us longs to return, to come back home or re-unite. Master Daie says that once the quick-witted hear about these things, their heart is aroused and trying to understand, their eyes stir immediately and they are trying to gain an understanding through their mind's discriminating intellect. I remember that when I came back from Japan, the questions that people asked and their ideas were quite bewildering.

Ideas can catch us quickly. The other day I had a letter from somebody who really ought to know better. Having gone into the neurological and chemical body changes, emotions and so on, he had convinced himself that his emotions were actually a chemical eruption in the brain and had nothing to do with him!

Any excuse that I can possibly find or fabricate, neurology or whatever, I will use in order to shield myself from the terrible insight that I am but a figment of imagination and I have spent my life so far in just holding up this figment of imagination, but not very successfully or otherwise I would not be reading this. Why persist in this foolishness instead of doing something helpful about it? And so 'As soon as intelligent, quick-witted people hear a spiritual friend mention these matters, their eyes stir immediately and they are already trying to gain understanding through their discriminating intellect.' It is translated here as 'discriminating intellect' but you might as well call it self-consciousness.

Trying to understand – but all intention misses the target. All intention is bound to go astray because all intention is I-conscious and that is just not enough. Master Daie continues, saying, **'People like this are creating their own hindrances and will never have a moment of awakening.'** Naturally not, because I am in the way. 'People like this create their own hindrances' – my pictures, my ideas, my this, my that, but all connected with I, me, mine. And so how can they see clearly?

'When devils from outside wreak calamity, it can still be remedied. But when one's own family creates disaster, it cannot be averted.' This our own family is our reliance on our understanding, on our intellectual discriminations, on our self-consciousness, on our judging and evaluating of this and that, yes and no. Although these have a place in our relative world of opposites, fundamentally they are not. This difference is difficult to understand unless we have done sufficient training to be aware of consciousness or awareness itself, and of self-consciousness which is based on I, and which has to do with 'I know' and is abstract and judgmental.

Consider the difference between the awareness 'it is hot' and the self-consciousness 'I am hot.' I already feel too hot, and knowing the opposite, I now set out to get cooler. Seems only reasonable, doesn't it? And if I cannot find anything cooler, I begin to think and invent, I get a fan and then an electric fan and then air-conditioning and with that the environment is ruthlessly used for anything that I need.

But when we think of our animal brothers and sisters, they also know hot and cold, it is the same consciousness. They also will seek a cool place in summer, etc. But they do not go out to create a cool spot, do not interfere with the environment – that is specifically human. When aware of the opposite, I cannot accept what is, but want to make it better!

The natural awareness inherent in all sentient being is 'choiceless awareness', without judging, without trying to manhandle the environment, without interference, *wu wei*. Self-consciously I say, 'Well, then what's the use of anything? If I have a toothache, shall I keep on with the toothache and wait until my tooth has rotted away and I am possibly developing blood-poisoning? Or if I still have my appendix and a pain in my tummy, should I not go to the doctor?' These are questions the discriminating I-consciousness is continuously pouring out to keep its supremacy up. But in that natural awareness, there is a pain and also awareness of what, within the given situation, can be done. We cannot go outside the situation and the situation is continuously changing.

Within the situation, we naturally gravitate to what is possible – like a cat naturally gravitates to the warmest spot in winter and the coolest in summer. And we, if the toothache is there, ring the dentist. If I happen to be on the North Pole and there is no dentist available, since we are always bound by a situation, well then whatever can be done about it is done and the rest will have to be endured. This is what is within the situation, the clear awareness of what is, without I coming in with my judgements. So Master Daie says, 'When devils from outside wreak calamity, it can still be remedied' because when something comes from outside, it can be adjusted to within the given possibilities. A Dutch sailing proverb says, 'God helps the sailor but steer he must himself.' 'But when one's own family creates disaster' – I, me, my mind.

This is further elaborated in the Yogacara teaching with its eight consciousnesses, the first six being 'one's own family' – my way of seeing, my way of believing, etc. 'When one's own family creates disaster, it cannot be averted' because then I am blind and deaf, can neither see nor hear, then disaster is inevitable. Master Daie then quotes Yoka Daishi (Yung Chia), **'The loss of the wealth of the Dharma and the decline of virtue** (strength) **all stem from** (the self-consciousness) **of the discriminating intellect.'** The loss of the wealth of the Dharma, all the wisdom and power of the Tathagata, is being veiled and not available, and I vainly try to get out of my misery. As to the decline of virtue, in Buddhism 'virtue' always means power/strength which is inborn in all sentient beings. Yoka Daishi says that the loss of the wealth of the Dharma, of this wisdom, and the decline of power, all stem from the mind's discriminating self-consciousness, being blinded by my ideas and notions and not being aware.

This needs to become really clear and it cannot become so by only thinking about it. This is why practice is so important. We need the practice to get ever clearer, and to check whether there still is all this I-judging, I-defending, I-this and I-that. Is there now strength to just stand and say, 'Yes'? Like the great master Joshu, who, when in front of a large audience, was asked one of those unanswerable questions, just said, 'I don't know.'

If you stand in front of a thousand people or even three people and they expect that you know, would you, even if you do not know, try to formulate some kind of answer in order to cover up your not knowing? Or would you just peacefully say, 'I don't know'? I don't like the idea that I don't know, do I? Even when scolded for something which we have actually done, though it is just, we do not like it, do we? I quickly defend myself, it was just an unfortunate slip, I am not really like that. But if I am scolded for something which I have not done, oh then I am up in arms, because I have not done it!

This is the point. If you think I have done something and I know I have not, well then what has that to do with me? It is your business, not mine. There is a Jewish story – an old couple, Isaac and Becky, live in a little house along a narrow road and opposite them lives their old friend Solly, a pawn-broker.

One evening Becky, rather tired, is in bed and wanting to sleep but Isaac walks up and down rather agitated. Becky calls, 'Isaac, I am tired, I want to go to sleep, come to bed.' But Isaac just continues his walking and Becky, more firmly, calls out, 'Isaac, I said go to bed, I cannot go to sleep.'

Isaac says, 'I can't.'

She says, 'Why not? I'm tired, come to bed.'

Isaac says, 'Well, I have a problem.'

'What is the problem? Tell me and just go to bed.'

Isaac says, 'You know Solly across the road?'

'Yes, of course I know him.'

'Well, I owe him hundred pounds.'

'So, you owe him hundred pounds, now do go to bed, Isaac.'

'But I have to pay it back by tomorrow morning.'

'Then pay it back tomorrow morning, but now go to bed!'

'But I haven't got the money!' At that, Becky jumps out of bed, opens the window and yells across the road, 'Solly!   Solly!'

Solly comes, his little white night-cap on, and calls, 'Yes, Becky, what is it?' Becky shouts across, 'Isaac says he owes you a hundred pounds.' 'Yes,' nods Solly. 'To be paid back tomorrow morning?' 'Yes,' says Solly. 'Well, he has not got it!' says Becky, slams the window shut and hops back into bed, 'Isaac, go to sleep, now it's his problem!'

Please remember this story. Your life might then have considerably fewer problems.

LETTER 5 to LO MENG-PI

The Text

The obstruction of the Path by the mind and its conceptual discrimination is worse than poisonous snakes or fierce tigers. Why? Because poisonous snakes and fierce tigers can still be avoided whereas intelligent people make the mind's conceptual discrimination their home, so that there's never a single instant, whether they're walking, standing, sitting or lying down, that they are not having dealings with it. As time goes on, unknowing and unawares they become one piece with it – and not because they want to either, but because since beginningless time they have followed this one little road until it has become set and familiar. Though they may see through it for a moment and wish to detach from it, they still can't. Thus it is said that poisonous snakes and fierce tigers can still be avoided but the mind's conceptual discrimination truly has no place for you to escape.

Ven. Myokyo-ni's Comments

'**The obstruction of the Path**' – the Path is, of course, the Buddha's Way, the Way of the Dharma. 'The obstruction of the Path' is brought about by '**the mind and its conceptual discrimination.**' Here is one of the few times where 'mind' is the correct translation of what we normally translate as 'heart' (*hsin*). There is the deluded heart from which we all suffer; and there is the heart that is cleared from the delusion – the main delusion being I, of course. So, if we carefully look at it, the mind, which is another part of 'I' – the thinking part of I – is different. I identify with the body as mine and I identify with the mind as mine. I don't identify so much with the heart as mine because when the passions arise, they have me much more clearly than thought-streams. But it is from thought-streams that we mostly suffer. It is our thought-streams which are in a way the mirror-image of what I think I am, and how I believe things should be. According to that, I react to anything in my environment. Without the thoughts and the thought-streams and the continuous running of the thought-streams, I very soon feel uncomfortable, get itchy and want to get away from it.

Conceptual discrimination cannot take place without thought and thought itself is bound up within conceptual discrimination. We cannot think without such discrimination. Whatever we think, it is either of this or that, and never both at the same time. It is either black or white or yes or no. Why are the conceptual discriminations, which are thought, so very bad? There is nothing inherently wrong with distinctions between this and that. A gong is a gong and a rose is a rose. They only arise by taking the gong as inanimate and the rose as a plant. Then we have Jack and Tom and we discriminate between those two. We evaluate, we judge and so never see things as they are, in their 'suchness', in their *tathata*. Because of that, we are actually blind. We cannot see properly when blinded by the Fires because of our discrimination, our ceaseless evaluating which is based on my notions and convictions. 'There are none so blind as those who do not wish to see.' That 'not wishing', if we carefully look, is the isolating factor which like a cocoon spins itself around us and separates us from everything. We then suffer from that separation and do not know that we are suffering from conceptual discrimination.

We need to be absolutely clear about the difference between natural distinction and conceptual discrimination, such as good and bad and all my likes and dislikes. Since these are not founded on actual input but on my discriminations, merely on my concepts, it is said that they are **'worse than poisonous snakes or fierce tigers. And why? Because poisonous snakes and fierce tigers can still be avoided.'** If you see them, you can avoid them. That is if you are open to your surroundings. But when we are closed to our surroundings and do not see them, they will get us. But 'intelligent people' – Master Daie particularly stresses **'intelligent people make the mind's conceptual**

discriminations their home.' Thomas Merton says somewhere in his monk's diary that the one thing that people nowadays need to know more than anything else is that our much-vaunted intellect does not function in a vacuum, where it would give exact information, but it is invaded from underneath by our appetites, notions, likes and dislikes. We are fooled by the belief that our intellect is neutral and can see things just as they are but it is by no means so. Yet we fall for it again and again.

'Intelligent people' – we all pride ourselves on being clever, etc. I may say modestly, 'Well, I don't think I am all that intelligent, really,' but deep inside there is the conviction that I am hub and centre of the universe. There is no doubt about that. Everything around is judged from that central point of the universe. And that is why I so desperately need to be someone, in my opinion, and why I'd rather be the worst than nothing at all. All that is slowly scraped off by our practice.

'Intelligent people make conceptual discrimination their home.' We live in our thoughts, notions, judgements and cannot be without them – we are them. Being active, doing something, distracts us from ourselves. And when we have nothing to do, we get desperate. So we must always be doing something and the irony is that we all complain that we do not have enough time. But when we really have got time, then it hangs heavy and we desperately look for means to 'kill time' because we can't bear not having anything to do, and because unbeknownst to ourselves we are frightened of suddenly conking out and becoming nothing.

This 'I' is our basic belief. We see and experience the world by judging and valuing it from that 'I'- orientation. In the Buddhist view, we blind ourselves against understanding what the Buddha-nature is, what our real true nature is, what we really are, by the delusion of thinking of myself as an 'I' and therefore separating myself. Of that

Buddha-nature, the Sixth Patriarch said, 'The peasant uses it all the time but is not aware of it.' But we make our home in our I-orientated discriminations, our notions of what is right and wrong, black and white, good and bad.

Master Daie continues, **'So there is never a single instant, whether they are walking, standing, sitting or lying down, that they are not having dealings with these conceptual discriminations.'** They have become our home. And losing one's home is painful. We cling to it, do not want to leave and have to be expelled from this spurious home. Why is this so? **'As time goes on, unknown and unawares, they become one piece with it.'** I have noticed, for example, here in the temple routine that something may creep in, be done or left undone 'just once'. Then the same occasion arises again and 'just once' creeps in again. Soon it begins to become a habit. And when asked how it has come about, 'But it has always been done like this!' Yes, 'Unbeknown and unawares, they become one piece with it.' This is how it goes, 'just this once'. It seems neither here nor there but it is enormously strong. This is the turning point. If 'just once' is given into, it will try to take over.

Therefore awareness is important, and not giving in, not sloping off 'just once' or 'unknowing and unawares, they become one piece with it **and not because they want to either but because since beginningless time, they have followed this one little road until it has become set and familiar'** Once 'it's become set and familiar', then sadly as we get older, this attitude becomes rigid. We all know old people who are thus rigidified. They have their firm opinions, get easily furious or 'must' have, and so are never happy. I remember a friend of my grandmother. She was a deeply unhappy woman. Her son came every day to visit her but she complained loud and bitterly day in and day out that the whole family ignored her, nobody ever came to visit her, nobody cared for her and said that with her son actually sitting by her. Fascinating. That is how once 'set and familiar', it rigidifies and screens what actually is. That is what Master Daie calls 'the obstruction of the Path by thought and its conceptual discriminations.'

Sadly, **'though they may see through it for a moment and wish to detach from it, they still can't.'** It has taken over, it is ingrained so that they have become it. Once poison has really eaten into them, even if 'they see through it for a moment and even if they wish to detach from it, they still can't.' It needs a major force, like the full power of the training. **'Thus it is said that poisonous snakes and fierce tigers can still be avoided but the mind's conceptual discrimination truly has no place for you to escape.'** So conceptual discriminations are worse, more dangerous, more frightening than poisonous snakes or fierce tigers. Avoid them before it is too late.

Start with the small things, because with the small things we can work. With the big ones, where we think we have our problems, we cannot work, they are too big, have as yet too much strength. This strength needs to be bled off them to become available for working with the problem. That happens by working with the small things. So, it is 'Yes' to the situation and 'Just once' is out, however tired I am, or whatever. To what extent is it really true that I can't anymore? We do not trust the body enough. If I really can't, I can't. It is as simple as that. But what I think I can't and what I really cannot is different. It is so with sitting zazen and it is so with everything else. If the legs really hurt, sooner or later, if they truly hurt over the limit, the body takes over, we can trust it. And if there is too much tiredness, the body takes over. It is as simple as that. But we do not believe it.

The Buddha said, 'Have I ever said, O monks, that there is a mind without a body or a body without a mind?' If we trust the body, it will give us a lot of information. But I am like the chap who was convinced he had cancer. All tests showed there was no cancer. He consulted the greatest specialists, no cancer at all. But he still could not let go, 'I still might get it.'

Discriminations are a mighty force and we have to be humble and modest; start with the little things that we can handle and work through them little by little. Then, not being fooled, but staying with the body, energy rises in the body and it is first felt in the body. At that moment the energy itself can be said 'Yes' to, and worked with, rather than with the 'picture' it paints. Only that way and very slowly is the whole process dismantled. Nowhere in Buddhism is it said that it is not possible to walk the Way, but it is not possible to walk the Way full of opinions. Only if there is sufficient willingness and sufficient humility to listen – and this is where the listening comes in. Learn to listen, it is a magnificent practice. Listen, not to the thoughts which we willingly give an ear to, but listen to what is actually in the surroundings, be aware of the surroundings rather than only of myself. Tune in with the surroundings, forgetting oneself. Then in that connectedness comes the joy, the playing, the warmth of heart and with that compassion.

LETTER 6 to HSU TUN-LI

The Text

Gentlemen of affairs often take mind which assumes there is something to attain, to seek the Dharma wherein there is nothing to attain. What do I mean by the mind which assumes there is something to attain? It is the intellectually clever one, the one that ponders and judges. And what do I mean by the Dharma wherein there is nothing to attain? It is the imponderable, the incalculable, where there is no way to apply intelligence or cleverness. Have you not read of old Shakyamuni at the assembly of the Lotus of the True Dharma? Three times Sariputra earnestly entreated him to preach. But there was simply no way for him to begin. Afterwards using all his power, he managed to say that this Dharma is not something that can be understood by thought or discrimination. This was old Shakyamuni taking the matter to its ultimate conclusion, opening the gateway of expedient means as a starting-point for the teaching of the true nature of reality.

VEN. MYOKYO-NI'S COMMENTS

'Gentlemen of affairs' – we all are such 'gentlemen of affairs' – **'often take mind** (thought) **which assumes there is something to attain, to seek the Dharma where there is nothing to attain.'** We almost always think that there is something to attain in seeking the Dharma. Otherwise, why are we sitting here? Why do we come to a *sesshin*? Because we think that there is something to attain. What we do not realise – do not want to realise – is that it is all clearly spelled out by the Buddha. On his own Awakening he exclaimed, 'How wonderful, how miraculous, all beings are fully endowed with the Tathagata's Wisdom and Power. Only sadly, human beings, because of their attachments, are not aware of it.' And so the practice is to let our attachments drop off.

But it is not just my attachment to this, that or the other which I now want to get rid of, because the focus of the attachment is of course myself. And there we come back to the Buddha's teaching of the Three Signs of Being – Change, No-I and Suffering. The state of No-I – I naturally cannot understand it, but it is the fulcrum of the whole practice. The training directly points to that and is concerned only with that. A kind of grinding away or washing off the dark, obscuring grime which I am – all my ideas, notions, convictions, opinions, likes, dislikes, preferences, etc.

I deludedly think I can attain whatever it is – peace of mind, happiness, freedom from suffering. But that is not how it is in our world. The Buddha's teaching points beyond that, and the training leads beyond that. The Buddha, from his own experience, taught the steps and stages of the Way. There is the Daily Life Practice, there is the meditation practice. And if properly followed, they lead naturally to the insight which is *prajna*, which is insight into the Dharma – but 'I' cannot have it, let's be quite clear on that issue. From the side of 'I' it is not possible to fathom what the Dharma is. Trying to make pictures of it and thinking about it will not bring us to it. As far as any 'I-doing' is concerned, it will not work because all intention misses the target. And therefore, as far as I am concerned, my way, my ideas, what I do to attain it, however I bestir myself, it is all quite useless in a way because it all only goes back to making 'I' the centre again. Therefore, all I have to do is to forget myself and diligently follow the Daily Life Practice and meditation. I do not need to bother about anything else. They are designed so that little by little they scrape off those bits of 'I' that are there, until finally the whole bundle can fall off. That is what the training will effect. What I do in order to get it only takes me further away.

It is difficult for us to understand that 'the doing' is actually 'without my doing' it, and that it is a question of my following the Buddha's footsteps. There is the Buddha's Way and there is my way, and those two ways very often cross each other. Am I following the Buddha's Way or am I following my convictions, my ideas, my whatever? If I follow mine, then I cannot at the same time follow the Buddha's Way. They are not the same.

'Gentlemen of affairs often take thought that there is something to attain, to seek the Dharma wherein there is nothing to attain.' Attaining the Dharma, but the Dharma is not to be attained, and nothing in the Dharma is attainable either. It is quite beyond. Huang Po (Obaku) says, 'There is nothing to be attained. Enlightenment is not to be attained. And he who has it cannot say he knows.' It is quite clear and decisive. Wherever I get stuck with my ideas, my wishes, my notions, my convictions, that is exactly the fulcrum where I need to put the spade in and start digging. When there is nothing left, then there is a natural falling into it. It happens of itself.

It does not have to be found because it has always been there anyway. I remember back in the fifties, I asked a visiting Zen priest about the saying, 'At the beginning of one's training, trees are trees and water is water. But then as we get into the training and everything becomes tenuous, trees are no longer trees and water is not water. And finally at the third stage, trees are trees again and water is water.' And I said, 'Isn't it rather sad that being born with that insight in any case, we have to grow out of it, struggling with difficulties and doubts, and then have to strive so long to regain the seeing a child has. Isn't it exactly the same, trees are trees, water is water? He smiled and said, 'Yes, yes. A small child has got it quite naturally but if something happens and it gets upset or frightened, it will yell out, "Mummy"! And, you see, in the third stage there is no need for that yell anymore.'

So that is the difference. This yell of fear or resistance or whatever, that is 'I' and that 'I' needs to fall off. That is what the training is for. So do not lay anything extra on, there is enough there to work through with, all my opinions and all my difficulties. The late Ven. Pannyavaddho told me he got rather 'holy', as one sometimes does during the training. He was a very long-standing smoker, and he decided to give up smoking. When his teacher, the Ven. Maha Boowa noticed it, he told him to smoke five cigarettes a day – not more – but no less than five cigarettes a day. Ven. Pannyavaddho said he had a real shock when he heard that. After all, he was doing it for the furthering of his practice, and then to be brought back down like that. And he added that it had taken him three or four years until he realised why.

This is how it goes. There are always two inside us, and there is one that tries to do some kind of special thing to feel good, but only to avoid looking at the real problem, quite unconsciously. In a way I do know it but in a way I don't, because I have never dared to look at it. As soon as I come closer to it and get uncomfortable, I then try to trump it with something else. Be very careful of that, it is something which we all know, and which we all try. But with it we have left the Buddha's Path and are once more fully engaged in my own follies. This is the 'gentlemen of affairs'. They think there's 'something to attain, to seek the Dharma, but in the Dharma there's nothing to attain.' On the contrary, there's only the losing of myself. With that we have a truly nasty, frightening feeling, 'But if I'm not there, what then? All kinds of things can happen.' That is only, once again, the clever one who tries to find all kinds of excuses. As a matter of fact, when that clever one is out of the way, the body and the mind together, the whole bundle of the five *skandhas*, functions naturally and perfectly smoothly. It is 'I' who am the spanner in the works.

So there is indeed 'nothing to attain', but there is a lot to get rid of. We try to do so with the help of the teachings and the training with its strictness. Yet we try to screen out what really goes to the bone, and that is what obstructs. It is like a deep black cloud that obscures the sun that is shining behind it.

Master Daie then explains who does the screening, **'It is the intellectually clever one, the one that ponders and judges.'** And he continues, **'What do I mean by the Dharma wherein there is nothing to attain? It is the imponderable, the incalculable, where there is no way to apply intelligence or cleverness.'** I believe that nothing is possible without my actually doing it, without my intention. And yet, can I fall asleep by an act of will? The ones who suffer from sleeplessness know quite well that however much they want to fall asleep, they can't. And during a long day's zazen, can I keep awake by an act of will? All the time? Sprightly? But it goes even further. Can I faint by an act of will? Yet, I do faint. Or rather, not I faint, the body does – without my wishing or permission! When it happens, it has nothing to do with me.

And so Master Daie goes on questioning. **'Have you not read of old Shakyamuni** (the Buddha) **at the assembly of the Lotus of the True Dharma?'** What happened there? **'Three times Sariputra'**, one of the main disciples, **'earnestly entreated him to preach.'** To say something, in other words, to expound the True Dharma, for that was the purpose of the Lotus Assembly. **'But there was simply no way for him to begin.'** The Dharma cannot be put into words, it cannot be put into concepts, it is beyond thinking. The moment we think of something, we already have one side of a pair of opposites, and the other side is left out or rejected. We cannot think but in opposites and so we can never fathom the whole. Therefore, although three times asked, he could not speak, not even the Buddha. But **'afterwards, using all his power'** and all his insight, **'he managed to say that this Dharma is not something that can be understood by thought or discrimination.'**

It cannot be understood in the head. Life, we cannot understand it, we can only believe that we can understand it. And yet we live it, willy-nilly, whether we like it or not. That is worthwhile pondering. The Dharma cannot be understood by 'thought or discrimination', it is the principle. And that is already wrong, because it is making it a something, even if it is only a mental thing. But it is a principle or Way which informs us and to which we all conform to an extent, whether we like it or not, it is inherent in all of us. Disobedience to it gives rise to delusion, makes our difficulties, our unhappiness, our dissatisfaction, in short, our suffering.

'Taking this matter to its ultimate conclusion,' saying that it cannot be understood, and with that **'opening the gateway of expedient means as a starting point for the teaching of the true nature or reality.'** 'The gateway of expedient means' – using analogies, using whatever is suitable under given circumstances, and to a given audience. Using 'expedient means as a starting point for the teaching of the true nature of reality.' How can the true nature of reality be expounded? Yet this is what Buddha did. Having had insight into it, he lived according to it. His living in accordance with this insight is the teaching. We may believe we know something but if this belief is in the head only, we cannot live according to it. In a way it is quite easy to say, 'Oh yes, it is not an intellectual thing,' but we do not know what it is. To really become one with 'the true nature of reality' means to forget myself and to live in accordance with it. With that arises not only wisdom but also compassion, the warmth of the human heart that feels related to everything, and to which nothing feels strange or frightening. When really warmed up, the fear is gone. When 'I' is truly out of the way, there is no more fear but instead a willingness to be of use to whatever is just in need of being given a hand. That is what the training is about. Not for me, but to find out what is underneath that delusion of I. This appears when the delusion of I which sticks like a burr has fallen off with all its pain, has been starved off by my walking the Buddha's Way, diligently, willingly, and without straying from it. The Buddha's Way is designed to make it shrink and fall off. Having fallen off, the sight is clear and the heart is not only warmed but is fulfilled and can really participate in being alive. Can we ponder that very carefully, please?

LETTER 6 to HSU TUN-LI (continued)

THE TEXT

In the old days Hsueh Feng, the truly awakened Ch'an master, was so earnest about this matter that he went to Mount T'ou Tzu three times and climbed Mount Tung Shan nine times. But circumstances were not met for him in those places. And so later when he heard of the teaching of Chou, master of the Adamantine Wisdom Scripture on Te Shan, he went to his place. And one day he asked Te Shan, 'In the custom of the school that has come down from of old, what doctrine is used to instruct people?' Te Shan said, 'Our school has no verbal explanation, nor does it have any doctrine to teach people.' Later Hsueh Feng also asked, 'Do I have any share in this business of the vehicle of this ancient school?' Te Shan picked up his staff and immediately hit him, saying, 'What are you saying?' Under his blow, Hsueh Feng finally smashed the lacquer bucket (of ignorance). From this we observe that in this sect intelligence and cleverness, thought and judgement, are of no use at all.

VEN. MYOKYO-NI'S COMMENTS

'In the old days' – we are in the T'ang dynasty in China – **'Hsueh Feng, the Truly Awakened Ch'an Master, was so earnest about this matter,'** that is the Great Matter, the matter of life and death, the Law or Dharma and he was so eager about it **'that he went up to Mount T'ou Tzu three times and climbed Mount Tung Shan nine times'** On each mountain was a famous monastery. **'But circumstances were not met for him in those places,'** that is although he went there repeatedly, nothing happened. **'So later, when he heard of**

the teaching of Chou, the master of the Adamantine Wisdom Scripture, on Te Shan, he went to his abode.'

When we read such texts, we assume that in those times monks hardly stayed anywhere for long, but walked about from place to place. But this is not true. As a young monk, you entered a monastery and you stayed there. Only if you were a well-attained monk might you go on pilgrimage – either because you had not completely penetrated and hoped to find some other place or master who would jolt you into it, or else because you felt you had nothing more to learn and you went to various masters to find out whether there was still something lacking. And if there was still something lacking, then you stayed there until that had become clear. So Hsueh Feng went three times to T'ou Tzu mountain and climbed nine times up Tung mountain but no insight opened, 'circumstances were not met for him.'

It has always been so. Four generations ago, it is said, a monk who had been in the monastery for eight years but still had not broken through, and feeling that 'circumstances were not met', decided that he would stay on until the end of Rohatsu *Sesshin*, and if nothing happened, he would leave. Nothing happened. The evening of the 8th he walked out during *kinhin* and suddenly came to himself, fighting for air! He had walked into the pond without noticing, the water was already over his mouth. That jolted him out of himself. In December the first frost usually comes, and the water must have been pretty nippy. He did not notice, he was so deep in absorption but the cold water brought him back from his thoughts, from the castles in the air, and the flowers in the sky, brought him back to himself. And that is what we all need. I'm not saying we need to go to Hampstead Heath and walk into the pond there, because that might not fit our circumstances. But something pretty stark usually has to happen.

And so Hsueh Feng found that he got nothing on either mountain, but then he heard about the teachings of Te Shan, and he went to see him. There he stayed. One day he asked Te Shan, **'In the custom of our school that has come down from of old, what doctrine is used to instruct people?'** All religions, not only Buddhism, expound instructions and customary teachings, so what does our school teach? How does it instruct people?

Te Shan replied, **'Our school has no verbal expression nor does it have any doctrine to teach people.'** That is stark but also accurate. Opinions have always been divided on that subject, one party saying, there is no teaching at all in the Zen School, which is quite true; but it is also a Buddhist School and is based on the Buddha-dharma, has grown out of the Buddha-dharma. We who have not grown up in familiarity with that Buddha-dharma, need to inform ourselves carefully about the Buddhist framework, or we will not find our grounding in the Zen School of Buddhism.

There is all the difference between looking up a way on a map and the actual walking on that way. You can comfortably sit with a most detailed map in your armchair at home and find, 'Ah, there is a nice little level stretch, good, but this is an awkward spot and there is a river to get across,' and you know the whole way in your head but you are still sitting in the armchair. Or you can decide that as it is clearly said in the Zen texts that there is no learning necessary, away with all those maps, and off we go. But it is highly unlikely you will ever get anywhere. Both need to work together, familiarity with the map but then to start walking the Way. If we follow that map carefully, we are not likely to go astray.

In the Southern Teachings, a Brahmin rather snootily asked the Buddha, 'Why do some of your disciples reach the goal but others do not?' The Buddha said, 'Do you know the way to Rajagriha?' The Brahmin answered, 'Yes, of course!' 'Then how would you describe it to someone?', asked the Buddha. 'You start walking out by the front gate, then you turn left, then etc. etc.,' replied the Brahmin. And the

Buddha said, 'And if in spite of your careful instruction, that person still goes wrong and misses the way?' 'Well,' said the Brahmin, 'that's nothing to do with me. I gave him the correct instructions.' The Buddha said, 'And so you see, Buddhas also only point the Way.'

We must inform ourselves of the Way before we can follow it, but then it is essential that we walk it by our own efforts. 'Te Shan said, 'Our school has no verbal expression, nor does it have any doctrine to teach people.' None of the old masters answered any questions, they did not give any instructions, did not spout any doctrines. They just pointed, as did the Buddha on Vulture Peak, when he lifted a flower before the assembly of monks without saying one word. It was only Mahakasyapa who realised and smiled and received the transmission with which the Zen School started. There is a world of difference between knowing something in the head only, talking about it, and actually knowing it in the body and living out of it.

I can see you swimming and want to learn it myself, so I carefully watch you. Then I read everything about swimming. Now it is a question of actually going into the water. I have never been in the sea and when the water is ankle-deep, I am already beginning to feel queasy. I wouldn't dare to go deeper, so it is a slow process of getting bodily familiar with the water, learning to trust it, intellectually knowing that the water will carry me if only I give myself to it. But I cannot relax as long as I am frightened. There is all the difference between thinking 'I know' which is thinking I understand, and knowing how to do it by actually doing it. Being a mammal, I float naturally. Why do we have to learn to swim? Actually, we don't because we quite naturally float. What prevents us from it is our fear of drowning. Truly, fear is the other side of I.

So it is not that I have to learn how to swim. Nor can I overcome my fear outright, because I am that fear. I have to gain confidence through experience, that the water will carry me. This then does away with fear and that is what it is all about. But that cannot be taught by the intellect, learned in the head as a teaching. It is a question of experience. Our training slowly edges us towards that experience. By having to endure this and being told that if we only follow the Buddha's Way, then little by little 'I' gets weaker and so the fear also gets less, and in proportion to that, inner strength and confidence grow until it comes to a breakthrough.

The old texts tell of only a few cases of insight opening in zazen meditation. That does not say that meditation is not necessary, but for an opening to real insight, just being hooked on meditation is not enough. We have the example of the Buddha. He was so deep in meditation that even the fear of Mara with his demons could not shake him. But it was only when he came out of meditation, his heart completely empty, fear also gone, that he saw the morning star and suddenly there was a response – he saw and became Buddha. Such stories you find throughout all the texts: one awoke at the smell of a peach blossom, another because he heard the clicking of a falling pebble, or still another heard the murmuring of the brook. When the heart is really empty, completely empty, and therefore also wide open, then what falls into that empty heart, reverberates and the heart responds and with that the reflective seeing is there. Not the 'I'-seeing with two eyes, double-vision and deluded, but what really is.

And so **'Hsueh Feng asked further, "Do I have any share in this business of the vehicle of this ancient school?" At that Te Shan picked up his staff and immediately hit him.'** Why do we so often have stories about the master hitting? One of the analogies likens it to the hen hatching out an egg. The hen has first to lay it. Then has to sit on it and hatch it out. If you have ever watched one of those excellent wildlife films, the bird has to sit on its egg in hot weather and in rain until the chick inside is fully grown and ready to come out. It will try from inside but will not be able to do it and so from outside the hen has to give a sharp peck. The shell breaks and the chick struggles out. Now if the hen would wonder whether it is ready and peck prematurely or if she would be overcautious and wait a little longer to be quite sure, the chick would suffocate. It has to be done at exactly the right time, inside and outside has to come together. How does the hen know?

And so when the conditions meet, real action or response happens and with it realisation can break through. But it never happens by explanation or by any verbal teachings.

So when Hsueh Feng heard, 'Our school has no verbal teaching,' he did not get the message. Obviously, he was a rather brainy person and was thinking and pondering a lot. So he asked again, 'Do I have any share in the business of the vehicle of this ancient school?' Have I anything directly to do with it? At that, 'Te Shan picked up his staff and immediately hit him.' Now, why hit? Do you see the question – 'Do 'I' have any share in the business of the vehicle of this ancient school?' 'I' is still there and is still coming up. Can 'I' do something about it? Have 'I' any business with it? And like a flash Te Shan hit him.

'Under this blow Hsueh Feng finally smashed the lacquer bucket' of his own ignorance. The instantaneousness, the livingness of the moment has nothing to do with 'I', has never known of any 'I' but is a direct and full response. This is why Te Shan hit him and why Hsueh Feng under this blow finally awakened. **'From this,'** says Master Daie, **'we conclude that in this school, intelligence and cleverness, thought and judgement are of no use at all.'**

But that does not mean that it can be immediately thrown away, it takes a long time to ripen. The great master Soen Shaku compared intellect to a hammer – a very useful instrument for all kinds of jobs. Lots of things could not be done without a hammer, but it is of no use to go fishing with a hammer! That is using it incorrectly. To know which tool to use also belongs to that insight. But that cleverness, merely thinking that 'I have grasped it', can never even come near it. In our school it is the right response which counts.

We need to ponder the way we have to go carefully. We have to inform ourselves about the Buddhist framework. We need a map and we have to follow the map, rather than go our own way and then be surprised that nothing happens. If we follow that map and go the way that is indicated on the map, we will certainly come to the understanding that actually it is something which is right here and what's more, which has always been known. And to some extent I have never believed it because 'I' have always been in the way.

So once again, as stressed in the Buddhist teaching, it comes down to the falling-off of that deeply ingrained sense of 'I' and 'I must do'. It is rather like one who has lost the fear of water and has become a good swimmer. He can freely open up and give himself to the water knowing that the water will carry him. All he has to do is to steer, to swim in the direction that he needs to go. If the water is quiet, and *sunyata*, the Great Void or Nature is quiet, empty, then he does not need to be frightened of the water. On the contrary, he can trust that it will carry him. What he has to do is the steering.

In Picture Six of the *Bull-herding Pictures*, the man is sitting on the gentled bull. It is not the man, but the gentled bull who knows the way home and also has the strength to carry the man home. But the man also has something to do. He sits on the bull and he plays his flute. He does not play a complicated air, but a folk song, a simple melody which lifts the heart towards home.

So perhaps we can ponder that and put it whole-heartedly but also humbly and modestly into our practice. And whenever we happen to see 'I' in its usual way striding and strutting about, then we can say in a friendly way, 'Now, now, just be a little bit reasonable' and try to understand, open up, as we would admonish a nice but naughty child. We can't let it go on running about with knives in the kitchen.

Look at our world! A little upbringing is very important. And before we want to bring peace into the world we better bring peace into our own heart and the rest will take place of itself.

LETTER 6 to HSU TUN-LI (continued)

The Text

An ancient worthy had a saying: 'Transcendent Wisdom is like a great mass of fire. Approach it and it burns off your face. If you hesitate in thought and speculation, you immediately fall into conceptual discrimination.' Yung Chia said, 'Loss of the wealth of the Dharma and destruction of Virtue all stems from the mind's conceptual discrimination.' Hence we know that the mind's conceptual discrimination not only obstructs the Path but also can make people mistaken and confused so that they do all kinds of things that are not good.

Once you have the intent to investigate this Path to the end, you must settle your resolve and vow to the end of your days not to retreat or fall back so long as you have not reached the Great Rest, the Great Surcease, the Great Liberation. There's not much to the Buddha-dharma, but it's always been hard to find capable people. The concerns of worldly passions are like the links of a chain, joining together without a break. Those whose resolve is weak and inferior, time and again willingly become involved with these passions. Unknowing and unawares, they are dragged along in them. Only if the person truly possesses the faculty of wisdom and willpower will he consent to step back and reflect.

'An ancient worthy had a saying, "Transcendent Wisdom is like a great mass of fire. Approach it and it burns off your face."' 'Transcendent wisdom' has not got any feelings of 'I' in it, or any ideas of anything. And as far as I am concerned, I cannot quite bear it, therefore 'approach it and it burns off your face.' The face that drapes itself over transcendent wisdom is 'I', if it is burnt off, then 'I' have no face, but the face beneath the 'I'-face is the real face. Just 'approach it and it burns off your face.' Nowadays, living in a time when there is 'much speculation and much thought', there seems to be no real religious or even cultural value left. We are not aware of it, but the heart longs for such value, has a sense of wonder which children still have and also the sense of awe which the religions taught us. Even in the times when they still had those values, 'transcendent wisdom could burn off the face.' For us, it really is burning off the face – all our fancy ideas that we have draped over ourselves.

And Master Daie continues, **'If you hesitate in thought and speculation, you immediately fall into conceptual discrimination.'** Naturally. 'If you hesitate in thought and speculation' – when we read the Zen stories, the Master very often hits. But he never hits when the student does not know. He only hits when he hesitates. That is to get us out of our hesitating thought – speculating and thinking about what I know, and what I do not know, must know, and all that. 'If you hesitate in thought and speculation, you immediately fall into conceptual discrimination' – what is better, what is worse, what is right, what is wrong, what is this, what is that. There is no end to it. One moment's hesitation and heaven and earth fall apart, says a Zen proverb.

'Yung Chia (Yoka Daishi) **said, "Loss of the wealth of the Dharma and destruction of Virtue all stems from the mind's conceptual discrimination."'** The Dharma, the great principle which IS. It is inherent in everything, informs everything and everything conforms to it. It is 'the wealth of the Dharma' and cannot be measured. 'Loss of the wealth of the Dharma and the destruction of Virtue' – when we read in Zen or Buddhist texts about 'virtue', the term stands for strength or 'power', not brute, coercing power but the real inner strength of full insight. So 'the loss of the wealth of the Dharma' and the loss of power, 'all stem from the mind's conceptual discrimination.'

When we want to hold our ground but cannot, what do we do? If we think or find we cannot stand on our own two feet, that is when there is not enough power. There is then not enough power for the realisation of what is there. 'I' who would like to secure myself against everything that is other, that 'I' is a very little thing, and it has very little power, unless blown up by the fire of passion and then I am blind, not there, carried away. The real power that stands on its own feet is like that of Bodhidharma in front of Emperor Wu. Knowing that his life was at stake, he nonetheless said that the emperor had gained 'no merit whatsoever' for his financial support of the Buddhist community, and when asked what the very essence of Buddhism is, he clearly stated, 'Vast emptiness, nothing holy.' That is where the real strength is. So we see that the 'loss of the wealth of Dharma', not being at home in the Dharma anymore, and the loss of the power that comes with it, all of this 'stems from the mind's conceptual discrimination', from our thinking and weighing of this and that, better and worse, should and should not. And when it really comes down to it, this is what we disport ourselves in for at least a good part of the day, instead of giving ourselves over to the wisdom and the power of the Dharma.

Master Daie says, **'Hence we know that the mind's conceptual discrimination not only obstructs the Path,'** obstructs which path? The Buddha's Path of course. Makes us either stray from it or not see it at all. So, the mind's conceptual discrimination not only obstructs the Path, **'but also can make people mistaken and confused.'** Naturally. If I don't know, I make up all kinds of stories. 'Mistaken and confused' I do hear and do not hear, and believe I have heard but have not really heard, rather like in the parlour game of Chinese Whispers. The third person has already got quite a few different words because we do not really listen, we cannot listen. We are stuffed so full inside that we cannot listen, and cannot see either.

In that kind of state, people **'do all kinds of things that are not good.'** What can be done about it? Master Daie spells it out exactly. **'Once you have the intent to investigate this Path to the end'** – here we can pause for a moment and ask ourselves, 'Have we got the intent to investigate this Path?' Yes, or we would not be sitting here. But have we got 'the intent to investigate this Path to the end'? If so, **'you must settle your resolve and vow to the end of your days not to retreat or fall back so long as you have not reached the Great Rest, the Great Surcease, the Great Liberation.'**

It is useful for us Westerners to look carefully at the Buddhist teachings. The Buddhist, if he is serious in striving to follow the Buddha's Path, is not interested in coming into a good incarnation, nor in being born into the heavenly realm, for that too is still revolving on the Wheel of Change. We all are on that Wheel – seemingly bound to it. Sometimes for better, sometimes for worse, difficulties are found in every state of that Wheel. Real deliverance does not come that way. So what the Buddhist wants is to get off the Wheel, not to be reborn.

Nowadays, when we hear about rebirth, and not being very familiar with the Buddhist teachings, we either incline strongly towards it because 'I shall be reborn, go on eternally, no reason to be frightened of death, we shall be together again.' Or on the other hand we think that it is all nonsense, 'How could I be reborn?' Yet the hope for that rebirth is very strong in us. The late founder and president of the Buddhist Society (Christmas Humphreys) had a theosophical background. And I know that whenever he gave a talk on the radio or on television and spoke about rebirth, he always received a lot of letters from people, saying, 'You have given me hope that I will again see…' my beloved father, husband, wife, child, whatever. That is how we take it, mistake it from the Western side.

So we must be very careful in trying to understand what is meant by rebirth, must be careful 'not to retreat or fall back so long as we have not reached the Great Rest, the Great Surcease, the Great Liberation' – where we are no longer bound on the Wheel. There is a release from the Wheel and that is precisely what the Buddha's Path leads us to, what the Buddha himself pointed out in his great one sentence, 'Suffering I teach, and the Way out of suffering.'

And so Master Daie, now really showing himself in his full strength and insight says, **'There is not much to the Buddha-dharma but it has always been hard to find capable people.'** 'There is not much to the Buddha-dharma' – it is only just seeing the way things really are. If not blinded by the mind's conceptual discrimination, it is natural to see the way things really are, and then there is not much to it. It is just as it is.

'But it has always been hard to find capable people.' 'Capable people' – courageous people who could let go of the whole bundle of 'I' and 'my' ideas and 'my' ideals, convictions, opinions and attachments. Master Rinzai says, 'If you meet the Buddha, kill the Buddha. If you meet the Patriarchs, kill the Patriarchs. If you meet your parents, kill your parents.' But is that not a frightful thing to say? Does he really mean that if you meet your parents, you should kill them? Do not mistakenly read it on the surface level only. 'If you meet the Buddha, kill the Buddha…' – said to an elderly monk who has spent the last fifty years in veneration of the Buddha, that must be absolutely shocking. But do you also remember the Buddha saying that as long as there are attachments you cannot become free.

It is only when everything is let go of that there can be liberation. The one who hangs onto something is 'I'. The life story of the great Master Kyogen (Hsiang-yen) is helpful in this context. We have all read about the sound of the pebble clicking against the bamboo trunk at which the monk was enlightened. But we very rarely know what happened beforehand. The monk to whom that happened was Kyogen, a very bright and intelligent young man. At the age of twenty-one, he had managed to learn many of the Buddhist scriptures by heart.

He was in the assembly of the great master Hyakujo (Pai-chang), but he died when Kyogen had only been his student for three years. His successor, Isan (Kuei-shan), had been the old head monk. Those who wanted to continue under him had to ask permission to stay or they could leave and go elsewhere. Young Kyogen asked Isan if he would please take him on as his disciple. Isan, knowing him well, said, 'You're a clever young man, are you really quite sure you want to continue, since you already know the scriptures by heart?' Young Kyogen, rather pleased that he was so well recognised, said, 'I think a year or two more would be quite useful.' At that moment Isan yelled, 'You young fool, if you know everything, tell me where are you going after you die?'

Kyogen was taken aback, for with all the sutras revolving in his head, he could not find the passage. He asked Isan, 'Will you please allow me to go into the library? I shall find it.' He was convinced that everything could be found in the scriptures, the teachings. Isan laughed and said, 'Go, you fool.' So Kyogen, sure he would find it, started going through the whole of the library. And you know how it is, he was young, and was also very much taken with his own cleverness. He was convinced it would be there, somewhere. He started looking but could not find it. He became so carried away that he forgot day and night, eating, drinking and sleeping, and for three days leafed through, ever more intent and desperate. Then he could not bear it anymore and ran to Isan. 'Tell me, please tell me, I cannot find it! I just cannot find it! Please tell me.'

Isan said, 'I would not rob you of your own insight.' Young Kyogen, having had no sleep, no food, quite overwrought, lost his head and grabbing Isan by the lapels, yelled, 'I'll kill you if you don't tell me!' And he meant it. Isan, being a Zen master, laughed straight in his face, 'And do you think my dead body will tell you?' At that Kyogen, utterly defeated, begged permission to leave. Knowing that having laid violent hands on his master, he would not only have to leave the monastery, but moreover that for the rest of his life he had lost all hope of release.

So he took his farewell and quietly vowed to himself – you see there is the vow again – that although in this life he had no more chance, he would never give up. He would just live as harmlessly as possible, wandering from monastery to monastery, begging for his food and a night's rest, and then would walk on. He would not give up but carry on in the next life, and life after life, until he could come to the end of the Path.

And that is what he did. For ten years he wandered about all over China and then he came to the tomb of the National Teacher Echu (Nanyang) who had been a Dharma-heir of the Sixth Patriarch. Its compound was rather overgrown and he decided he might as well spend the rest of his life looking after it, keeping it weeded and swept. He had a little hut, and if the odd pilgrim came by, he could put him up and feed him; and that is how he spent the next ten years. Altogether twenty years had gone by when one day, as he again was sweeping the grounds, he threw his bucketful of pebbles into the bamboo thicket as he had done daily for the last ten years. But this time his heart was truly empty and that click of the pebble reverberated.

And the great insight, 'the great rest, the great surcease' happened. And as he himself in his record says, at that realisation he very carefully put all his tools away, heated the bath, and for the first time in twenty years got into his ceremonial robes. Then he climbed to the top of the mountain behind the pagoda and there in the direction of the Isan's monastery made nine full prostrations, thanking his master that even threatened with death he had not robbed him of his own insight. It is quite a story, well worth pondering it in detail, worthwhile remembering it. 'Vow to the end of your days not to retreat or fall back so long as you have not reached the great rest, the great surcease, the great liberation.'

'There is not much to the Buddha-dharma but it has always been hard to find capable people,' because **'The concerns of worldly passions are like the links of a chain, joining together without a break. Those whose resolve is weak and inferior, time and again willingly become involved with these passions.'** 'With weak resolve' – not capable of sticking to it. 'Time and again willingly become involved' in this chain of old habits, passions 'joining together without a break.' And again we fall right into it.

'Those whose resolve is weak and inferior, time and again, willingly become involved with the passions' and **'Unknowing and unawares they are dragged along by them. Only if a person truly possesses the faculty of wisdom and willpower will he consent to step back and reflect.'** The wisdom and the willpower – not the 'I'-willpower, but when the whole heart really inclines. It is quite incredible what we can bring off if the heart really inclines. It is also incredible what we can bring off in an act of passion, though that usually leads to tragedy – but nevertheless there is a great deal of energy/strength which is not at 'my' disposal, for this willpower as well as the wisdom is in the heart, not 'I'. With regard to this, it is said in the Southern Scriptures, 'The heart naturally tends towards Nirvana, inclines towards Nirvana, slides towards Nirvana.'

If that is really felt, the *bodhicitta*, the aspiration towards enlightenment, and is really listened to, given over to it, that will pull us through even if I feel I can't go any further. 'Only if the person truly possesses that faculty of wisdom and willpower,' strength of heart, 'will he consent to step back and reflect.' Will he consent to 'step back and reflect'? Even if the passions flare? And thereby hangs the story. Perhaps we can also say, will he have the strength and the wisdom of jumping right into the fire and letting himself be burned away? In our case then, it is useful if we are quite clear about our priorities. If the priorities are clear, then even if the passions rear up, it is quite possible to stick to the priorities. But if we only hop about in the mind's discriminating ideas about this and that, and are unaware of our priorities, then an uproar of the passions is certain to sweep us along. But if we are clear about the priority, then it's not so difficult.

So perhaps before we have acquired that complete Wisdom/ Power to stick it out, we might try to be clear about our priorities. Do we truly want to come off that Wheel? Do we truly want to go the Buddha's Way? Are we aware that we cannot go that Way for ourselves alone? It is not possible, because we are not alone. We are not separate, we do it for everybody, including ourselves. Do we really want to contribute to that? Or do we want to go on in our selfishness and usual unhappiness? Well, we can peacefully consider that in meditation and find out where the heart's resolve, where our real priority is, where the heart really wants to go. And since that heart slides and tends towards nirvana, then we can safely vow that we will follow it for our own sake as much as for the sake of all sentient beings.

THE TEXT

Yung Chia also said, 'The real nature of ignorance is identical to the nature of enlightenment. The empty body of illusory transformation is identical to the body of reality. Once you have awakened, there's not a single thing in the body of reality. Original, inherent nature is the naturally really enlightened one.' If you think like this, suddenly in the place where thought cannot reach, you will see the body of reality in which there is not a single thing – this is the place for you to get out of birth and death. What I said before, that one cannot seek the Dharma which has nothing to attain with the attitude that there is something to attain, is just this principle.

Gentlemen of affairs make their living within the confines of thought and judgement their whole lives: as soon as they hear a man of knowledge speak of the Dharma in which there is nothing to attain, in their hearts there is doubt and confusion, and they fear falling into emptiness. Whenever I see someone talking like this, I immediately ask him, 'Is this one who fears falling into emptiness himself empty or not?' Ten out of ten cannot explain. Since you have always taken thought and judgement as your nesting place, as soon as you hear it said that you shouldn't think, immediately you are at a loss and can't find your grip. You are far from realising that this very lack of anywhere to get a grip is the time for you to let go of your body and your life.

Yung Chia, whom we know as Yoka Daishi and from his *Song of Realisation*, is quoted here again by Master Daie: **"'The real nature of ignorance is identical to the nature of enlightenment.'"** Ignorance and enlightenment are only words, thoughts; and when it really comes down to the absolute principle, there is neither the one nor the other. They have been made up for purposes of explanation, and have then acquired their opposites, but 'there is neither good nor bad but thinking makes it so.' **'The empty body of illusory transformation is identical to the body of reality.'** 'The empty body of illusory transformation'– insubstantial shapes and shadows, going and coming, coming and going, always changing – 'is identical to the body of reality.' There is no reality different from illusory transformations. There is no ignorance that is not enlightenment. The two are the same. They are the same, and yet not the same. They are the two poles of the one thing behind. And that one thing behind, which is not a thing and which is not behind, cannot be grasped by a thought and cannot be imagined; but rather like life it can be lived.

Yoka Daishi goes on to say, **"'Once you have awakened, there is not a single thing in the body of reality.'"** Can't find anything. As far as conscious awareness goes, there is nothing. He continues, **"'Original, inherent nature is the naturally real enlightened one.'"** It's already there. It does not need to be looked for, it doesn't even need to be discovered. It only needs to be uncovered. That was the quotation from Yoka Daishi.

Master Daie goes on, **'If you think like this, suddenly in the place where thought cannot reach, you will see the body of reality in which there is not a single thing.'** On the surface this is a contradiction, but we have to look not at the finger pointing at the moon, but at the moon itself. The place where 'thought cannot reach' – do we know that place? 'I' do not know it; 'I' cannot know it. But there is a continuous abiding in it. 'In the place where thought cannot reach, you will see the body of reality in which there is not a single thing. **This is the place for you to get out of birth and death.'** If there is not a single thing, there is no 'I'; and where there is no 'I' that is the place without birth and death, without continuing on the Wheel of Change, the place of liberation from the Wheel.

Master Daie says, **'What I said before that one cannot seek the Dharma wherein there is nothing to attain with the attitude that there is something to attain, is just this principle.'** Thought cannot reach it. It is the place to get out of birth and death, but it is not something that I can get. It's not even something that I have, though it is there. It is simply the absence of the delusion of 'I'.

Master Daie goes on, **'Gentlemen of affairs make their living within the confines of thought and judgement their whole life long.'** That is actually what we are all doing – making our living within the confines of thought and judgement. **'As soon as they hear a man of knowledge speak of the Dharma in which there is nothing to attain, in their hearts there is doubt and confusion, and they fear falling into emptiness.'** But I don't fear falling into emptiness, I say. Well, if you get up in the small hours of the morning and go outside into a very dark night in the country, or if you sit, all alone, in your darkened room, is there no feeling of fear? In the long sittings, doesn't fear creep in a little bit?

As a matter of fact, since fear is the other side of 'I', whenever I am not actively constellated, or not keeping myself actively employed, fear creeps in. And with that fear comes the whole psychological hinterland too. Falling into emptiness – or losing control, which is another aspect – is the fear of every 'I'. It is just under the surface, and we all know it; and we all play our particular games, or our individual games, so as not to be invaded and swallowed by that fear, and so as not to show it either. Real training is nothing other than facing that fear, having the strength to face that fear, seeing it for what it really is, without any roundabout notions, recognising it as an old friend, and suddenly the whole thing gives. It is not about getting something, but seeing what is there.

Master Daie, aware of this fear of falling into emptiness, then says, **'Whenever I see someone talking like this, I immediately ask him, "Is this one who fears falling into emptiness himself empty or not?" Ten out of ten cannot explain.'** We might usefully ask ourselves that question again and again.

And, says Master Daie, **'Since you have always taken thought and judgement as your nesting place…'** And I like that phrase 'nesting place' – sitting there, pontificating about everything, particularly about what we don't understand. We have great opinions in that nesting place. He continues, **'As soon as you hear it said that you should not think, immediately you are at a loss and can't find your grip.'** Isn't it so? Isn't it just so? You shouldn't think. Should I therefore make the mind a blank? Is that it? How do I do it? But all these questions when really looked at are just an excuse for not doing it, because if I really wanted to do it, then I would try.

So as soon as you hear it said that you shouldn't think and can't find your grip, then **'You are far from realising that this very lack of anywhere to get a grip is the time for you to let go of your body and your life.'** As a matter of fact, in a way we know it, and this is why we are so frightened. This very lack of anywhere to get a grip, this is the place to look for, this is the place to strive towards, the place where 'I' finally cancels out. That is something to take home from the *sesshin*. When that grip is gone, it's only a thought, when that is gone, there can be now. Carefully look. When that is gone, then there is no more worry about body and life. Can there be anything that can frighten? The fear goes with it. And without that fear one can stand squarely, on one's own two legs. So, it really comes down to that. You find it again and again in the teachings, throw off, or let go of, body and life. If that is not my worry anymore, what else can I be worrying about?

If we look very carefully at these old texts, we find ourselves being directly addressed with our various gripes and difficulties. They do not just hop about on the surface, they point straight to the real thing. If we really experiment with this, we find that I and fear are like the palm and back of the hand. To get away from the fear is to get away from I. Since I cannot get away from I by an act of will or by a thought, it is necessary to do the practice. We do the practice in order to get the strength to look at what we know anyway and, in a way, have always known, but what we have never had the courage to look straight at. The strength accumulates from enduring the practice, from getting on with the practice, from not stopping with the practice; gradually a little bit more strength and a little bit more strength, accumulates. And then it is suddenly possible to look at what has always been known, but what we have always refused to see. Then it looks quite different, and with that there is a coming together. With that everything, that in our best moments our heart genuinely wants, is also fulfilled. What we unrealistically want to do, what we think we should do, is suddenly quite unimportant, because what really needs to be done has nothing to do with 'I'. The answer is a very simple and direct one. I'm sure that we all want to be reasonably decent, and reasonably good. In Buddhism, that means in all three ways – in deed, speech and thought. But in spite of all of us really wanting it, and most human beings do really want it, look at our collective history. Have we always been really good and decent human beings? Look at ourselves. Have we always been really good and decent in deed, speech and thought? Have we? So we have got a good bit to learn, until we have the strength to look at ourselves, to recognise ourselves, and to open up.

Master Rinzai liked to say that it is like a man ripping himself open and showing stomach, spleen, liver and gall, all those things that we prefer not to show, and prefer not to be aware of either. So it's a pretty hefty thing, but it's a useful thing, to take home and to chew over, and to chew over, again and again until it finally begins to nourish.

LETTER 6 to HSU TUN-LI (continued)

THE TEXT

> Tun-li, my friend in the Path, when we met at Pien in 1176 you were of mature age and already knew of the existence of the Great Matter. But with your vast erudition you have entered too deeply into the Nine (Confucian) Classics and the Seventeen Histories. You are too brilliant and your lines of reasoning are too many, whereas your power of stable concentration is not enough. You are being dragged along by your daily activities as you respond to circumstances. Thus you are unable to make a clean break right where you stand.

> If correct mindfulness is present at all times and the attitude of fear for birth and death does not waver, then over long days and months what was unfamiliar will naturally become familiar and what was stale will naturally become fresh. But what is this stale? It's the brilliance and cleverness, that which thinks and judges. What is the unfamiliar? It's enlightenment, nirvana, true thusness, the Buddha-nature, where there is no thought or discrimination, where figuring and calculation cannot reach,

where there's no way for you to use your mental arrangements.

Suddenly the time arrives: you may be on a story of an ancient's entry into the Path, or it may be as you are reading the scriptures, or perhaps during your daily activities as you respond to circumstances. Whether your situation is good or not good, or your body and mind are scattered and confused, whether favourable or adverse circumstances are present, or whether you have temporarily quieted conceptual discrimination — when you suddenly topple the key link, there'll be no mistake about it.

VEN. MYOKYO-NI'S COMMENTS

This is the end of a very long letter to Tun-li who seems to have been a very old disciple of Master Daie's. And now Master Daie addresses him, **'Tun-li, my friend in the Path, when we met in Pien in 1176 you were of mature age and already knew of the existence of the Great Matter.'** So when Tun-li became his disciple, many years ago apparently, he was already of 'mature age', probably about forty or so. He also seems to have been a very cultured man, and probably held a rather high position. Before meeting Master Daie, he already knew of the existence of the Great Matter. In Zen texts, the Great Matter means the Great Matter of Life and Death, the Great Matter of being born and dying. 'You already knew of the existence of the Great Matter' – in other words, when Tun-li met Master Daie, he was not a complete beginner knowing nothing about Buddhism, but was already quite well-read in it.

'But,' says Master Daie, **'with your vast erudition you have entered too deeply into the Nine Classics and the Seventeen**

Histories.' The Nine Classics – these are the Confucian classics. In other words, Tun-Li had deeply studied all the Chinese philosophies and writings, the Nine Classics and the Seventeen Histories, all from the very beginning, with all the legends, and was therefore naturally acquainted not only with Confucianism, but with Taoism as well. He was a truly cultured Chinese Gentleman. But the difficulty with this is **'you are too brilliant and your lines of reasoning are too many'** – having read so much, the head gets rather full. We haven't read nearly as much and are not nearly so well-trained, but our own 'lines of reasoning' are nevertheless likewise far too many.

'And your lines of reasoning are far too many, **whereas your power of stable concentration is not enough.'** We can check it out at the *sesshin* here. Are our 'lines of reasoning too many'? Do they swirl about like a swarm of bees? Are our powers 'of stable concentration' too few? Can we sit peacefully in the zendo in stable concentration?

But we have to be very careful with the term 'concentration' because we so easily fall into the trap that I must concentrate. And what happens if I concentrate? What can I concentrate on? Yes, of course I can concentrate – I can concentrate on an individual item, for example. But the more I concentrate, the more focused this object becomes. And the more it excludes everything else, doesn't it? With this 'I'-concentration, everything else is shut out. But the Buddhist concentration, on the other hand, being Eastern, is to open up, and like a mirror to take in just what is, without any kind of exclusiveness. Such concentration takes in just what is, and like a mirror, when it turns away a little bit to something else, it lets what was in it before drop, and takes the new picture in. Please do not forget, the Buddhist concentration is the mirror. That's why Buddhism so often talks about the heart mirror. Whereas 'I'-concentration is 'I'-focusing and is totally exclusive. So perhaps 'concentration' is not exactly the right translation here; perhaps we could say your power of 'stably beholding, stably remaining in the situation.'

'You are being dragged along by your daily activities as you respond to circumstances:' Being dragged along, we can't let go, we must continue, and we get involved, personally involved in the circumstance and situations. That is what happens when the power of 'stable being' is not strong enough; we get pulled off our feet and dragged along. Being dragged along by circumstances as they are, **'thus you are unable to make a clean break right where you stand.'** To make a clean break means to just let go, to just drop it. If the one who gets so easily dragged is dropped, then the stable concentration or the stable openness or the stable being is there of itself; it need not be learnt as it is in any case our natural state.

So Master Daie continues, **'If correct mindfulness** (awareness) **is present at all times, and the attitude of fear for birth and death does not waver...'** Correct awareness is not 'I am aware of this or that' but just that openness of the heart mirror. 'If correct awareness is present at all times' – in other words if there is no interference by 'I' anymore, 'and the attitude of fear of birth and death does not waver' – as long as I am there, there is naturally the attitude of fear. Whatever I'm frightened of, at root it boils down to death, and is closely connected with death, with Birth and Death, with the Great Matter, or as the Buddha expressed it, coming to be and ceasing to be. And however much I would like to live forever and be eternal, that is not what the Buddhist wishes for. The Buddhist is far too wise, and wants to come off that Wheel of Birth and Death, where endlessly every death is followed by a birth, and every birth is followed by a death.

'Fear of birth and death' – that is what gets the Buddhist into training and spurs him on. The only way to come off that Wheel of Samsara, off the Six States, is to become one with the doing, and to let 'I' drop off. But that also means going deeper and deeper, because there are four stages – to forget 'I', to forget the human being, a living being and a life. When the life has dropped off and 'if the correct awareness is present at all times and the attitude of fear of birth and death does not waver, then' says Master Daie, **'over long days and months, what was unfamiliar will naturally become familiar and what was stale will naturally become fresh.'**

And he asks, **'But what is this stale? It is the brilliance and cleverness, that which thinks and judges.'** That is what we, being silly, think is our best aspect, and what we ideally want to be – brilliant and clever. That is also thinking and judging. Cleverness and brilliance are only possible in the presence of thinking and judging, that's obvious. And with that we are, not only in 'I'-activities but in a personal line of thought where I can no longer see or hear correctly. If we really look into it, it is quite impossible in our state, to look at something. If there is 'something', it already implies that there is also another thing, because in this way of thinking, we are in the pairs of opposites. As long as there is one thing, there is also the other. And that is already a judgement – this and that, and light and dark. A closer example, consider a flower. Can we really see a flower, just as it is? Or in the moment that we see the flower, do all kinds of further judgements come in? A flower – first of all, the naming, then the descriptions, a red flower, in full bloom, yet in bud, beginning to wilt, vase, water – the whole range of things comes in. We cannot really see just that flower. The ability to 'just see' has to be cultivated by correct awareness. In our usual seeing or hearing or any sense perception, we cannot take in what is. It's overlaid at once, at source, by our opinions, notions, convictions, conditions, and so on. Therefore Master Daie quite rightly says, 'What is this stale? It is the brilliance and cleverness, that which thinks and judges.'

Master Daie continues, **'What is the unfamiliar? It's enlightenment, nirvana, true thusness, the Buddha-nature.'** So many words. True nature or anything – it doesn't matter what you call it. That is the unfamiliar. It will always remain unfamiliar, and not-known and ungraspable, because whatever ideas we have about it, whatever concepts we make of it, however we try to form it into something that is graspable, that again is only an idea and has nothing to do with it.

It's not even a thing. It is literally inconceivable. And if we think that we can somehow manage to grasp the inconceivable, then in our own misunderstanding we are only trying to shrink, what is by nature truly inconceivable, down into some kind of concept again. But then it remains only a concept and has nothing to do with what actually is. Therefore what is the unfamiliar is enlightenment, nirvana, true thusness and the Buddha-nature. It is no thought, no discrimination, it is Right Seeing, Right Thinking, all the way through the Noble Eightfold Path. Master Daie repeats it, all the Zen Masters say it, **'where there is no thought or discrimination, where figuring and calculating cannot reach, where there is no way for you to use your mental arrangements.'** This is how Master Daie describes enlightenment. We can carefully look at it once more: where there is 'no thought or discrimination, where figuring and calculating cannot reach, where there is no way for you to use your mental arrangements.' Being a Westerner and fairly conditioned, even being familiar with Buddhist literature, we believe that enlightenment is an experience. It isn't. As long as there is an experience, there is also I the experiencer. Enlightenment is a state different from the state that 'I' know. That is what Master Daie is trying to say and he says it beautifully, because if there is no way for you to use your mental arrangements, 'suddenly the time arrives', if the training goes on.

'Suddenly the time arrives: you may be on a story of an ancient's entry into the Path, or it may be as you are reading the scriptures, or perhaps during your daily activities as you respond

to circumstances. Whether your situation is good or not good, or your body and mind are scattered or confused, whether favourable or adverse conditions are present, or whether you have temporarily quieted conceptual discrimination – when you suddenly topple the key link, then there'll be no mistake about it.' Everything truly falls off.

It is usually a sudden thing. Remember the Buddha, sitting in long meditation, so deep that nothing, no circumstances, could take him out of it; and when on that last night under the Bo Tree neither Mara's daughters nor Mara's demons, neither lust nor fear, had any inroad anymore? Because he was not there anymore. Or no 'I' was there anymore, nothing which, so to speak, could have been 'got' by Mara. But in that condition, he did not become 'enlightened', which is in any case a bad expression. Enlightenment did not open whilst he was sitting there in meditation. It was in that moment when he came out of meditation and looked up and saw the morning star – with a completely empty heart, with no thought, before thought had arisen, in that complete reflection which is the state of beholding and not 'I'-focused or 'I-seeing'. In that moment, when the sense-impression falls into such an empty heart, that heart reflects it. In that the awareness truly arises. 'When you suddenly topple the key link, there'll be no mistake about it.'

When there is only a beholding, there is no seeing as I see; there is no hearing as I hear and therefore things are truly seen and heard, as they are. With that awareness, comes the response. Use this *sesshin* to come into that awareness – the true beholding, the true hearing, where there is no judgement of nice and not nice, of annoying or not annoying, or whatever it might be, where there is just the seeing and the hearing. It is at such times that there is nobody who hears. There is only the hearing. There is nobody who sees, there is only the seeing. This is why there are no judgements with it. When the see-er and the hearer have vanished and have become one with the activity, that is where the entrance is. Experiment, please.

LETTER 7 to LI HSIEN-CH'EN

THE TEXT

A gentleman reads widely in many books, basically in order to augment his innate knowledge. Instead, you have taken to memorising the words of the ancients, accumulating them in your breast, making this your task. Depending on them for something to take hold of, you are far from knowing the intent of the sages in expounding the teachings. This is what is called counting the treasures of others all day long without having half a penny of your own. Likewise in reading the Buddhist scriptures, you must see the moon and forget the fingers. Don't develop an understanding based on words. An ancient worthy said, 'The Buddhas expounded all teachings to save all minds. I have no mind at all so what's the use of all the teachings?' If they can be like this when reading the scriptures, only then will people with resolve have some comprehension of the intent of the sages.

VEN. MYOKYO-NI'S COMMENTS

'A gentleman reads widely…' – What is a gentleman? Not born, as we very easily mistake it. A gentleman is made – by education, by upbringing, to endure whatever emotion and emotional energy rushes up, without being hindered in what is being done, in whatever is to be done at the moment. That is what a gentleman is. And the opposite of a gentleman is a barbarian, who may be a very nice person indeed, but his passions are uncontrollable; when they rise, they have him. As a result, the difference between the gentleman and the 'barbarian' is that the gentleman can be trusted to continue the course which he is engaged in without being swerved by any kind of flare-up whatsoever. In the Southern Scriptures, too, we read about the sons and daughters of a noble family and as with the gentleman, 'noble' has nothing to do with birth, but with upbringing so that the emotions cannot run away with them anymore.

Such a gentleman, says Master Daie, **'reads widely in many books,'** because naturally he wants to have role models and inspiration along the Way that he is engaged in, and **'basically in order to augment his innate knowledge.'** Then his demeanour and conduct will also confirm it and confirm him on his course and in his activities.

Master Daie writing to his correspondent tells him that instead of looking for role models, instead of having examples, **'you have taken to memorising the words of the ancients, accumulating them in your breast and making this your task. Depending on them for something to take hold of.'** 'Memorising the words of the old masters' – even if the whole compendium of scriptures is known by heart, what is only in the head is of no use. When suddenly a very difficult task or a calamity befalls you, what is only in the head will be of no help. You go down with it and get yourself thoroughly upset and into all kinds of states. When it's only in the head – even the whole compendium of scriptures is no good.

This is where one really has to change gears. Has the practice truly sunk into the heart? Has the heart truly been gentled? Is it possible to bear up in a human way under the pressure of adversities? Or do we snap and crack up? We need to be clear that this is what the Zen training is about. Master Daie is actually telling Li-Hsien-ch'en that he has only head-learning and that the practice is missing. **'You are far from knowing the intent of the ancients in expounding the teachings.'** They gave the teachings, but not for the words alone. This goes right back to the beginning of the Zen school with Bodhidharma's – 'A special transmission outside the teachings, not standing on words and phrases.' Yet we go on insisting, 'But this is what is said here, this is what it must mean.'

That is not what is meant by it. In the Zen School there is the lovely story of the great Master Joshu, who only started teaching when he was eighty and he lived until a hundred and twenty. You know the story of the monk, who having just read the *Nirvana Sutra* where it is clearly stated that all beings have Buddha-nature, came to check out what his teacher would say. So, he asked Master Joshu, 'Does a dog have Buddha-nature?' And Master Joshu very firmly said, 'No.' The monk was quite shocked. Such a great master denying it, he ought to know it. He had come to Master Joshu without any problem – now he had a problem to take away with him! That was the greatness of Master Joshu.

But another monk also came to Master Joshu, who had not necessarily heard about this incident, or perhaps had heard about it, but who in any case was genuinely concerned about it. And he asked Master Joshu, 'Does a dog have Buddha-nature?' And Master Joshu said, 'Yes.' You read that and think, Now, now what is this – to one he says, 'Yes' and to the other he says, 'No.' Doesn't he know his mind? Doesn't he know what it is?' That is what we will never learn in the scriptures but which we learn in the training, that to different situations we respond in different ways and yet in that different way it is always the same response.

Without recognising that we will not get far in our training or in our life or in our understanding of things as they are, because we are far from knowing the intent of the teachings of the old masters. **'This is what is called counting the treasures of others all day long without having half a penny of your own.'** This is a famous saying, at least I know it in different variations in the Zen texts, I expect it's a Chinese proverb. 'Counting the treasures of others without having a penny of one's own.' We wonder how much our friends earn, how much they know, how many books they have read, that I have not yet read. All concerned with 'the treasures of others.'

'Likewise in reading the Buddhist Scriptures,' says Master Daie, **'you must see the moon and forget the fingers.'** I have often told this story but I will nevertheless tell it again because it is such a good example. In my early days in Japan, I was just getting used to reading the Chinese koan texts in the *Rinzai Roku*, which is difficult to read. I used to translate and try to get the meaning out of the passage the Roshi would give in the next teisho, so that I would at least know what he was talking about and could follow the commentary better.

And there, the passage for the next day was what an enlightened person can do – they can go into the woods and not be molested by the wild beasts and can go into the three deepest hells and play about in them as if it was a fairground. And I must say, my heart sank and I thought, 'When they get into those eulogies, even the Zen School, even the staid Zen School, gets carried away. What about that famous compassion – playing about in the three deepest hells as if it was a fairground?' I was really looking forward to the next day, to see what the Roshi would say.

And he took it right up and said, 'If you look at it with your two eyes, which is the way in which 'I' look, it seems really callous. But this is not how you are ever supposed to read scriptures. You have to look where it points to.' He said, 'If a person is going into those frightful places where there is nothing but the most terrible suffering, they go of their own free will. But if they go there and are caught up in the pain and suffering, then they only become another inmate, making it worse for everybody. They must remain free because otherwise if they don't remain free, they cannot hold out a helping hand.' So, this is forgetting the finger, not mixing up the finger pointing at the moon with the moon itself. Fingers point at the moon but the fingers can come from all different directions. Which one reveals the true meaning? We suddenly look at those lines in a different way.

Master Daie warns, **'Don't develop an understanding based on words.'** We know all about this with our Bible-thumping – 'This is what is says, this is what is written right here!' But the Buddhist scriptures are not like that. The Buddhist scriptures are explanations, expounding, sometimes for this and sometimes for that audience just as the Buddha himself also did, depending which people he had in front of him. To merchants he would speak in a language which was natural to them and give examples and analogies that went with their life styles. And to warriors he would talk in another way. And we, without even knowing it, do exactly the same. When we talk to a small child, do we use the same language as we use when we talk to our boss in the office? Or do we talk to our boss in the office in the same way as we talk to our spouse at home? We don't try to make it different, it quite naturally is different.

Master Daie continues, **'An ancient worthy said, "The Buddhas expounded all teachings to save all minds. I have no mind at all so what's the use of all the teachings?"'** They 'expounded all teachings to save all minds' – that is to address all people, to be of use to all people. And this is why we have such an enormous number of scriptures. They are all saying the same thing, from the simplest to the most complicated, but in different ways for different audiences. Just like that old master who said that the Buddha expounded all teachings to help all people, we too vow that every day when chanting the Four Vows, don't we? But that old master continues, 'I have no mind at all so what's the use of all the teachings?' What might that possibly mean? 'I have no mind at all,' I have no opinion at all, 'so what's the use of all the teachings?'

All the teachings come down to the same one. However, a framework is necessary, especially for us Westerners. If you really look, the Three Signs of Being, the Three Poisons, the Four Noble Truths, the Six Paramitas, the Eightfold Path, the Twelve Links, each one explains the same thing, in either a simpler or more complicated manner. But as time went by the teachings like the four Noble Truths and the Six Paramitas, etc., were studied more deeply, further explained and commented on so that they seemed like new teachings, and in this way the whole enormous Buddhist canon came about. That is how the scriptures, how the written word misleads if you follow it up instead of just looking where it points to. And therefore: 'I have no mind at all so what's the use of all the teachings?'

The letter concludes, **'If they can be like this when reading the scriptures, only then will people with resolve have some comprehension of the intent of the sages.'** When they can be like this – simple, straightforward, responding to circumstances as they are, immediately and without hesitation. All other living beings in the Six Realms do exactly that. If we think of our nearest neighbours, the mammals, and also as a matter of fact all animals, a mouse will always, reliably, behave as a mouse behaves, under all circumstances good, bad and indifferent. And so will an elephant. And so will a tiger. But we as human beings, do we always respond like that? Not only respond like this, but in the Buddhist way, in deed, word and thought? If we look at our collective history, we know that we don't. And if we look at ourselves, have we never in deed, word or thought had any moment that made us less than human? 'I could have punched him, I could murder him!' Has nobody ever thought that?

We may excuse ourselves saying, 'Well, it is only all too human.' But it isn't truly human. It is just showing that we are not yet truly inhabiting the human state. So we go into the training and learn, not to be misled by pointing fingers or by erudite knowledge and swallowing book after book but by sorting ourselves out so that we do not mistake the finger pointing at the moon for the moon. Only then will we have any understanding of what the old masters really pointed at, which then comes down to simply sitting zazen and directly responding to what is, under all circumstances, in all situations. Not to be toppled over by this, that and the other.

LETTER 8 to TENG TZU-LI

The Text

These days in the Ch'an communities they use the extraordinary words and marvellous sayings of the ancients to question and answer, considering them situations for discrimination and beguiling students. They are far from getting to the root of their reality. When the Buddhas reached the Dharma, their sole concern was that people wouldn't understand; though they had recondite and obscure things to say, they would then bring in other comparisons and similes to make sentient beings wake up and understand. For example, a monk asked Ma Tsu, 'What is Buddha?' And Ma Tsu said, 'Mind itself is Buddha.' At this the monk was enlightened and entered the Path. What discrimination is there here? But if the monk hadn't awakened from this, then this very 'Mind itself is Buddha' would have been a situation of discrimination.

Ven. Myokyo-ni's Comments

'These days in the Ch'an communities they use the extraordinary words and marvellous sayings of the ancients to question and

answer, considering them situations for discrimination and beguiling students.' Well, looking at the old texts, seeing what the old masters said, with question and answers, trying to understand, getting the meaning – all very nice, but abstract and in the head.

When I was young and green in Daitoku-ji, a priest there spoke very good English and he befriended me. From time to time I was allowed to come to his temple and we would talk and I would ply him with questions, asking for the meaning. And one day he grinned and said, 'You foreigners, all you want is to understand the meaning. What's the use of it?' I looked rather surprised. We were sitting on the veranda in front of his main shrine room and we were both smoking and he said, 'I'll give you an example. There was a master and his student and the student had just asked, "What is the meaning of the Buddha-dharma?" or something like that. But the master didn't say a word. He put his hand down, took up a brown leaf and rolled it up tightly, and put it into his mouth and then he set fire to the other end. He sucked and blew out a big cloud of smoke. The student was thinking, "Now what is he trying to show by this? Is he perhaps showing that whatever is considered in this world of secondary truth goes up like smoke and vanishes into thin air? What could it be?"' Then Kobori-san looked at me and said, 'But, you see, the two of us,' and he blew out a big cloud of smoke, 'we know the old boy was just smoking!'

This is a beautiful illustration of what is always going on. The true kernel is not in the words, is not in this or that and can't be caught in thought or with understanding. In the same way that you cannot describe how cold or hot the drink in the cup is – you have to taste it yourself. You can say it's hot, but you cannot describe how hot it is. What is hot to one person is barely lukewarm to another.

But says Master Daie, **'They are far from getting to the root of their reality,'** of what those extraordinary words and marvellous sayings of the old masters actually point to. He then carefully explains, **'When the Buddhas reached the Dharma'** – when they had true insight – **'their sole concern was that people wouldn't understand.'** Because it was too straightforward, too direct. **'And though they had recondite and obscure things to say, they would then bring in other comparisons and similes,'** simple ones, **'to make sentient beings wake up and understand.'**

In the Mahayana, it is said that the Buddha preached the Dharma in Five Cycles, because after his own awakening and after carefully pondering, he could not see any way in which he could bring the meaning over so that people would be able to understand. First he tried by preaching what came to be known as the *Kegon Sutra*, the *Flower Ornament Sutra*. The main theme is that one is all and all is one. It's quite easy to put it into words and even intellectually to understand it, it's not too difficult when put that simply. But to actually realise it and live out of it, truly live out of it, that is quite another thing. So, in order to really bring that point across, he then started preaching the *Agama Sutras* which in the Southern Tradition are called the Pali Canon. That was the second cycle. And the following cycles then contain the more profound Mahayana sutras.

So, 'all the Buddhas who reached the Dharma, though they had recondite and obscure things to say, they would then bring in other comparisons and similes to make sentient beings wake up and understand.' In one of the Southern teachings the Buddha said, 'Which are the more numerous, the few leaves I have here in my hand, or those up in the trees of the grove? Of all the leaves, I've taken up a handful. These I show.' Those things which should be taught and practised – were equal to the number of leaves in his hand.

Here Master Daie by way of illustration says, **'For example a monk asked Ma Tsu** (the great master Baso Doitsu in the Japanese) **"What is Buddha?" Ma Tsu said, "Mind** (heart) **itself is Buddha."**

At this the monk was enlightened and entered the Path. What discrimination is there here?' A rhetorical question, because there is of course no discrimination. Heart itself is Buddha.

But the full story shows how discrimination can be made out of it. Whatever Master Ma Tsu was asked he used to declare, 'Heart is Buddha. Heart is Buddha.' A young monk gained his insight from just this. Eventually he left Ma Tsu's assembly and spent many years on pilgrimage and when he found that there was nothing lacking, he settled down on a faraway mountain, and a community began to form around him. Years later, news of it reached the old master who, by that time, had found that many imitated his 'Heart is Buddha' without relevant insight, and so he now firmly taught, 'Neither heart nor Buddha.' Ma Tsu sent an experienced monk to find out what his erstwhile disciple taught and to tell him about the old teacher's change of style. The emissary arrived and duly asked about the teaching. Told that it was 'Heart is Buddha', he delivered his message. 'You know, our Master has of late changed his teaching. He no longer says, "Heart is Buddha." Nowadays he teaches "Neither heart nor Buddha nor anything."' But Master Daibai, which means 'The Great Plum', firmly replied, 'I don't know what the old man is up to. He can teach what he likes. I got my insight under him, Master Ma Tsu, and I got it from the insight into "Heart is Buddha". This is the insight that I teach and the insight that I show. I know no other.' When the messenger returned and told what had happened, Ma Tsu nodded and said, 'I distrusted The Great Plum, but now I know it is ripe.' This is self-reliance derived from truly knowing. It is the confirmation, the realisation, of which Buddhism talks so much. Once realised, one can put it to use. Nothing could deflect him, not even a test by his old teacher.

Master Daie asks, 'What discrimination is there here?' 'Heart is Buddha.' And then the other says, 'Neither Heart nor Buddha.' Now you can go on, finding reasons, and pondering it, why this, why that, instead of straight away seeing. Seeing what? Seeing! What goes through the head will not hold when the moment comes and puts it to the test. Therefore it has to be taken in with the body too.

Because there is one thing which we tend to forget, particularly we Westerners tend to forget, that a thought without a body is quite useless. It's only when the body is included, that the thing becomes whole. We may have been shown exactly, and intellectually know how to swim, or how to touch-type or how to play the piano or whatever it is, but when it then comes right down to doing it, we still won't be able to bring it off because the body is missing. Without the body, it's a kind of ghostly thing. On the other hand, what is once learned with the body, as different from what has been learned with the mind only – in the head only – is not so easily forgotten, as a matter of fact isn't forgotten at all.

'But if the monk hadn't awakened from this, then this very Mind (Heart) **is Buddha, would have been a situation of discrimination.'** Or a situation of, 'What did he mean by it? What does it mean that the Heart is Buddha?' Or if you want, 'What can be meant by the True Face?' Thinking and thinking about it, trying and trying to find it.

Much simpler, much more straightforward, 'Heart itself is Buddha.' That's that. We either get it or we don't get it. If we get it, there's nothing more to be said about it; and if we don't get it, we will not get it by discriminating and thinking but rather by realising it. That's what it is about, at this moment here and now being able to express it. If it is realised, it can be expressed. If it is not realised and only thought about, it goes into long thought-streams and means nothing. So please, again, when it comes to the Buddhist texts, and particularly to the Zen texts, don't look for any meaning but go directly for what it says.

LETTER 8 to TENG TZU-LI (continued)

The Text

When people engaged in meditation read the scriptural teachings and the stories of the circumstances in which the ancient worthies entered the Path, they should just empty their minds. Don't look for the original marvel or seek enlightenment in sounds, names and verbal meanings. If you take this attitude, you are obstructing your own correct knowledge and perception and you'll never have an entry. P'an Shan said, 'It's like hurling a sword at the sky. No talk of whether it reaches or not.' Don't be careless! Vimalakirti said that the Truth goes beyond eyes, ears, nose, tongue, body and intellect. If you want to penetrate this Truth, first you must clear out the gates of the six senses, leaving them without the slightest affliction. What does 'affliction' mean? It means to be turned around by form, sound, scent, taste, touch and phenomena and not detaching from them. It's seeking knowledge and looking for understanding in the words and phrases of the scriptural teachings and the ancient worthies. If you can avoid giving rise to a second thought about the scriptural teachings or the stories of the ancient worthies entering the Path, and realise directly what they go back to, then there will be nothing in your own realm or in the realm of others that is not according to your will and nothing of which you are not the master.

Ven. Myokyo-ni's Comments

'When people engaged in meditation read the scriptural teachings and the stories of the circumstances in which the ancient

worthies entered the Path, they should just empty their minds.' It doesn't say not to read them – but not to read them and create more ideas while trying to understand them and ponder what they might mean. I remember when I was in Daitoku-ji, I think it must have been my second year when I was told to stop reading anything to do with Buddhism, philosophy and psychology. I was rather surprised and, seeing my astonished face, was told, 'If you do not stick to your own training, and you read a lot, you can't help but relate to every new thing you come across and will continuously try and compare it to what you have found out yourself. All these ideas will clutter your training and obstruct you from going deeper into your practice.' And how absolutely true it is. I was deeply grateful and still am deeply grateful for that advice. A good many of you know this, because I have told you the same! We have to be very careful with this, because it does not mean that the framework of the texts is not of absolute importance, and it does not mean that we shouldn't have a good grasp of the Buddha-dharma, but that is something quite different.

When we first hear about the Buddha-dharma, we cannot help but naturally look at it and try to understand it against our own Western framework that we are a part of, and which has a doer, and without a doer it is quite impossible to see and understand anything. But when we read that into the Buddhist texts, then we very much misread them and are unable to understand them properly. If we have done our training thoroughly and then look at the texts, we'll see what they actually mean. Also, the advice that I was given continued, 'When you have clearly seen what it means, then you can read the teachings. Then they will make real sense and you will appreciate their enormous beauty and awesomeness, something which will lift your heart.' And those are the things that you can pass on, just as they are needed; you can say the same thing to a child and the same thing to an older person – but the wording in which you give the same message is likely to be very different.

So Master Daie says that they should make their hearts empty. And in order to see to it that the heart becomes empty, we do not need teachings, we need the training. If the heart is truly empty, then whatever falls into it is reflected back and we will not misread, misunderstand, or misapply the Buddha's teachings. To empty the heart means to get rid of our thought patterns, which is another way of saying to forget about myself. So Master Daie suggests, **'Don't look for the original marvel or seek enlightenment in sounds, names and verbal meanings.'** 'The original marvel' – the pebble clicked against the bamboo trunk and the monk was enlightened. Don't seek 'in sounds, names and verbal meanings.' The sounds that move – the sound of the single hand. And verbal meanings – what is the meaning of Bodhidharma's coming from the West? **'If you take this attitude, you are obstructing your own correct knowledge and perception and you'll never have any entry.'** When thought patterns get in the way, it doesn't work. **'P'an Shan said, "It is like hurling a sword at the sky. No talk of whether it reaches or not."'** Do we see what this means? One will say, 'What's the use of hurling a sword against the sky? You know, it's silly to do so. It will not reach the sky.' The other says, 'Of course it will reach the sky.' And with all this, they forget to just hurl that sword and have done with it!

An anecdote from the Sixth Patriarch's community makes the same point rather nicely. Two monks, having read all the Mahayana teachings, were standing in the yard and saw the temple flag fluttering in the wind. One monk said to the other, 'Do you see, it is the wind that flutters and moves the flag?' And the other said, 'No, no, it's the flag that flutters itself.' They were getting into a hefty discussion when fortunately the Sixth Patriarch himself came across the yard and heard them vying with each other. He looked at them and said, 'It is neither the wind that moves the flag nor the flag that moves of itself. It is the hearts of the two eminent monks that flutter.' So perhaps if we do not let our heart flutter, because we have made it empty and then it cannot flutter, this is how we begin to see and also see where Master Daie points.

Master Daie then says, '**Don't be careless. Vimalakirti said that the Truth goes beyond eyes, ears, nose, tongue, body and intellect.**' We can translate 'the truth', which is a convenient Western word as the Dharma. So, the Dharma 'goes beyond eyes, ears, nose, tongue, body and intellect.' Those are the Five Functions or five senses, plus a sixth here translated as 'intellect' but usually understood as 'thought' or 'mind'. But they are also very often referred to as the thieves, as the robbers, because they carry us away. Therefore very clearly we are told by Vimalakirti, '**If you want to penetrate this Truth, first you must clear out the gates of the six senses, leaving them without the slightest affliction. What does 'affliction' mean? It means to be turned around by form, sound, scent, taste, touch and phenomena and not detaching from them.**' In other words, quite rightly, the 'thieves' or 'robbers' as they are sometimes referred to, take you away, carry you away with them. With the six senses we come to the eighteen *dhatu*: form and colour from the eye, sound from the ear, scent from the nose, taste from the mouth, touch from the body, and phenomena. They carry us away unless the gates are cleared. So, not to be turned round by them, that is the important thing. It's not to do away with them, it's not not to see them, it's not not to perceive them, but just not to be carried away. Not detaching from them, but just not clinging to them. Not detached from the senses, because there's nothing wrong with the senses. On the contrary, they are not only important for our survival, they're also very often a joy. But to be carried away by them, to cling to them, to be attached to them rather than detached from them – then we are in trouble, as we know to our cost.

'It is seeking knowledge and looking for understanding in the words and phrases of the scriptural teachings and the ancient worthies.' In other words, to believe it can be found, can be got from somewhere outside; and when I get it, then I have entered the Path. But this is precisely where the delusion sits. First of all, the wisdom of the Buddha is, in any case, inborn and inherent. As long as I seek it outside, it cannot be found, least of all when I'm convinced that I must unearth it somewhere in the scriptures and the sayings of the old masters. And though inborn, it cannot be found inside either, because it's not a thing. As long as I seek, my seeking covers it. Looking for it, looking for it, where is it?

But Master Daie says, **'If you can avoid giving rise to a second thought about the scriptural teachings or the stories of the ancient worthies entering the Path and realise directly what they go back to, then there will be nothing in your own realm or in the realm of others, that is not according to your will, nothing of which you are not the master.'** 'If you can avoid giving rise to a second thought,' you can realise directly where something is pointing to. We can take it in this way or in that way or the third way, but we'll not cling to the words but follow them to where they point. The caution, which we have heard and read so often, is not to mistake the pointing finger for the moon. But we are rather attached to those fingers and stick with the finger and then we see twenty fingers pointing to the moon from all different directions. One from this side and one from that side and they seem to contradict each other and we say, 'Now what does that mean? Do I know it? What could it possibly be?' Instead of realising there are different ways.

I remember, in a much more concrete way, a particular mountain on the Austro-Italian border that looked like a three-humped back, rather beautiful, quite high. I had lived in a little town from which the view of that mountain was on clear days, very beautifully seen, and I liked that mountain very much. Then I had occasion to be driven up to that valley at the foot of that mountain. And as we drove up the valley, there was another mountain that looked just like Mount Fuji. And I said, 'I've never seen that mountain before. What is it?' And the name that I was given was exactly that same one, that large, long, three-humped one. I said, 'Are there two Mittagskogel (that is its name)?' They said, 'No, no, why should there be two?' I said, 'Well, what about the one that one can see from where I live?' 'Well, yes, course it's the same, only this is from one side and that is from the other side.' So unless you go round the mountain, you will not recognise that it is the same mountain that looks different from this side and different from that side and still different from a third side. So there we have to be really careful. Empty the heart, find out for yourself.

Therefore, 'If you can avoid giving rise to a second thought about the scriptural teachings and realise directly what those stories go back to, then there will be nothing in your own realm, or in the realm of others, that is not according to your will, nothing of which you are not the master.' That sounds rather lofty, most fascinating, but it's certainly not meant like that. We have already mentioned the section in the *Analects* where Confucius speaks about the changes he went through every ten years or so, starting with his studies at the age of fifteen. By the time he was sixty, he found himself completely in accord with the will of the Tao or we could say Dharma. And finally at the age of seventy, he could do whatever he liked and it would not transgress the Dharma. In other words, that complete accord with it, which is also found in the Tao Te Ching, where it says, 'Man obeys the laws of the Earth, Earth obeys the laws of Heaven, Heaven obeys the laws of Tao – or Dharma if you want to – and Tao obeys its own inherent nature.'

If man can but bring himself to be in accord with the laws of the earth, that brings him into that complete accord with everything, and then he can follow the dictates of his heart without transgressing; that is what is meant here. It is not according to your Tao, not according to your will, because the will and the Dharma and the Tao are all one thing and there is no possibility of transgressing any more. This is what makes a human being a really whole human being, a master. That does not mean that there is nothing else left because to a full human being there also belongs the human stature and the human heart, and the human heart is something that has a lot of qualities, such as gratitude and joy and warmth and compassion. With that there is also the re-linking to everything that is – nothing separate, only 'I' is separate. A human being at one with everything is also acting from that understanding and in good will. That, please, take to heart and just little by little by your own practice, let it emerge.

LETTER 9 to LU SHUN-YUAN

The Text

In the old days the military commander Li Wen-ho studied with the Ch'an master Ts'ung of Tz'u Chao, at Shih Men, and awakened to the essence of the Lin Chi School. He had a verse which said:

> To study the Path, one must be an iron man:
> Get hold of the mind and settle the issue immediately!
> Directly seizing supreme enlightenment,
> Don't concern yourself with right and wrong.

How marvellous these words are, they should be considered an aid for making the seeds of illumination unfold their potential.

'Buddha' is the medicine for sentient beings. Once the disease of sentient beings is removed, the medicine has no further use. If the disease is removed but the medicine kept, though you enter the realm of enlightenment (Buddhahood), you are unable to enter the realm of delusion (Mara). This disease is equal to the disease of sentient beings before it is removed. When the disease is cured and the medicine removed, and both Buddhahood and deluding influences are swept entirely away, only then will you have a bit of accord with the causes and conditions of this Great Matter.

Buddhas are those who have comprehended and completed things in the realm of sentient beings. And sentient beings are those who have not comprehended and completed things in the realm of Buddhas. If you want to attain Oneness, just give up both Buddhas and sentient beings at once. Then there is no comprehended and completed or not comprehended and completed.

Ven. Myokyo-ni's Comments

'In the old days the military commander Li Wen-ho studied with the Ch'an master Ts'ung of Tz'u Chao and awakened to the essence of the Lin Chi School.' – that is the Rinzai School. Of course, what he awakened to cannot be said in detail, but as so often happens, he composed a verse, because the closest you can come is through poetry. That's why we often have capping verses.

His verse begins, **'To study the Path, one must be an iron man.'** If we give up just because it gets a little bit difficult or if we give up because for the moment we have got a nice easy stretch and we think we don't need any more training, that won't hold for any length of time and won't stand up in the face of difficulties. To really 'study the Path, one must be an iron man,' in other words, not give up under any circumstances. That alone already says it. But the man of iron does not give up, does not stop, is not deflected; he just steadily moves on. He doesn't rush, has no express train to catch; just plods on steadily. And that is precisely what I do not like – plodding on steadily. I'm quite willing to make an absolutely incredible effort for a day or two, then, 'Nothing has changed, oh dear, what am I doing this for, why should I?' Then I settle down into lethargy, until something happens and I pull myself together again. But this does not work. It's the steady plodding on that's needed.

Such a man of iron, not deflected by anything, is told, **'Get hold of the mind** (heart) **and settle the issue immediately!'** What issue? 'I', always 'I', everything revolves around me. Soko Roshi told me that he once had a young mother visit him, with a small child. She said she would do anything for that child, she would willingly kill for that child. Soko Roshi said, 'Yes, that is normally what mothers feel. But when it really comes down to it, it's not for the child but because you love yourself best. It's not the child.' And she was very perturbed by that. But it's worthwhile really thinking about it. 'Get hold of the heart and settle the issue immediately.' To be very clear about things – how dear am I to myself. How far does that root go. And as far as that is concerned, how far is the separation from everything else. **'Directly seizing supreme enlightenment'** – the moment that root is really pulled out, there is nothing more to be done.

'Don't concern yourself at all with right and wrong' – whether I do it the right way or the wrong way or whether I fail to do it altogether; whether I slip up in my work, in my normal life, or in zazen. 'Do I count the breaths? Am I giving myself into the count? Do I count to ten? Do I just go on counting?' All these questions that we have, they're all concerned with 'I' doing right or wrong. But we do not need to worry, because even if 'I' do it right, it's still wrong. So, I might as well give up doing the right thing, just in order not fail. It does not really matter which is the best method, the most effective method. It's just the plodding on and not stopping which does it.

To give a very mundane example or analogy: when I was a geology student in Austria, which also meant studying mineralogy, our mineralogy professor was a very short and very wiry man and he was an excellent mountaineer. At least once a year in summer we used to go into the high mountains with him to collect various bits of whatever it was that we were working on. Right from the beginning in the morning, he started walking and we young students couldn't bear his slow walking, plodding along, and we just zoomed ahead. By about midday, we were all thoroughly exhausted, had to sit down a couple of times and had lost sight of him completely. When we arrived exhausted at the spot where we were having lunch, he would already be sitting there comfortably having arrived there an hour before us. Never changing his speed, just plodding on. And we, having lost our wind, lost our strength because we had run about too much, were far behind. So, you see, it is from the simple counting all the way through to mountain walking, just plodding on gets us there.

And 'don't concern yourself at all with right and wrong.' If you want to rush ahead, go run along and see for yourself that it doesn't work. We learn from our mistakes rather than from not wanting to be making a mistake. The great teacher is not what somebody tells us, because that makes no inroad at all. The great teachers are our own mistakes, because from those we really learn. So, quite rightly, 'don't concern yourself at all with right and wrong.'

Master Daie says, **'How marvellous these words are. They should be considered an aid for making the seeds of illumination unfold their potential.'** This illumination is in all of us, only, as the Buddha said, because of our attachments we cannot see it. Our attachment is of course to myself. Master Daie continues, **'Buddha is the medicine for sentient beings.'** He has taught the way out of suffering, to the peace and the warmth of the heart. He is truly the medicine for sentient beings. But **'once the disease of sentient beings is removed the medicine has no further use. If the disease is removed but the medicine kept, though you enter the realm of enlightenment, you are unable to enter the realm of delusion,'** the realm of Mara. 'The medicine for sentient beings' – that is walking the Buddha's Way. If walking the Buddha's Way is really the cure, then once the disease of sentient beings is removed, the medicine has no further use. Because 'if the disease is removed but the medicine kept, though you enter the realm of enlightenment, you are unable to enter the realm of delusion.' Then you are only good.

I remember a speaker at a Buddhist Society Summer School, long ago, well before I went to Japan. He gave a talk on Mahayana Buddhism, and at that time very little was known about Mahayana. I remember him standing there with a big smile on his face and saying that the easiest way of differentiating between Theravada and Mahayana is that in Theravada you have to be good, and in Mahayana you don't have to be good. You don't do anything harmful in either but in Theravada you still have to be good, but not in Mahayana. What is meant is that when you are all-good, holy and careful, you cannot enter the realm of delusion at all, and therefore are of no use to ordinary beings.

There is a Zen story which I rather like of an old Master who had chosen his head monk as his heir, a very apt heir. But though that was settled, the head monk himself, heir presumptive, had some worries about it. He was not absolutely sure. So he asked the master on his deathbed, 'Whilst you are still alive, if there is anything you think I should still do, anything I should still achieve, will you please tell me whilst there is still time? I'll do my best.' The old Master said, 'Well, really, I can't find any fault in you whatsoever. You have got everything: You have got the stability, you have got the strength, everything. But there is one little thing that still worries me about you – you still stink of Zen!' You can't enter the realm of delusions with only good. This is where we come back to it once again, with only good you are frightened of and dislike the realm of the bad, and can therefore not know or understand it.

Yet those two, the realm of delusion and the realm of Buddha, counterbalance each other. The one cannot exist without the other. We always fall into our 'disease', we are split into this and that. Our whole world and all our concepts and notions are split into opposites. There's nothing we can say of which the opposite cannot be said too. We arrange ourselves on the side of our notions, on the side of good opposed to the other – and with us it's not just the other, as it is in the East, it is the enemy, that must be fought, that must be exterminated. Consequently, we have got the frightful aggression and the frightful greed from which we also suffer, and into that we dare not step.

'This disease,' says Master Daie, **'is equal to the disease of sentient beings before it is removed.'** The disease of one only, of only the cure, of the medicine, of keeping the medicine. If you have been ill and got a reasonably strong medicine and it did effect a perfect cure, what will happen if you go on using it, taking it nevertheless? It begins to poison you. So whenever we get totally one-sided or even reasonably one-sided, we are already taking the medicine as poison and are made ill by it.

But Master Daie says, **'When the disease is cured and the medicine removed, and both Buddhahood and deluding influences** are swept entirely away,' Buddhahood – what I have thought about and wanted, because it was something great and beautiful – to be swept away entirely; and also the deluding influences – my judgements of this, that and the other – to be got rid of. Only when this has happened, **'Only then,'** says Master Daie, **'will you have a bit of accord with the causes and conditions of This Great Matter.'** The Great Matter is what in the Zen School usually refers to as the insight into the way things really are. We could also say insight into this principle, which is inborn in all of us and informs everything, all sentient life; and not only the sentient life, but everything on this planet of ours.

Everything conforms to this 'information' and therefore goes in harmony, whether up or down, like the wonderful analogy of the ocean and the waves. All the individual waves go up and down, form and dissolve, but inherently are nothing but ocean. To realise that, not in the head, but really in the living body, that means accord with the Great Matter. Under those circumstances I don't actually have to try and be good anymore, because the natural way of a human being, is not that of a fighting demon. We all know what a true human being is, with decent behaviour, with a warm heart, with understanding, kindness and helpfulness, all of which I want to be, but do not always bring off. All this is what the human being naturally is, and couldn't be different from, just as much as a mouse can never be different from the way of a mouse, but it's only because we human beings whirl about in the Six States of the Wheel that we are not yet true human beings.

It is only from the human state on the Wheel that liberation is possible. For that we have to forget the 'I' which is the delusion that I am separate from everything else and therefore afraid of it and feel I need to get rid of it. Actually, there is absolutely nothing that I need to get rid of. On the contrary, I have to find out what it is that I refuse in order to come into the totality. Master Daie then goes on, **'Buddhas are those who have comprehended and completed things in the realm of sentient beings,'** which means having become Buddha. As in Bodhidharma's verse, 'Directly pointing to the human heart, Seeing into its nature and becoming Buddha.' So, 'Buddhas are those who have completed and comprehended things in the realm of sentient beings, but **'sentient beings are those who have not comprehended and completed things in the realm of Buddhas,'** not yet come to it.

Master Daie tells us, **'If you want to attain Oneness, then just give up both Buddhas and sentient beings at once.'** 'If you want to attain Oneness' – to again be one with, not separated out as an 'I', 'just give up both Buddhas and sentient beings at once' – because Buddhas and sentient beings are another pair of opposites in our notions. As long as those notions are there, 'I' am also there, and therefore there is no Oneness. But we all know this Oneness in any case, only we are not aware of it. When we are completely absorbed in something we enjoy and are skilled at, like a sport or playing a musical instrument, then, in the midst of the activity, we are no longer aware of ourselves.

'If you want to attain Oneness, just give up both Buddhas and sentient beings at once, **'then there is no comprehended and completed or not comprehended and completed.'** This is because all those things are only my ideas of something, something interesting, nice and good that I have heard about and that I would like to have, something to comprehend and to complete. No need to bother about it, just go on, do the training, step for step; various things have already been comprehended and completed in a small way. A good tennis match is played, who plays it? Being a fool, I afterwards say 'I' did. If I'm good at the piano and love the music and play it, it will come out as good as my skill allows and sometimes even exceeding. But has it really been I consciously playing it? Along there lies the entrance. Experiment, please.

THE TEXT

An ancient worthy said, 'Just perceive nothingness in the midst of things. When seeing form and hearing sound, don't be blind and deaf.' This man knew the truth that the contrivances of the worldly are empty, false and unreal. When he was faced with situations and circumstances as they suddenly popped up in front of him, he didn't go along with them, so they were taken under control by him.

In general, since time without beginning, you have overdone the familiar and left undone the unfamiliar. Even though you may see through it for a moment, in the end your power in the Path cannot overcome the power of your actions. And what is the power of your acts? It is what is familiar and stale. And what is the power of the Path? It is what is unfamiliar and fresh. Basically, however, there is no fixed measure to the power of the Path and the power of acts. Just observe whether or not you are befuddled in the conduct of your daily activities. When you becloud the power of the Path, then it is overcome by the power of acts. And when the power of acts prevails, then you get stuck wherever you go. And when you get stuck wherever you go, then you become attached everywhere. And when you get attached everywhere, you consider misery to be happiness. This is why Shakyamuni said to the Kindly One (foremost among his chief disciples in expounding the Dharma), 'You use the characteristics matter and emptiness to overturn and eliminate each other in the Repository of Thusness. And the Repository of Thusness accordingly becomes matter or emptiness extending everywhere throughout the cosmos. For this reason, within it the wind stirs and the air clears, the sun is bright and the clouds are dark.'

'An ancient worthy said, "Just perceive nothingness in the midst of things."' Look at it like a shadow-play, unreal, swirling about, changing into this and changing into that – none of them having any substance, none of them prevailing. That is how the Buddha suggests we should look at it. As it is said in the *Diamond Sutra*,

> Thus shall you look upon this fleeting world:
> A star at dawn, a bubble in a stream,
> A flash of lightning in a summer cloud,
> A flickering lamp, a phantom and a dream.

'Just perceive nothingness.' Do not take it as empty in the sense that I see nothing, just do not take it as something substantial and real or lasting. If you look into a kaleidoscope at how things form and continuously change, or if you look out of the train window, you know it's all passing, and you don't feel that you must cling to it. 'Just perceive nothingness in the midst of things.' And in the same way we should also see ourselves.

Hence there is the warning, **'"When seeing form and hearing sound, don't be blind and deaf."'** Some people are convinced by false emptiness, thinking that there's nothing to be seen, nothing to be heard, nothing to be perceived, that it's all empty. But this is the greatest delusion, seeing form and hearing sound, don't be blind and deaf. Master Daie continues, **'This man,'** this old master, **'knew the truth, that the contrivances of the worldly are empty, false and**

unreal,' that they do not last, are not really actually concrete.

So, **'When he was faced with situations and circumstances as they suddenly popped up in front of him, he did not go along with them,'** as we usually do; getting carried away by the circumstances and situations in our daily life, 'This is too much, oh the pressure, the stress of it all.' 'Why can't I have this? I have tried and worked hard and it's still not coming about.' But the old master, not being swerved by circumstances, did not go along with them, did not get carried away by them. So it is said that **'they were taken under control by him.'** But that also is not quite right. He just did not get carried away, he did not get attached to them, he did not react to them. That is the thing: Let them be. Neither attaching, nor fighting against — just let them be.

This is like the story of Mara and the monk meditating. Mara didn't like him because he was coming too close to insight, so he climbed up on the door and began swinging, causing the hinges to creak. In the quietness there is nothing more annoying, as you all know, than a noise breaking in, not too loud but persistent. Mara went on swinging and, being by nature impatient and not getting any reaction out of the monk, got rather upset and annoyed and gave the door a real good, 'CREEEAK!' The monk peacefully said, 'I see you Mara, go on with your antics as much as you like,' and continued sitting. Mara gave a few more creaks, but the monk just did not react and peacefully went on with his meditation. Mara being impatient soon went away. If we can think of our reactions, they are actually Mara. And if we don't let them carry us away, then they soon go away and we settle down again. If we feed them, that, of course, is another thing. A promising little bit of wood to go onto the fire which already burns, well that feeds them. So it's not a question of controlling, it's a question of not feeding, it's a question of not attending, of not giving attention, but getting on with what is in the process of being done.

Doesn't that sound rather like our Daily Life Practice?

'In general,' says Master Daie, **'since time without beginning, you have overdone the familiar and left undone the unfamiliar.'** 'Overdone the familiar' – 'But I have always done it this way, this is how we've always done it, it's how it's always been' and the unfamiliar, which I do not like, I have not done. So, 'overdone the familiar and left undone the unfamiliar.' Trevor Leggett used to say that in the early days of Judo when it was first brought over from Japan, a good bit of it was unfamiliar. However, once students started becoming familiar with it, they very soon found that they had a particular way of working which resulted in a good throw. When that was settled, the teacher would then say, 'Now stop doing it that way and do it with the other arm or with the other leg,' or whatever. And that made those who had become rather good by that time, really very awkward beginners again. Some really tried and they got very good at it. But others just could not bring themselves to do it, because it was unfamiliar and they were not comfortable with it. Even though they were trying, sometimes at the last moment, they again reverted to what they were used to. That is something that we need to consider carefully. 'Overdone the familiar and left undone the unfamiliar.' Work with those parts in us that are unfamiliar, because we do not wish to see them.

'Even though you may see through it all for a moment, in the end your power in the Path cannot overcome the power of your actions.' Though you 'see through it for a moment' – may realise that the other side needs to be trained too, to come up to a balance – if in the end, you are not able to achieve that, then 'your power in the Path is overcome by the power of your actions' – by what you're actually doing. And that is what is called karma.

'And what is the power of your acts?' Master Daie tells us, **'It is what is familiar and stale.'** This is our complacency when the practice is going well and our effort slackens, and we then become despondent when it all falls to pieces. That is exactly when it is necessary, with whole-heartedness, to really wade in and work. This is the situation from which we learn. Not when all goes well.

'And what is the power of the Path? It is what's unfamiliar and fresh.' Sesso Roshi once said, 'There are various stages in the training where you feel you can now really settle yourself down. But it's only because you don't look. Because if you do look, you see that you are only sitting on a very narrow ledge and further up there is a huge mountain.' In other words, do not stop. That is what the texts also tell us.

That is why in Master Torei's *Inexhaustible Lamp*, we are reminded of the Four Great Vows, to vow to assist all sentient beings. But in a wider sense it may be understood as helping all things that we come in contact with, help them come to their proper function; the needle to be used for sewing, and the cooking spoon used to stir the food with, and the pot to cook in – reverently, gently, seeing that all can fulfil their proper function, including ourselves, seeing that we can fulfil our proper function in the circumstances as they arise and go away again.

'And what is the power of the Path? It is what's unfamiliar and fresh' – that is what we yet have to learn, have to get used to. **'Basically however, there is no fixed measure to the power of the Path and the power of the acts.'** It is very important to realise this, that as they slowly approach each other and balance out, the one has become the other. There is neither this nor that. However, as long as we are here, we always put names on it, make pictures of it – it's important to realise that too. But then in the end when it really comes down to the one truth, there is neither the one nor the other.

'Just observe whether or not you are befuddled in the conduct of your daily activities,' by your ups and downs, your likes and dislikes.

'**When you becloud the power of the Path, then it is overcome by the power of the acts.**' The power of the Path is therefore not seen, is not made use of and slips away. Then that is overcome by the power of acts – the karmic, familiar, all the same reactions, again and again.

'**And when the power of acts prevails, then you get stuck wherever you go,**' – in every situation always the same reaction, again and again. This now becomes a long series, one after the other, 'when the power of the acts prevails, then you get stuck wherever you go.' '**And when you get stuck wherever you go, then you become attached everywhere. And when you get attached everywhere you consider misery to be happiness,**' and this is the tragedy of becoming attached. You get attached to insubstantial things which float about, there's nothing to hold onto.

'**This is why the Buddha said to the Kindly One (foremost among his chief disciples in expounding the Dharma), "You use the characteristics matter and emptiness to overturn and eliminate each other in the Repository of Thusness."**' Thusness – *tathata*, the way all things are, now, here. Matter and emptiness – one of the great pairs of opposites and when they come together, they cancel each other out. When there is matter, then emptiness cancels out. When there is emptiness, then matter is cancelled out. '**"And the Repository of Thusness accordingly becomes matter or emptiness extending everywhere throughout the cosmos."**'

In the *Heart Sutra* we chant, every morning and evening, 'Form is emptiness and emptiness is form.' It's the same thing. The one is the other, changing. But not in the sense that either of them is fixed, but extending as a principle everywhere throughout the cosmos. This is what we are made of, our planet is made of, the same principle, you cannot put your hand on it. Form is emptiness, emptiness is form. It's not empty, it's not form, doesn't last. '**"For this reason, within it,** (within the thusness, within the principle) **the wind stirs and the air**

clears, the sun is bright and the clouds are dark.'" That is the way things really are, the sun is bright – that is its nature. And the clouds are dark, that is what clouds are. The mountains are high, that is what mountains are; and valleys are low, that is what valleys are. But we tend to make judgements; the one is better than the other and this is how we go wrong, instead of seeing things as they really are. Matter and emptiness, emptiness and matter – one becoming the other, like night and day alternating, 'extending everywhere throughout the cosmos. For this reason, within it, the wind stirs and the air clears. The sun is bright and the clouds are dark.' That's just how it is.

If we willingly go along with it, there will be no difficulty, and there will be an opening up of the heart, of our human heart, in its looking up, in its joy, its kindliness and in its warmth. And in that, not only does the heart find its fulfilment but it also has again become what it always has been, part of what is. In that there is no estrangement anymore, no separation nor fear anymore, but there is a commonality which is the true heart of being a human being. Shall we take that home and ponder it, please?

LETTER 9 to LU SHUN-YUAN (continued)

The Text

> Sentient beings, stifled by delusion, turn their backs on enlightenment and join the dusts, thus giving rise to sensory affliction and the existence of worldly forms. These are the ones who dim the power of the Path and are overcome by the power of their actions. Old Shakyamuni also said, 'I formed the Repository of Thusness with subtle illumination that is

neither destroyed nor born.' And the Repository of Thusness is only illumination of sublime enlightenment shining throughout the whole cosmos. This is why within it the one is infinite and infinity is one. When the great appears within the small and the small appears within the great, the immutable field of enlightenment pervades all worlds in all directions and one's body contains limitless space in all directions. On the tip of a hair you manifest the Land of the Jewel King. And sitting within an atom of dust, you turn the Great Wheel of the Dharma. This is not dimming the power of the Path in one's activities, and mastering the power of actions.

Ven. Myokyo-ni's Comments

'Sentient beings, stifled by delusion, turn their backs on enlightenment and join the dusts,' 'Stifled by delusion' – we human beings know that delusion is the prime cause of our difficulty. So here, quite rightly, Master Daie says, 'stifled by delusion', by not-clear seeing. What does the delusion really consist of? Seeing pictures, having ideas and notions; and it is not I who have them, but I who am them. The delusion is that I am separate from everything else. Then of course with that delusion also comes fear, which is the other side of I. Because if I am separate, other than everything else, then of course I am insecure and frightened, of course I feel unhappy and feel that there ought to be more, and I want and want and want.

Therefore, 'stifled by delusion, we turn our backs on enlightenment and join the dusts' – will not open the eyes and see, but 'join the dusts' – are carried away by the dusts, the robbers, as they are called, the thieves of sensory perceptions. With those sensory perceptions, rather like Don Quixote with his windmill, we either like them or we hate them, and with them we build our world and our difficulties. Master Daie continues, **'thus giving rise to sensory afflictions and the existence of worldly forms.'** This is because we project these worldly forms from inside out. 'This is what I would like to have, that is what I would like to be, that one has to be somehow eradicated,' so that I can feel comfortable in my world where I am safe and King. Whatever threatens me – which is everything else of course – sends me into despair.

But it is obvious in both cases, that taken to their ultimate conclusion, they are self-destructive and catastrophic. This is why delusion, the delusion of a separate 'I' is not only a tragic but also an extremely dangerous thing. The Buddha himself said that because we have attachments – and we are the attachment – we cannot be aware of what we actually are, cannot be aware of our inherent wisdom.

Delusion is the mother of both the wanting and the wanting to get rid of – they are the same thing. Both of them, the wanting and the aversion, are perfectly visible, and we can feel them in the body too, because the wanting is the desperate urge of 'I' to secure itself a position, to make itself invulnerable. So it is wanting more and more and that wanting can never be stilled. We can say it is rather like eating and eating until everything, the whole world, is eaten up and I have incorporated it. Then there is nothing more to be feared. The opposite of course is the aversion, of killing off and killing off everything, until there is nothing left but I. And again, I am safe.

So by 'giving rise to sensory afflictions and the existence of worldly forms,' we build these forms – myriads of them. And the sentient beings who give rise to these forms, **'these are the ones who dim the power of the Path and are overcome by the power of their actions.'** These people, these sentient beings are the ones 'stifled by delusion,' who cannot see clearly and so 'dim the power of the Path,' – the power of the Way, the power of the Tathagata. Thus they are 'overcome by the power of their actions,' the karma of their actions.

'Old Shakyamuni also said, "I furnish the Repository of Thusness with its subtle illumination that is neither destroyed nor born;" 'The repository of Thusness' – where things are just as they are and bestowed with that 'subtle illumination' which is the awareness that is no longer clouded and distorted by the notions of delusion. This 'Repository of Thusness,' which is as it is, 'that is neither destroyed nor born,' has no beginning and has no end. It just is. To say that it 'is' is also wrong because it is not a thing. And **"the Repository of Thusness is only the illumination of sublime enlightenment shining through the whole cosmos."'**

It's rather beautifully expressed and that is actually what it really comes down to. However, I, the insecure, separate fool, always want something. I must want, that urge is inborn, it belongs to the very nature of I – desperately looking for something great, high, beautiful, sublime, whatever it might be. As the apt Chinese expression puts it: 'painting flowers in the empty sky and looking for the flowers there.' But I do not see what is actually around me, that 'sublime enlightenment that shines throughout the whole cosmos.' Layman Pang used to say, 'How wonderful, how miraculous, carrying wood and fetching water.' When we see our ordinary daily surroundings, we hardly ever notice them, except that we mostly do not like them. But if we see those same surroundings shining, lighting up with that 'subtle illumination', then we are no longer deluded. That is what it really comes down to. We do not need to have fancy ideas, they are only so many magic-lantern shows, not real. Real is what is here, and that shines. If we see that, we do not need any further great ideas of this, that or the other.

Of this 'illumination of sublime enlightenment shining throughout the whole cosmos' Master Daie says, **'This is why within it the one is infinite and infinity is one,'** Within that shining, that sublime enlightenment 'the one is infinite and infinity is one.' The one is the other and the other is the one. One could also say, as Master Hakuin said, 'Not one, not two.' You cannot say they are two, you cannot say they are one. You cannot say it's infinite without taking the one in two. Because, perhaps as an analogy, like life – you cannot see life itself. It's only an idea in the head and yet it exists. But it exists only in forms; swaddled in forms, we can perceive and have an idea of it. But without the form, life does not exist either. All the forms die out, suddenly, life itself – where is it? Can you point at it? It's not a thing. In our delusion, we think that life is something, is a thing, that it exists.

Master Daie continues along the same lines, **'This is why the great appears within the small and the small appears within the great, the immutable field of enlightenment pervades all worlds in all directions and one's body contains limitless space in all directions.'** Whatever we think or see, in the state of illumination, in the state of enlightenment, that is not something special. It is only when the delusion has dropped off and we see things as they really are, then it shines and 'pervades all worlds in all directions and one's body contains limitless space in all directions.' When the sense of 'I' has gone, so has the limit of the body, which I feel very clearly as 'I'. But actually when the sense of 'I' dims and retreats, somehow things begin to grow, not like Alice in Wonderland, but there is a space where the body has not really got any particular directions or limits. Occasionally when we are sitting really well, we lose the sense of a limited I, and the body and things open up. Though it doesn't last very long, this is heading in that direction.

Master Daie continues, saying, **'On the tip of a hair, you manifest the Land of the Jewel King and sitting within an atom of dust, you turn the Great Wheel of the Dharma.'** When we read a statement like that, we are frightfully tempted to take that personally, instead of understanding it as an analogy, showing that 'one is in all and all is in one,' which is the main teaching of the *Kegon Sutra*. These analogies are completely interacted and interacting, 'One in all and all in one' – that is not an intellectual understanding. But if we can but live out of it, instead of only having an intellectual understanding of it and no longer fall back into delusion, then it truly has ripened and that is what Buddhahood is.

'Sitting within an atom of dust you turn the Great Wheel of the Dharma.' An atom of dust, naturally, equally turns the Great Wheel of the Dharma, it reveals it. Since there is no 'I' any more, there is the atom of dust that reveals it and there is the body that reveals it, there is the oak tree that reveals it, that comes into a quite useful analogy too. If you take one of those chestnut trees out there, they have just come into leaf. And if you look at the chestnut leaves, you will find that each single one is unique there are no chestnut leaves on the same tree or on any chestnut tree that are exactly the same. Yet each leaf, on each tree, is unmistakably a chestnut leaf. And each reveals in its uniqueness, the wholeness of the chestnut tree. That is perhaps a feeble analogy of how it is.

This revealing of what is in the individual unique form is what the whole thing is about and Master Daie says, **'This is not dimming the power of the Path in one's activities and mastering the power of actions.'** 'The power of the Path' and 'one's activities' have become one. Just that is 'mastering the power of actions,' and the actions are always at one with the Path and never diverge from it, not because I make them so, because I am no longer there, but because this is just how it is.

And this 'just how it is', is the important thing – to be free from any kind of ideas or planning and to just be at one with whatever it is. I would again like to quote from verse 25 of the *Tao Te Ching*, because it best expresses this:

Man obeys the laws of Earth,
Earth obeys the laws of Heaven,
Heaven obeys the laws of the Tao (the Way),
and the Tao obeys its own inherent nature.

In other words, to be once more truly at one with ourselves and at one with everything that is; acting out of one's single uniqueness of individuality and in accordance with it. That is 'mastering the power of actions.' Ponder that very carefully, because this is the way along which we have to go, where the 'I' has finally lost its insecurity and its fear and where something else has opened – a wide realm, that Bodhidharma described as 'vast and limitless'.

LETTER 9 to LU SHUN-YUAN (continued)

THE TEXT

Nevertheless, both are ultimately empty falsehoods. If one abandons the power of actions to grasp the power of the Path, then I would say that this person does not understand the skill in means of all the Buddhas in expounding the truth as is appropriate to the occasion. Why? Have you not read how Shakyamuni said, 'If you cling to the truth aspect, you are attached to self, personality, living beings and life. If you cling to the non-truth aspect, you are attached to self, personality, living beings and life.' Therefore you should not cling to truth (Dharma) and you should not cling to what is untrue (adharma). This is what I said before, that basically the power of the Path and the power of actions have no fixed measure. If you are a man, a real man of wisdom, you will use the power of the Path as an instrument to clear away the power of habitual action. Once the power of actions has been cleared away, the Path too is empty and false. Thus it is said, 'The Buddha only uses provisional terms in guiding sentient beings.'

VEN. MYOKYO-NI'S COMMENTS

'**Nevertheless, both are ultimately empty falsehoods.**' Now Master Daie explains, '**If one abandons the power of actions to grasp the power of the Path, then I would say that this person does not understand the skill in means of all the Buddhas in expounding the truth as is appropriate to the occasion.**' Perhaps this reminds us of picture number ten of the Bull-herding series where it is said, 'Sometimes he speaks Mongolian, sometimes he speaks Chinese' – it depends on the occasion and it depends on to whom one is speaking.

Therefore, 'to abandon the power of actions and to grasp only the power of the Path' and talk from that position, that is misunderstanding the situation. As Master Daie says, 'The skill in means of all the Buddhas in expounding the truth' – he would talk to merchants in analogies that they would understand and to farmers according to how they perceived things. That is really important. It's no good talking in highfalutin terms to people in a totally different world. Therefore, once again the importance of our Daily Life Practice, in becoming what the situation demands. This becoming – not I doing it – but truly becoming, fusing into it, that is the important thing. To a child we talk in a different way than to a grown-up. We do not need to learn that, it comes perfectly naturally. But if we cling to the aspect of talking to a child, or cling to the aspect of 'I am an adult', we mess the whole thing up and we are not understood. This is one of the things we find, particularly in our present time, and is why we so often talk about the difficulty of relationships. It's not a difficulty if we are willing to become what the situation demands, rather than sitting in our own nest and expecting everything to go in the way I see it. So do not 'abandon the power of actions' in order 'to grasp the power of the Path.' And 'the power of the Path' cannot be expounded properly if it is not 'appropriate to the occasion.'

Master Daie then asks, **'Why? Have you not read how Shakyamuni said, "If you cling to the truth aspect, you are attached to self, personality, living beings and life. And if you cling to the non-truth aspect, you are attached to the self, personality, living beings and life."'** Now that sounds very odd, doesn't it? 'If you cling to the truth' – that's the same as 'if you cling to the non-truth' – but it's not, and this is where our split arises, and we Westerners in particular suffer from it, though all human beings do. This is the split that we make between light and dark, between good and bad, and right and wrong; the one must be right and we cling to it and the other has to be annihilated. But this is not true. They are both halves of the same thing. They are different in aspect but not in essence. Therefore to cling to one is to refuse half of life. This is what is particularly stressed in Buddhism.

'If you cling' – it's the clinging, whether it's to this or to that, the clinger, the attachment is 'I'. And 'I' can't help but being split. So, 'if you cling to the truth aspect, you are attached to self, personality, living beings and life.' There are four parts of 'I', because 'I' has got a very deep root, therefore a self, a personality, a living being and life itself. Only when that has truly been seen into and the fear of not only being diminished but of losing life has truly gone, then the 'I' is truly lost too. It goes that deep.

So whichever aspect you cling to, you are still attached to 'I'. 'I' is still there in one or the other of its manifestations. That is what we really need to take into our very heart so that we do not take this part or the opposite part, but move freely between them.

'Therefore' Master Daie says, '**you should not cling to truth (Dharma) and you should not cling to what is untrue (adharma) – this is what I said before, that basically the power of the Path and the power of actions have no fixed measure.**' Either they have become one, or they are in the usual way parted halfway through. You can't say there is more power of the Path or more power of actions. In a way the two, as we said earlier are one. They are either harmoniously one or they are disturbed, inert and obscured by 'I'.

Master Daie continues, '**If you are a real man of wisdom, you will use the power of the Path as an instrument to clear away the power of habitual action.**' This 'Power of the Path' is the insight and the strength to help 'clear away the power of habitual action.' But you will insist, 'I have always done it this way, surely there is nothing wrong with it? It is not going against the Dharma, it's just a habit of mine.' Are we quite sure about those kinds of attitudes? Or is there still a clinging to it? That clinging prevents the free flow of going with things as they are, the continuous becoming. And with the becoming also comes the continuous dying – continuous becoming and dying. If that really becomes a natural habit, a free flow, then there is no more 'I' that obstructs it and with no more 'I' the fear is also gone. And our final fear of death is also no longer there. As long as 'I' am there, there is fear. Fear and 'I' are as inseparable as the palm and the back of the hand. I would like to keep 'I' but lose fear. If, however, I would like to have insight into the Dharma, but not to give up life, then I'm on a very wrong path, or not wrong but on a path that will not answer.

'The power of the Path and the power of the action have no fixed measure.' The lifting of a box of matches and the lifting of a heavy pot, it's the same. And yet it is not the same because they are different weights, or sizes or whatever it might be. But neither is better or worse. But that is what we do with our judging. So particularly in Zen, we are often put in front of things like what is better and what is worse, just to get out of that habit. Seeing differences but without judging and evaluating them. We usually cannot see difference without at the same time judging that one is better or worse or whatever it might be.

'Once the power of action has been cleared away, the Path too is empty and false.' Our habitual actions obscure, but once they have been cleared away, then the Path as such is another concept in the mind. So Master Daie says, **'Then the Path too is empty and false. Thus it is said that the Buddha only uses provisional terms in guiding sentient beings.'** He did not lay down anything hard and fast, he didn't even say that he had found something new, he only said that he had re-discovered an ancient Path that leads to an ancient city. What he explained was in 'provisional terms' as fitted the background and lifestyle of the person or the audience. Sometimes he said this and sometimes he said that.

Doctors will not prescribe the same medicine for every ailment. And when the patients get well, they certainly do not expect them to go on using that medicine. Because what was useful as medicine for the illness is likely to poison when they are well – so there are 'provisional terms in guiding sentient beings.'

Whether we follow the Buddha's teachings or mistake them or are too lazy or too hell-bent on our own things, that depends on us. They are 'only provisional terms in guiding sentient beings.' What we can take home from the *sesshin* therefore is also this rather beautiful pointer of 'provisional terms' for our guidance. The important thing is that while we ourselves are doing our practice and following the Way, we do not, unbeknownst even to ourselves, change the practice or the terms of the practice so that it is more palatable to me and no longer really the Buddha's Way, as we often do. Or just downright forgetting it because, 'I am so busy.' How often have I heard, 'I am too busy, I was so busy I couldn't do the practice.' 'I was ill, I couldn't do the practice.' Well, what is the Daily Life Practice, if not our ordinary daily routine, our day-to-day being? That and our surroundings, that is our practice-ground, our arena. That 'I am too busy, I am ill, I am this, I am that' means that I do not even understand the very basis of what the Daily Life Practice is.

I cannot 'do' the practice, I can only give myself, give myself into every moment; and when I forget, then to immediately bring myself back again. Slowly a new, more wholesome attitude is created, more being given, more at one with things. Little by little 'I' is squeezed out, is less and less clamorous. With that, life becomes much more rounded, much more enjoyable but also much more warm-hearted, because it is only 'I', always separate and therefore always insecure who flails around to keep myself up. If that is no longer there, then there is a true commonality with an understanding and with warmth in the heart for each other. With that we have really reached not only the human state proper but our feet are firmly on the Path that the Buddha indicated. Can we take that home from this *sesshin* and work at it until we meet again?

LETTER 9 to LU SHUN-YUAN (continued)

THE TEXT

> Before you have managed to see through it, you are beset with countless difficulties. After you see through it, what difficulty or ease is there? As Layman P'ang said,

The capacity of ordinary people's will is meagre:
Falsely they say there is difficulty and ease.
Detached from form, empty as space,
You reach complete accord with the wisdom of the
Buddhas.
The form of discipline too is empty as space:
Deluded people consider themselves upholding it.
Unwilling to pull out the root of the sickness,
They just fool with the flowering branches.

Do you want to know the root of the sickness? It is nothing else, just this clinging to difficulty and ease, arbitrarily giving rise to grasping and rejection. If this root of disease is not utterly extirpated, you will float and sink in the sea of Birth and Death without ever getting out.

As soon as the source of sickness was pointed out to him by an old adept, Chang Ch'o the famous scholar in the old days, understood enough to say:

Trying to eliminate passion aggravates the disease;
Rushing towards True Suchness is also wrong.
There is no obstruction in worldly circumstances
according to one's lot:
Nirvana and birth and death are equally illusions.

If you want to cut directly through, don't entertain doubts about Buddhas and Patriarchs or doubts about birth and death — just always let go and make your heart empty and open. When things come up, then deal with them according to the occasion. Be like the stillness of water, like the clarity of a mirror, so that whether good or bad, beautiful or ugly approach, you do not make the slightest move to avoid them. Then you will truly know that the mindless world of spontaneity is inconceivable.

'Before you have managed to see through it, you are beset with countless difficulties.' 'To see through it' – to see through the delusion, the delusion that 'I am' which paints everything and distorts everything. **'Before you have managed to see through it, you are beset with countless difficulties. After you see through it, what difficulty or ease is there?'** If there is no obstruction, there is neither ease nor difficulty and it just flows. That is what Master Daie tells us and then he quotes Layman P'ang, who says, **"The capacity of ordinary people's will is meagre"**– their will is not strong, they are not willing to really exert themselves. So, going on as usual, clinging to what they have always clung to, they see in double vision, and therefore they falsely say there is difficulty and ease. They make little or no effort to truly and energetically work on overcoming themselves. This question of overcoming ourselves is the basis of the teaching. If we do not overcome ourselves, then 'I', the good old delusion, always remains.

Master Daie continues to quote from Layman P'ang, **"Detached from form, empty as space, you reach complete accord with the wisdom of the Buddhas."** This has been continuously spelled out since the Buddha, and all the old Patriarchs have said the same thing. Though we listen and may think it is right, we don't really put it into practice. Yet, if we really look clearly, 'detached from form, empty as space' – without any judgements at all – that is not blind, that is not dead, that is simply clearly seeing things as they are, without clinging and without revulsion.

'Detached from form, empty as space, you reach complete accord with the wisdom of the Buddhas.' To be that empty, to go with what is, this is what the Buddha tried to convey, tried to teach us. If we go with things, there is no difficulty. If we stem ourselves against things, there is an enormous amount of difficulty. Whatever we refuse, whatever we push against, that we give power over ourselves. If we do not do it, there is peace. Therefore the great formula of *wu wei*, so often mistranslated as 'non-action' which it certainly is not, it is 'non-interference' – let be, let go. But we are great meddlers, we human beings. We do not like to let go. Because we are full of opinions, we like to meddle. 'If I were you, I would do it this way, you know.'

But that is not all, for the quote from Layman P'ang continues, **"The form of discipline too is empty as space."** Why do we need the discipline? To become empty. But, **"Deluded people consider themselves as upholding it."** Like the raft that carries to the other shore, but once across it is no longer necessary to go on carrying it. These are things that are easily misunderstood. As Layman P'ang says, 'Deluded people consider themselves as upholding it,' the discipline. They have not yet got used to it and stick to it for reasons that are not helpful. Because as it was said before, 'Ordinary people's capacity is meagre.' And not only is it meagre, but they are also **"Unwilling to pull out the root of the sickness, they just fool with the flowering branches."**

Master Daie then goes on to clarify Layman P'ang's statement, **'Do you want to know the root of the sickness? It is nothing else, just this clinging to difficulty and ease, arbitrarily giving rise to grasping and rejection.'** – 'Oh, this is difficult, I don't really think I've got the time for it, not just now anyway. I'll have to get myself into a better state for it because it is so difficult. Isn't there anything that is easier? This training, it just goes on and on and nothing comes out of it, there surely must be something that is much easier.' Whatever it is, as long as I am there I judge as difficult or as easy, as what I like and what I do not like. And so 'arbitrarily give rise to grasping and rejection,' that is the illness.

'Arbitrarily' – without reason – 'giving rise to grasping and rejection.' This is what I want and this is what I want to get rid of, and I never realise that in the course of my life, I have changed what I want to grasp and what I want to get rid of umpteen times. What I wanted to grasp and what I wanted to get rid of as a child is quite different from what it was when I was a young person, and different again when I am middle-aged and when I am old. The objects of our desires continuously change. They are not constant. What is constant is our grasping and rejection, which is 'I'. 'I want this, I want that.'

And so Master Daie says, **'If this root of disease is not utterly extirpated, you will float and sink in the sea of birth and death without ever getting out.'** The root of disease is of course the assumption of a self-nature, of an 'I'. If 'this root' – with all my notions, opinions and ideas, judgements, fears, likes, dislikes – 'is not utterly extirpated, you will float and sink in the sea of birth and death without ever getting out.' That is what the Buddhist most fears. This floating and sinking in the sea of birth and death, bound on that Wheel of Change, again and again whirling round and whirling round, 'without ever getting out.'

Master Daie quotes another poem, **'As soon as the source of the sickness was pointed out to him by an old adept, Chang Ch'o, the famous scholar in the old days, understood enough to say, "Trying to eliminate passion aggravates the disease; Rushing towards True Suchness is also wrong."**

Don't we vow, in the second line of the Four Vows, to eliminate all the passions? And now we are told that 'trying to eliminate passion aggravates the disease.' Trying to get rid of the passions by energetically pushing and holding them down, siting on them, is like the cork in a champagne bottle. Unsurprisingly, sooner or later of course they break out. Trying to get rid of the passions therefore only increases them. And 'Rushing towards True Suchness is also wrong,' because 'I want' the True Suchness. With a head full of Zen stories of sudden enlightenment, I want to get it – the quicker the better.

The quote continues, **"There is no obstruction in worldly circumstances according to one's lot."** One just goes with it, clearly seeing it as it is; there is no judgement, no evaluation, no stemming against, no wanting to manipulate. That is the situation as it is and you flow with it, as part of that situation, taking part in it. Sometimes it goes well, sometimes things are hard. Sometimes it's night and sometimes it's day. Sometimes it's health, sometimes it's sickness. Sometimes it goes smoothly, sometimes the going is difficult. But that's just how it is. There is no evaluation in it.

Layman P'ang concludes the quote from Chang Ch'o, **"Nirvana and birth and death are equally illusions"** – now this sounds unbelievable, doesn't it? But look at it. Nirvana, birth and death are just concepts in the mind. We do not really know what they are. They are just particular terms for concepts, equally illusions. All we need to do is to peacefully go with things as they are. There is nothing special about it. But I want to have something special. But who is that 'I' who wants to have something special? 'I' the deluded one, not realising that it is the delusion that blinds us from perceiving the miraculous and the beauty of all that is around; that stops us from seeing how it all is interconnected – much more than I can actually conceive. An inkling is there and so I want to have something that is special, not realising that I'm in any case in the midst of the miracle and wonder of life as it is in this world.

So Master Daie then says, **'If you want to cut directly through, don't entertain doubts about Buddhas and Patriarchs or doubts**

about birth and death – just always let go and make your heart empty and open.' 'Don't entertain doubts about Buddhas and Patriarchs' – about who they were and what they did, or 'doubts about birth and death' – what will happen. Just stop it. Only 'always let go.' Let go, let go. 'And make your heart empty and open.' Doesn't that remind us of the Sixth Patriarch? 'Before thinking of good and bad, what is the True Face?' It sees what is. When it acts, it acts in accordance with circumstances, in accordance with the situation.

Master Daie goes on to say, **'When things come up, then deal with them according to the occasion.'** That's all. **'Be like the stillness of water, like the clarity of a mirror, so that whether good or bad, beautiful or ugly approach, you do not make the slightest move to avoid them.'** Just 'deal with them according to the occasion.' Because that's where it is and that's how it is now. And it is to that now, and in that now, that we react in terms of that now and of that situation. Not rigidly, not with the idea of how I should react, because that's certainly going to be wrong again. But really 'let go.'

'Then you will truly know that the mindless (empty) **world of spontaneity is inconceivable.'** 'The empty world of spontaneity' – because only when empty is the natural response also spontaneous. If it is calculated, then as we have often heard, 'All intention misses the target.' If it is truly in accord with the situation, then it is also spontaneous. If you think of any sport – tennis for example – obviously you have to be trained in it, but then do you think of how to hit the ball? You haven't got time to think. That is truly from the empty heart. We are quite aware of this state in sport or in something that we know well and are skilled at.

But the moment I come up and I feel self-conscious, the whole thing falls down again. In the training, we begin to be prised away from our dear self-consciousness towards the clear awareness, which Krishnamurti called the 'choiceless awareness' of what actually is, and to be in accord with it. To be in accord with it, is not as a kind of mote of dust, but as a specific human being, with the humanity of a warm heart and understanding and the feeling of being truly at one with all that is. Out of that comes good will, the compassion, sympathetic joy and the serenity – the Four Brahma Viharas. Please ponder it carefully. And as Layman P'ang and Master Daie tell us, do not think that your capacity and will is meagre, but just apply yourself to the task of letting go.

LETTER 12 to SECRETARY LOU

THE TEXT

Since we parted I don't know whether or not you can avoid being carried away by external objects in your daily activities as you respond to circumstances, whether or not you can put aside your heap of legal documents as you look through them, whether or not you can act freely when you meet people, whether or not you engage in vain thinking when you are where it's peaceful and quiet, whether or not you are thoroughly investigating This Matter without any distracting thoughts.

Thus Old Yellow Face (Buddha) has said, 'When the mind does not vainly grasp past things, does not long for things in the future and does not dwell on anything in the present, then you realise fully that the three times are all empty and still.' You shouldn't think about past events whether good or bad. If you think, that obstructs the Path. You shouldn't consider future events. To consider them is crazy confusion. Present events are right in front of you. Whether they are pleasant or unpleasant, don't fix your mind on them. If you do fix your mind on them, it will disturb your heart. Just take everything in its time, responding according to circumstances and you will naturally accord with this principle.

This is a letter to a person called Lou, who was a government secretary, which is quite a high position. He had obviously been in contact with Master Daie for some time and had also visited him. Now he has written to him and Master Daie replies, **'Since we parted I don't know whether or not you can avoid being carried away by external objects in your daily activities,'** It has been some time since they parted and what has happened and how he continued, Master Daie of course does not know. 'I don't know whether or not you can avoid being carried away by external objects in your daily activities as you respond to circumstances.' We can't help but 'respond to circumstances'– but whether we respond in harmony to the circumstances, as human beings – or whether in a confused state, that is the question.

He then goes on, **'whether or not you can put aside your heap of legal documents as you look through them,'** – so the government secretary must have had a lot to do with legal things. Could he put them aside, that whole heap of them? We can ask ourselves too, in our jobs, as we go through the various tasks, can we put them aside once we have looked through them? Or do we carry them along? Excited or disturbed by them, annoyed or pleased by them. Or have they been looked at, been dealt with and then put aside?

And the next question is, **'whether or not you can act freely**

when you meet people,' – can we? Can we really act freely under all circumstances, with whomever we meet? Or do we become self-conscious? I'm sure when somebody looks over our shoulder and breathes down our neck, we somehow feel hampered, don't we? Can we then act freely?

He continues further, **'whether or not you engage in vain thinking when you are where it's peaceful and quiet,'** When there's nothing to do – do we engage in vain thinking? When there is an opportunity to sit down in a comfortable armchair with a big sigh, can we relax into it? Or do thoughts at once arise of this, that or the other?

And **'whether or not you are thoroughly investigating this matter without any distracting thoughts.'** – are we? Can we thoroughly investigate this matter without any distracting thoughts? – this matter of birth and death, the Buddha's teaching, where we come from, where we go, who we are. These are all the possibilities and Master Daie has not left any one out: the daily work, being with others, in peaceful times and when there's nothing to do – do we investigate?

He then quotes the Buddha, **"When the mind** (heart) **does not vainly grasp past things, does not long for things in the future and does not dwell on anything in the present, then you realise fully that the three times are all empty and still."** It's useless to grasp at things. They change in any case, they will not stay. Even if they stayed, in the end they would not be giving that fulfilment that we hope for. Whatever we grasp at is in vain, especially when we think of what has happened in the past – 'Oh that was such a pleasant day, oh why can't I go back to it? When I was young, when I was healthy, when this happened,' – it's all in the past, it's all gone away, only memories, phantoms in the mind. If 'the heart does not vainly grasp past things,' then it does not cling or hang on to them, does not want to replicate them – all that is involved with that grasping. Just let past things be gone. And if it 'does not long for things in the future' – 'Hopefully tomorrow will be just as nice a day as today,' – tomorrow, this, that and the other. 'Perhaps I can juggle things around a little bit in my job too' or whatever it is. The heart that does not grasp for the past, long for the future or dwell on anything in the present echoes a phrase from the *Diamond Sutra*, 'Cultivate a heart that does not dwell on anything.'

When there is no being tied to an experience, either with memories from the past, or with plans and anxiety about the future and does not dwell on anything in the present, then there is just what is here to be dealt with now, that's all. And to be dealt with in a human fashion, without judgement – whether the situation is easy or difficult, whether it is happy or annoying – without any of those feelings to just carry on. But can we really do that? Because we somehow feel, 'Oh, it's all so cold. So totally without any feeling. It's not really worth living.'

That is how we completely and utterly deceive ourselves. There is a beautiful example of this in the Southern Scriptures, in *The Questions of King Milinda*. The king had a very wise *bikkhu*, Nagasena, at his court. Having just read about the 'afflicting passions' and how they contribute to our unhappiness and our difficulties, King Milinda asked, 'Surely a life completely without passions is bland, without excitement and not worth living?' And Venerable Nagasena said, 'Oh no, that is by no means the case because on the contrary,' and then he gives an analogy. He says, 'If you are invited to a banquet and are served an absolutely delicious dish, the best you have ever eaten, you order your cook to get the recipe and have it on the menu tomorrow. All day long you are already anticipating that lovely dish and savouring it in your imagination. But when the dish comes, it's nothing like what you expected, it does not taste like it did yesterday. The dish is the same, but you do not just taste the food, you taste your memory and your expectations. But without passion you taste it truly, as it is, and you find it delicious. Then it is gone because you have eaten it. And when you get the dish again it is equally delicious, because you do not entertain such imaginings, and just taste and savour it afresh, as for the first time. So life without passions is not bland: on the contrary, it makes it possible to savour things exactly as they are each time they come up.'

When not longing for things in the future nor dwelling on anything in the present and not vainly grasping past things, 'then you realise fully that the three times are all empty and still.' Instead of getting stressed out by this, that and the other, you peacefully flow along with them. Acting in accordance and being part of what is happening. As a situation is never still either, it means being part of and taking part in and responding to the changing situations. An hour ago, some of you were working in the garden, some of you were in the house. Then a bell rang and you cleaned up and went to have tea and when the tea was over, you went into the zendo and now you are sitting here and it all moves along from one thing to the next.

If you just follow what is, it goes smoothly, quietly. If you want it to go quicker or want to change it or whatever, then there is trouble. Then there is no flowing with it and we ourselves obstruct the Path. Master Daie, having quoted the Buddha, now continues to admonish us. **'You shouldn't think about past events whether good or bad. If you think, that obstructs the Path.'** This is not only because past events are no longer there, but because our thoughts are dwelling on past events, we are not here. And not being here means we fail to respond to the situation as it is now and here. We don't see it, we don't hear it – we are far away. We all have experienced this. Hung up on some thought-streams or other, whatever they might be, we have lost our senses; our sense inputs are not available any more.

We do not see, we do not hear, and this is exactly where the difficulties, the failures, the mishaps and the accidents occur. You know the story of the Master Tree Pruner, which in Japan is a very highly regarded profession because it means pruning in a specific way so that the branches grow at exact angles and it often involves very high trees. The Master Pruner had an apprentice who was just coming up for the examination of Master and he had to prune a very high and quite dangerous tree. The whole town had assembled to see that feat. The young man started pruning right at the top and slowly worked his way down. The Master stood underneath, without saying one word, only carefully watching. Just as the apprentice was lowering himself down to the last branches, only a couple of metres above the ground, the Master suddenly yelled, 'Take care!' One of the bystanders asked the Master, 'I can't understand. When the apprentice was up there, where it's really dangerous, you just let him be. Why did you call out when he was almost down to the ground. Even if he had fallen here, nothing much would have happened to him.' And the Master said, 'Well, when he is right up at the top, he knows himself that it's very dangerous and he really takes great care. But when he is nearly down, almost at the end of his job, and he's a little bit tired by that time, that is where the accidents occur.'

But it's not only with trees, it's in all situations – in the kitchen, workshop, up a ladder. That is where the accidents occur, when we are not with what we are doing. Now you see the importance of our Daily Life Practice, of always being given into what is there without being hung up on thoughts, imaginations, notions, or whatever. So 'you should not think about past events whether good or bad' because 'if you think that obstructs the Path.'

Master Daie says the same about considering future and present events and concludes, **'Whether they are pleasant or unpleasant, don't fix your mind** (heart) **on them. If you do fix your mind** (heart) **on them, it will disturb your mind** (heart). **Just take everything**

in its time, responding according to circumstances.' When this crops up – respond according to circumstances. When that crops up – respond to those circumstances. The sun shines, the ground is dry – the garden needs watering. It's pouring with rain – take the umbrella. So, taking everything in its time and responding to circumstances as they arise, then says Master Daie, **'You will naturally accord with this principle.'**

But when we fix our heart, then it becomes 'always' and again that obstructs the Path and so 'it will disturb your heart.' 'Just take everything,' says Master Daie, everything 'in its time, responding according to circumstances, and you will naturally accord with this principle,' nothing special about it. Just don't keep the eyes, the mind and the thoughts glued on something that is not there. Do not rebel against what needs to be done now either. The garden urgently needs watering. 'I don't want to do the watering. I want to continue with my book. I wanted to go out this afternoon.'

With regard to that, I remember growing up as a child in rural Austria where there naturally was a lot of livestock about but very few motorised vehicles. Well, if an animal was ill, there was no question about it – you couldn't go to sleep that night, you had to look after it. Or when there was a calf to be born or when a horse had colic or whatever, there was no question of, 'Now it's my time to go and have my rest.' And when at harvest time, regardless of whether it was lunchtime or a Sunday, which was usually a day of rest, if the stooks stood out, already dry and there was a thunderstorm threatening, well you hitched the horses and brought the sheaves home before they got wet. But nowadays, if our plans or our routine has been disrupted, do we naturally go according to circumstances? Or do we stick to 'our rights' of this, that and the other? But 'just taking everything in its time,' and 'responding to circumstances' as they come, then 'you will naturally accord with this principle.'

Perhaps this is a useful reminder, because when doing just that, there are no extraneous thoughts necessary. Thoughts of themselves begin to fade away. There is therefore a very clear seeing of circumstances as they are. Because again if I remember, our farmers at that time, were remarkably wise with regards to the weather. Not only just wise with the weather, they were wise in many things. Weather forecasts did not exist in those days. But just not being distracted by any kind of thoughts, of this, that or the other, they observed and were rarely wrong.

'Responding according to circumstances and you will naturally accord with this principle.' Live at peace with what is and with yourself and everything around. And not only at peace but in harmony and goodwill.

LETTER 12 to SECRETARY LOU (continued)

The Text

Unpleasant situations are easy to handle, pleasant situations are hard to handle. For that which goes against one's will, it boils down to one word, patience. Settle down and reflect a moment, and in a little while it is gone. It is pleasant situations that truly give you no way to escape, like pairing magnet and iron. Unconsciously, this and that come together in one place. Even inanimate objects are thus, how much the more so for those acting in ignorance, with their whole beings making a living within it. In this world if you have no wisdom, you will be dragged unknowing and unawares by that ignorance into a net. Once inside the net, won't it be difficult to look for a way out? This is why an early sage said, 'having entered the world, leave the world completely.' This is the same principle. In recent generations there has been a type who lose track of expedient means in their practice. They always consider acting in ignorance to be entering the world, and so then they think of a force pushing away as the act of leaving the world completely. Are they not to be pitied? The only exceptions are those who have pledged their commitment, who can see through situations immediately, act the master and not be dragged in by others.

VEN. MYOKYO-NI'S COMMENTS

'Unpleasant situations are easy to handle, pleasant situations are hard to handle.' This goes smack against what we feel, doesn't it? We think that it is easy to handle the pleasant situations, but that the unpleasant ones are our trouble. Here, Master Daie tells us that this is by no means so – the unpleasant ones are easy to handle, and it is the pleasant situations that are hard to handle. And why is that so? He explains it very carefully: **'For that which goes against one's will, it boils down to one word, patience.'** If something goes against my will, it will go on churning inside me, won't it? And I will try to somehow find a way to manipulate it and get my way and thereby be as active as possible in just finding some way round it. But that is only furthering the situation, being dragged away by it. Master Daie said, 'it boils down to one word, patience.' Nothing will last forever, and if I do not give in to all the likes and dislikes that immediately arise, and to the notions and opinions, and whatever is really niggling me, if I don't give into them, then the next time when something comes up there will be a little bit more strength to resist being dragged into it. Therefore, 'That which goes against one's will, it boils down to one word, patience.' Well, I would love to have it, but I just can't, humph, humph, humph! I would like to have it, but I just can't patiently sit it out.

As Master Daie says, **'Settle down and reflect a moment and in a little while it's gone.'** That is if there is the patience, and if there is the strength. Three things are said to be necessary if we want to seriously go into Zen training: a great root of faith, a great ball of doubt, and resolute determination. The great root of faith is not just belief in the Buddha's teachings, but it is to have *faith* in the Buddha's teaching, to really know that they work. In Christianity, too, there is the saying, 'faith can move mountains.' In other words, faith is a very strong force, because it connects not with the head but with the heart. And patience arises from the strength and the warmth of the heart. Without faith, patience is almost impossible. And the great ball of doubt means not to believe those whisperings of my likes and dislikes, but to see through them and not get carried away. And the almost fierce determination is to stay the course, to go the Buddha's Way, even if everything inside roars, 'I want! I won't!' So, in cases where something goes against one's will, it boils down to one word, patience. 'Settle down and reflect a moment, and in a little while it is gone.'

'It is pleasant situations that truly give you no way to escape, like pairing magnet and iron. Unconsciously, this and that come together in one place.' Like the magnet attracts the iron filings and pulls and pulls. Unconsciously this and that come together in one place – the picking and choosing – and it brings together the object and the inner energy, and that does make a strong glue. There is no peace, now I've got this, a little bit more of that, and still a little bit more. Like magnet and iron 'unconsciously, this and that come together in one place.' Master Daie continues, **'Even inanimate objects are thus, how much the more so for those acting in ignorance; with their**

whole beings making a living in it.' This world of desire in which we live is ruled by Mara, the Lord of Desire; look at the Wheel of Life out there. 'With their whole beings making a living within it.' This is how I would like it to be, this is how I'm trying to have everything, from my personal things to how the world is ruled, run according to my notions, my wishes. The Third Patriarch warned about this when he said, 'The Great Way is not difficult, it only avoids picking and choosing.' Picking and choosing – we do it all the time in our thought-streams; watch them for a while, how they go, what they revolve round, it's all picking and choosing. How I would like it, what I would like, what I am going to do, what I don't want to do, but must do. Is there one thought that is not I-centred and connected with my likings and loathings? With my notions, my opinions? 'With their whole being making a living within this world of ignorance.'

Master Daie continues **'In this world, if you have no wisdom, you will be dragged unknowing and unawares by that ignorance into a net.'** The net is made up of our wants, of our picking and choosing, and likes and dislikes. That is the net, our ignorance. Always stick to your own part, to the Fires, to the energy, the strength inside that roars as the fire, and not to the object. We all know that if we really, energetically want something and finally get it, after a bit of delight about it, the object does not really answer, it doesn't make me happy for ever after. It changes, it pales; and then, with luck, I find something else that I can now chase after. Or possibly, if my karma is really good, I begin to realise that it's not the object. But as long as I am there – we are now in the Buddha's teaching – as long as I am there, I can't help it. I am in the world of opposites, and I will always want, and I will always refuse. Instead of being fooled by the objects, look at the energy itself, and work with the energy itself. In the Zen training we know that energy as the Bull. It is very useful then to realise that being frightened of the Bull – because he is so much stronger, and wild as well – is of no help, because the Bull needs to be gentled. It is only the Bull, the gentled Bull, that has both the wisdom of knowing the Way home and the strength of carrying us home. I can never know the Way, nor have I the strength to walk it. So it is necessary to come together, and to gentle that Bull. But to be able to gentle that Bull we must first discover him; and then have the strength and humility to allow the acquaintance with him, even if it is hard to bear. Otherwise, we'll be 'dragged, unknowing and unawares by that ignorance' of refusing the other part of ourselves.

Master Daie asks, **'Once inside the net, won't it be difficult to look for a way out?'** It's difficult enough to look for a way out in a building; but if caught in a net, it's very difficult. And just because of this situation, **'An early sage said, "Having entered the world, leave the world completely." This is the same principle.'** A strange saying, isn't it – 'Having entered the world, leave the world completely.' Monks and nuns are called home leavers, but that is not necessarily what is meant by this. Entering the world, this relative world which we take for real; but then leave the world completely. How can one leave the world? How can one leave this relative world which we consider reality but which is really the world of opposites? To leave it completely, what could that mean? Could that possibly mean not to be fooled any more by the objects? There is a whole Buddhist school, the Yogacara, often translated as Mind Only, or Heart Only, or Consciousness Only, which says that all the objects in the world are all mind-made, are all thought figurations – not real. Seeing them as not real, so not to be fooled by them anymore. Leaving the world completely refers to what the Buddha calls our attachments, in the sense of not getting ourselves caught up or attached to things, not hanging our hearts on anything. This doesn't mean being callous or uncaring, just not becoming attached to things.

There is the rather beautiful Indian story about a very devout

Raja. In his kingdom, lived a renowned goldsmith, who could make the most fantastic jewels with wonderful properties, rather like wish-fulfilling gems. He had the goldsmith come to see him and asked him to fashion him some kind of jewel that would make him humble in the hour of triumph, and give him hope and peace of mind in the hour of despair. The goldsmith agreed to undertake it and left. After a year he came back with a little parcel which he unwrapped carefully and in it was a plain ring, rather like a wedding ring. The Raja was infuriated – this was the famous goldsmith, who was going to give him what, from the sincerity of his heart, he had asked him to do. He felt he was being mocked with a simple plain gold ring and he was just about to have him punished when the goldsmith said, 'But just look inside,' and there in the most beautiful, delicate, Indian *devenagari* script inside the ring was written, 'It will pass.'

That's not bad advice for any of us. 'It will pass.' Whatever we get het-up about, it will pass. I have often suggested a useful exercise for this 'it will pass', or will it? If we are really riling against something, upset about someone, or desperately want something which we can't have, whatever it might be, then just settle yourself down and find out what we really depend upon. Imagine that you only have another five minutes to live. What kind of wishes, dislikes, or anything will be left? What kind of problems will be left? Five minutes and you are gone. I'm sure that most of us have got various attachments. I'm also sure that during those five minutes before we are gone, that most of them will have dwindled away. 'Having entered the world, leave the world completely.' Do not hang onto anything nor be careless, because having really left the world completely, there is the same principle and that is the true awareness of the interconnectedness of everything with everything. In that interconnectedness there is a warmth in the human heart that begins with the goodwill, the compassion and the understanding that we are all connected, not only with human beings, but with everything that is. But again without the attachment.

'In recent generations,' says Master Daie, **'there has been a type who lose track of expedient means in their practice.'** 'In recent generations' – you often read this in the Zen texts and it is still used nowadays as well. 'There has been a type who lose track of expedient means in their practice.' Such people **'always consider acting in ignorance to be entering the world, and so then they think of a force pushing away as the act of leaving the world completely.'** I have known quite a few who played that game, I'm sure you have too. They display an attitude of indifference, regarding everything as the same and meaningless. But you can only play that game for some time before it suddenly explodes and what has been pushed down is guaranteed to sooner or later come up with a vengeance. For that I know the story told by the great Swiss psychologist Carl Gustav Jung who talked about a Swiss church warden, a Calvinist, who was getting more and more stern and more and more holy until – these are now Jung's actual words – until he was 'nothing but a sombre pillar of the church.' And at the age of about fifty-five his wife woke up in the night with him sitting straight up in bed next to her laughing his head off and saying, 'I have found it, I know I'm nothing but an old scoundrel.' And from that day on he began to live the life that he had missed before, and lived accordingly. It may have done him some good, but it might have been rather sad and hard on the poor wife. So sooner or later it comes out.

Patience and expedient means in the practice and the awareness of it, this is important. Therefore when pushing away every kind of feeling, which is after all a natural thing for every human being to have, there is then no awareness of the connection and interconnection. And isn't it interesting that having lost track of that, we now talk so much about the lack of relationship. Because we are so I-centred, so completely only in our world of ignorance, we cannot see, cannot be aware, cannot feel that interconnection. How can one possibly say, 'Oh, I'm so lonely.' Not only are we surrounded by everything that is connected with me, but we are also really pampered a lot. Do we ever consider what has had to come together for me to be able to drink a cup of tea? Not only did the water have to be boiled, nowadays usually in a kettle; the kettle run by electricity, which comes by some kind of cable, which has to be made in various fashions, through various processes, and then it also has to be generated somehow. And the kettle has to be made, whether it is plastic or whether it is metal, and that has to be fashioned. Then it has to be delivered to the shop where we had to go to buy it. And that is now only the kettle. And the water that has to be piped. And the tea that had to be planted somewhere. And the leaves picked, and then it had to be processed in a plant which also had all kinds of needs to come into being. And from there it had to be transported, and the means of transport had also to be fashioned. By the time we have had that cup of tea, three-quarters of the world have worked for me, and there I say, 'Oh dear! I'm so lonely, nobody does anything for me.' I mean quite honestly, it's partly ludicrous, but it's really rather sad too. That we do not understand, and instead of being bowed down in gratitude and gratefully doing our poor little best to help in this general process, we moan. That is where we go wrong. To forcefully push away is not leaving the world completely. Leaving the world completely is not to be attached to things, but to be grateful for the enormous amount that we actually, not only are surrounded by, but always get. Quite rightly Master Daie says, **'Are they not to be pitied?'** Those forceful pushers-away.

Master Daie then says, **'The only exceptions are those who have pledged their commitment.'** Who have vowed that they will continue on the Buddha's Path, and those **'who can see through situations immediately.'** The situation as it is, not as I want it, not as I dislike it, but just as it is. And **'act the master and not be dragged in by**

others.' 'Act the master' means not to manipulate but to respond in terms of the situation, and not as others want me to or try to make me do, or try to make me avoid it – whatever it is – but simply respond to the situation in terms of the situation. In order to do that, one needs to be able to see through the situation, see through it immediately, and that is exactly what I cannot do, because my seeing is focused. If I really focus on this book here, I do not see anything around, do I? I just see the book. Therefore I miss the connections, I miss the situation, I have no idea what is going on. When not 'I'-focused, then the situation as a whole is clearly there. To the extent that it is clearly there, it is also clearly taken in by the sense organs. If there is no 'I' that sorts out and focuses on particular things, then the situation is clearly seen. But if that is not the case, then it's, 'I didn't see it', 'it slipped my mind', and whatever other idioms we have for it. This is blindness, which is ignorance, which is 'I' and which is also fear, because only 'I' can fear. That is precisely being caught in that net of ignorance, instead of seeing the situation immediately. Tending house plants and a garden are very good examples, because if I am too much taken up with other things, I won't see it until it's too late, that the plants are wilting. The garden is a very helpful thing, not for nothing do Zen monasteries usually sport large gardens, because they are great teachers. Responding to the situation in terms of the situation is the oneness of the Way we are striving to walk. There the human heart is liberated, released from the trammels of 'I'; liberated from that cave and net and can act freely, warm-heartedly, with understanding. It doesn't need to make plans; the answer to every situation, the response to every situation is different as the situations differ. We have already had a good example of this in Joshu's 'Mu-koan', where to the same question of whether a dog has Buddha-nature or not, Joshu gave each monk a different answer. To one he said 'No' and to the other he said 'Yes'. The response to the situation is in the situation, it does not need to be deliberated on, it cannot be deliberated on. The situations are never the same and they are changing, from moment to moment, as everything changes. But with the heart that is full of goodwill, and not turned into selfishness there is a natural going with it. Perhaps we can leave it at that for today.

LETTER 12 to SECRETARY LOU (continued)

The Text

Hence Vimalakirti said, 'For those with the conceit of superiority, falsely claiming attainment, the Buddha just says that the detachment from lust, hatred and ignorance is liberation. For those with no conceit of superiority the Buddha says that the inherent nature of lust, hatred and ignorance is identical to liberation.' If you can avoid this fault so that in the midst of situations favourable or adverse there is no aspect of origination or demise, only then can you get away from the name 'conceit of superiority' (applied to one who thinks he has attained, but hasn't). Only this way can you be considered to have entered the world, and be called a man of power. What I have been talking about thus far is all my personal life experience, even right now I practise just like this. I hope that you will take advantage of your physical strength and health and also enter this stable equilibrium.

Master Daie continues with a quote from Vimalakirti who said, **'Hence for those with the conceit of superiority, falsely claiming attainment, the Buddha just says that detachment from lust, hatred and ignorance is liberation.'** The Three Fires, here translated as lust, hatred and ignorance, we usually think of it more as desire and wanting, and dislike and hating and delusion. Detachment from those, but how do they hang together? It is from delusion that wanting and disliking arise, and the delusion is another way of saying 'I', and therefore it cannot detach from I. Only little by little can we cultivate a way that makes I less and less important. Even if it is only something we really like, we can forget ourselves in that. That is why pets are so useful, why they are considered a real help, not only for older people but also for various patients. They take 'I' out of our desires and enable us to forget them because of something that is more than 'I'. That puts us on the Way and this is how we get liberated from our wants and hatreds, and our ignorance too. The 'conceit of superiority' is what every 'I' feels and thinks. On the surface I may modestly say, 'Well, I know I am not all that much,' but inside – oh there is something different! And that is the superiority. The likes of us therefore have to work through that, to detach from the three fires – liking, disliking and delusion.

But **'for those with no such conceit the Buddha says that the inherent nature of lust, hatred and ignorance is identical to liberation.'** Do we recognise that recurrent Mahayana phrase? 'The inherent nature of lust, hatred and ignorance is identical to liberation.' We know it in the coupled phrase – 'the passions are the Buddha-nature, and the Buddha-nature is the passions.' It is the same energy. If we get clear on that, then we can understand how very much 'I' warps the whole thing. Without 'I' there is a willing participation in life and appreciation of what life is. We also have to understand that life has a vested interest in being lived, and if we refuse to live it wholly, the unlived life piles up against us, either making us more rigid or unhappy or more irritable. The heart longs for its fulfilment, for becoming aware and once more participating in what is. That is why it is said in the Southern Scriptures, 'The heart tends to, inclines to, strives towards Nirvana.' This is where we need to have faith, then it can go much easier.

'If you can avoid this fault,' says Master Daie – this fault means the conceit – **'so that in the midst of situations favourable or adverse there is no aspect of origination or demise, only then can you get away from the name conceit of superiority.'** Within a situation we have a certain amount of leeway and can accommodate what is most acceptable, or most comfortable. But we are bound by the situation, and we cannot step outside the situation, or if we do, we really get ourselves into trouble as we often do. Since we are never without a situation, we are always bound. And if we feel ourselves bound instead of comfortably settling in, we make our life a misery, and we suffer from the 'conceit of superiority'.

If you can detach from the 'conceit of superiority', which means detaching from 'I', then 'in the midst of situations favourable or adverse', there is no favourable or adverse, is there? Because there is no judgment, when 'I' is forgotten, there is just the situation. That is another thing where we can really learn from animals; there is just the perception of the situation. A dog or a cat invariably finds the warmest place in winter, and the coolest place in summer, it does not need to be taught – it goes quite naturally to it. If it cannot, then it gives in, and when it is ill it learns to cope with it as best it can. I remember a three-legged cat that played about and caught mice as if it had four legs, and did not make any fuss and bother about it. It just lived with what actually was. We with our reflecting consciousness have to a certain extent learnt to alleviate painful situations, and there is nothing wrong with that. But this tendency can become exaggerated and nowadays it is almost an insult if I get ill, and my demands for my health, for my rights, for my this and my that – have gone rather far, have they not, if one really thinks about it?

'So that in the midst of situations favourable or adverse there is no aspect of origination or demise' – there is no aspect of coming to be or ceasing to be, and between those we make our Way. That means that in situations, whatever they might be, there is no aspect of I, of I being there or of I dying, or whatever – all this is gone. If this coming to be and ceasing to be has truly become neutral, not concerned with I anymore, then there can be no flurries any more, and only then can you get away from the name 'conceit of superiority'. You can also possibly think of it as 'conceit of I'. Master Hakuin would call that 'to die the Great Death'. Not just the ordinary death, which we are usually frightened of. Why? Because I cannot see what happens when I am out of the question. And yet often enough during the day for a short time I am exactly that.

One of the great old masters said: If a man hangs on a cliff face with one hand holding on to a stout root, the other hand and both feet already dangling over the abyss, can he let go? If he does let go, after that, Master Torei says, begins another life. Most of us have hung on that cliff, because life too hangs us on that cliff, at least once or twice in our lifetime. But not knowing what to do and the fact that we are all sitting here means that by tooth and nail we have managed to scramble up on top of it again. And now we come to the Zen training, only to find that it also is trying to hang us on that cliff, which we had hoped to get away from.

The only thing that is different is that the Zen training tells us what that root is, which we hold on to so desperately, and why it is necessary to let go. What is that root? There is a proverb that says: 'A healthy man has a thousand wishes; a really sick man has only one.'

It all comes down to that one. That is that root. When nothing else matters any more but this, 'I can't let go, I can't let go,' and if this is understood and declutched from, and if there is enough courage and the strength from the Daily Life Practice, then we can really let go. Well, that is the Great Death, after which another life begins. Only if that is possible and there is no more aspect of coming to be and ceasing to be, then there is also no more concern and conceit of superiority. **'Only this way,'** says Master Daie, **'can you be considered to have entered the world and be called a man of power.'** To enter the world without being driven about by it, by the seeming objects; and so not being driven about by the objects, the man of power is not perturbed by them anymore.

Master Daie finishes by saying, **'What I have been talking about thus far is all my personal life experience,'** he has not been relying on head knowledge, he has not been reading books about it, it is his personal life experience, and **'even right now I practise just like this.'** Because the practice never ends, and the Way never ends, only 'I' believe there is a place where I am really on the top, and above everything. But that is precisely the conceit from which I suffer and then get disappointed because I will naturally never reach any top. On the other hand, I could go and play the part that, within the situation is mine, and play it wholeheartedly, without thinking of something far ahead or something far away, but just as it is right here and now. 'Even right now,' says Master Daie, 'I practise just like this.' I think that is rather wonderful for us at this *sesshin*. He ends with, **'I hope that you will take advantage of your physical strength and health and also enter this stable equilibrium.'** This stable equilibrium of being willing to obediently and joyfully go with what is, without judgment, but with warmth and with a true understanding that comes from the human heart, not from any ideas. This is after all what we also vow in the first of the Four Vows, to assist all beings. How do we assist them?

By talking to them until we are blue in the face and they have stopped listening? Or by just living our life in that joyful obedience which has a lot of humility in it, and which is there to help or not to help as the case requires. And not even 'I' wanting to help, but just responding to the situation. It is that which actually speaks and teaches most loudly.

I remember Sesso Roshi attending the very rare conference meeting of all the Rinzai Roshis. That was in the late fifties when it was just beginning to be known in Japan that the West was greatly interested in Zen. They had all gathered together to debate whether Zen should perhaps loosen up its rather old-fashioned ways and should go out and do a bit more teaching. At the end of the day, it was noticed that Sesso Roshi had not taken part in that discussion at all, and so he was asked directly what he thought about it. And I think I quote him correctly when he said that he had listened carefully to the whole discussion, and had carefully pondered it and that to the best of his understanding he could not say what *active* harm such a resolution could do, but he could for the life of him not see what good it could do. His reasoning was that if a man listens to the most eloquent talk, so beautiful that it is like a burbling mountain stream, and so clear and true, then by the time he comes home and settles himself down to the family supper he has forgotten half of it. If there was a real serious wish to propagate the Buddha-dharma, then the onus would be on the would-be propagators to settle themselves down and once more really go through the training so that they had completely worked themselves out. You see, not the slightest intention left anymore, and he said, 'by doing so a fount of warmth springs up in the human heart which is so great that it cannot be contained in a human heart, but needs to flow over and flow out.' When that heart-flow reaches other human hearts, they respond and are so touched by it that words are not necessary. There is a kind of feeling that, 'that person, he has got something – Oh I wish I could be like that.' And they follow that feeling and start the training. It is rather beautifully expressed, and that is really the great teaching that comes through all those stories.

As Master Daie said, 'What I have been talking about thus far is all my personal life experience,' and naturally they all do talk, because without it, it does not go either. It is quite interesting the way in which this and that come together, that the Zen school, which mostly talks about not talking, has a comprehensive library of all the records most of the Masters always left. So it is the one and the other, the one is the active helping, the other is the finger pointing to something that cannot be put into words.

So perhaps we can remember Master Daie's closing words – 'I hope that you will take advantage of your physical strength and health and also enter this stable equilibrium' – and take that home with us. And with Master Daie wishing us good speed, get on with our training.

LETTER 13 to TSENG T'IEN-YU

The Text

> Having read your letter carefully I have come to know that you are unremitting in your conduct, that you are not carried away by the press of official duties, that in the midst of swift flowing streams you vigorously examine yourself. Far from being lax, your aspiration to the Path grows ever more firm as time goes on. You have fulfilled my humble wishes solidly and profoundly.
>
> Nevertheless, worldly passions are like a blazing fire, when will they ever end? Right in the midst of the hubbub you must

not forget the business of the bamboo chair and reed cushion (meditation). Usually you set your mind on a still concentration point, but you must be able to use it right in the midst of the hubbub. If you have no strength amid commotion, after all it is as if you have never made any effort in stillness.

I have heard that there was some complicated situation in the past, and now you are experiencing the sadness of the outcome. Alone, you do not dare to hear your fate; if you arouse this thought, then it will obstruct the Path. An ancient worthy said, 'If you can recognise the inherent nature while going along with the flow, there is neither joy nor sorrow.'

VEN. MYOKYO-NI'S COMMENTS

Among Zen Master Daie's many disciples, there were not just monks, but lay disciples too, some of them in high government positions. During his period of exile, they occasionally visited him but very often they dealt with him by letter. This is an ideal text for us, because in his letters he always deals with lay people.

So this letter is to one of his lay disciples; and apparently a very diligent, long-standing and a very advanced one. Master Daie answers him, saying, **'Having read your letter carefully, I have come to know that you are unremitting in your conduct, that you are not carried away by the press of official duties, that in the midst of swift flowing streams you vigorously examine yourself.'** Now, are we doing that? If we really look at it, is our effort unremitting in all our conduct, all day long, or do we forget the Daily Life Practice? Only too easily, only too often, either because we are carried away by something or because we just are not sufficiently collected, not sufficiently interested, is it not always there. But when it comes right down to it, the Daily Life Practice, which is after all giving ourselves into what is being done here and now, at this moment, that is all there is to it. But seemingly so easy, do we really do it; or do we only do it when we remember it? Do we only do it when we feel there is nothing more important or interesting to do? These are questions that we might usefully ask ourselves, and find out. Because if we do not really put serious effort into it, if we do not wholeheartedly give ourselves – only do it half-heartedly or when the occasion is there for it, then nothing will happen.

And so Master Daie acknowledges that his correspondent, despite being a high government official with many duties, is 'unremitting in his conduct' and 'that in the midst of swift flowing streams', when things really go in a rush, 'you vigorously examine yourself.' What does that actually mean, 'you vigorously examine yourself'? Does that mean that he stands there in the midst of a swift flowing stream and observes himself and thinks about how he is doing? Or whenever a thought of 'I' comes up, does he just give himself back into what is being done, and is not carried away by that hubbub around? That is what the training helps us to come to, that we can hold onto our own stability, our own balance, and not be stampeded by this, that or the other from the outside. And to use the words 'our own' is also, of course, in this respect the wrong designation, but to give it its technical name – our True Face, our True Nature.

Master Daie tells his correspondent that he is rather pleased with him, **'Far from being lax, your aspiration to the Path grows ever more firm as time goes on.'** There are two possibilities when we do the training. The one is that after the first enthusiasm has worn off and the practice has become routine, it just hobbles along somehow. And the other is that if we are really serious, then we do not let it become routine, we carry on with it. The strange thing is that the more energy we invest in it, not because of what I want out of it, but just because the heart really pulls, the more the aspiration grows, the more interested we become. This can be cultivated – everything can be cultivated, our habit patterns have been cultivated unconsciously and though they seem to be completely ingrained now, that is not true. Little by little we can cultivate ourselves out of them too; it takes time and it takes unremitting effort, but it is possible. So perhaps we could also think that with this unremitting effort and the aspiration of the Path, we can get ourselves out of the whole caboodle of I want, I will not, I this and I that, which are all manifestations of 'I' and which in Buddhist terms means the great delusion. Of the Three Fires the main one is delusion. And what is the delusion? It is the belief that there is such a thing as a separate 'I' – which I think myself to be, unrelated to anything. Therefore, underneath, I naturally feel alone and frightened; and consequently also insatiably wanting and aggressive if I do not get what I want. If I forget myself, then none of these troubles exist, and so the whole thing is a question of forgetting myself. We come back again and again to the Daily Life Practice of giving myself; I cannot forget myself by an act of will, but I can give myself fully into the moment here and now. This was what this correspondent has done, and the Master Daie tells him – and it is quite something to be told that by ones Master, **'You have fulfilled my humble wishes solidly and profoundly.'**

Naturally Master Daie wants his disciples to come to that inner quiet in all circumstances. But then it is very tempting to sit down on that place and think, 'Ah, I have got it,' so he warns, **'Nevertheless, worldly passions are like a blazing fire, when will they ever end?'** Worldly passions, whatever it might be, a new dress, a new car, a new house, the top job, ambition. Then I am crossed by something, and whoosh up I come! 'Worldly passions are like a blazing fire' and I can't help having them, they erupt of themselves, the wild primitive energy.

'When will they ever end?' They will only end when there is no 'I' anymore that gingers them up. As we often point out, 'the passions are the Buddha-nature, and the Buddha-nature is the passions.' Of course, it is not that the one is the other, but it is the same energy, which in the presence of 'I' is stirred up and soars into want and dislike, into want and anger, want and fear. If there is no 'I' present, then it returns to what it always has been, or remains what it always has been, the Buddha-nature, inherent in all sentient beings; I cannot eradicate myself, but I can voluntarily give myself away, by giving myself into this moment, this moment here as it is now, and now, and now, which incidentally is also the only moment that we have, everything else is thought. We think of the sixth Zen Patriarch who put it very succinctly by saying, 'Before thinking of good and bad, before a thought has arisen, without thinking, what is the True Face?' That 'without thought' cannot be thought of, cannot be conceived, but certainly can be lived, and is lived whether we know it or not.

So the 'worldly passions are like a blazing fire, when will they ever end?' We all know what it is to be really angry. We may try to get away from the anger, but we cannot. We may try to reason ourselves out of it, and we cannot. But flaring energy, being dynamic, sooner or later burns itself out. Having reversed again and again, round and round it goes, and then after an hour or after a day or after a week, depending how strong it was, it has burnt itself out. Then there is a little bit of peace, only to focus on something else again, because as long as I am there, I cannot help picking and choosing, picking and choosing. So truly 'worldly passions are like a blazing fire, when will they ever end?' They end when I am no longer there to stir them up.

Master Daie puts the finger right on the spot, **'Right in the midst of the hubbub you must not forget the business of the bamboo chair and reed cushion.'** Here we sit on Japanese-style cushions on the floor, but in the T'ang dynasty, the Chinese used to meditate on a low bamboo chair with no back or armrest, but with matting and a reed cushion. In other words, in the midst of the hubbub you must not forget the meditation. The attitude of sitting meditation is simple quietness, and that is what we start to work with. **'Usually to meditate you set your mind on a still concentration point,'** and that is what we do. To begin with we either follow the breath, which is more like the Southern School, or we count the breath, which is more the practice of the Northern School. But we are already looking at it the wrong way if we see it as 'I' doing it, I follow the breath or I count; that won't lead anywhere. It is the same as with the Daily Life Practice, it is I giving myself to the count or to following the breath. I give myself into, which means I become it. The moment I am given in to, am given away, it is quiet already, perhaps only for a moment and then it comes back again. Just patiently go on with it until it truly, really becomes quiet. Hopefully as it has become quiet when I sit motionless on the cushion, 'I' has fallen off. However, as soon as we get up from the cushion, I am already there again and the quietness is gone.

Daito Kokushi, founder of Daitoku-ji, Great Master Daito, when he had completed his training under his master Daio, he was told to go and mature his insight in another place. For some years he chose to go live under the fourth bridge in Kyoto over which all the main traffic goes. As the bridge is very wide and is sheltered from rain, a lot of beggars used to live there. Daito mixed himself amongst the beggars and lived there for some time. From him comes the saying: 'If you cannot sit as peacefully and quietly right under the Fourth Bridge as you would sit on the mountain top of Hieizan in the lonely wilderness, then you do not know what meditation is.'

So in order to cultivate that quietness, not just when on the cushion, we do *kinhin*, walking meditation. Do not think that *kinhin* is now a rest from the sitting and an opportunity to stretch my legs. On the contrary, this is to see that the same quiet attitude also prevails in the walking. As Master Daie quite rightly says, **'you must be able to use it right in the midst of the hubbub.'** What is the use of sitting quietly in a Zendo if the moment I am up and about in daily life, things begin to flare and burn again. Learning or getting used to that quiet attitude, not only in the stillness of sitting, but in movement too, is very important. Then when it is beginning to hold in movement, there is no particular difficulty anymore, because it is only 'I' who have problems. In fact, there are no problems, things are the way they are. And Master Daie adds, **'If you have no strength amid commotion, after all it is as if you have never made any effort in stillness.'** Or to turn it the other way round, what is the use if we truly have stillness when sitting, and it all falls to bits the moment we are on our legs again? What use, any use? None whatsoever!

Master Daie then continues to this particular correspondent, **'I have heard that there was some complicated situation in the past, and now you are experiencing the sadness of the outcome. Alone, you do not dare to hear your fate.'** Whatever it was, something quite serious must have happened that deeply engrained itself in him; and that still has its repercussions. Now that he is alone, he has his job, yes, but he is alone and 'you do not dare to hear your fate.' We do not know what it was, perhaps a serious illness, perhaps something else – an intrigue that could lead to being exiled. Anyway, something that really shakes. Master Daie tells him, **'If you arouse this thought, then it will obstruct the Path.'** If you allow that thought, not daring to hear your fate, to dwell on the complicated situation in the past, to be gripped by that, carried away by it, 'then it will obstruct the Path.' We know from our own experience how it goes – 'Why should it happen to me? How can I change it, I cannot bear it,' etc., and the hubbub takes over.

Master Daie continues, **'An ancient worthy said,'** that is Yoko

Daishi incidentally, **"If you can recognise the inherent nature while going along with the flow, there is neither joy nor sorrow.'"** The inherent nature – what we really are, and what everything else really is – the Buddha-nature, the True Face, whatever you like to call it; the life force, in all that is formed, and acting and functioning in everything according to its nature. 'If you can recognise the inherent nature' is putting it a little bit awkwardly, because it is not that I can recognise it, but that there is an awareness, an insight of the inherent nature. Whilst that awareness is there, which means that 'I' is no longer in the driver's seat, then while going along with the flow with things as they are – in sickness and in health, in happiness and in sorrow – 'there is neither joy nor sorrow.' Sometimes the sun shines, sometimes it rains, that is just as it is. The joy is if I get what I want, and the sorrow, if I do not get what I want, or if what I have is taken away from me. To see that as quite natural and not to cling to either – is to go along with the flow as it is. Again, that is something which is very difficult for 'I' to consider, because 'I' think I should be above such things, and naturally I am not – on the contrary 'I' am the point of the hubbub. To be above things is truly not to be carried away by them.

The, great Shaku Soen, who goes back four generations, was the Zen Master of Engaku-ji monastery. He was extremely well known, and was in the habit of going for a walk to the little village of Kamakura in the evenings after *sanzen*. One evening he heard loud crying coming out from one of the houses, and he walked in to see what had happened. The whole family was sitting there crying – the householder, a relatively young man, had just died, leaving a young wife and four little children unprovided for. Shaku Soen settled himself down with them, and he cried with them. One of the old uncles suddenly noticed who was sitting there with them, and stuttered, 'You here? I thought that at least somebody with your insight should be above such things!' And Soen Shaku with tears on his cheeks is supposed to have answered, 'But it is just that which puts me above such things.' To make that clear, a quotation from Master Rinzai, 'To cry but not to be carried away by tears, to laugh but not to be carried away by laughter.' It is a human quality, but it is just a matter of not being carried away by it. That is exactly what Yoko Daishi means, 'If you can recognise the inherent nature while going along with the flow, there is neither joy nor sorrow.' There is a natural smile and a natural tear, it would be inhuman if that were not so. But to take it beyond that and to make one's difficulties out of it, and one's fate, that is not necessary.

Confucius also said that things and events are always neutral, in other words, they just are as they are. It is the 'I'-reaction to them which makes my fate. What I make out of them makes my joy and sorrow. If they are taken as they are, then they release us from being caught up by events. But there is something else that happens which is very important, and that is nicely shown with Soen Shaku's story, because what then happens is that this opens the warmth of the heart, and the heart can flow over. The human heart, being by nature a warm heart, can touch. Since we all have such a human heart, it can be touched by that warmth that flows and with that there is a natural relationship with everything, for whatever is touched by that somehow responds. That is what it actually comes down to, 'If you can recognise the inherent nature while going along with the flow there is neither joy nor sorrow.' But there is a lot of warmth and a lot of understanding, and willingness to be there for others.

LETTER 13 to TSENG T'IEN-YU (continued)

THE TEXT

Vimalakirti said, 'It is like this, the high plateau does not produce lotus flowers, it is the mire of the low swamplands that produces these flowers.' And the Old Barbarian (Buddha) said, 'True Thusness does not keep to its own nature, but according to circumstances brings about all phenomenal things.' And he also said, 'Proceeding to effect according to circumstances it extends everywhere while always here upon this seat of enlightenment.' Would they deceive people? If you consider quietude right and commotion wrong then this is seeking the real aspect by destroying the worldly aspect, seeking nirvana, the peace of extinction, apart from birth and death, when you like the quiet and hate the hubbub, this is just the time to apply effort. Suddenly when in the midst of hubbub you topple the seat of quietude, that power surpasses the meditation seat and cushion by a million billion times.

VEN. MYOKYO-NI'S COMMENTS

This letter ends with a lot of quotations, all pointing to the same thing. **'Vimalakirti said, "It is like this, the high plateau does not produce lotus flowers, it is the mire of the low swamplands that produces these flowers."'** And what is more, though they come out of the mud they are not stained by it, when they open they are beautifully clear – worthwhile considering. We always like to split things into this and that, into good or bad, but perhaps it could be looked at in another way. **'And the Old Barbarian said,'** that is the Buddha, **"True Thusness does not keep to its own nature,"** True

Thusness, the way things are, just as they are, 'does not keep to its own nature.' It is not a thing, that True Thusness, it is a principle, in itself it is nothing. And so it cannot keep to its own nature, not being a thing, **"but according to circumstances brings about all phenomenal things."'** From an acorn comes an oak tree, from a spring bulb comes a daffodil. 'According to circumstances' in spring everything breaks into flower, in autumn the leaves fall, and they do not do so with a purpose, but according to their own nature. There is a rather nice Japanese Zen saying, 'In the landscape of spring there is nothing better or worse, the flowering branches grow naturally, long or short.' Is a long flowering branch better than a short one? 'According to circumstances' this Thusness 'brings about all phenomenal things.' But again, we must not fall into the trap of seeing two, because there is no Thusness without phenomenal things, and there are no phenomenal things which have not got that structuring principle of Thusness. It is like palm and back of the hand, you cannot separate them out. It is only 'I' the fool who can separate myself out, or think I can separate myself out.

Master Daie continues quoting the Buddha, **'And he also said, "Proceeding to effect according to circumstances it extends everywhere while always here upon this Seat of Enlightenment."'** 'Proceeding to effect' means proceeding to some result depending upon circumstances. 'The effect according to circumstances': the squirrel hops onto the tree, the bird flies, the dog runs, according to circumstances and to what is. That is again the principle, the True Thusness, that 'extends everywhere' to everything that is formed, to all the ten thousand phenomena, and yet never leaves, is 'always here upon the seat of enlightenment.'

There is a rather helpful analogy about a monk who lived nearly three hundred years ago in Japan. He was good at wood carving and carved thousands of figures of the Bodhisattva Kannon, a good many of which are still in existence. Though they are rather folksy and rough, they are very impressive. He himself was a very quiet man, and when he was already elderly, the young monks in the monastery stood in great awe of him, not because he was fierce or anything, but because there was seemingly nothing that could shake him. So one night a group of them hid themselves in a dark corner of the corridor where they knew that first thing in the morning, long before it got light, it was the elderly monk's task to bring the Buddha-tea to the founder's altar. And sure enough, they heard him shuffle along in the darkness, carrying the tea. As he passed them, like so many young devils, they came out growling, 'Graaaah!' He did not falter or miss one step, but quietly went along the winding corridor until the next bend where, although one could not see it, he knew there was a little table. There he carefully set the tea down and then he leaned himself against the wall, 'Oh! What a shock!' Master Sesso, who told me that story, gave his own interpretation by saying, 'So you see, there is nothing wrong with the emotions, only you should not let them interfere with what you just happen to be doing.' So, 'proceeding to effect according to circumstances it extends everywhere while always here upon this seat of enlightenment.'

Master Daie then asks, **'Would they deceive people? If you consider quietude right and commotion wrong, then this is seeking the real aspect by destroying the worldly aspect, seeking nirvana, the peace of extinction, apart from birth and death.'** There are people, and we ourselves have also fallen into the trap at one stage in our training, usually quite early on, who do not want to have too much commotion. When we start with meditation practice, it is useful to have a quiet place and the right surroundings, because we are very easily jolted out. But once it has settled in a little bit, then to say it all must be quiet, and commotion is all wrong – that is denying half of life. That is 'seeking the real aspect by destroying the worldly aspect.' As we are naturally always splitting things into this and that, we cling to this and we want to destroy that, because those two sides of us, which are in us, are always at war with each other. And to bring that war to an end, to establish real peace in our own heart, this is the way the Buddha points out to us.

But even if I have managed to get into the real quietude of meditation, and remain sitting there, that can miscarry too. To be worried that it does not hold in the midst of the commotion – who is worried about that? Who does not like the commotion? Why take it personally? 'If you consider quietude right and commotion wrong then this is seeking the real aspect by destroying the worldly aspect, seeking nirvana, the peace of extinction, apart from birth and death.' Who is still here to do the seeking, who is still here to do the judging and the evaluating? The wanting and disliking? The same old 'I'.

Master Daie continues, **'When you like the quiet and hate the hubbub, this is just the time to apply effort.'** Because then, **'Suddenly when in the midst of hubbub',** when everything crashes around you, **'you topple the seat of quietude – that power'** opens up, says Master Daie and **'surpasses the meditation seat and cushion by a million billion times.'** In other words, you sit in meditation as a stage, as a part of the training, but if it is not applied and does not go into the fullness of the daily life, then it remains dead; there is no life in it and there is no power in it. The whole power of life, that is the important thing, not 'my' power, which in any case is not much, but the power with which things grow. If grass wants to grow and a stone is on top of it, it wriggles itself out from underneath and comes out by the side, still a little bit yellow as it emerges, but out it comes. Or it can even burst a stone – a root can – that is real power; that kind of real power does not come from me, that comes from the inherent nature, and being one with that inherent nature. We previously quoted the *Tao Te Ching* where it says, 'Man obeys the laws of the earth, earth obeys the laws of heaven, heaven obeys the law of Tao, and the Tao obeys its own inherent nature.' So, if I want to be in accord with the Tao, I first have to be in accord with the laws of the earth, and the rest takes place by itself. This is what it really comes down to, but I, not wanting to obey the laws of the earth, because they do not suit me, want to go and look for the Tao, and naturally cannot find it. That is, frankly speaking, our dilemma. I will not accept this planet on which we live, and I will not try to understand it and accept it, I will not have it that on Sunday, just as I want to go out, it starts pouring with rain, I will not accept that it gets dark in the evening, and light in the morning. And the last thing that I want to do is to bow my head and go with things *just as they are.* Thus I rob myself, I have sprung myself out of this living accord. Therefore as a separate, lonely thing, I err about, trying all sorts of fancy ideas that I believe will give me peace. Naturally I cannot find it, following my own bright ideas without taking into accord the laws of the earth and willingly obeying them, instead of bowing my head, and saying, 'Yes' to them. The great Yes. Think of it, ponder that a little bit.

Just giving ourselves into our daily life, flowing freely with it, just as it comes, neither giving preference to this or that. But 'when you like the quiet and hate the hubbub' Master Daie says, 'this is just the time to apply effort.' When I feel that I must have some time to myself – when it's all too much – that is just the time to apply effort. What kind of effort? Well, look. Just for a moment stop and look. Who is making all that hubbub? Is it the outside, or is it I myself, because I won't have this, and I can't have that, and I want to do this? This is just the time to apply effort, and rein it in. Then 'Suddenly, when in the midst of hubbub, you topple the scene of quietude,' – just when it all becomes too much, and the effort is applied, it suddenly topples round. The power that comes with that, in the midst of hubbub, looks at the hubbub, sees the hubbub, but does not take part in it. There is a quietness inside, a power that, Master Daie says, 'surpasses the seat and cushion.' The seat and cushion are, as we heard, the bamboo chair and the reed cushion, the meditation seat – in other words, that surpasses meditation, sitting in meditation, 'by a million billion times.' That is where the real power of the Tathagata comes in. 'In the midst of hubbub, you topple the seat of quietude.' This is the translation, but in fact it's not that *you* topple it; it topples of itself. 'And that power surpasses ordinary meditation by a million billion times.' The wisdom and power of the Tathagata does not just sit quietly in meditation.

From Soko Roshi, I had a lovely story which he told me once when I visited him in Daishu-in. He said, 'You know when I was still the head monk at Daitoku-ji the monks hated me, I know that quite well. Now years later, older and abbot of Daishu-in, strangely enough, they are rather fond of me here and from time to time they think that they would like to do something special to give me some real joy. I can see it coming in their faces, the far-away look in their eyes. And I resign myself to a period of great difficulty, because to tell them right away would only hurt them, they would not understand. But since they now have only their great good deed in mind, they forget to open the gate in the morning, they burn the rice, they spoil the vegetables. After four or five days when we are all suffering from stomach ache, I say to them, "Now please, please, please, do you see what is happening? Just forget that great good thing that you want to do for me, just stick to the ordinary, normal chores of opening the gate, of looking after the cooking, there is nothing more, and nothing greater that you can do for me, and nothing that gives me more joy."' That is when we are willing to accept things, not the great which draws us, but that which is actually here and now. This, please, take to heart and remember it when you come back to your daily life again after this *sesshin*. It is the small things, and the obedience and giving in, and the willingness to work with them.

LETTER 14 to K'UNG HUI

The Text

Once you have achieved perfect stillness of body and mind, you must make earnest effort. Do not immediately settle down in peaceful stillness. In the teachings this is called 'The Deep Pit of Liberation', much to be feared. You must make yourself turn freely like a gourd floating on the water, independent and free, not subject to restraints, entering purity and impurity without being obstructed or sinking down. Only then do you have a little familiarity with the school of the patch-robed monks. If you just manage to cradle the child when it is not crying in your arms, what is the use?

Ven. Myokyo-ni's Comments

'Once you have achieved perfect stillness of body and mind (heart).' That peaceful stillness is the first stage, *samatha*, which the Sixth Patriarch described as 'before thinking of good and bad.' Here the translator says 'Once you have achieved perfect stillness,' and this is a good place to carefully look at the translations again. Of course, 'I' cannot achieve peaceful stillness, it is quite impossible for 'me' because 'I' am the one who hops about, 'I' am the thoughts, the wanting, the emotions, the attachments, and therefore peaceful stillness is not something that 'I' can have. The peaceful stillness of itself opens when I am not there, and so once again 'before thinking', once again the Buddha's teaching of No-I. So once peaceful stillness of body and heart has started – it is not 'I' that has it, it is automatically there when 'I' am absent. To say that it has arisen, has started is also wrong, because actually it is our normal, natural state, without 'I'.

The Sixth Patriarch also said that the peasant uses it all day long but is not aware of it, that is the True Face. And with that True Face, there is a peaceful stillness that is not shaken.

When I recall my childhood, eons ago in a very remote corner of Austria, if you went walking up into the hills on a Sunday afternoon, you could see the individual houses of the peasants with their small fields down in the valley. In front of each house there would usually be an apple tree or chestnut tree with a bench underneath. And there they would sit; it was Sunday, so there was nothing to be done, and they would sit comfortably resting. They did not talk with each other, they just sat. And I would like to see whether we could manage to bring that off with a real restfulness, sitting for a couple of hours in the afternoon, side by side on a bench, looking out, sun shining perhaps, and just resting. Do you think we could?

So, 'Once perfect stillness of body and heart' has happened again **'you must make earnest effort.'** Is that not strange? But there is a reason for making an earnest effort. Master Daie, says, **'Do not immediately settle down in peaceful stillness. In the teachings this is called the "deep pit of liberation", much to be feared.'** If I think I have got it, if I think I have arrived, if I think anything, that peaceful stillness of body and heart is by no means there. For that we have a very helpful record of the great Master Hakuin who thought he had had an insight deeper than anybody had had for two or three hundred years, and he went around to have it certified – from one master to another. But none of them certified it, none of them agreed. Finally he decided to go up into the mountains, the Japanese Alps, where there was a renowned master of incredible strictness, and he would present himself and his insight to him. And he did so. But he was told by old Master Dokyo Etan, 'No, no, show your real insight.' However much Hakuin tried to convince him, old Master Etan was not having it and he called him a 'little devil sitting in a cave filled with the slime of his own self-accredited achievement.' That is what Master Daie here calls the 'deep pit of liberation, much to be feared.' 'I have got it. Have you got it?' 'Yes, I have got it too, but mine is better than yours! Mine is deeper than yours…' and there we are again, in the 'deep pit of liberation, much to be feared.'

Master Daie continues, **'You must make yourself turn freely like a gourd floating on the water, independent and free, not subject to restraints, entering purity and impurity without being obstructed or sinking down.'** During my twelve years in Japan, I came back to England for nine months between Sesso Roshi's death and continuing my training under Kannun Roshi; and since I love cargo ships, that is how I travelled there and back. We were nine passengers and I found that first evening out of Southampton very difficult. I realised that most of them were elderly, well-off people, retired and widowed, who went around the world because they were unhappy and lonely and they made these round trips on the cargo ship because they found new people with whom they could exchange their stories. The first evening I sat next to a retired police inspector from Hong Kong, who talked about his unhappiness and so on. I wanted to say something sympathetic and encouraging, but after having spent so much time in a traditional Zen monastery, my mode of expression was almost entirely Buddhistic. I knew perfectly well if I started talking about Buddhism on a cargo ship like this, I would be the odd one out and would ruin the unity of the passengers and all that – I could not talk about Buddhism, and I did not know what to do. So I shut myself off to hatch it out. And on the third day I started laughing at myself, and I thought what a silly goose I am – here I am, having spent ten years doing nothing but blab Buddhism this, Buddhism that, without realising that actually it is so much a short-hand code for our common human problems, dilemmas and sorrows and can easily be translated into ordinary language for the benefit of all. And with that I peacefully and happily mixed with the passengers again, and we started talking quite naturally. We got on very well with each other. A couple of them even wrote to me for a couple of years afterwards, they thought I was teaching English in Japan.

So, 'You must make yourself turn freely like a gourd floating on the water', within the circumstances, not outside the circumstances. Not offending against the circumstances, being aware of them. 'Independent and free, not subject to restraints.' It is not a restraint if I cannot talk about something, as my experience on the cargo ship proved. So, it is just a matter of fitting into the situation in which we find ourselves.

Another teaching story that comes to mind is of the two monks by a river crossing. The ford was a little bit under water because the river was in flood, and a girl in all her finery stood there obviously wanting to go across. One of the monks simply took her piggy-back and carried her across, putting her down on the other shore, and the two monks then wandered on. The second monk started murmuring, 'You know this is against the rules. You know that a monk is not allowed to touch a woman; and there you go and carry her across. This is surely not the right thing to do,' and on and on he went. After about half an hour the other monk, who had carried the girl across, peacefully turned to him and said, 'You know, I set her down on the other side of the ford. You are still carrying her!' 'Not subject to restraints, entering purity and impurity without being obstructed or sinking down.' That is a very important thing, entering freely into whatever situation presents itself without being obstructed, without being gobbled up by it. **'Only then do you have a little familiarity with the school of patched-robed monks.'**

Master Daie uses a Chinese proverb as an analogy, **'If you just manage to cradle the child when it is not crying in your arms, what is the use?'** A child that is happily playing, what is the use of trying to console it? So, 'Do not immediately settle down in peaceful stillness.' You must make an earnest effort to freely enter all situations 'without being obstructed or sinking down.' We are never free of a situation. Within that situation we can wriggle a little bit, outside the situation we cannot go. And we usually moan because we do not like the situations in which we find ourselves. But within the situation we are actually all in the place where we most want to be. For the very good reason that if it were not so, we would not be there. If I did not want to live in the temple any more, there is nothing that can hinder me from going right out by the front door, or from leaving in the middle of the *sesshin*. But the consequences of our acts usually prove that by comparison we are better off where we are. Every other place is still less preferable than the one we are in, or we would not be there. It is literally as simple as that. So we do the Zen training, we go to *sesshin*s, the legs hurt, and we wish we were somewhere else; well why are we not somewhere else? Let's be quite honest and instead of complaining about this or that, this is the place where we most want to be, so make good use of it, free and unobstructed. 'Entering purity and impurity without being obstructed or sinking down.'

Perhaps we can all remember when we first heard about Buddhism and possibly even enlightenment and those kinds of things, and then when we went into training all we heard about was the Daily Life Practice and just giving myself into what I am doing... 'Yes, and then what, and then what, and then what?' But it always comes back again to just giving myself into the Daily Life Practice. 'Yes, but I am giving myself!' The very voice shows that I haven't got a glimmer of what it means to really give myself. Not until something really grips me and flares up as either a WANT, MUST HAVE, or a HATE THAT! Then suddenly there is strength there and strangely enough I think I am doing it whole-heartedly, but I am not doing anything, it is the emotional energy that is doing it whole-heartedly. Has anybody never had at least one moment of real rage? Then we all know what we are talking about. And by golly, doesn't a real rage make you feel almost like God? This is the wisdom and power of the Tathagata, either in the form of the wild bull or otherwise in the whole strength of the Buddha-nature. That is the strength that is necessary to give myself away, that has to be cultivated ruthlessly, with whole effort until it happens of itself. 'You must make earnest effort,' particularly when things have become very much routine or just a little bit easy. If something is crucial or urgent, we are quite willing to make some effort, but when things have settled down, then it is not so easy, and this is where we then have to pull ourselves together and think of the teachings. That 'deep pit of liberation, much to be feared' has to be jumped out of as hastily and as quickly as possible!

LETTER 15 to YEN TZU-CH'ING

The Text

> Lin Chi said, 'If you can put to rest the mind that frantically seeks from moment to moment, you will be no different from old Shakyamuni Buddha.' He wasn't fooling people, even Bodhisattvas of the seventh stage seek Buddha knowledge without their minds being satisfied. Therefore it is called 'affliction', really there is no way to manage, it is impossible to apply the slightest external measure.

> Several years ago there was a certain Layman Hsu who was able to find an opening. He sent me a letter expressing his understanding that said, 'Empty and open in my daily activities,

there is not a single thing opposing me; finally I realise that all things in the three worlds are fundamentally non-existent. Truly this is peace and happiness, joyful liveliness having cast it all away.' Accordingly, I instructed him with a verse:

> Don't be fond of purity:
> Purity makes people weary.
> Don't be fond of joyful liveliness:
> Joyful liveliness makes people crazy.
> As water conforms to the vessel,
> It accordingly becomes square or round, short or long.
> As for casting away or not casting away,
> Please think it over carefully.

Ven. Myokyo-ni's Comments

'**Lin Chi,** (that is Master Rinzai) said, **"If you can put to rest the mind** (heart) **that frantically seeks from moment to moment, you will be no different from old Shakyamuni Buddha."'** He also asked his monks on another occasion, 'Why are you running about getting flat feet from your rushing? What do you expect to find?' But here, 'If you can put to rest the heart that frantically seeks from moment to moment, you will be no different from old Shakyamuni Buddha.' The heart that frantically seeks. 'Well,' you might think, 'I don't necessarily frantically seek – I may be seeking, but frantically seeking? And from moment to moment continuously frantically seeking?' But if we look carefully into it, isn't there a longing inside each one of us? We do not know what it is. Usually we misinterpret it as something from outside; an object, or ambition, or whatever it might be. But there's always something, some kind of wanting. It is only natural, because if we look at the Buddha's teaching, the belief in 'I' and look at the identity that we have forged with this ghost of an 'I', we see that it is very strong. And it separates us from all other things. This longing for something, this longing for being – well, the correct word for it would be 'whole' – is inborn. Naturally, because the heart, which is different from the head, the heart knows and longs for that coming together in wholeness.

And there is a kind of feeling that it is there, but I can't get hold of it. However hard I try, it's not possible, because as Master Mumon said, the treasures, the heirlooms of the house do not come in by the front door; they are already there. So it's not something that I need to get – it is something that, once the sense of 'I' has really fallen off or been seen through or penetrated, it is found that it always has been there. Nor is it unfamiliar to us. At moments when things are rather tight, or in moments when something beautiful happens, suddenly we are with it.

The heart longs to get away from the 'I'-separation, and wants to participate, to participate in the whole of life as it is, as it lives itself. 'If you can put to rest the heart that frantically seeks from moment to moment, you will be no different from Shakyamuni Buddha.' Having entered the state of I-lessness, like the Buddha, there is no seeking anymore, there is no trying to become this, that or the other anymore; neither to become rich nor to become holy, not to become anything. It is all a question of putting the 'heart that frantically seeks' to rest.

Master Daie says, Lin Chi **'was not fooling people, because even Bodhisattvas of the seventh stage seek Buddha knowledge without their hearts being satisfied.'** The Bodhisattvas of the seventh stage – doctrinally in Mahayana theology, there are ten stages on the Bodhisattva Path of training and it's at the seventh stage that the dichotomy of subject and object is overcome. Well, not quite, because the discriminating knowledge is still somehow there. The difference between the discriminating knowledge and the differentiating knowledge is also something we need to be clear about. As long as 'I' is there, we can only think in opposites. There is no thought, there is no idea that does not also have an opposite. And since we all think in opposites, we also immediately put a value judgement on everything. A rose is beautiful; the sunset today was not nearly as lovely as yesterday. We can't leave things alone; we always put a judgement on them – this is better than that. That is the discriminating knowledge, which is the 'I' judging. This is the cause of all our troubles, both personally – with wanting what we haven't got and disliking what we have got – but it is also that which makes us quarrel with each other, because of our ideas and our convictions. 'My way is better than yours is' – and so we come to fight and aggression takes sway. **'Therefore it is called affliction,'** says Master Daie.

Differentiating knowledge is something quite different. It is to see things as different, in that clear seeing which is the Buddha-seeing, to see things as different but without judging them – the mountain is high and the valley is low. That Garry has this opinion and favours this idea, and Myokyo-ni favours that idea can be quite neutrally seen. We can talk about it without heat, and in the end can say, 'Well, I see your point, but I think I'll stick to mine.' There is no heat in it, it's just that neutral seeing, the way things really are – this is the Buddha-seeing, differentiating but not discriminating.

This tendency to see everything through the veil of my ideas, my notions, my convictions: this is what is called affliction. And **'really there is no way to manage it. It is impossible to apply the slightest external measure to it.'** It has to be truly worked through, in the very heart.

Master Daie then goes on with a story which is of great help to us, **'Several years ago there was a certain Layman Hsu, who was able to find an opening.'** He came into the quiet, in other words, from the hubbub. And **'he sent me a letter expressing his understanding in which he said, "Empty and open in my daily activities, there is not a single thing opposing me. Finally, I realise that all things in the three worlds are fundamentally non-existent."'** This sounds pretty good does it not? But if we look a bit closer at it, what he has managed to do is to get himself into a state where he has bludgeoned himself out, where he has deadened everything inside – that is firmly intentioned and something quite different from 'I' actually really being out of the way. This is where we have to be careful, we are only too easily tempted by 'everything is empty, everything is the same,' and to a certain extent we can, if we are strong and persistent enough, get ourselves into that. But sooner or later something happens, and it backfires – our friend the Bull breaks through with energy. That is not it, that is the empty emptiness which Master Etan referred to as 'that cave filled with the slime of one's self-accredited achievement.' 'Empty and open in my daily activities, there is not a single thing opposing me.' He has blunted it and driven it all out, and finally Layman Hsu said, 'I realise that all things in the three worlds are fundamentally non-existent.' Well, he has really cleared it all out, hasn't he? There he sits now, having forcefully driven it all out. **'"Truly this is peace and happiness, joyful liveliness having cast it all away."'** This is the story of the frog who sits on a lotus leaf, legs crossed in the meditation posture, hands folded in the lap, teeth closed, tongue on upper palate, deep in meditation – nothing. Behind him a huge snake rears up! Does he know? Does he not know? On the lotus leaf sits a frog, legs crossed, hands in lap, tongue on upper palate, deep in meditation... 'LOOK OUT!' We love to be the frog, because that is the only thing that I can conceive – to try and wipe it all out, but casting it all away is not it.

And so, Master Daie having read this letter from Layman Hsu, now tells his correspondent, **'Accordingly I instructed him with a** verse: Don't be fond of purity, purity makes people weary.'** We are reminded here of Bodhidharma's answer to Emperor Wu, who asked what the essence of Buddhism was and got the reply, 'Vast Emptiness, nothing holy.' That 'nothing holy' is the important thing. 'Don't be fond of purity, purity makes people weary.' Being overly careful about this, that and the other. And then taking it a step further, **'Don't be fond of joyful liveliness, joyful liveliness makes people crazy.'** That is getting above oneself.

But now comes the more important line of the verse, **'As water conforms to the vessel, it accordingly becomes square or round, short or long.'** In a cup, water is round, in something else it is square, long or short – in other words, being part of the situation I am in, not standing outside, not holding myself aloof, and not refusing to take part and play my role in that situation. So depending on what the situation demands and what my part in the situation is, I am sometimes friendly, sometimes helpful, sometimes hostile, depending on the circumstances. But I object, 'Surely this is not right, there is no consistency in it, surely a person well qualified, well advanced on the Way, must be consistent.' Yes, consistent in conforming to the situation, not consistent in some kind of fancy idea.

'As for casting away or not casting away, please think it over carefully.' I want to get rid of this, I want to get rid of that; all the things I do not like, I want to get rid of. Why do I want to get rid of things? Because of my judging, and when I want to get rid of something, it is as if I was cutting my living flesh off, because I don't like it. For which Master Rinzai has a fitting comment, 'Why gouge out healthy flesh to make a wound?' Why? Because I do not know any better. So it is perhaps useful to once again carefully look at the Buddha's basic teachings: the Three Signs of Being, the Three Fires, the Five Skandhas, the Noble Eightfold Path, the Six Stages of the Wheel, and the Twelve Destinies. With that, I slowly begin to wonder, whether I can really do it and why I have started to follow this teaching? Most likely for what I can get out of it. But as I go on with the practice, does the attitude of 'what I can get out of it' remain, or does it widen out as it gets a little bit further away from I? Do I occasionally get a glimmer of the fact that, like a little child I cannot go on wanting, looking for what I can get, and that it is also a question of giving as well as receiving. We chant, 'To be of assistance to all sentient beings.' So perhaps we can be like the water, conforming to whatever situation we are in. That is not judging, that is being free – in the situation. As long as 'I' am there, I want to be free of the situation, which is not possible. But when that has been seen into, then within the situation there is freedom, and there is therefore the free conforming to the situation as it is, and the joy of that conforming, playing, as we used to play as children. Now when we are grown up with our so-called cares, in other words with our likes and dislikes, we can't play anymore, we take ourselves too seriously and carefully cover over what we really are, so that we are not seen by others. Master Rinzai said, 'Just be your ordinary selves, don't give yourself airs.' So perhaps we can think along those lines and ponder them on the way home, then we will sit easier with ourselves and with the world.

LETTER 16 to HUANG PO-CH'ENG

The Text

> In the daily activities of a student of the Path, to empty objects
> is easy, but to empty the mind is hard. If objects are empty but
> the mind is not empty, the mind will be overcome by objects.
> Just empty the mind and objects will be empty of themselves.

If the mind is already emptied but then you arouse a second thought, wishing to empty its objects, this means that this mind is not yet empty, and is again carried away by objects. If this sickness is not done away with, there is no way to get out of birth and death. Once this mind is empty, then what is there outside the mind that can be emptied? Think it over.

'In the daily activities of a student of the Path, to empty objects is easy, but to empty the mind (heart) **is hard.'** In our daily activities, in our Daily Life Practice, 'to empty objects is easy.' Objects are made by myself, without I, there can be no objects. Furthermore, I believe that I can know objects, but I cannot, I can only know my perception of objects, the reflections in my heart. There is a whole Buddhist school based on that, the Yogacara School. But if we really, concretely, look — can we really know even that old table over there? No, we can only see what is reflected in our mind. Master Torei in the *Inexhaustible Lamp* gives a rather nice example of a master who draws a circle. On seeing the circle, someone who is a bit greedy immediately thinks, 'Ah, a bun!' Another one, who likes money, thinks of it as a gold coin. Only very few will simply see it, as it really is, an empty circle. When we see something, and the same applies of course to the other sense data as well, we immediately form our own ideas about it, jump in and think that is what we see, but it is not. It takes a lot of skill to really see, to empty out. Perhaps hearing is a better example because we all know that if we really want to listen to something that is a bit faint, we cannot think at the same time as we listen, or rather we do it often enough, but then we don't hear. But if we really listen, first of all the ear turns a little bit towards the sound, then the whole body tilts forward, and it is an automatic emptying out so that the sound can actually fall in.

So 'In the daily activities of a student of the Path', that is in our Daly Life Practice, 'to empty objects is easy', says Master Daie, because by giving ourselves into our activities, into the doing, the objects pale by themselves, the things, the thoughts. But 'to empty the heart itself is hard' for as long as I, the final object, am still there, to empty the heart is not possible. Our conceptions, ideas, and opinions are well ingrained and go very deep. I can't even imagine how deep they go because they go right to the root of 'I'. Therefore to get rid of them, to work them out means to work out the root of 'I'. To empty the heart is to root out I, and that is hard.

Master Daie continues, **'If objects are empty but the mind** (heart) **is not empty, the mind** (heart) **will be overcome by objects.'** So even if there are no objects outside, if the heart is not empty, it will throw up objects. A good example for this goes back to the last century, when in the sixties scientists started conducting sense deprivation tests. The people who took part in these experiments were hand-picked for their stability and even-mindedness. In a dark and soundless space, they were immersed in tanks, in liquid of body temperature and viscosity so the body floated. And within hours, even the most settled ones began to hallucinate, heard voices and I don't know what else. 'If the heart is not empty, it will be overcome by objects.' And if there are no outside ones, it will start producing the inside ones, because without good solid training, the heart is not empty, because I am still ghosting about.

Therefore, Master Daie suggests, **'Just empty the mind** (heart) **and objects will be empty of themselves,'** because if there is no clinging and no wanting, no opinions and preconceptions, etc., then the objects cannot get hold of what is not there. 'Objects will be empty of themselves' – the work is not, as I so often mistakenly think, with the objects, the work is with the own heart. This is why we have *sesshin*s, because *sesshin* literally means a collecting of the heart. The heart hops about from object to object, from wanting and dislikes, from this and that, planning and scheming, that is what we normally only too easily engage in. But in a *sesshin* we collect the heart – there is no going out, there is no specific entertainment and there are long hours of sitting. During these long hours of sitting, if we really make use of them, we begin to become more aware – is the heart getting empty, or are there still so many little devils hopping about with all kinds of ideas; are we being carried away by them, following them, or are we just letting them hop about and peacefully carry on with the sitting, giving ourselves into the count. Think of the Buddha on the last night before his awakening, tempted by Mara – first by his daughters and then Mara's demons hopping about. Did he pay attention to them, did he try to stem himself against them, did he try to shoo them away, get rid of them? No, he just peacefully continued sitting, and that is all there is to it, and that is what a *sesshin* is about, to just peacefully continue sitting, taking up the count, and always back again to the count.

But Master Daie then gives another very helpful hint, not only, 'just empty the heart and objects will be empty of themselves', that is certainly so, but there is one temptation – if there is still a root of I fluttering about – **'If the mind** (heart) **is already emptied but then you arouse a second thought, wishing to empty its objects, this means that this mind** (heart) **is not yet empty, and is again carried away by objects.'** Do you see, this is what so often happens to us, hardly have we had a bit of quiet, and the heart is already empty, then up comes the thought, 'is this a real thing', stirring about, 'is there no other thought at the moment there?' and up comes the whole caboodle. 'Then you arouse a second thought, wishing to empty its objects': the heart itself doesn't have objects, I make them. I do not need to empty it of its objects, just be with this peaceful quiet sitting. But at that moment of peaceful, quiet sitting, 'is it really empty?' We begin to look and stir about, that is where we have to be really careful and get a grip on ourselves, and let be, because when we 'arouse a second thought, wishing to empty its objects, this means that this heart is not yet empty, and is again carried away by objects.' The Buddha's heart was certainly empty, neither Mara's daughters nor Mara's demons could do anything; nor did he think about whether they were objects, or not objects, or anything, he just had no truck with them. This having no truck with means leaving it alone, instead of stoking it up, which I like to do to convince myself.

'If this sickness is not done away with,' this trying to check up on ourselves, this sickness of making objects, and of somehow not being able to leave things alone, then **'there is no way to get out of birth and death.'** Birth and death – coming to be and ceasing to be – that also is definitely connected with I. There is a beautiful Buddhist analogy of the ocean and the waves. One individual wave could be compared to an 'I', an individual 'I' – up, existing for a time, and then falling down again once more. And if such a wave would have any feeling, just as it is up at the top, at a crest, in the process of breaking down, hemmed in by other waves all around, would it not be frightened? But if that wave were in any case aware that, whether up or down or any other way, it is nothing but ocean, and all the other waves around are also nothing but ocean – would there still be any need for this concern and anxiety? The way out of birth and death.

But Master Daie tells us, **'Once this mind** (heart) **is empty, then what is there outside the mind** (heart) **that can be emptied?'** Once this heart is empty, empty of I, that is what it really comes down to. You can also say, 'Once this heart has become one with everything,' with just what is; though perhaps not with everything, that is too abstract, just 'one with whatever there is here and now' – then there is nothing separate any more. There is a great difference between trying to know whether my heart is empty and having become the empty heart itself. Whenever in our daily life we whole-heartedly give ourselves into what we are doing, that is becoming. If we are whole-heartedly given into what we are doing, we have given ourselves away and we have become one with the doing. That is the enormous difference. A good example would be a sports reporter, who sits comfortably in a booth above the pitch and gives his rapid, excited comments on the progress of play. But he is not playing football or whatever the game might be, that would mean jumping down into the arena and taking part himself. This is what the separate heart prevents us from doing and is why life always seems so unsatisfactory to us, because we are sitting on the side lines, not taking part, not playing, not playing the game of life. That is the difference – being really part of it, playing the part, and partaking. And strangely enough in that partaking, having become it, the thing is alive and therefore it is joyful as well as rewarding, and even if it is painful, it is still rewarding and joyful – that is something that we need to find out ourselves. But if we opt out and are spoil-sports, 'nothing ever happens that I like,' and sit there continuously moaning, then we will never find out. So again repeating Master Daie, 'once the heart is empty then what is there outside of the heart that can be emptied? Think it over.' With that empty heart going into situation after situation, because the situations change, it is only if I am stiff and do not want to change that there is trouble. Master Daie suggests, **'Think it over.'** And that is what we had better do. Listen to Master Daie and think it over.

LETTER 17 to CHEN-JU

THE TEXT

If your mind does not run off searching, or think falsely, or get involved with objects, then this very burning house of passion is itself the place to escape the three worlds. Didn't the Buddha say, 'Not depending on or abiding in any situation, not having any discrimination, one clearly sees the vast establishment of Reality and realises that all worlds and all things are equal and nondual.' Thus a bodhisattva of the Far-Going Stage goes beyond all in the Two Vehicles by virtue of the power of knowledge and wisdom which he practises; though he has attained the treasury of the Buddha-realm, yet to teach he appears in the realms of delusion; though he has transcended the ways of delusion, yet he appears to practise the stuff of delusion. Though he appears to act the same as outsiders, he does not abandon the Buddhist Teachings; though he appears to go along with all that is worldly, he is perpetually practising all world-transcending ways. These are the real expedient devices within the burning house of passion.

VEN. MYOKYO-NI'S COMMENTS

'If your mind (heart) **does not run off searching, or think falsely, or get involved with objects'** – 'if your heart does not run off searching' – why does the heart run off searching? Because it feels incomplete; it feels separated off. As long as this feeling is there, the heart must go on running off searching. Therefore it also naturally can't help but think falsely, erroneously; having thoughts about what it is looking and searching for, and getting involved with objects from outside. Wanting to get something from outside in order to feel complete.

In the *Diamond Sutra*, the Buddha himself said, 'Who searches for me in form, who looks for me in sound, his footsteps go astray. He will not find the Tathagata.' It's not outside; and as long as we go on running and thinking that I can get it – this or that will be the thing, this will be it – we think falsely and can't help but get involved in objects.

Master Daie says, if your heart does not run off in this searching and thinking, **'then this very burning house of passion is itself the place to escape the three worlds.'** This burning house of passions refers to the parable in the *Lotus Sutra* – 'This house is on fire, burning with the Three Fires of greed, hatred, and delusion. There is no staying in such a house.' Yet if the heart does not run off searching, having notions and ideas and getting involved in opposites, then this very burning house of passions is the place to escape the three worlds, for if the heart is at peace, the passions are not rising. It is just like the quiet sea carrying a good swimmer.

Master Daie then quotes the Buddha, **"Not depending on or abiding in any situation, not having any discrimination, one clearly sees the vast establishment of Reality."** Not depending on or abiding in any situation – 'If only this would happen, then everything will be all right with me.' And if it is all right with me, then I want things to stay that way, and to this I cling. It is this clinging which is our difficulty, because that comes together with the searching. The analogy that comes to mind is freely floating along, hopping along, like a gourd dancing on the water in a quick-running brook. It doesn't say, 'Now I want to go this way, now I want to go that way. I will not have it this way or that way.'

'Not depending on or abiding in any situation, not having any discrimination, one clearly sees the vast establishment of reality.' But with our notions and discriminations, we cannot see it, this realm, the vast establishment of reality. We cannot see reality, because our thoughts all run in opposites and along with that come all our judgements and evaluations. This is round and that is square; round is better, more complete; the square has edges. The mountain and the valley – well, the mountains are high, the valleys are low. We cannot see that there simply are mountains and there are valleys. That's all there is. Neither is better, neither is worse. We cannot see things just as they are? Our bundle of notions, ideas and evaluations immediately drape themselves over the object like a vast garment. And for this reason, we cannot see the vast establishment of reality.

But when one clearly sees the vast establishment of reality the Buddha concludes, then **"one realises that all worlds and all things are equal and nondual."** As long as I am full of my notions, I will only pay lip-service, 'Everything is the same. All things are equal and nondual.' But they are only equal and nondual if there are no discriminations. The mountain is not better than the valley; they are equal and nondual without discrimination. What is better, a racehorse or a cow? If in the middle of the desert you are dying from thirst, a racehorse is no help at all, though a cow will give you milk and you may survive. But if you want to have a race, then you do not have a race with a cow, do you? So without notions there is also the appropriateness of things. If there is no depending or abiding and no discrimination, then all things can be seen, and if worked with, left in their proper place.

Now Master Daie continues, **'Thus a bodhisattva of the Far-Going Stage goes beyond all in the Two Vehicles by virtue of the power of the knowledge and wisdom which he practises.'** There are ten stages in the Bodhisattva Path, and the Far-Going Stage is the seventh. Such a bodhisattva 'goes beyond all in the Two Vehicles by virtue of the power of the knowledge and wisdom which he practises.'

He is a fully-fledged bodhisattva by now, which means fearless; which means without I.

Master Daie says, **'Though such a bodhisattva has attained the treasury of the Buddha-realm, yet to teach he appears in the realms of delusion.'** If he only shows himself as the bodhisattva of the seventh stage, he is not perceptible to most, only to a few other bodhisattvas. 'He has attained the treasury of the Buddha-realm; yet to teach, he appears in the realms of delusion,' where you and I abide. That's why it is important to realise that what is somehow inconceivable, that is something I cannot imagine. Fondly in my delusion I believe that I can imagine everything; my imagination is free and can soar. But can it really? It cannot get out of or beyond what I actually truly know. The great difficulty of science fiction writers and film makers is to make aliens and other worlds look really alien. But do they manage it? They may create strange beings, but they don't really depart from what we actually know; it is not possible.

Therefore, the bodhisattva, 'though he has attained the treasury of the Buddha-realm, yet to teach he appears in the realm of delusion.' And **'Though he has transcended the ways of delusion, yet he appears to practise the stuff of delusion.'** He blends in with what is. If you really think about it, it is essential that we are capable of doing that. If for instance you were to meet a retired gardener, who has spent all his or her life tending plants and has an enormous store of wisdom and understanding of it, and try and talk to them about the finer points of cooking, you just wouldn't be able to connect with them, there's nothing there for them to identify with. It has to be familiar, it is through a familiar analogy that we can understand each other and that we can make points that are helpful to one another.

So, **'Though he appears to act the same as outsiders, he does not abandon the Buddha's teachings. Though he appears to go along with all that is worldly, he is perpetually practising all**

world-transcending ways.' We often misunderstand when reading things like this. We think there is complete freedom, that bodhisattvas can do exactly as they like. But this is by no means so; because, if they could do as they liked, they wouldn't be bodhisattvas. There would still be an I there, wouldn't there? And so there is no bodhisattva there, not even of the first stage, and certainly not of the seventh.

To take on the forms that are required for practising and for expounding the Buddha-dharma, even quite wordlessly if necessary, that is what bodhisattvas of the seventh stage are actually engaged in. They are perpetually practising all world-transcending ways and, says Master Daie, **'Just these are the real expedient devices within the burning house of passion.'** This energy of the passion – that is precious energy which a bodhisattva will often show rather than talk about. These are the real expedient devices within the burning house of passion. Not to be mistaken as 'now I can do as I want to.'

There are some very great figures in the history of Zen who lived and acted exactly like this, and had a great following and a great impact on people. You know about the eccentric itinerant monk Fuke Osho (Chin. Puhua) who knew Master Rinzai and is mentioned several times in the *Record of Rinzai*. He was beloved in the town because he mingled with the people in the market and in the taverns, and in a strange way because they liked him very much, they got a little bit interested in Buddhism which they would not have otherwise done. Then one day Fuke Osho went through the town saying that he needed a new robe and many came and offered him a new robe. But he refused all, until a joker presented him with a coffin. And delighted, he put the coffin on his back, walked through the town with it and said, 'This is my new robe. Tomorrow I'm going to die at the East Gate.' So the whole town flocked to the East Gate in the morning to see Fuke Osho die. And truly, he was there sitting on the coffin, and when everybody was there he said, 'I have decided against it, it is going to be tomorrow morning at the South Gate.' The next day everybody came to the South Gate and the same thing happened, 'No, tomorrow, definitely at the North Gate.' Only a few people came then, for they thought it one of the pranks of Fuke Osho. After the third day nobody came anymore, but at mid-morning on the fourth day, a traveller came into town and said, 'I've had the most incredible experience; just outside the West Gate, there was a coffin by the wayside, and in it lay somebody. He called out to me and said, "Please, nail the lid on." But I said that I couldn't possibly do that. But he continued to beg and so I nailed him in left him there.' Everybody streamed out to the West Gate and truly enough there was the nailed coffin. They prised the lid open – and there was nobody in it. But far, far off in the sky came the tinkling of his little bell which he always had.

That is the story of Fuke Osho. He could enter purity or impurity. Being obstructed by it, he could not have done it, but without being obstructed – this is what he showed. If you want to liberate yourself and do exactly as you want and do all the things that in our rules we shouldn't do, that's fine enough; but then you also have to allow yourself to be nailed into the coffin. Then it is really true, then there is no abiding in any situation, no depending on any situation, but making use of the situations for the benefit of everything. And if it is for the benefit of everything, it includes oneself too; but that is of little importance. It is for the benefit of everybody. It is not intentionally willed as a do-gooder, but done because there is a true warmth and a true understanding that in that warmth there is no separateness; that whatever is done is done to everything. And strangely enough, if that is seen into, then everything also responds.

The Text

> If people who study transcendent wisdom abandon these expedients and go along with passions, they will certainly be controlled by the demons of delusion. And while yielding to sense objects, to impose theories and say that affliction is itself enlightenment and ignorance is itself great wisdom, to act in terms of existence with every step while talking of emptiness with each breath, without admonishing oneself for being dragged along by the power of habitual action, to go on and tell others to deny cause and effect – the vicious poison of misguided delusion has entered the guts of people who act like this. They want to escape from passion, but it's like trying to put out a fire by pouring on oil. Aren't they to be pitied?

> Only having penetrated all the way can you say that affliction is itself enlightenment and ignorance is identical to great wisdom. Within the wondrous mind of the original vast quiescence – pure, clear, perfect illumination – there is not a single thing that can cause obstruction. It is like the emptiness of space. Even the word Buddha is something alien, to say nothing of there still being passions or afflictions as the opposite.

Ven. Myokyo-ni's Comments

'If people who study transcendent wisdom abandon these expedients and go along with passions, they will certainly be controlled by the demons of delusion.' Those who study transcendent wisdom, which is *prajna*, the Buddhist ideal, and who come to it, thus spring free of the Wheel of Change, from birth and death. The teachings themselves are the expedient means, because following them, living according to them, little by little they whittle away the strong root of I. But 'if people study transcendent wisdom and yet abandon these expedients and rather go along with passions' – if we do not hold on to the expedient means of the teachings – then the objects will once again exert their allure, and they will start to be 'controlled by the demons of delusion.'

What is it that brings up an eruption of the passions? Whether it's wanting, greed or hatred, it is first of all the delusion of 'I' and then the judgement of some object, which suddenly is not that object anymore because it is as if my heart has jumped out, and like a shimmering veil has draped itself over the object. It is either complete attraction, or otherwise a real aversion, 'must get rid of it.' If we go along with passions, when the Fires flare up, when the volcanoes erupt, then we certainly are controlled by the demons of delusion. Because then, whatever comes up in that eruption, we take for real, and we believe it and we believe it with that same fierceness with which the eruption comes.

This is why throughout the ages there have been means of repressing it – which is not helpful, but nevertheless it's better than going out and murdering someone. But why are the passions so dangerous? If we consider for a moment: if they go all the way, they are always catastrophic, as our personal and collective history demonstrates only too well. But it's useful to look at those things and recognise that it is the own heart that drapes itself like a veil over the object. Because it is my own heart, I feel so strongly about it.

There is the story of the golden ball, which I know from Venerable Maha Boowa, and I'll tell it again because it is so useful. A monk is sitting in the jungle, a good old monk, well grounded in meditation. As he sits peacefully there, he sees a little golden ball just in front of him, hopping up and down, up and down, as if to say, 'Grab me! Grab me!' The monk goes on meditating, but the ball is insistent, 'Grab me! Grab me!' and comes closer. Before he knows what he's doing, his hand goes out to grab that ball, and at that moment, the ball has hopped a bit further away. The monk, by now forgetting his meditation, leans forward a bit out of the meditation position to get it. The ball goes still further away; and before he knows where he is, the monk is up, running after the ball; and the ball hops in front of him, always just within reach. Then finally the ball bounces up a tree, and out onto a big stout branch. By now the monk is in hot pursuit and follows right after it until he comes to a rather slender extended part of the branch. As the branch begins to sway, he comes to his senses and sees that he is in an exposed place, and he is frightened. The ball has gone. He yells for help, but it takes a couple of hours until his brothers find him and help him down. And I see the Venerable Maha Boowa sitting on his high chair, spitting out betel nut juice, and laughing, 'Ha, ha, ha! It serves him right! Why did he let his own heart escape?' It's a good story, that golden ball story, and it's something that we all know.

Master Daie says that if we abandon these expedient means of the teachings that help us, and if we go along with passions, then we will certainly be controlled by the demons of delusion. The delusion of not knowing that it is one's own heart that escapes, not knowing that the delusion is I, and as long as I am there, I see things in opposites: liking and loathing.

He goes on to say, **'While yielding to sense objects'** – being carried away by sense objects, and please remember that these are not just outside objects, but also mental objects, and yielding to these and having read the teachings to then arrogantly **'impose theories and say that affliction is itself enlightenment and ignorance itself great wisdom'** – 'that is what it says in some of the books, I have read it myself!' It's easy to talk about that, and yet **'to act in terms of existence with every step'** – being controlled by the demons, the passions, **'while talking of emptiness with each breath without admonishing oneself for being dragged along by the power of habitual action'** – without taking a breath and looking and seeing what we are once more up to. This is where we need the practice, where we need the strength to really hold together, rather than **'going on and telling others to deny cause and effect – the vicious poison of misguided delusion has entered the guts of people who act like this.'** 'The vicious poison' he calls it, 'of misguided delusion.' With no training and no framework, the whole thing explodes. Yet such people, **'want to escape from passion,'** but how can you escape from the passions if you allow them to carry you away again and again? **'It is like trying to put out the fire by pouring on oil.'** What happens if there is a fire and you pour oil on it? **'Aren't such people to be pitied?'** This, and Master Daie really lays it on, is a careful warning, that not only in our talking, but also in our thinking we have to keep to the practice, to the framework and not continuously allow our own ideas, our own passions, our own weaknesses, to obstruct and rule us. Because says Master Daie, **'Only having penetrated all the way through can you say that affliction is itself enlightenment and ignorance is identical to great wisdom.'** It is not only in talking, it is also in our reading; having just read that affliction is itself enlightenment, ignorance is identical to great wisdom, 'Now I know! Now I'll have no more trouble!' And then I wonder where the trouble and obstructions come from when, after all, I know it. I have only ensnared myself even more.

But Master Daie tells us, **'Within the wondrous mind** (heart) **of the original, vast quiescence – pure, clear, perfect illumination – there is not a single thing that can cause obstruction.'** You remember the Sixth Patriarch, 'Before thinking of good and bad,' before thinking, when there is nothing – we must not misunderstand that 'nothing' either, for it is not that there is nothing, but that there is no obstruction because there is just one. Master Daie calls it 'pure, clear, perfect illumination,' and being one, and having become one with it, there is not a single thing that can cause obstruction. **'It is like the emptiness of space, and even the word Buddha is something alien'** to this vast emptiness, like space. The word Buddha doesn't belong to it. That's only made up by us. **'To say nothing of there still being passions or afflictions as the opposite'** of that vast quietness. There is just nothing.

LETTER 18 to HSU TUN-CHI

The Text

This affair is like the bright sun in the blue sky, shining clearly, changeless and motionless, without diminishing or increasing. It shines everywhere in the daily activities of everyone, appearing in everything. Though you try to grasp it, you cannot get it. Though you try to abandon it, it always remains. It is vast and unobstructed, utterly empty. Like a gourd floating on water, it cannot be reined in or held down. Since ancient times, when good people of the Path have attained this, they have appeared and disappeared in the sea of birth and death, able to use it fully. There is no deficit or surplus. Like cutting up sandalwood, each piece is it.

'**This affair is like the bright sun in a blue sky, shining clearly, changeless and motionless, without diminishing or increasing.**' This great affair is the great matter of life and death, which means the Buddha-dharma or the Zen Way, if you like. Clouds may obscure it, but it is shining. And it shines on everything, because shining is its nature.

'**It shines everywhere in the daily activities of everyone, appearing in everything.**' Master Daie is very careful in really trying to point the finger towards it. In the daily activities of everyone, whatever we are doing, it shines through it and appears in everything like the sun shining clearly. It cannot be hidden. The Sixth Patriarch said of this true nature, of the Buddha-nature, 'The peasant uses it all day long, but is not aware of it.' So, in the same way but much more warped by our picking and choosing, it is also with us. It shines everywhere in all our daily activities, appearing in everything. There is a vague awareness of it, which comes from the practice, because that practice of giving ourselves into what at this moment is being done, is giving myself away into and becoming it. With this awareness, I then begin to wonder about it, however, '**Though you try to grasp it, you cannot get it.**'

Though you try to grasp it, to see it, to hold it, to look at it, you cannot get it. The knife that cuts but cannot cut itself, the eye that sees but cannot see itself. This is the delusion of 'I', thinking that it can grasp it, and look at it as if it was something extra, something separate. But it – if you want to call it the True Face, because we are mostly concerned with that – cannot be seen, it cannot be grasped, but it works. You cannot get it. And '**though you try to abandon it**' – this is the other side of it – '**it always remains.**' You cannot see it, and you cannot get rid of it either. It is in the oneness, in the total union with it, and the functioning in that union, which takes the body in as well as the mind and the thought and the heart – the whole lot. But it has no 'I' with it, as observer.

'Though you try to abandon it, it always remains,' for this we are reminded of the story of Lazy An, which Master Daie mentions in Letter 3. When asked by his master, 'What do you do these days?' Lazy An said, 'I look after my bull. The master asked, 'How do you look after your bull?' He said, 'Well, whenever he goes into another field, I pull him by the nose ring, and by now he's so used to me that there's no need to pull the nose-ring any more. He just goes with me wherever I go; and even if I tried to push him away, he wouldn't go.' What is really mine – and that is useful to realise – that I cannot get rid of. The things that I fear to lose: they are not really mine.

Master Daie says, **'It is vast and unobstructed, utterly empty.'** That genuine insight, what we really are. Vast and unobstructed, and utterly empty. It has no intentions, has no wants, has no dislikes. **'Like a gourd floating on water, it cannot be reined in or held down.'** It's a well-known and favourite Zen analogy. A gourd floating on water cannot be reined in, it just flows with the water. If you try to hold it down, it bobs back up. If you think of all those analogies with regard to the true nature or inherent nature or whatever you want to call it – do not try to grasp and do not try to understand, because it's quite useless. With the intellect we can understand something which is objective, material. We can also understand something abstract, like arithmetic or algebra. But that is all within the conscious intellect. But it does not go deep enough, the intellect does not go deep enough to grasp what actually is there. Nor does the intellect understand the powers of which we are so proud, that in fact it is not really as clear and objective as we think; because it is from underneath, and quite unbeknownst to myself, it is coloured by my wants and my dislikes, by my notions, convictions, and fancies. That I see according to those is something which I first of all, do not believe, and secondly, I will not accept.

'**Since ancient times, when good people of the Path have attained this, they have appeared and disappeared in the sea of birth and death, able to use it fully.**' That is, those who have followed the Path, the Great Way, and have come to an insight into this, have realised who they really are – 'they have appeared and disappeared in the sea of birth and death, able to use it fully.' Now, we must not take that as a kind of reincarnation or something like that; but rather as how it goes on the Wheel. 'Appeared and disappeared in the sea of birth and death, able to use it fully.' Coming up here, going down there. Coming up here, gone down there. But not haphazardly as if bound on that Wheel which is the fate of the delusion, of I, but fully and freely going into this or that form. In that there are also all the karmic connections. Once that insight has really cleared, then the karmic connections do not really come into it any more, unless there is something done which produces them again.

In the *Ratnakuta Sutra* there is a rather beautiful passage, in which the Buddha relates, how in some bygone age, when he was still a bodhisattva he travelled with a caravan of forty-nine merchants, trading up to the north of India. They were very successful, and on the way back loaded with goods, they camped in a remote place in the wilderness of the mountains. One evening one them was overcome by greed and of thought of killing all of them and returning home with all the wealth, and saying that he alone survived the attack of bandits or wild beasts. The bodhisattva was of course aware of this evil thought, and before that crime could be committed, he killed the would-be murderer, thus saving forty-nine lives.

But a killing is a killing and therefore the karmic price has to be accepted. So in a later incarnation, still a bodhisattva, he joined another caravan of merchants and travelled with them up to the north of India, and they were equally successful. On the way back, again camping in a remote area and sitting around the campfire, he told that story. He said that it was he, who had killed the merchant and that for every killing there is a price to be paid, and that the time was now ripe. Suddenly a large thorn grew out of the ground in front of him, and with all his strength he trod on it so that the thorn pierced his foot. At that moment one of the merchants rushed forwards and threw himself at the feet of the bodhisattva, crying, 'I myself have planned such an evil deed for tonight. I confess, having heard your story, I repent! Please help me, forgive me.' The bodhisattva nodded. The thorn withdrew back into the ground and the foot was healed.

This is very important, because we tend to think of karma mostly in terms of cause and effect. But you see, it not only goes back again to be repaid, it also goes forward – how it saved that person from trying to do the same deed. So we must never think of karma as a simple line, but as an intricate web that is connected with all our volitions. And we hang in that, all connected with this that and the other. But it was the bodhisattva himself who could choose where and as what he was going to emerge, as a merchant being of most use – once to prevent, once to save, appropriately responding to each situation, appearing and disappearing in the sea of birth and death, able to use it fully. Though the two situations seem unconnected, nothing in this world is separate – there is a thread running through them.

Now I would like to couple that story from the *Ratnakuta Sutra* together with our temple cat, Ginger. Our merchant-bodhisattva was now reborn at a time when the Zen school was flourishing in the middle of the T'ang dynasty. He became a Zen monk and was so outstanding that very soon he became a master. Many, many monks wanted to stay in his community and train and learn with him. It now grew so big that his normal zendo could not sleep and house all of them; so another one was built opposite and there were now two halls.

Then along came a pussy cat, as pussy cats do. Sometimes it went to one, and sometimes it went to the other hall. The monks befriended it and gave it food. But then they began to be a bit jealous of each other, and got the best food for it to make it more attached to them. Quite soon things became rather acrimonious, human nature being what it is. 'It likes us better!' 'No, it likes us better!'

One of the five most serious crimes is to disturb the peace of the Sangha. It means immediate exclusion from the community. So when the master heard that the monks were practically fighting with each other over that cat, he got hold of that cat and a kitchen knife and said, 'If you can say one word, the cat is safe. If you can't, I will kill it.' The monks were absolutely stunned, horrified and numb. – Whack! – and one half went to this side, and the other to that side.

Now with the monks deeply contrite and realising what they had been up to, the peace of the Sangha was restored, which is a good thing. But a killing is a killing. And so, there is naturally a debt to be paid. So the next time this bodhisattva-master appeared in a cat's body. As part of that debt to be paid, something happened to him when he was still practically a kitten. He was badly treated, lost a bit of his tail, and was generally quite traumatised. He managed to escape and then he lived wild for at least a year or two. Then, looking to find some food one day, he found that in one particular place there was something that was familiar. He was a cat, he didn't know what it was, but there was something definitely familiar, and that happened to be a Zen temple. He was seen slinking along the borders at the edge of the garden, terrified of everything. One person, seeing him day in, day out, brought him a saucer of milk, and though obviously very hungry, he ran away. So he left the saucer there and went away and hid, and the cat came and lapped it up. It took him three months to feel safe about coming from the border at the end of the garden to the kitchen steps. Every week about a metre closer.

If you see him now, having paid his debt, he is free. But whilst he is still in the cat's body, he can undertake his teaching, which he does, there is no doubt about it. However, he is still in the cat's body and is still imprinted, so loud or sudden movements, make him run away. That is the debt that is still in the process of being paid; but otherwise, having paid most of that debt, he now has a good life, and the life of a teacher for the rest of his life as a cat. Then no doubt with a clean slate he'll become a Zen master once more.

Now what do you say to that story? That is how the karmic con-cat-enations and webs really work! So perhaps we can take that to heart and realise that it is not just what we have done, but what we are doing which has its repercussions in the future too. If really free, then as Master Daie says, 'good people of the path who have attained this, appear and disappear in the sea of birth and death, able to use it fully,' as it is of best use for everything, because everything is interconnected, like Indra's net, which is the famous analogy for it. It is an infinite net, spread in all directions, with a multifaceted jewel at each node in the net. And each crystal reflects every other crystal and is itself reflected in every other crystal – a continuous interconnection. If we can feel that our life is like that, and realise that we reflect each other, then we can go along smoothly, appearing and disappearing in the sea of birth and death, and using it fully – not to the detriment, not to the harm, but to the benefit of everything.

'There is no deficit or surplus' in that use. Master Daie compares it to **'like cutting up sandalwood, each piece is it.'** You cannot increase it, you cannot decrease it, neither more nor less, it just is. In everything, in every action. In cutting a piece of bread, in lifting a finger, in whatever it is, in response to the demands of the situation. Like cutting up sandalwood, each piece is it. And when it comes to that, then things work together in harmony.

If we feel connected all round like that, then we are beginning to take our first step in the Four Divine Abodes, the *Brahma-viharas*. The first one is good will which naturally flows out of the human heart. The next one is compassion; and we must never mix up compassion with sentimentality, because compassion can be quite energetic when necessary. I remember in my professional time, as a geology student, there was a lot of mountain work. In the beginning we always went with a guide, and on difficult and exposed spots we were roped together. If somebody got mountain sick, usually on a rather difficult and exposed place, you could notice them becoming quite pale; when the guide noticed something like that, he shinned up to that person and whacked him in the face. And you think, 'My goodness me! He's already in that frightful state. How cruel, how unbelievable!' But on the contrary, with that whack, as the aggression comes up in the smacked person, they're over it. But you don't do it automatically. You have to see the conditions. So compassion is understanding, and compassionately doing what is necessary at that moment. That is the second of the Divine Abodes.

The third one is the joy, the joy of seeing that somebody has got something that pleases, and having joy with him or her instead of feeling, 'Oh, I wish I had that myself.' You see the difference? It is sympathetic joy. The last one is equanimity. But equanimity, not in the sense of indifference, but rather that which cannot be upset by anything. Fully compassionate, seeing what is necessary and doing it. So with that equanimity – perhaps it is better translated as serenity – there is also the fully warm-hearted looking and seeing; seeing that life is also suffering; and to live, not by going and doing something about the suffering at the other end of the world, but to be here, right here where we are, with willingness to take part and to help wherever a helping hand is needed. Not with the feeling that I should do it, but with quiet naturalness. If you are walking behind somebody and that person stumbles, you do not need to think, 'Shall I help?' Your arm shoots out by itself. Isn't it so? And it is in that sense too that the

Brahma-viharas have taken over instead of the sense of I. Now, can we take that home, and in our own life, be a little bit less concerned with my feelings, with my this and my that – and instead open up and take part in what is.

LETTER 18 to HSU TUN-CHI (continued)

The Text

Where do the passions of birth and death arise from? Where can it be located when gathering the causes to produce the effect? Since there is no place to locate it, Buddha is illusion and Dharma is illusion. The three worlds, twenty-five states of being, the sense organs, sense objects and consciousnesses, are utterly empty. When you get to this realm, there is no place to put even the word Buddha. If even the word Buddha has no applicability, where is there True Thusness, Buddha-nature, Enlightenment, or Nirvana? Thus the Great Being Fu said, 'Fearing that people will give rise to a view of annihilation, we provisionally establish empty names.'

Students of the Path who do not understand this principle are always going to the stories of people of old entering the Path looking for mysteries and subtleties and marvels, seeking interpretations and understanding. They are unable to see the moon and forget the pointing finger, unable to cut directly through with one blow. This is what Yung Chia called understanding the empty fist as though there were actually something in it, falsely making up wonders within the senses and their objects. Such people vainly imprison themselves within the passions of the five clumps, the sense-organs, objects, and consciousnesses of sensation, the twenty-five states of being – the Tathagata said they are to be pitied. Haven't you seen Yen Tou's saying? 'Just have no desires and depend on nothing, then you'll be capable of goodness.'

This is Master Daie at his most direct. **'Where do the passions of birth and death arise from?'** The passions of birth and death; coming into samsara, the world we are in and suffer from. Birth, and the moment birth is there, death is guaranteed. But we in our normal life rejoice about birth and fear death. Where do those passions – wanting and not wanting, liking and loathing – where do they arise from? It couldn't be more directly pointed at, could it? Where do they arise from, do we know? And the next question, **'Where can it be located when gathering the causes to produce the effect?'** In other words, the karmic connections.

Where is that place, where can we find it? **'Since there is no place to locate it,'** where the passions arise from, karmic causes coming together, **'Buddha is illusion and Dharma is illusion.'** We are here in the teachings of Nagarjuna's Madhyamaka, where everything is mind only, thought only, illusion, not real. 'Since there is no place to locate it, Buddha is illusion and Dharma is illusion', concepts of the mind, both Buddha and Dharma and everything else. Though useful perhaps as stepping stones, but the moment you cling to them, they become the great obstacle. In the same vein, Master Rinzai warns, 'If you see the Buddha, kill the Buddha; if you see the Patriarchs, kill the Patriarchs....' Do not stick to them, because otherwise there is no free movement within the circumstances.

We cling passionately to our thought formations. Master Daie in this particular passage is desperately trying to take them away. Buddha is illusion and Dharma is illusion. **'The three worlds, twenty-five states of being, the sense organs, sense objects and consciousnesses are utterly empty.'** The three worlds – of desire, form and no form. The world of desire in which we live is the six states of being on the Wheel of Change. The world of form is pure thought, the meditative states, and the world of no form is empty consciousness; in the first two we have our being. Altogether they make up the twenty-five states of being, starting from animals through to the human state, through to the Arhat state with the Two Vehicles and the Five Vehicles and the bodhisattvas. Then we have the sense organs, sense objects, and consciousnesses, all of which are special teachings in Buddhism: and yet they are utterly empty, says Master Daie.

'When you get to this realm, there is no place to put even the word Buddha; if even the word Buddha has no applicability, where is there True Thusness, Buddha-nature, Enlightenment, or Nirvana?' Just so many empty words. **'Therefore the Great Being Fu, said, "Fearing that people will give rise to a view of annihilation, we provisionally establish empty names."'** When everything is taken away, I get frightened. I then also get the idea that the entire Buddha-dharma might be about annihilation, which is obviously not true. Therefore provisionally empty names are established. And though knowing right from the beginning that they are empty, yet we work with them. We do not need to know or go into all the details of the entire Buddhist canon, which fills libraries; but we need to be very well acquainted with the basics of the Buddha's teaching, because with those we have to work, and with those we have to confront ourselves, so that the passions of birth and death can be clearly seen into, and with that the whole delusion begins to get a little bit wobbly.

Master Daie then continues, **'Students of the Path who do not understand this principle'** – this principle that there is nothing to hold on to or cling to – **'are always going to the stories of the old masters entering the Path,'** looking to see how they did it, **'looking for mysteries and subtleties and marvels and seeking interpretations and understanding.'** Whatever interpretations, whatever explanations, they are all in the field of I, in the field of opposites and within the parameters of 'my' understanding. What is beyond understanding – well, that we can't talk about, can we? But that is what really matters. The heart inclines to it, and the heart wants to participate in that. In a way you could say it is mysterious, but if you then put the mystery into pictures, you have already made it into something quite different.

Searching for mysteries and interpretations, **'they are unable to see the moon and forget the pointing finger.'** We usually stick with the finger that is pointing – and the moon we do not see, because we are riveted on the finger. We want to look at the moon, but are not yet ready. We haven't got the strength; we are also a bit frightened. Because, unable to see the moon to which the finger points, they **'cannot cut directly through with one blow'** so that it opens up. One blow – and suddenly the whole caboodle of I with my notions, convictions etc. is shattered, and what is actually there, and always has been there, becomes perceptible. Why is it not perceptible if it has always been there? Because superimposed on what has always been there, is the whole bundle of our opinions, likes, dislikes and convictions. That whole bundle is, of course, I – because of that, what always has been there is not seen.

'This is what Yung Chia (Yoka Daishi) **called understanding the empty fist as though there were actually something in it,'** You know the game, we have played it with children, holding up an empty fist and asking, 'Which hand is it in? Which hand?' Somehow understanding and believing there are all kinds of things in it, whatever it might be, from a handkerchief to a jewel. Understanding the empty fist. Not only are we eternally curious, but we also believe there are all kinds of wonders and fantastic things, **'falsely making up wonders within the senses and their objects.'** This is the natural delusion of I. **'Such people vainly imprison themselves within the passions of the five clumps,'** – the five aggregates, the five *skandhas*, **'the sense organs, objects and consciousnesses of sensation,'** – these are the eighteen *dhatus*, **'the twenty-five states of being'**; in other words, in all the formations that we can go into and get deluded by. **'The Tathagata said they are to be pitied.'**

Master Hakuin phrases it as, 'In the midst of water, pitifully crying from thirst.' Well, it is the nature of I. And the more we get into Buddhism, the more we see that it turns on that question of I, and No-I. It is the nature of I not to be able to accept what is here and now, because we think there is something better, greater, more beautiful and we will not accept what is. Because we do not see the wholeness and the fullness of what is, we feel we need to make special wonders. The Buddhist analogy for this is painting horns on the hare and legs on the snake – more than what is, there must always be more than what is.

Master Daie then asks, **'Haven't you seen Yen T'ou's** (Ganto) **saying, "Just have no desires and depend on nothing, then you'll be capable of goodness."'** Just have no desires! But I can't help having desires. This is then exactly where it comes down to the basic Buddhist teachings of the Three Fires: delusion, desire, and aversion. So 'just have no desires' – it is naturally not possible for me, however much I might try. And I immediately say, 'But how can you live without desire? It's not possible. If you are hungry, you must eat, and you can't help but have preferences.' It is also important that we look clearly into that. If desire is something, which I must have, then it is hot, and that is a passion. When it is just a natural liking, a preference for something without any kind of heat, there's nothing wrong with that, and the same also with the other things. If I want to get rid of it because I have an itch, I scratch it. That's all there is to it. There are preferences on the one hand, and then on the other hand the heat of the Fires when 'I must have' or 'I must get rid of' – and we often confuse the two.

'Just have no desires and depend on nothing.' Do not lean on anything, do not attach to anything, depend on nothing, stand on one's own feet. In twelve years of the traditional Zen training, under two different masters coming from different lines, but teaching as they all do with one voice, what I heard from them most was: 'Look at the place where your own feet stand!' In my experience, it proceeded something like this: 'Yes, yes, I do know that place in any case… but, what is over there? What is over there? That is what I have come for – I already know the place where I am standing.' But then slowly, looking down, perhaps half way down to the navel, a quiet voice came up, urging – 'what do you think it's saying?' And the initial reaction is always, 'Better not look!' But it is with that 'Better not!' that one has to grapple, because only then, says Ganto, 'will you be capable of goodness.'

With that goodness that Ganto speaks of, we again come to *metta* or *maitri*, goodwill, the first of the Four Divine Abodes – the *brahma viharas* that goodness, which is the warmth of the heart. How does that come about? I do not have to 'send it', as in our 'I the doer' delusion we always understand it to mean. For if there are no more desires, and there is no more depending on anything, goodwill spreads from a heart that is freed from the shackles of 'I only' and flows out and naturally warms all it touches. Because there is the real awareness that in any case the world is marvellous; it all is – yes, even pains and horrors and darkness – but it is just a marvellous, beautiful, incredible thing in which we take part; and also realise that it's us taking part, being part of it, that has made it as it is. With that comes a first understanding of contrition and repentance; and consequently a greater willingness to bow down, because our behaviour is not only hurting ourselves, but it is also hurting others. Whatever we do, it inevitably touches others.

Freely partaking in what at this moment is, means being in harmony with everything that is, a harmony that goes well beyond what I can understand and that affects others too. So then to freely flow with it, as Master Ganto says, you'll be capable of goodness. Take that home with you, and let it flow out freely in your individual circumstances, surroundings, and jobs and family.

LETTER 18 to HSU TUN-CHI (continued)

THE TEXT

All this time there has just been a lump of flesh born of your parents. Unless you come up with a bit of energy, it is subject to the control of others. What else is there outside the lump of flesh? What can you hold to be wonderful, mysterious, or marvellous? What can you take to be Enlightenment or Nirvana? What can you take to be true Thusness or Buddha-nature? You wanted to investigate this affair to the end, but from the first you have not come to the root of its reality. You just wanted to seek knowledge and understanding from the public cases of the ancients. Even if you had a thorough knowledge and understanding of the entire Buddhist canon, on the last day of your life, when birth and death comes upon you, you won't be able to use it at all.

We are still reading from this long letter to somebody called Hsu Tun-chi; he seems to be a high government official, and very intelligent. He was apparently talking in his letter to Master Daie about all kinds of intellectual understanding. And so in this long letter, Master Daie continues, **'All this time there has just been a lump of flesh born of your parents.'** That's all there is, isn't it? A lump of flesh born of your parents. Master Rinzai also using that same phrase 'a lump of flesh' says, 'In this lump of flesh, there is somebody who goes in and out all day long through the sense gates. Have you met him yet?'

Master Daie continues, **'Unless you come up with a bit of energy, it is subject to the control of others.'** Unless you come up with a bit of energy, it – that is that lump of flesh – is subject to the control of others. Not only others around, not only people, but also to circumstances and to the control of the passions, of the Fires. This is what we need energy for. And the energy comes from the Daily Life Practice, which consists of giving ourselves into what at the moment is being done anyway. It also consists of keeping the Precepts. It also consists of sticking to the timetable; and it naturally also includes zazen. That, really religiously kept, actually creates, or rather produces, the energy which is necessary. We cannot make the energy, it's not ours; but it can be cultivated. If it is relentlessly cultivated, then sooner or later it is sufficient to look, to stand, and not to be subject to the control of others.

Now Master Daie says, 'Unless you come up with a bit of energy, it is subject to the control of others.' When we look at our Daily Life Practice – 'Well, I should have got up at six, but I was so tired. Well, not today perhaps. No, actually, it would be much better if I did it the other way, not according to the timetable.' So it goes all day long – 'And if I now have my lunch a little bit earlier, then I could have a little bit longer afterwards for this, that, or the other,' – and so it goes throughout the whole day. Though we believe we do it in order to make life easier for us, it really only means that we just haven't got sufficient energy, have never cultivated it, and are thus continuously subject to the control, not only of others, but also as it is implied here too, of our own whims. And so nothing will change. And then I say, 'Oh, for twenty years I have done this practice, and nothing much has changed.' Well, naturally not. Because I have not thrown myself into it sufficiently, the energy has not been cultivated; and it is only with this energy that something begins to change. Otherwise, we are subject to the control of others.

Master Daie then asks, **'What else is there outside the lump of flesh?'** Look! It's clearly limited. What else is there outside that lump of flesh? Anything? Oh yes, there are the trees, and there is heaven and there is hell – but that is not outside that lump of flesh, that is only in the mind, in thoughts. Concretely what else is there outside the lump of flesh?

Master Daie now goes on asking, **'What can you hold to be wonderful, mysterious, or marvellous?'** That's what I'm after, something more than what is already here in any case, which are just my ordinary daily things. I'm after something 'wonderful, mysterious, or marvellous.' Something that really grips me, that is what I'm after. **'What can you take to be Enlightenment or Nirvana?'** – which I also want. **'What can you take to be True Thusness or Buddha-nature?'** All these things, I want them; and the question is: Why do I want them? If I really look carefully, there is I wanting them, for the very good reason that I feel myself insufficient and want to be lifted, actually, to be absolutely secure. Isn't it incredible that all those things that I lust after are things to lift me out of myself. And that is exactly where the Buddha's Way points. It's just that I do not want to go that way. I want to 'have'; and this is where the delusion comes in – I want to be enlightened, I want to be lifted out of myself. That is looking at it the wrong way. Again, it is not that I need to have it in order to become secure, it is much more the question of I myself, being the delusion, getting out of the way. Because once out of the way, things are as they are, whether you call it True Thusness, Buddha-nature, Nirvana or Enlightenment – they are all different names for the same thing – and it is seen that there is no I at the centre. There are two types of consciousness: the one which is ego-centred, that wants the 'wonderful, mysterious, marvellous' to make me secure; and the other one, that just – perhaps the best word would be 'behold' – beholds things just as they are.

Master Daie then continues to his correspondent, **'You wanted to investigate this affair to the end, but from the very first you have not come to the root of its reality. You just wanted to seek knowledge and understanding from the public cases of the ancients.'** 'You wanted to investigate this affair to the end' – this affair, the Great Matter of birth and death, which is in Zen language precisely the Buddha's Path, until it opens into True Thusness, or we could also say into No-I. 'You wanted to investigate this affair but from the very first,' says Master Daie, 'you have not come to the root of its reality.' From the beginning you did not really want to get into it. 'You just wanted to seek knowledge and understanding from the public cases of the old masters.' Knowledge and understanding – so we read books, swallow them by the dozen, go to lectures, read more and more, acquire more and more details and don't even realise that they are all different aspects of the same thing – just swallow and swallow, believing that we will come to the root in that way.

We might then ask ourselves, why we are told we should do a bit of study, if Master Daie speaks against all this studying and reading of the texts. Well, perhaps we can say that without the framework it does not work. But the framework though good is not enough, the rest has to be filled in by our own practice. If we do not practise wholeheartedly, if we do not work sufficiently to cultivate that energy, then whatever we read is only intellectual understanding, intellectual knowledge. But being foolish and deluded, we actually believe that what we understand in the head, what we have read and now believe we know, that this really is true. But it isn't, because it leaves the body out. Therefore, when it really comes down to it, when it comes to the crunch, it caves in, it will not hold. Only what is learned in the body, what is familiar, really becomes one's own; and that can then not be forgotten any more.

Think of riding a bicycle. Once you have learned how to cycle and ridden in the past, then even if you haven't ridden a bicycle for thirty years and you suddenly come into the situation where you need to ride a bicycle, you don't have to relearn it, you don't have to remember how to do it. You just get on it; and perhaps the first couple of pedals might be a bit wobbly, but after that you can peacefully ride away. That's all there is to it. But if you have read something, and really believed you understood it, and for thirty years – or even five years – have never had occasion to think about it, do you think you'd remember it?

What we need as our framework is only the basics: the Three Signs of Being, the Fires, the Four Noble Truths, the Paramitas and the Chain of Causation. The rest we leave as frills and flounces, which do not really help us on our way. But in our practice we are diligent, so that the energy is cultivated and increases.

As far as the body is concerned, it's not from thinking about it, but from keeping it up, and keeping it up, that the energy arises. To seek knowledge and understanding only from the old records, or from the public cases of the old masters, that is not possible, because as Master Daie says, **'Even if you had a thorough knowledge and understanding of the entire Buddhist canon, on the last day of your life, when birth and death comes upon you, you won't be able to use it at all.'** It is not possible by thought, by intellect, or by reasoning, to come even near to the living thing, the living point. 'Even if you had a thorough knowledge and understanding of the entire Buddhist canon' – the entire Buddhist canon fills about three rooms completely; to read all of it is practically impossible in one lifetime. Even if you had a thorough knowledge and understanding of it, 'on the last day of your life, when birth and death comes upon you, you won't be able to use it at all.' As to this last moment, Master Sokei-an said most beautifully, 'When that moment comes, there's nothing further you can do. You fold your hands and you go with it, to where you always have been.' Always have been – the Sixth Patriarch: 'Before thinking of good and bad, what is the True Face before mother and father were born?' Always have been; before mother and father were born; they all say the same thing. I haven't got a clue about that. And as long as I hop about in thoughts, this living point, out of which the whole of life comes, will always be unknown, and there will always be a separate I, and the other side of I is fear. To know where we have always been; that is what is found if the training is thoroughly followed, if it is truly cultivated. That cannot be found in books, that cannot be found in scriptures, that comes from one's own experience, and that is where the Buddha's Way brings us. Or as an old Master said, 'Then begins another life.'

LETTER 18 to HSU TUN-CHI (continued)

THE TEXT

> There is another sort: as soon as they hear a wise adviser speak of such an affair, they still use their conceptual minds to figure it out, and say, 'If it's like this, then won't I fall into emptiness?'

Ten out of ten gentlemen of affairs entertain this kind of view. I have no choice but to tell them, 'You haven't ever reached emptiness, so what are you afraid of? It's as if you are trying to leap out of the water before the boat has capsized.' When I see that they don't understand, I don't spare the mouth-work, but try once more to create trailing vines for them. I say, 'This one who fears falling into emptiness – has he been emptied or not? If your eyes aren't empty, how can you see forms? If your ears aren't empty, how can you hear sounds? If your nose isn't empty, how can you smell scents? If your tongue isn't empty, how can you taste flavours? If your body isn't empty, how can you feel contact? If your consciousness isn't empty, how can you distinguish the myriad phenomena?'

VEN. MYOKYO-NI'S COMMENTS

Master Daie cites somebody else, who is equally trying to grasp where the road actually goes. **'There is another sort: as soon as they hear a wise adviser speak of such an affair, they still use their conceptual minds to figure it out, and say, "If it's like this, then won't I fall into emptiness?"'** Using the conceptual mind, we get frightened. This diminishing of I is what we are afraid of. We only need to scratch the surface a little bit, and what happens? Resentment and fear immediately crop up, and I have to cover it up to make myself somebody, in my own eyes and in your eyes too, because whatever I want has nothing to do with the fact that factually I am nothing. We carefully repeat the Buddha's teachings, but we still don't believe them – *anatta*, No-I. But I cling to that 'I' with everything I've got. Therefore, it is very difficult for us, particularly in these days when we haven't got anything but that 'I' to hold onto. We have neither religious nor cultural values anymore; we are only left with the dreary little 'peeps' of I, and to that we cling, and so we are easily frightened. We cannot get away from it, and the training therefore presents real difficulties for us. Because actually all the training does is to peel away one layer of I after another until there is nothing left. I resist this becoming nothing, not realising that with that the fullness opens.

So, when this sort of person tries to figure it out intellectually, then fear comes up – 'If it's like this, then won't I fall into emptiness, won't I vanish?' **'Ten out of ten gentlemen of affairs,'** says Master Daie, **'entertain this kind of view. I have no choice but to tell them, "You haven't ever reached emptiness, so what are you afraid of?"'**

What are you afraid of? Like with each of the other Fires – and fear/aversion is one of them – if you have got it, reason does not make any inroad into it. I think I have told you often enough of a simple analogy. We human beings always have had the same concerns. Yet I feel, 'No, mine are special.' They seem so to me because I am something special, am I not? If you have a phobia about spiders and I have a phobia about mice, we have to see it that way. We may laugh at the others' phobia, while taking our own very seriously. But neither of us realises what it really is, that what we are both suffering from, is the real terror of fear. What we really need to see is the common ground, explain to each other that what you feel when you see the spider is exactly what I feel when I see the mouse. Then we know exactly how we both feel and that it has nothing to do with the object. We mistakenly always pin things on the objects, rather than seeing the experience, the living thing itself that is in ourselves. If we can deal with and reverently and carefully face the tremendous power that is in us, whether it manifests as fear or as anger or whatever, and give it houseroom, while still keeping the form – and this is why we are so careful about the form – then it can emerge in its human form instead of as the primitive energy, which is destructive.

So, trying to figure it out intellectually and then wondering, 'Won't I fall into emptiness?' – Master Daie puts that very accurately when he says, 'Ten out of ten gentlemen of affairs entertain this kind of view.' In other words, that's what we all feel. Defensive of our 'I', whatever it is, we must, I must, be something. Naturally, I would like to be the best, or the greatest or whatever – but if I can't be that, then I can at least be the worst. Better than nothing. Anything but nothing.

Master Daie continues, because this is how they feel, he has no choice but to tell them, 'You haven't ever reached emptiness, so what are you afraid of?' That is a very helpful question. We are not afraid of something that we actually know. We are afraid of something that we do not know. We have not reached emptiness, so what are we afraid of? I do not feel at one with a mouse, so I am afraid of it. By and large we do not know death, so we are afraid of it. We know pain, and of course are frightened and do not want to have it; but there is a great difference between worrying about it and actually suffering from it; and we can certainly blow things up in our minds with worry and anxiety.

Master Daie cites a lovely analogy, **'It's as if you're trying to leap out of the water before the boat has capsized.'** – while you are comfortably sitting in the boat, trying to leap out and swim for safety. Actually, that is an ideal thing to remind ourselves of when next we create a problem again, to think: Are we trying to leap out of the water while still sitting comfortably in the boat?

Having told them that, Master Daie then continues, **'When I see that they don't understand, I don't spare the mouth-work'** – in other words, I go on talking – **'and try once more to create trailing vines for them'** – trailing vines, wisteria vines are usually meant by that. It means trying to explain with words, and getting more and more wordy, though it's not really necessary. But he sees that they don't understand, and so out of sheer compassion he doesn't spare the words, spare the mouth-work, and once more gives them a few trailing vines to hold on to. **'I say: "This one who fears falling into emptiness – has he been emptied or not?"'** That's a good question, isn't it? This one who fears falling into emptiness, this one who fears becoming nothing, this one who fears vanishing, has he been emptied or not? Or has he still got a whole bundle of opinions, notions, ideas, convictions, wants, dislikes inside? And not only just inside. Is he perhaps nothing but a bundle of ideas, notions, convictions, and attached to them? That attachment to the whole bundle – is that bundle anything but delusion? That is exactly what 'I' is. And this one who fears falling into emptiness – has he been emptied or not? Empty out first: is there any fear left?

Master Daie now very kindly explains in detail, **"'If your eyes are not empty, how can you see forms?'"** We have got all kinds of ideas. If your eyes aren't empty, if they are full of dust, how can you see clearly? There is a Zen proverb which says, 'Though gold dust is precious, in the eyes it obscures vision.'

"'If your ears aren't empty, how can you hear sounds?'" If your ears are full of 'boom, boom, boom, boom', you can't hear the wind in the trees. To hear, the ears have to be empty. But with our body we do know it. If we really want to see something very clearly, don't we direct the eyes and focus? If we want to really listen, don't we turn the ear to the sound? Emptying ourselves out so that there is nothing there, and so that what comes in, as 'I' goes out, can be clearly distinguished. Can I hear something whilst thinking of something quite different? I will hear a few garbled words, and have a garbled idea about it, but I won't have heard what is said. If your ears are not empty, how can you hear sounds?

"'If your nose is not empty, how can you smell scents? If your tongue is not empty, how can you taste flavours?'" Try to have a lump of sugar on your tongue, and see if you can taste something savoury. It won't work, will it?

"'If your body is not empty, how can you feel contact?'" If you are really engrossed in a conversation with a friend or having a hefty argument and someone tries to get your attention by tapping you on the shoulder, you won't be able to feel it. If your body isn't empty, how can you feel contact?

And **"'If your consciousness'"** – intellect, mind, however you like to translate it – **"'isn't empty, how can you distinguish the myriad phenomena?'"** If I have an idea of what something looks like, how can I really see it? If I have a clear understanding of something, as I believe I do, then I can see only that; 'how can you distinguish the myriad phenomena?' A pebble on the road, a leaf on a tree; if I hold on to it, I can't see the tree, because I'm only seeing the road. If that intellect/consciousness is not empty, how can you distinguish the myriad phenomena?

This is why in the Zen School and also in the Mahayana in general, there is always talk of the Heart Mirror. The Heart Mirror reflects exactly what is before it. It doesn't cancel anything out; it doesn't highlight the important things. It just reflects whatever falls into it, just as it is. If it is turned away, it doesn't hold on to the old object or try and superimpose it on top of the new object. 'If your mind is not empty, how can you distinguish the myriad phenomena?'

Consequently, we tend to see as if through a veil; there is something of our mind draped over things so that we do not see what is actually there. The heart is not addressed, is not satisfied, because it is not lived, since we live in our head only. So from time to time the heart – in a desperate attempt I like to think – jumps out so that I really need to take cognisance of it. And it drapes itself over an object, like a shimmering veil. That object then becomes absolutely fascinating, irresistible. That is the story of the golden ball that we told previously. That is exactly what happens when something suddenly grips us like that, whatever it may be. But there's only one possibility then, and that is that it has to come to a sobering event, like the monk stranded out on the branch. This is also a good example of why the Fires, the passions of must have, violent rejection and fear – all of them coming from the delusion of I – why they invariably lead to some kind of misfortune, why they are dangerous and destructive.

Therefore emptying out is an absolutely essential thing, for when the 'I' is emptied out, I can see what really is. Normally I can't – for instance looking at the Buddha image over there, suddenly I'm thinking, 'I'm glad Maggie is here because it needs another brass cleaning, she can do it during the work period tomorrow, and it will look really nice then. She's always done it so well.' And I do not really see the Buddha-rupa at all, do I? I've only got my ideas about it, whatever they might be. It's the same with our ears.

Listen to Master Daie. Listen to yourself. Listen into yourself. When that fear arises, then look at that fear too. Open up to it. Do not close up against it and try to shove it away. The closing up against and trying to shove away is our greatest enemy. Open up and look at it, and give it houseroom. But don't let it carry you away. Give it houseroom, try to become acquainted with it. Make friends with it. Then things begin to look different. When that fear is gone, and the true emptiness has opened up, in which there is a free flowing with everything that is, and no obstruction at all, then things begin to look a little bit different. Could you please ponder that.

LETTER 18 to HSU TUN-CHI (continued)

The Text

> Didn't the Buddha say that there is no eye, no ear, no nose, no tongue, no body or mind; no form, no sound, no scent, no

flavour, no touch, or phenomena? No sense-organs or sense-objects or consciousnesses of sensation; no twenty-five states of being? Even sravakas, pratyekabuddhas, bodhisattvas, and buddhas, as well as the doctrines preached by the Buddha: Enlightenment, Nirvana, True Thusness, Buddha-nature, along with those who expound these doctrines, and those who listen to these doctrines, those who make up these teachings and those who accept these teachings – none of these exist. When you reach such a realisation, do you call it empty or not empty? Do you call it Buddha, bodhisattva, sravaka or pratyekabuddha? Do you call it Enlightenment or Nirvana? Do you call it True Thusness or Buddha-nature? Let those who say they are intelligent and quick-witted and not fooled by others try to determine what's what here. If you can settle it correctly, you should stay in a grass hut by yourself and live beyond the gate of the monastery. If you cannot determine for sure, just don't open your big mouth to speak of things that are beyond you.

'Didn't the Buddha say there is no eye, no ear, no nose, no tongue, no body or mind; no form, no sound, no scent, no flavour, no touch, or phenomena? No sense-organs or sense-objects or consciousnesses of sensation; no twenty-five states of being?' You know that we chant it at least three times, most likely four times a day? Where does it come from? The *Heart Sutra*, isn't it. Then you can ask, but what does it actually mean? If we are really willing to look at it and not just chant it mindlessly, we note – no eye, no ear, no nose. No things. All wiped out. Not only an empty room, but no room either.

Master Daie takes it further, '**No sense-organs, or sense-objects or consciousnesses of sensation; and no twenty-five states of being.**' He already mentioned these twenty-five realms of existence earlier in this letter, but he now goes on to include, '**Even sravakas, pratyekabuddhas, bodhisattvas, and buddhas, as well as the doctrines preached by the Buddha: Enlightenment, Nirvana, True Thusness, Buddha-nature, along with those who expound these doctrines, and those who listen to these doctrines, those who make up these teachings and those who accept these teachings,**' and he concludes, '**none of these exist.**' That is a radical emptying out, isn't it? Nagarjuna's Great Negation.

With that we come deep into the realm of the Mahayana: the *Kegon Sutra* or *Flower Ornament Sutra*, which is the teaching of One in All and All in One, but also One is All and All is One. For this we have already had the analogy of Indra's net: a room full of netting, and at each cross section of the net hangs a clear jewel, and this clear jewel reflects every other jewel, and is itself reflected in every other jewel.

This also takes us to the doctrine of the Two Truths: on the one hand, the principle of the real, which is *sunyata*, that emptiness we are so frightened of, and on the other, the shifting unreal things which we are, as well as everything else that is formed. The Two Truths — seen from this side there is a continuous shifting, like a flowing river, but with its continuous shifting, where nothing lasts, nothing is real. But that which actually gives it form, which is in the river, which is in all being, we do not know, we cannot know, much as we try to; but we can live it, it can be lived. As a matter of fact, it is lived whether we know it or not, sometimes to the detriment and to the unhappiness of the being, and sometimes, if it is seen into, then there is a smooth flowing with it, satisfactory, quite joyful.

In order to arrive at this point, then whatever we believe in, whatever our convictions tell us, whatever ideals we have – all of which, to some of us at least, are dearer than life itself – all that has to go by the board. Therefore, Master Daie is very careful to include everything, even the entire teachings. It belongs to the shifting unreal, it's only ideas in the head, systems made out of it. Even if they're correct as systems, they're only systems. Words in themselves are nothing, shifting. The real truth, which is beyond it, is the principle that informs all those shifting forms. And all conform to that principle, knowingly or unknowingly.

Master Daie then asks, **'When you reach such a realisation,'** the realisation that none of these exist, **'do you call it empty or not empty?'** Either way, you just make something out of it, and it's wrong. Or **'Do you call it Buddha, bodhisattva, sravaka, pratyekabuddha?'** Since earliest times we have tried putting names to things in the hope of understanding them. It is true that Palaeolithic magic consisted in knowing the name of a thing, because knowing the name of a thing gives power over the thing. But today things are very much changed. Today we only have empty names without any understanding of them. So, what do we call it? Just another name. **'Do you call it Enlightenment or Nirvana, or True Thusness or Buddha-nature?'** – you see, all those things, different names – do they point to the same thing or not? That is what we need to find out.

Master Daie then says, **'Let those who say they are intelligent and quick-witted and not fooled by others, try to determine what's what here.'** Find out by doing the training, find out by yourself. Without that, to quote the Zen phrase, it's only 'licking the spittle of others.' **'If you can settle it correctly, you should stay in a grass hut by yourself and live beyond the gate of the monastery.'** In other words, you are then not in need of any further training. There's nothing lacking, or 'no more learning' as the texts say. When we read in the Zen stories of the monks, going on pilgrimage, going from place to place, we have the impression that any monk could do it. But actually this is not so, because when a would-be trainee came to a monastery, that's where they stayed and trained. They might stay there for their lifetime. But if it was somebody who really had looked into it, and had insight, then they would go on a pilgrimage from monastery to monastery, from master to master, asking questions – and this is where we have the texts with the questions – asking questions, to see whether there was still something lacking. If they found that there was still something lacking, they would stay at that monastery until that was seen into. So those pilgrim monks were very well settled already.

If completely settled, there is no need for any training. There is nothing lacking, or there is the state of 'no more learning' and just participating in the circumstances as they are. In other words, live life as it is within the situations. But, says Master Daie, **'If you cannot determine for sure, just don't open your big mouth to speak of things that are beyond you,'** which we really like to do, greatly taken by such fascinating things as *satori*.

LETTER 18 to HSU TUN-CHI (continued)

THE TEXT

> When men of power want to investigate this one great affair to the end, they all break down their facades, and with bold spirit draw their spines up straight. Do not go along with the feelings of others. Take your own constant point of doubt and stick it on your forehead. Always be as if you owed someone millions, with nothing to repay with when pressed for payment, fearful

of humiliation by others. Only thus will you have some direction in the task of finding urgency where there is no urgency, getting busy where there is no pressure, and finding importance where there is no importance. Work diligently day and night, while eating and drinking, when joyful or angry, in clean places or unclean places, in family gatherings, when entertaining guests, when dealing with official business in your job, when concluding a betrothal – all of these are first class times to make efforts to arouse and alert yourself and awaken.

Ven. Myokyo-ni's Comments

Master Daie puts it very clearly, **'When men of power want to investigate this one great affair to the end'** – men of power do not give up, really want to go into it, through the emptiness, through the fear of the emptiness, through the whole lot, to find out where we come from, where we go back to, who we really are. This one great affair that lifts out of the narrow confines of 'I' into what actually is, and of which there is only a partaking, not a looking and speculating about. This one great affair, they want to investigate this one great affair to the end.

It is not possible to investigate this one great affair with thought and reason, thinking about it and forming intellectual ideas and notions about it. This is not the one great affair. The one great affair has to be penetrated all the way through. Therefore, if they want to investigate this one great affair to the end, **'they all break down their facades, and with bold spirit draw their spines up straight.'** Their facades, the armour, in which we hide comfortably or uncomfortably from the outside, so that it cannot hurt us. The facades, the masks that we have, behind which and with which we confront our surroundings, those facades – the businessman, the high official, the merchant, the clever one, the humble one, the one that doesn't understand anything – all those facades, the roles that we play, all are broken down resolutely 'and with bold spirit draw their spines up straight.'

You know what that 'spines up straight' actually means; let's go through the whole thing once more, physically: 'I am oh, so tired! I'm in such a state. I really can't go on any more. Oh dear, what shall I do?' Go into that physical 'Oh dear, oh dear, what am I going to do? How can I hide myself from all the terrible things that there are about?' But then Nicky looks at Myokyo sitting like that, and says, 'What's the matter with you, Myokyo-ni? You've gone all to pieces. Pull yourself together!' and just pulling oneself together – easy thing with a straight spine, isn't it? Is that a different feeling?

So 'with bold spirit they draw their spines up straight.' But one other thing happens when they pull their spine up straight. It has to be a bold feeling, because that side is then freely available. This is what Master Rinzai means when he says, 'show liver, spleen, stomach and gall,' to open up – that is what the fearlessness is about.

Now with bold spirits and spines drawn up straight Master Daie says, **'Do not go along with the feelings of others.'** What someone else says, what someone believes, what someone feels. Do not go along with the feelings of others. **'Take your own constant point of doubt and stick it on your forehead.'** That constant point of doubt: what is it? 'I don't know. I don't know. I'm not sure.' Take it and stick it on your forehead. Stay with it. When you read in the Zen texts about a monk asking the master a question, and the master hits him, it is not because the monk does not know, that is not when they hit; it's when the monk hesitates, that's when he hits. Therefore, your own constant point of doubt, stick it on your forehead. Let it freely be there. Air it, and see what happens. Stick it on your forehead, and go on doubting, and stick to it.

'Always be,' says Master Daie, **'as if you owed someone millions, with nothing to repay with when pressed for payment, fearful of humiliation by others.'** Always be as if you owed someone millions, with nothing to repay with when pressed for payment. That's a rather urgent situation, isn't it? You can't forget it. Or can you, what do you think? Can you? This pressure of 'What am I going to do?' Master Hakuin has quite a good analogy for that, though it does not have to do with millions. He tells about somebody going to a market with three gold pieces to buy whatever he needs. It's a rainy day and the dust has turned into mud. And somebody jostles him and the three gold pieces fall down into the mud. What does he say – with lots of people milling about – does he say, 'Excuse me, please step aside a little bit, I want to look in the mud to see whether my gold pieces are there?' Or does he jump in and shout, 'Out of the way!' That is the urgency with which we are supposed to look for it. Though we may come to that point, and occasionally we are at that point, it doesn't last very long, and then it's back to a slow, 'Oh, yes…' So act as if your gold pieces are at stake, or as if somebody presses you to repay the millions that you owe, fearful of humiliation by others, laughed at, 'Why do you run up such enormous debts?'

Another example of the urgency is from my own experience. I was in hospital sometime at the very end, or after the war, I can't exactly remember, but anyway, they had few anaesthetics at that time. So they asked whether I would agree, to have chloroform. Now, all I knew about chloroform was from detective stories: you know, where you drive with the villain in the car and he puts a wad of cotton wool full of chloroform on your face and you are out. So I happily said, 'Alright!' That was that, and then they put the thing on me, and it was quite all right too. But when my breathing began to be a little bit difficult, and I felt that I couldn't breathe any more, I very politely said, 'Please take it away for a moment, I need to catch my breath,' but they didn't take it away. So more urgently I said, because I was getting breathless, 'Please take it away!' and they didn't take it away. And really, I didn't think about doing it, but my whole body rose up: 'Grrrr!' – and that was the last I knew. So that is the urgency. Whilst it goes fairly well, we don't mind, but when it really comes to an urgency, the whole thing rears up; and this whole thing, body as well as mind, is what Master Daie is talking about here.

'Only thus,' he says, **'will you have some direction in the task of finding urgency where seemingly there is no urgency, getting busy where there is no pressure, and finding importance where there is no importance.'** Usually it's, 'Yes, of course I want to find out. Of course, I want to, I'll put my absolute utmost into it,' and perhaps I really do, to a great extent, but it doesn't last long, and then I get tired of it and it just limps along. 'But, after all I'm doing my training, am I not?' That will bring nothing. Where there is no urgency, nothing will come about.

But, 'Getting busy where there is no pressure, and finding importance where there is no importance' – that is what we have to instigate with skilful means, so that we have got that drive behind it. The training, the Daily Life Practice, the giving ourselves into what at the moment is, is the way towards it. Normally we more or less do it, though certainly not whole-heartedly all the time, and very often we do it just by trying to watch ourselves instead of actually really giving into the doing. But it is the giving and the giving continuously which is important, for in that, little by little, a certain amount of that strong will of 'I' is ground away, until it comes to the point where it really comes to the jump.

I have often told you (see comment to letter 2) about my frightening experience during an early sanzen interview with Sesso Roshi, which ended with him saying, 'Now you know all that you need to know – Jump!' and rang the bell. And I slunk back along the corridor, thinking, I remember distinctly, 'Yes, yes! This is what I want to do! This is what I came to Daitoku-ji for! But not now! Not now! Not now!' And this 'Not now!' is usually also what holds us back, and over this, if really urgent, we need to jump.

So to come to that point, Master Daie says, **'Work diligently day and night: while eating and drinking, when joyful or angry, in clean places or unclean places, in family gatherings, when entertaining guests, when dealing with official business in your job, when concluding a betrothal.'** In other words, in all situations of the ordinary daily life. Work diligently day and night. While eating and drinking – 'No, surely I can't work while eating, it will spoil the taste of my food.' When joyful, we forget. When angry – 'In that state I could not possibly work.' But these are the good opportunities, **'– all of these are first class times to make efforts to arouse and alert yourself and awaken.'**

Again, I remember the various problems and my concerns that arose, during my early days in Daitoku-ji. I used to think, 'If I can only get over this distraction or problem now and things begin to quieten down a little bit, how well I will meditate then! But this one thing, I must somehow get over that first.' And always by the time this one thing had gone, another had naturally come up. So it always went, thinking how wonderfully I will meditate once this or that is out of the way. But this attitude is what was holding me back. And it took quite some time until it dawned on me that to work diligently, in spite of all one's problems and likes and dislikes, that is what the Daily Life Practice actually is about, and that is why it is the Daily Life Practice. It's not just saying, 'Yes, yes, yes,' to everything as we assume to begin with, but it is a real getting into the activity and giving ourselves into it. Not becoming stiff by trying to be untouched by anything, but a full going with it as a human being. That is why we work diligently day and night, eating and drinking, when joyful or angry, in clean places or unclean places, when it's really urgent, but not being carried away but going with it.

This is also how mindfulness is misunderstood. Before I went to Japan there was very little known about mindfulness, but when I came back after twelve years there was great deal of talk about it. At the Summer School that year, I saw a young man diligently walking – lifting his foot up, forward, down, up, forward, down, up, forward, down, and it went very slowly. There was a visiting *bhikkhu* from Cambodia attending that year and seeing that young man walking, he asked me, 'What is he doing?' I said, 'He is trying to walk mindfully.' And the *bhikkhu* laughed so much that he actually fell off his chair. That gave me the confirmation that that is a Western idea, and it comes from watching oneself instead of doing it. That is the main difficulty that we have in our practice, because we are too easily tempted to watch ourselves. Please, with the Daily Life Practice be natural, smooth, normal, and don't dawdle and don't hesitate – because this is when things go wrong.

'Work diligently day and night, while eating and drinking, when joyful or angry, in clean places or unclean places.' But 'I must have a quiet, clean place; I cannot meditate otherwise' – well remember, that Daito Kokushi meditated for years with the beggars under the most busy bridge in Kyoto; and he said, 'If you cannot meditate like that under such circumstances, and you need the quiet peak of Hiezan for that, then you haven't any idea what meditation is.'

So, work diligently 'in clean places or unclean places, in family gatherings, and when entertaining guests,' – in different situations: in family gatherings when you feel you can be yourself, and when entertaining guests, where you watch your manners, in other words where we put a mask on. And 'when dealing with official business in our job,' again there is another mask on; 'and when concluding a betrothal' – this is a text of Master Daie's time, where in China that was a very important business. But 'all of these are first class times to make efforts to arouse and alert yourself and awaken.' To make efforts to arouse and alert yourself, to come out of those roles that we play and to really give ourselves into the situation and to be natural and straightforward. Make efforts to arouse yourself and alert yourself, and awaken. Because it is at such times, when we are really open and really naturally at one with the circumstances that the heart is empty. Then if something strikes, there is a response, and that is awakening. Can we ponder that for this first day of the *sesshin*?

LETTER 18 to HSU TUN-CHI (continued)

THE TEXT

In the old days the military governor Li Wen-ho was able to study Ch'an and attain great penetration and great enlightenment while in the thick of wealth and rank. When Yang Wen-kung successfully studied Ch'an, he was dwelling in the Imperial Han Lin Academy. When Chang Wu-chin studied Ch'an, he was the minister for transport in Kiangsi. These three elders are examples of this 'not destroying the worldly aspect while speaking of the real aspect.' When has it ever been necessary to leave wife and children, quit one's job, chew on vegetable roots, and cause pain to the body? Those of inferior aspiration shun clamour and seek quietude: thence they enter the ghost cave of 'dead tree Ch'an' entertaining false ideas that only thus can they awaken to the Path. Haven't you seen Layman P'ang's words:

Just have an empty mind as to the myriad things:
Then what hindrance is there when myriad things
  surround you?
The iron ox does not fear the lion's roar:
It's like a wooden man seeing a picture of flowers and
birds –
The wooden man's body itself has no feelings,
And the painted birds are not startled when meeting
the man.
Mind and objects are Thus – only this is:
Why worry that the Path of Enlightenment will not be
fulfilled?

Ven. Myokyo-ni's Comments

Yesterday we heard about pulling the spine up straight; and in the middle of things, whatever the circumstances outside or inside – joyful, angry or whatever – to just diligently carry on. It's not the circumstances that are in the way, it's ourselves.

Here Master Daie gives a few examples. **'In the old days the military governor Li Wen-ho was able to study Ch'an and attain great penetration and great enlightenment while in the thick of wealth and rank.'** If we really have a mind to work on it and we really do put ourselves into it, then there's nothing that can keep us from doing it, if we really want it. If we do not really want it, if we have lots of things going on, spread all over, then it's not so easy; as a matter of fact, it becomes impossible. It's not the lots-of-things situations, it's the single-mindedness; and so it is useful for us to consider to what extent we really want to follow the Buddha's Path. Is that the most important thing in my life, or is it just one amongst the various things that I would like to do? If we are clear on that and know this is the most important thing for us, then whatever our circumstances, we can carry it through.

Master Daie then gives another example: **'When Yang Wen-kung successfully studied Ch'an, he was dwelling in the Imperial Han Lin Academy.'** In other words, he was a teacher there, which meant a great scholar, very busy indeed; and yet pushed through and came to an insight.

'When Chang Wu-chin studied Ch'an he was the minister for transport in Kiangsi,' and had more than enough to do – and yet managed it.

Having cited **'these three elders'** Master Daie says they 'are examples of the **"not destroying the worldly aspect while speaking of the real aspect."'** When it comes to the real aspect, when it is really seen into, then it is portrayed by anything and everything, all the actions, all the words. It can't be otherwise.

There is a very apt Hassidic Jewish story for that too. When a famous rabbi came to give a talk in a particular town, the very well-known rabbi living there was asked, 'Are you also going to the talk? Do you think you need to?' And he said, 'Oh yes, I certainly am going to the talk, but I am not interested in listening to the talk. What I want to see is how he ties his shoelaces.' That's what it comes down to. These are also things that we learn from: to express it in all our actions. If it is expressed in all our actions, and if we train ourselves to really wholeheartedly give ourselves into what is being done here and now, then slowly we get into the habit of it really being expressed. The worldly aspect does not hinder when speaking or portraying the real aspect. Speaking is not needed, the portraying is even more important

And when we do so another thing arises. We begin to be careful, and we begin to have respect for the things that we handle, not only people. With that we come back to having respect for ourselves, which nowadays we very rarely have. We may think we are a hell of a so-and-so, but we have not got respect.

This question of respect is a very important one, because it comes together with carefulness and with goodwill, and taking care. Once we've really got used to taking care of everything, from the cup to the rake to the knife, then we actually have very little time to think about ourselves, and with this are released from the straitjacket that I am. In a monastery for example, when a new monk arrives, he is summed up by the way in which he can adapt, and by the way in which he handles things. Useful to remember.

Master Daie tells us, 'These three elders are examples of not destroying the worldly aspect while speaking of the real aspect.' If all our actions speak of it in the midst of all situations, then that worldly aspect does not need to be shunned or destroyed, because it is clearly carried out. Apart from us human beings, all other sentient beings express the real aspect, because they have no thoughts that disturb that real aspect. An ant will under all circumstances, good, bad, and indifferent, only act as an ant. And an elephant under all circumstances, good, bad, and indifferent, will only behave like an elephant. But we have all kinds of ideas. We know how an ant acts, and how an elephant should act, but we are sometimes like this and sometimes like that and have to go through the six realms continuously, bound in them, because we are not really human yet.

Master Daie then asks, **'When has it ever been necessary to leave wife and children, quit one's job, chew on vegetable roots, and cause pain to the body?'** You will say, 'Well, but this is what monasteries are about.' Yes, this is what they are about; but they are not necessary. It is helpful to train in the monastery, to go through the earlier stages. But if our circumstances do not allow it, then we can use the circumstances as they are.

'Those of inferior aspiration shun clamour and seek quietude.'

We feel it must be quiet, must be properly this, that and the other. Enough air. Enough sunshine. No sound. Well, I will admit that the continuous 'thump, thump, thump' that we hear nowadays sometimes is not exactly an ideal thing, but it can be blended out, or endured. It does not need to drive one up the wall and halfway across the ceiling. Again the example of Master Daito: sitting under the bridge the continuous noisy traffic of crunching wheels and stamping horses overhead didn't deter him from doing zazen.

Because they shun clamour and seek quietude, **'Hence they enter the ghost cave of "dead tree Ch'an" entertaining false ideas that only thus can they awaken to the Path.'** There are conducive circumstances, and there are naturally also the opposite, not conducive circumstances. But there are no circumstances that can possibly hinder somebody who really wants to do it. And in a way, if it is not so easy, it has an advantage, because more strength is needed. The more strength that has to be gathered and gained in order to do it, the more strength comes out in the end.

To exemplify this, he now quotes Layman P'ang, **'Just have an empty mind** (heart) **as to the myriad things.'** Do not clutch, do not hold on to them. Just have an empty heart as to the myriad things. When we travel by train and look out of the window and know the train won't stop, we just look in a quite neutral way. Sometimes there is nice scenery, sometimes it is through a town, and it passes by. We do not clutch on to it, we do not hang on to it, we know we are not stopping. That also is an example of an empty heart, not attached to anything. When there is an empty heart that is not attached to anything, **'Then what hindrance is there,'** asks Layman P'ang, **'when myriad things surround you?'** – and he gives an example: **'The iron ox does not fear the lion's roar.'** The iron ox is an often-used example or analogy in Zen training. The iron ox does not fear the lion's roar; the lion can roar however much he wants to. And what's more, **'It's like a wooden man seeing a picture of flowers and birds – the wooden man's body itself has no feelings, and the painted birds are not startled when meeting the man.'** Well, we have to be careful when we read things like this, and we have to read it with the Single Eye of Zen, otherwise we misread it. The wooden man has no feelings, so then I begin to think that maybe I should be detached, be without any feelings for anything. But, apart from the fact that it is not possible, that is merely callousness.

I have often told you about Sesso Roshi's comments on the passage in the *Rinzai Roku* where the bodhisattva plays in the deepest hells as if on a fairground (see letter 7). He said that if we look at it with our ordinary ideas, then it is merely callousness. But you have to look at it with the Single Eye – and this is how these texts need to be read, otherwise we do not understand. Then you see that nobody asks the bodhisattva to go into these fearful places. He goes there by his own volition because he wants to help beings; if he is caught up in their misery, he only becomes another inmate, and only increases the suffering; then he is certainly not capable of reaching out a helping hand to those who are there. He must remain free.

That is what is meant here; and we come again to the teaching of non-attachment. Do not think that non-attachment means that there is no feeling left. Look at the Buddha, who after his enlightenment, wandered about all over north-eastern India until his death, full of friendliness and compassion. If not open to normal human feelings, that is definitely 'I' trying to do something – different from being fully opened, and experiencing them truly, but without attachment, and without being carried away. As Master Rinzai says, 'To laugh but not to be carried away by laughter. To cry, but not to be carried away by tears.'

'The wooden man's body itself has no feelings, and the painted birds are not startled when meeting the man.' Pictures, pictures.

'Mind (heart) **and objects are Thus – only this is.'** 'Thus' – that is Tathata, just that. So, 'Heart and things are Thus. Only this is.' That is all. **'Why then worry that the Path of Enlightenment will not be fulfilled?'** To see it as it is. Just this, 'Thus'. Why then worry? Who is the worrier? Who is this, that, and the other, seeing it like this, and like that? 'Only this is,' says Layman P'ang, and he knew what he was talking about. Can we take this home with us from this weekend *sesshin*, and ponder it very carefully? What is in the way, as the Buddha recognised and realised on his own enlightenment, is our attachment – not only attachments, because we have many – but the fundamental attachment to I. Once that is gone, things fall naturally into place.

LETTER 18 to HSU TUN-CHI (continued)

The Text

> If you can manage not to forget the matter of birth and death while in the midst of the passions of the world, then even though you do not immediately smash the lacquer bucket (of ignorance), nevertheless you will have planted deep the seed-wisdom of transcendental knowledge. In another lifetime you will appear and save your mental power. You won't fall into evil dispositions. You'll overcome that sinking down into the defilement of passions.

> Not seeking escape, some say this affair should not be treated casually, and make of it an object of veneration and faith. Views like this are countless.

As a gentleman of affairs, your study of the Path differs greatly from mine as a home-leaver. Leavers of home do not serve their parents, and abandon all their relatives for good. With one jug and one bowl, in daily activities according to circumstances, there are not many enemies to obstruct the Path. With one mind and one intent, home-leavers just investigate this affair thoroughly. But when a gentleman of affairs opens his eyes and is mindful of what he sees, there is nothing that is not an enemy spirit blocking the Path. If he has wisdom, he makes his meditational effort right there.

Ven. Myokyo-ni's Comments

'If you can manage not to forget the matter of birth and death while in the midst of the passions of the world' – thrown about by the passions, wanting, aggression, must have, must get rid of – and if in the midst of that, says Master Daie, 'you can manage not to forget the matter of birth and death, **'then even though you do not immediately smash the lacquer bucket, nevertheless you will have planted deep the seed-wisdom of transcendental wisdom.'** If you can manage not to forget the matter of birth and death – this is what really concerns the Buddhist; that striving to get out of the world of birth and death, off the Wheel of Change, in the midst of all the passions that get hold of us in the normal way. Yet not to forget, and still to go on striving. Master Daie says, if that is the case, 'then even though you do not immediately smash the lacquer bucket...' – the lacquer bucket is a metaphor for our normal ignorance and delusion; you can't see through black lacquer which is thick and opaque – so even if you do not immediately smash the lacquer bucket – that delusion which actually is I – 'you will nevertheless have planted deep the seed-wisdom of transcendental knowledge.' Transcendental knowledge, or transcendental wisdom, *prajna*.

To the extent that it is possible not to be swerved or be carried away by the passions, we must try not to forget the Great Matter, the great matter of birth and death as it is also called, that keeps us returning again and again on the Wheel. This is the basic Buddhist conception. It is foreign to us Westerners, and we have difficulties with it, because we can't quite see that we go round and round on that Wheel, birth after birth. Even if we do somehow get a picture of it, it is I going round and round; but this is also not the case, because it is not I going round and round; it is the bundle of the Five Aggregates – body, sensation, perception, volition, and consciousness – that bundle is what goes round and round. Using that metaphor of the cart, the Buddha carefully pointed out that you can ride in it, but if you take it apart – axle, wheel, framework, etc. – then where is the cart? Thus an analogy for the non-existence of I: there is the body; there are feelings and sensations; there are perceptions; there are volitions; and there is consciousness; but nowhere in that bundle that works perfectly smoothly – nowhere do you find an 'I' in it.

Intellectually, it is possible to see this. But to really get into it, to really fall into it, and to really live out of it, is another matter. So, as long as you do not forget that Great Matter of birth and death – Master Daie tells us – even if you do not immediately smash the lacquer bucket, even if you do not immediately awaken, you will nevertheless have planted deep the seed-wisdom of transcendental knowledge: that habit of not forgetting and of striving on and on. It goes with the bundle, and will find itself another form; and what it has brought along will go into that other form.

Therefore, **'In another lifetime you will appear and save your mental power.'** There's a lesson here: it is a matter of not wanting to 'get', but at the same time of just not forgetting, of striving on and not forgetting, but not wanting something. This is the important thing. We have got many stories in the old texts where old masters, for some reason or other gave up hope of ever coming to enlightenment, but nevertheless they just went on with their training. Then one day, suddenly something happens. And so, 'In another lifetime you will appear and save your mental power.' It may be another lifetime, but you never know. The most famous one is Master Kyogen, who wandered about for twenty years, not expecting anything anymore, and just wanting to wear out this present lifetime, and hoping that in another life he would have better *innen* – better affinity links – and be able to get on more with his training. Then he settled in a derelict temple and for the next ten years restored and cared for it. One day as he cleaned the backyard and threw a mass of leaves and pebbles against the bamboo thicket, one pebble hit the bamboo. And as he heard that click, suddenly he awoke.

Another master awakened by hearing the murmuring of the brook. But it is an empty heart which is the important thing for us to realise. An empty heart has no wishes; and an empty heart has no fears; and an empty heart does not throw itself about. It just goes with what is. So, 'In another lifetime you will appear and save your mental power. **You won't fall into evil dispositions.'** Not possible with such an approach. And Master Daie says, **'You'll overcome that sinking down into the defilement of passions. Not seeking escape, some say this affair should not be treated casually.'** 'Not seeking escape' – this is different from the caution 'Not to forget' and this is very carefully taught. 'Not to forget the Great Matter of birth and death' is not seeking escape. Escape is getting away from it, and is different from seeing into and awakening. Whatever we try to escape from, whatever we try to push away – to that we actually give power over ourselves. We all know it in our own experience of things which we dislike and really want to get rid of: it goes round and round in my mind, on and on and won't even let me sleep.

So, 'not seeking escape, some say this affair should not be treated casually, **and make of it an object of veneration and faith. Views like this are countless.'** 'They're only seeking escape' is easily said of someone who just quietly goes along with circumstances. But really seeking escape is throwing oneself about. And the other side of it, the opposite of that seeking escape, is seeking something, is that affair of making 'it an object of veneration and faith.' Again, making an object; and thereby hangs a story. If it is an object, something outside, something to escape from, something to get, something far away and to look up to – these do not work. It's all object, it's all outside; and whatever is outside has nothing to do with the heart itself. As a matter of fact, it only clutters the heart. What is important is that the heart becomes empty. Empty of seeking, empty of objects, empty of everything. Finally, empty of I.

Then Master Daie says something which is very helpful for us to consider. **'As a gentleman of affairs, your study of the Path differs greatly from mine as a home-leaver.'** Gentlemen of affairs in the world? This is something we can also take note of, whether it is in the Southern or the Northern texts: it is always a son or daughter of a noble family, a gentleman of affairs. Why do you think that is? Is it that only the nobility can get to it? But this is not so because one is not born as a gentleman or gentlewoman. One is educated, one is made one. What does a gentleman or gentlewoman mean? A person who is gentled is not carried away, not subject to rages or violent ambitions, etc. A gentleman or gentlewoman is literally what it says: a gentle man/woman. As such, they can stay a course without being thrown off it. And as such they can be trusted, they are responsible. That is what a gentleman or gentlewoman is. Nowadays when we have lost our cultural values, we first need to educate ourselves to being such a gentle person. To keep the form, not rigid; to be trustworthy and helpful, kind; gentle in other words.

And so, Master Daie says, 'As a gentleman of affairs, your study of the Path differs greatly from mine as a home-leaver.' And why does it differ so? Because, and this is the interesting part: **'Leavers of home do not serve their parents, and abandon all their relatives for good.'** He doesn't say they don't strive after money or ambition, but goes much closer: 'do not serve their parents, and abandon all their relatives for good.' We must not forget that this is T'ang dynasty China, where the Confucian values of filial piety were still very strong. Leavers of home go into a monastery and cut their bonds with their family. **'With one jug and one bowl'** – going begging with it, getting their daily food that way – **'in daily activities according to circumstances, there are not so many enemies to obstruct the Path.'** They haven't got anything much, so they don't need to be frightened of losing it. They are not supposed to have anything much, so they don't need to covet it. But rather in daily activities, according to circumstances, on their begging rounds, in their religious observances, in their meditations, there are not so many enemies to obstruct the Path.

'With one mind and one intent, home-leavers just investigate this affair thoroughly.' This affair, this great affair of birth and death. With one mind and one intent, without much obstruction, investigate this affair thoroughly.

'But when a gentleman of affairs opens his eyes and is mindful of what he sees, there is nothing that is not an enemy spirit blocking the Path.' 'I want this.' 'This is not right.' 'That is beautiful, I would like to have it.' 'This needs to be got rid of.' All these things come in: nothing that is not an enemy spirit blocking the Path. All these things are there. His path is by no means empty.

But **'If he has wisdom, he makes his meditational effort right there.'** If he has the wisdom, then he can really settle himself down in meditation right there. All these enemy spirits blocking the Path: all the wants, likes, dislikes, and loathings. Just sit down in meditation; not to get rid of them, but to look at them, to look at them clearly and recognise them. In that recognition, they lose their power. And that is an important point.

LETTER 18 to HSU TUN-CHI (continued)

THE TEXT

> As Vimalakirti said, 'The companions of passion are the progenitors of the Tathagatas: I fear that people will destroy the worldly aspect to seek the real aspect.' He also made the comparison: 'It is like the high plateau not producing lotus flowers; it is the mud of the low-lying marshlands that produces those flowers.'

> If you can penetrate through right here, as those three elders Yang Wen-kung, Li Wen-ho, and Chan Wu-chin did, your power will surpass that of us leavers of home by twenty-fold. What's the reason? We leavers of home are on the outside breaking in; gentlemen of affairs are on the inside breaking out. The power of one on the outside breaking in is weak; the power of one on the inside breaking out is strong. 'Strong' means that what is opposed is heavy, so in overturning it there is power. 'Weak' means what is opposed is light, so in overturning it there is little power. Though there is strong and weak in terms of power, what is opposed is the same.

Yesterday we heard Master Daie saying that the home-leavers have it easier than the people in the world. And he quotes Vimalakirti, **'The companions of passion are the progenitors of the Tathagatas.'** The Mahayana saying is: 'The passions are the Buddha-nature, and the Buddha-nature is the passions.' That does not mean that if I give full vent to my fury, that I am now going to produce my Buddha-nature. What it really means is that the same energy gives rise to it. In the presence of the delusion of I, filtered through my likes and dislikes, it comes out as the passions, which have a tremendous power, when it really comes down to it. If there is no I to judge, to choose, to pick, then the Buddha-nature carries like the quiet sea carries a good swimmer. So it is not that I need to get rid of, or to cut off the passions – which I can't in any case, except by suicide – but it's a question of transforming them. And to transform them, there are ways and means.

Just how important that is, is beautifully portrayed in the Bull-Herding Pictures, where in Picture 6 you see the gentled bull carrying the man home. In other words, it is first of all only the bull, not the man, who knows the way home – the man does not know it – and secondly it is also the bull who has the strength, the power, to carry the man home. The man doesn't have to guide him. The bull does that quite comfortably by himself. But the man also has something to do. He sits on the back of the bull and he plays his flute, a simple melody; and step by step by step, the bull carries him home.

Hence transformation is the important thing. That is what it is all about. It is not 'I' that have to transform it. It takes place by itself. I have to do a certain amount of practice, a certain type of practice; and that by itself will see to that transformation. It's not always easy; I have to endure a good amount of the onslaught of that power to be slowly ousted from the driver's seat, which I think I need to occupy, because I believe it doesn't go without me. As a matter of fact, it goes much better without me.

'The companions of passion are the progenitors of the Tathagatas.' But Vimalakirti then also continues, **'I fear that people will destroy the worldly aspect to seek the real aspect.'** That is trying to destroy the worldly aspect completely, to get away, hide myself in a cave or on a mountain-top in order to do it. That is not how seeking the real aspect really works.

So Vimalakirti also made the comparison, **'It is like the high plateau not producing lotus flowers; it is the mud of the lowlying marshlands that produces these flowers.'** Useful to realise. Not to avoid difficult situations, but not to be carried away by them either.

Master Daie then continues, **'If you can penetrate through right here'** – listening to this, and seeing it the right way, then **'as those three elders Yang Wen Kun, Li Wen Ho, and Chan Wu Shin did, your power will surpass that of us leavers of home by twenty-fold.'** Those three are very high government officials, with a tremendous amount of responsibility and many duties. Yet, in spite of all of this, hearing about the Buddha-dharma, applying themselves to it, they penetrated right through. So, you have to penetrate right through here, now – because it is only here and now where we can penetrate right through, there is no tomorrow for that, it is only here, now that it cuts. That here and now is this living moment. As a matter of fact, we never live anywhere but here, now in this living moment. A second ago is already gone; and a second further is not yet here. Have we ever thought that we always live in this living moment here, now, which invigorates, but which we refuse to live because of our ideas of what I would like, and our thoughts that carry us away, far into the past or into the future, whatever it is, So we long for that aliveness, that vividness of the living moment. Yet we are in it all the time, we just refuse to see it. Again, as Master Hakuin liked to say, 'In the midst of water, pitifully crying from thirst.' So, 'if you can penetrate through right here, into this moment now, your power will surpass that of us leavers of home by twenty-fold.'

And why? **'What is the reason? We leavers of home are on the outside breaking in; gentlemen of affairs are on the inside breaking out. The power of one on the outside breaking in is weak; the power of one on the inside breaking out is strong. "Strong" means that what is opposed is heavy, so in overturning it there is power. "Weak" means what is opposed is light, so in overturning it there is little power.'** Strong and weak means that what is opposed is either heavy or light. If what is opposed and in the way, is heavy, namely I with all my likes and dislikes, then a strong power is necessary to push it over. Whereas, from inside, 'weak means that what is opposed is light.'

But, says Master Daie very carefully, **'Though there is strong and weak in terms of power'** – to push through – **'that which is opposed is the same.'** That which is opposed is of course, I – my notions, my this, my that. That is very humbly said; but right from the beginning, the Zen School has always been open to everybody, male and female, monk and layman. So what Master Daie says is rather on the humble side; because as a matter of fact in the Mahayana, as different from the Southern School, it is said that there is no difference between monks and laypeople. They get the same teaching, the same training. They have the same opportunity. Some may have to work more; some may have to work less. But what is inside will want to come out, whatever the circumstances: whether at home, or having left home.

I remember when I went to Japan, a very, very good friend of mine, who was having a good amount of trouble in his marriage, used to write flaming letters to me: 'You! You in your cloistered peace! What do you know of the troubles that beset us in the world?' He knew jolly well that I was not living in a monastery; as a woman I lived outside and only went there for the training. But I didn't say, 'Well, you know I'm not living in a monastery,' which he knew in any case. I simply wrote back, 'Whether I get furious and upset and hurt and grieved that my boss does not appreciate me as I think I should be appreciated; or whether I am getting upset and hurt and grieved that the head monk scolds me for something that I haven't done; whether I am getting annoyed that my colleagues push all kinds of work onto me which I should not really do, which is theirs; or whether I am getting furious that the monks leave me the most unpleasant things to do, scraping the leaves out from under the trees with bare hands, etc. – it is all inside me. Whatever it is, the circumstances will differ, but the same thing will come out.'

That's what it really comes down to. There is no cloistered peace in the monastery, and there is no uproar in the world. It's all inside. It is my reaction to it. That's all there is to it. In this country here, or in the West, where we are free and can do what we want, if we are truly, clearly, willing to admit that it is not the circumstances, but that it is our reaction, then we are, all of us, in exactly the place where we most want to be. But I complain, 'No, it's not true, I would prefer to do this, that, or the other.' But is it really true? If I carefully look at the consequences of my choices, then I will find that after all where I am is where I most want to be.

We may dream of change and our dreams carry us all over the place; and they carry us into very strange byways. So, when it really comes down to it, whether it is a monk or whether it is a layman, the Buddha-dharma is the Buddha-dharma, and the scheme of things is exceedingly fair. Each one has his or her own difficulties to go through, depending on how individually we are geared. There are easier and there are harder places, but they are the same for everybody. Some may find that mountain-climbing is easy, whereas going through a swampy landscape is difficult. Others may find the swampy landscape is easy to go through, but haven't got the eye for mountains, or whatever it is. But we each have our difficulties. So it's no good saying, 'He's got it easier,' and 'She hasn't got it so hard.' – there are just different circumstances, but we all experience the same difficulties.

When it comes down to it, as far as the Buddha-dharma is concerned, we bow our head, and instead of our usual 'I this, that and the other,' we listen to the Buddha. We listen to the Daily Life Practice, which tells us, that in the framework of Buddhism I is the arch-delusion which is keeping us away from the full life that the heart is longing for. If that arch-delusion is given in to again and again, if I am thinking and watching myself constantly, and possibly even scolding myself – that is only further I-delusion – instead of pulling up my socks, then I will never get into this moment. At this moment: there is no I. There is just this living moment. And to come back into this living moment, into the relationship that is here in this living moment, and into the forms that are here in this living moment – this is what the heart longs for. I, being a fool, think that if I can understand it, there will be peace. Not a bit of it: the heart is not interested in understanding. The heart is only interested in participation, and that participation, that whole-hearted participation, is only possible in this living moment of here, now.

So please do not forget that living moment, and the Buddha-dharma that helps us into it, again and again. In the Daily Life Practice, it does not matter how often we forget; but as soon as we become aware of having once more drifted off somewhere far away, we should jump back into that living moment – whatever at that moment is being done. If only consistently done, and immediately done – it will slowly begin to become habitual. There is nothing which cannot be cultivated. All our habits have been cultivated over many, many years, so to think that we could then cultivate such an attitude within five minutes is simply silly. We need to have the strength, or the power, and the determination.

This is why it is said there are three things necessary for the Zen training: a deep root of faith, a great ball of doubt and iron determination. Faith in the Way that the Buddha pointed out, a way he had gone himself, that he knew by his own experience. We can have faith in that. The great ball of doubt – all the I-whisperings saying, 'Is this really the right way?' 'Can I believe all this?' Whatever 'I' whispers, however clever, to all those murmurings – a great ball of doubt. And an iron determination, that dispels the doubts and gets on with it.

And as we get on with it, we need strength as well as determination. We know it with all skills that are physical – and the training is much more physical than we believe to begin with – slowly, as the skill improves and the strength improves, things begin to flow much more naturally. Then we are truly on the Way. So can we take that home from this weekend *sesshin* and instill it as much as possible into our ordinary everyday life.

LETTER 19 to TSENG SHU-CH'IH

The Text

There has never been anything to give to people. There have only been some who have been able to point out the road for people. An ancient worthy said, 'Having some attainment is the jackal's yelp; having no attainment is the lion's roar.'

The Buddha was someone who had mastered adaptation. In the course of forty-nine years, in more than three hundred and sixty assemblies where he taught the Dharma, he guided people according to their individual faculties. Thus he preached with one voice through all realms, while sentient beings each obtained benefits according to their kind. It's like one gust of the east wind, and the myriad grasses all bend down: the Dharma preached by the Buddha is also like this.

If he had had the intent to create benefit in all realms, then this would have been preaching the Dharma egotistically. To want to cause myriad beings to gain deliverance according to their kind: isn't this after all impossible?

Ven. Myokyo-ni's Comments

'There has never been anything to give to people.' There is no need. There is nothing to give. Realising this on his own awakening the Buddha said, 'How miraculous, how wonderful! All sentient beings are fully endowed with the Tathagata's wisdom and power.' Nothing to be given. Only with regard to us humans, he also realised that because of our attachments, we sadly are not aware of it. So quite rightly, there has never been anything to give to people.

But there were always **'some who have been able to point out the road for people.'** That is possible. It's not to give, because there is nothing to give. It's all there already. As Master Mumon said, 'The treasures of the house – the heirlooms of the house – do not come in by the front door.' They are already there; but since we are not aware of it, there is a pointing finger showing the way to come to that realisation. So Master Daie quite rightly says that there were some who have been able to point the way for people – a path to be walked with our own feet, the Buddha Way; and it is very well signposted.

Right from the time of the Buddha all the old patriarchs walked the road following those signposts, and they left those signposts. They are still there, and we can follow them; or we can think that they are old-fashioned, no longer fitting our time, and go our own way. We couldn't be more mistaken.

This brings to mind the wonderful story I've already told you about my friend who went to a large meeting in India, which was held for foreigners in English. He happened to sit next to an American. The teacher giving the lecture said, 'It's a long way, an arduous way, taking years and years,' and the American nudged my friend and said, 'You know, that's their way; I bet if we got hold of it, we'd do it in a few months!'

Buddhas do but point the Way. Whether we are willing and want to follow it, or whether we very soon want to make it our way, depends on us. The fact is that the Buddha's Way and my way very often cross; and when it comes to such conflicts, then the question is: Do I follow the Buddha's Way, or do I go my way? Which one wins? That decides the issue.

'An old master said, "Having some attainment is the jackal's yelp. Having no attainment is the lion's roar."' Now, what do we make of a saying like this? 'Having some attainment' – 'Hmmm, I must have a little bit, after fifteen years of practice.' Having some attainment is the jackal's yelp. But having no attainment is the lion's roar. 'But then why do I need to do all this practice, if I know I won't have any attainment?' But what is behind all of this? Well, first of all, I do not quite believe that I have no attainment at all, because that puts me too much in the line of nothing – 'having no attainment, no, I'm sure a little bit must have been achieved. In any case, having no attainment – why should I then trouble myself? Why should I sit at the *sesshin*, cross-legged until the legs hurt, or on a chair until the back shrieks? Why should I, if no attainment is the lion's roar?'

But having no attainment, am I then capable of roaring like a lion? Or does it very quickly come to nothing? We always come back to the story of Bodhidharma's encounter with Emperor Wu, because it contains so many good pointers. The Emperor, a very pious Buddhist, wanted to know how much merit he had accumulated for allowing many monks to be ordained and for having endowed many temples. But the great monk just said, 'None whatsoever.' The Emperor was not pleased, but being a good Buddhist, and this being a famous monk, he then asked, 'Tell me, what then is the essence of Buddhism?' And Bodhidharma said, 'Vast emptiness, nothing holy.' Rather perplexed, and by now rather annoyed, too, the Emperor said, 'Then who is it who stands in front of us?' Bodhidharma, fully aware that his life now was literally on a hair's breadth, said, 'Not known.' That is the Lion's Roar. Not giving himself any airs whatsoever, just clearly standing on that inherent wisdom and power. That is the Lion's Roar. None whatsoever – no merit, no attainment.

Master Daie then goes on, **'The Buddha was someone who had mastered adaptation.'** 'Mastered adaptation' – is a funny way of putting it, because the Buddha was someone who naturally adapted to whatever the circumstances were, whoever the people were. This is when we are truly at one with whatever is, not holding on to I, which is a delusion, which is separation, and which is fear. Being truly at one with whatever is, that is mastered adaptation – we don't actually need to master it; we become it.

With a fool – become a fool; with a merchant talk about business; with a farmer about the weather and the harvest; with a cook about cooking; with an office worker about work in the office; as it fits: 'who had mastered adaptation.' Therefore, having a smooth relationship, being one with – that is what mastered adaptation really means. Not standing out; not wanting to do anything; just naturally adapting to what is. Speaking to a child and speaking to a grown-up, we use a different voice, no need to try – to a certain extent we do it naturally. Then we become self-conscious and suddenly the whole thing has gone, and we become stilted and artificial, because we have not completely given ourselves into the circumstances; have remained outside. Someone who had mastered adaptation means somebody who has completely emptied the heart, and is therefore naturally flowing into whatever is touched.

Because he had mastered adaptation, Master Daie says, that **'In the course of forty-nine years, in more than three hundred and sixty assemblies where he taught the Dharma, he guided people according to their individual faculties.'** So, in all his talks to all the assemblies where he taught the Dharma, and also when he talked to people directly, he guided people according to their individual faculties. But here it is particularly mentioned that he taught the Dharma to three hundred and sixty assemblies. Well, how in such large assemblies can you teach the Dharma and guide people individually? That is something that is very useful for us to realise. We always believe that we have to be given things individually, directly, according to the way I see things and have it explained accordingly. Teaching the Dharma is teaching the Dharma – that's all. It's not so difficult: the Three Signs of Being; the Three Fires; the Twelve Links; the Four Noble Truths; and that's about all that we need to know and Daily Life Practice to put it into practice. Just giving yourself into the doing and becoming aware of what the Dharma actually says. Guiding people according to their individual faculties – well, some will be able to naturally give themselves into it; some will have much trouble. 'My difficulty is this, my problem is this' – all quite unimportant. It is just giving oneself, and continuing to give oneself. sila practice, the *Paramitas*: none of them have anything much, or anything at all, to do with I. They only show what needs to be done. But if I only want to see what happens to me, that is surely the opposite of the way that we want to go, because that all leads back to I again.

So the Buddha 'guided people according to their individual faculties.' Individual faculties? Well, we find them out ourselves. It is important for us to be aware of our individual emotional household, but not to dwell on it, not to be carried away by it, but see it as signposts, or as red lights, so to speak: 'Careful – here she blows.' If I know that I easily get irritated, then I can make that a help in my practice. In the irritation there is energy. Make use of the energy. Get ready to catch it when it blows, so that it does not carry away.

So, in the course of forty-nine years, the Buddha guided people according to their individual faculties. **'Thus he preached with one voice through all realms, while sentient beings each obtained benefits according to their kind.'** He preached with one voice – he just preached the Dharma – the Way. He never said what the Dharma was, or what his insight was. The Dharma – 'one voice, through all realms, while sentient beings each obtained benefits according to their kind.' Following completely, or half, or not at all; depending on how we listen, whether we listen at all – because sometimes we don't even listen, though we think we do. And when we have listened correctly, then also putting it into practice.

Master Daie makes a comparison – sentient beings each benefiting according to their kind, **'It's like one gust of the east wind, and the myriad grasses all bend down.'** There's just one gust of wind and all the grasses bend down. **'The Dharma preached by the Buddha is also like this.'** It's the same Dharma, reaching all who come in touch with it. But to what extent they are touched by it; to what extent they even hear it – that is another question.

There is a rather good analogy of Mara, the king of the demons, who one day swallowed the sun and proudly told his subjects, 'I'm not going to spit that sun out, I'm going to keep it forever!' But on earth all became dark, nothing grew anymore and living beings got hungry and were despairing. They went and begged the Buddha. 'Please help us, please, please go and speak to Mara and help us in our despair.' And the Buddha sent for the king of the demons, and he said, 'Look here, the poor beings on earth have nothing, they are dying; it is dark and unpleasant, and nothing grows, just because you have swallowed the sun. Do spit it out and give the sun back to the world.'

But even before the Buddha had finished speaking, Mara said, 'Ohhh!' and ran back to his own realm, spitting the sun out on his way. When he got back to his own realm, all his subjects asked, 'But what happened? What did the Buddha say? After all, you said you would never, ever give the sun back again – and now look how you come running back! What did he say?' 'Well,' said the king of the demons, 'What he said was, that if I did not spit out the sun, he would catch me and crush me to bits, he would grind my bones and he would mix them with my marrow, and he would roast it – he said all those terrible things; and I knew he would do it! I couldn't help it!' Yes, it's a good analogy, isn't it? Because what we hear is very, very often not what is really said, but what filters through our consciousness. That is why Chinese Whispers is such a funny game.

So perhaps one of the good training devices is to learn to listen. And for that I have a funny true story. Many years ago, at a Buddhist Society Summer School, two Benedictine monks from the nearby Prinknash Abbey came to visit us. A young man who at that time was staying with us in Shobo-an, the Zen Centre, was having great difficulty with obedience. During a coffee break he asked the Benedictine monks about obedience. The elder of the brothers said, 'Well, the word comes from the Latin and actually means listening, to listen,' and then went on to explain. When later asked what else had been said, the young man ruefully admitted that he had been so startled by the initial statement that he did not hear anything more after that. The Dharma preached by the Buddha is like one gust of the east wind, and the myriad grasses all bend down. All get touched. Whether the Path is then followed or not is up to us.

Master Daie continues, and this is equally a very, very important point: **'If he had had the intent to create benefit in all realms, then this would have been preaching the Dharma egotistically.'** If he had had the intent to create benefit everywhere: lecturing, proselytising, trying to convert, then this would have been preaching the Dharma egotistically. You cannot preach the Dharma egotistically. You remember that all intention misses the target; and we also know what a real do-gooder is – well, that's why we have got the word. The intention sticks out, and we resent it. It is not really meeting the purpose.

'To want to cause myriad beings to gain deliverance according to their kind: isn't this after all impossible?' And quick as a flash I come and say, 'But in the Four Great Vows, isn't it said that sentient beings are numberless and I vow to assist them all? And here he says that's wrong, that it's egotistical to want to cause myriad beings to gain deliverance according to their kind and is impossible?'

Here we come again to that one gust of the east wind and all grasses bending, but not to pushing the Dharma down unwilling throats. As long as there is any want, there is also ego. As long as there is ego there is intent. And as long as there is intent, it goes off the rails and goes wrong. It creates dissent, it creates aggression, but it does not come to any benefit. If only we could begin to realise that and learn it.

What is behind those Four Vows is something very different, because there we again go into the *Brahma Viharas*, into the Four Divine Abodes. The first one is *maitri* or *metta*, which is often translated as loving-kindness, but we will call it simply goodwill, because if the heart is really freed from the stranglehold of I, then its natural warmth, which is inherent in it, begins to flow of itself. It is in this flowing of the heart which touches, and it is in this touching that the Buddha-dharma is best spread; spreads itself readily. There is no more 'I' and there is no more wanting; there is just a natural adaptation and a oneness with whatever is. That is what is meant by the Four Great Vows. And 'I want' – that does not come into it anymore, because there is no I that can want. It naturally reveals itself, it naturally flows, and it naturally touches, because the human heart is the human heart, and since we all have such a human heart, in the outflow of such a really completely empty human heart there is only warmth and with it the understanding that touches immediately and cannot be gainsaid.

That is what the Four Vows are about and if we really bow our head and listen to the Buddha-dharma and wholeheartedly practise it, that will empty the heart and also bring the warmth and the understanding which not only is the fulfilment of our own heart but which is also for the sake and for the benefit of all beings. Shall we leave it at that, please?

LETTER 19 to TSENG SHU-CH'IH (continued)

THE TEXT

Haven't you read how Sariputra, at the assembly where the Perfection of Wisdom was preached, asked Manjushri, 'Don't all Buddhas, the Tathagatas, awaken to the realm of truth?' Manjushri said, 'No, Sariputra. Even the Buddhas cannot be found: how could there be Buddhas who awaken to the realm of truth? Even the realm of truth cannot be found: how could it be realised by the Buddhas?' See how those two men spurred each other on this way. When did they ever set their minds on anything? All the Buddhas and all the Patriarchs since antiquity have had a style like this in helping people. It's just that later descendants have lost the essence of the school, and set up their own individual sects, making up strange things and concocting marvels.

Master Daie asks, **'Have you not read how Sariputra, at the assembly where the Perfection of Wisdom was preached, asked Manjushri,'** The assembly where the Perfection of Wisdom was preached – we have already mentioned how the Buddha's teachings were divided into periods (s. letter 8). He first preached the *Kegon Sutra*, the *Flower Ornament Sutra*, but nobody could understand what it was about. So he decided that he had to start, so to speak, from scratch, and in the next period he preached the *Agama Sutras*, which in the Southern Tradition are known as the Pali Canon. And when that had properly settled in, he began introducing Mahayana themes with sutras like the *Vimalakirti Sutra*. After that he preached the full negation – based on Nagarjuna's teachings – with the *Prajnaparamita Sutras*, the Perfection of Wisdom, a radical taking the ground from under the feet. As an old Zen master put it, 'Last year I had still enough ground to put an awl in. This year even that has gone.' Nothing left. That is the Perfection of Wisdom, the *Prajnaparamita* cycle.

So Sariputra, at the assembly where the Perfection of Wisdom was preached, asked Manjushri, **'Don't all Buddhas, the Tathagatas, awaken to the realm of truth?'** Sariputra was one of the great disciples of the Buddha and Manjushri of course is a Bodhisattva. Sariputra asks the Bodhisattva, 'Don't all Buddhas, the Tathagatas, awaken to the realm of truth?' In a way it's a perfectly reasonable question, isn't it? But in a way it need not even be asked, because obviously all Buddhas awaken to the realm of truth – that is what makes them Buddhas, wouldn't you take it as that?

But Manjushri said, **'No, Sariputra. Even the Buddhas cannot be found: how could there be Buddhas who awaken to the realm of truth?'** Even the Buddhas cannot be found – what does that actually mean? Where is he, the Buddha? Why 'all the Buddhas?' That is where we come to Nagarjuna's Four Negations: neither is, nor is not, neither both is and is not, nor neither is or is not – neither, neither, neither; cut off, and cut off, and cut off, until there is no thought possible any more.

To begin with, and especially whilst one is young and full of 'I' and reason, that can be extremely annoying. I remember one time in Japan one of the Zen priests who spoke very good English was demonstrating this to Ruth Sasaki's zendo disciples. Holding up a book, he said, 'What is this?' 'Well, a book.' 'No.' 'A paper.' 'No.' And whatever we said, it was just 'no' and 'no' and 'no'. I remember that I got really cross and thought that was just sheer sophistry, absolute nonsense. It took quite some time until I understood. What is it? Fancies in the head, thoughts, all coming from 'I' which is a delusion, and which loves making further delusions; and 'I' likes nothing better than putting frills and flounces on those delusions, and creating more and more details about the delusions; whether it is about I or whether it is about the teaching, it doesn't matter.

So, if we have a carrot to help us on the way, we do not need to take it for real. If we have a finger pointing at the moon, we do not take the finger as the real thing; and even the moon might be a picture in the mind. So if we really follow through, led on by Nagarjuna and the Buddha's teachings, we are simply left with nothing. And the 'we' which is left with nothing is also not there. So if even the Buddhas cannot be found, how could there be Buddhas who awaken to the realm of truth? And it goes on, **'Even the realm of truth cannot be found: how could it be realised by the Buddhas?'** You see, from whatever angle you come, it can be dismantled at once. It is not seen.

By this time, I am likely to say, 'Then why have I been doing the training, if all this is just ideas in the head?' Well, we already mentioned that the Buddha actually realised this problem when he first preached the *Kegon Sutra* and found that it was too difficult for people to understand. So he started with the more basic teachings of the *Agama Sutras*. But even so, when the Buddha then started with the *Prajnaparamita* teachings, many arhats suddenly realised that there was in fact something else – as a matter of fact there was much more than they had originally thought and they got very upset. Not only were they very angry that there was something more, but also that it was something which they could not grasp. Because so far, they had been able to grasp it with their reason, but this was now beyond it; it was all taken away. The story is that half of the assembly left.

So, it's not so easy, unless we really bow into it and try to begin to see what is happening in our head, with our thoughts, with the pictures. That, in the Southern Teaching, is when the Buddha on his awakening said, 'Now I have seen you, builder of the house. Never will you build houses again.' But you can also say, 'Now I have seen you, maker of pictures. Never will you make pictures again.' Because this builder/painter makes pictures of objects that I want, need to have. 'Look around,' I say, 'There are objects all over the place.' And then we read in the *Prajnaparamita Heart Sutra*: 'No eye, no ear, nor nose, nor tongue' – and I say, 'No eye, no ear? But I see you and hear you. What is all that about?' However, if we are really doing something that we truly like, that we are really interested in, whatever it might be, are we then aware of ourselves? Where am I then? Have we ever really asked ourselves that?

So 'Even the Buddhas cannot be found. How could there be

Buddhas who awaken to the realm of truth? Even the realm of truth cannot be found. How could it be realised by the Buddhas?'

Master Daie continues, **'See how those two men'** – Sariputra and Manjushri – **'spurred each other on this way.'** Back and forth with questions and answers. **'When did they ever set their hearts on anything?'** Is it ever said, 'This is it'? I may have the idea that I see our head monk, Sogen, sitting there with his eyes carefully closed; but what do I actually see? Do I see Sogen? I see a form that, whilst it is in existence, has a certain shape, changing all the time, and has a certain name. But what it really is, I do not know. How can I know? Of course, I know Sogen, and his foibles, etc., but all these are machinations of my own mind. And if my own mind is object-oriented, as every 'I' is, then it's likely to be full of fancy ideas; otherwise, when not full of ideas, it's quite clear. That is what the Sixth Patriarch meant when in response to the verse, 'Carefully always wipe the mirror on its stand so that no dust can settle there,' he replied with, 'The bright mirror has no stand. When there is nothing at all, what dust can settle anywhere?' The mirror is not there, the dust is not there, nothing is there – that is the question, isn't it?

'When had those two ever set their hearts on anything?' But when we set our heart on something, as every 'I' inevitably does, then we can't see a way out. And when for a moment we forget all about it and are naturally there, it looks quite different. When playing, in the midst of playing, is the heart set on anything? Or does it just smoothly run with it?

Master Daie continues, **'All the Buddhas and all the patriarchs from of old have had a style like this in helping people.'** In the Zen training there is the caution not to show too much grandmotherly kindness; because then, **'It's just that later descendants have lost the essence of the school, and set up their own individual sects, making up strange things and concocting marvels.'** The palace of the Buddha, the greatness of the Mahayana, it's just all so many ghosts in the head. But once we have truly realised those ghosts for what they are, then the ground is taken from under our feet. And with that the fear, which every normal I is naturally possessed of, is gone. Because, like the palm and back of the hand, I and fear are inseparable; and as long as I am there, separate as I feel myself naturally from everything else, there is also fear. Hence, I try to shore myself up, and to make myself secure.

And this is where we come into the basic Buddhist teachings of the Three Marks of Existence, of which *anatta* – No-I – is one. In my ignorance I see myself as separate; and because I see myself as separate and am afraid, I want to make myself secure. There are two ways of doing so: one is by gobbling up and gobbling up until I have made myself the whole universe and am secure – by which time I have long since burst of course! In other words, it is not possible. The other way is by hitting out and thrashing and trying to get rid of everything. Or finally not wishing to reveal what a frail little being I am, I make pictures of myself which I try to project, claiming that I am completely cool, nothing can upset me. But if I think that I have reached permanent coolness without any feelings, how could that be walking the Buddha's Way? The Buddha was known as the All-Wise but also as the All-Compassionate One, and nowhere is it said that he no longer had feelings, or was beyond any kind of feelings. On the contrary, out of sheer compassion, in the forty-nine years of his teaching he walked all over India, willing to talk to whoever asked.

So if we think of the Buddha and his warm-heartedness, his great compassion, then we know that there is no Buddha beyond all that. Then we can admit, that yes, it's only that ghost of an I with its fancy ideas that thinks feelings are not necessary and we realise that it is not useful to go beyond all that in order to feel secure. Topple it over, throw it away, and comfortably settle yourselves down to peaceful training, walking the Buddha's Way, saying yes, and willingly walking it, trustingly walking it and eventually it will open out. It cannot open immediately, because particularly nowadays our 'I' is so entrenched that to really get a little bit away from it is a major undertaking.

As Master Daie already said, 'It's just that later descendants have lost the essence of the school, and set up their own individual sects, making up strange things and concocting marvels.' But with all of this they do not produce anything. As a matter of fact, it only leads to nothing – but to the empty nothing, not to the full, brim-full, alive, rolling, warm-hearted nothing, which naturally spreads itself without any kind of intention, just because it is there – like the sun that simply shines because shining is its nature. And we can realise that this is what our nature is, the Buddha-nature, that has no wanting, that feels, that laughs but is not carried away by laughter, and that cries but is not carried away by tears.

Perhaps we can take that home with us and allow that Buddha-nature – which is after all inherent in all of us – allow it a little bit of air, rather than pressing it down into a bottle, which is the body, by my fierce determined, clutching, calculating, manipulating I. No, let out what is there. Trust it. And with that trust comes the warmth; and with that comes a feeling of at-one-ness, related with everything that is. Can we take that home, please?

LETTER 20 to HSU SHOU-YUAN

The Text

A Patriarch said, 'As long as there is mental discrimination and calculating judgement, all the perceptions of one's own mind are dreams. If mind and consciousness are quiescent and extinct, without a single thought stirring, this is called correct awareness.' Once awareness is correct, then in your daily activities, twenty-four hours a day, when seeing form, hearing sound, smelling scent, tasting flavour, feeling touch, or knowing phenomena; whether walking, standing, sitting or lying down; whether speaking or silent, active or still, there is nothing that is not profound clarity. And since you do not engage in wrong thinking, all is pure, whether there is thinking or not. Once you have attained emptiness, when active you reveal the function of profound clarity, and when inactive you return to the essence of profound clarity. Though essence and function are distinguished, the profound clarity is one; like when you cut up sandalwood, each and every piece is sandalwood.

'A Patriarch said, "As long as there is mental discrimination and calculating judgement, all the perceptions of one's mind are dreams."' Mental discrimination: this is nice, this is ugly, this is high, that is low. And calculating judgment: this is better, that is worse, this is expensive, that is cheap. As long as there is any thinking, that's how it goes. If we carefully look into that, we cannot think except in pairs of opposites: white and black, high and low, etc. And so, in our thoughts we discriminate and judge. As long as this continues, 'all the perceptions of one's own mind are dreams' – that's what the patriarch said. It is actually as if each of us was a grid, consisting of our own notions, our own convictions, our own ideas and ideals; and through this grid we perceive. We cannot see directly; it is always filtered through that. So, quite rightly, 'all the perceptions of one's own mind are dreams.' They are not really there.

If I look at the altar over there, I only see my conceptions of it. We can only see our ideas and perceptions. We cannot see what is. There is a difference between my seeing, which is always I-focused, and which is filtered through my notions, and the Buddha-seeing, which is simply seeing like a mirror – what falls into it is reflected back.

As long as there is discrimination and judgement, all our perceptions are dreams. But, continues the patriarch, **"If mind and consciousness are quiescent and extinct, without a single thought stirring, this is called correct awareness."** If all thoughts, all consciousness, I-consciousness that is, are calmed and have died out, have fallen off, then there isn't a single thought stirring and this is called correct awareness. Then it is just reflecting; like a mirror, as we said, that exactly reflects, down to the last hair, what falls into it. It doesn't add anything; it doesn't take anything away. And it doesn't hold on to it either.

'Without a single thought stirring, this is called correct awareness.' That's what the patriarch said and we are reminded of Bodhidharma, with his 'directly pointing at the human heart, seeing into its nature, and becoming Buddha.' Or we can think of the Sixth Patriarch: 'Before thinking of good and bad, what is the True Face before father and mother were born?' Before thinking of good and bad – again we are the thinking; before thinking of good and bad, before thinking of anything. That quietness – not quietness only, but also that vast openness – that is what we are slowly going towards as we walk the Buddha's Way. 'Without a single thought' also means without I, because I am only a thought. That might seem a rather strange statement. Then we think of our Western philosophical tradition – 'I think, therefore I am' – which is perfectly true, because I am the thinker. But what happens if there is no more thinking? What happens then to I-I-I-I? That is what I am frightened of. And this is why we need that long and thorough training.

When it really comes down to it, before a single thought stirs, without any thinking – which also means without I, or I-consciousness – this is then called correct awareness.

That ends the quotation of the patriarch and Master Daie then goes on to explain, **'Once the awareness is correct,'** – and there are no thoughts and no I ghosting about – **'then in your daily activities, twenty-four hours a day, when seeing form, hearing sound, smelling scent, tasting flavour, feeling touch, or knowing phenomena, whether walking, standing, sitting or lying down,'** – all four positions – **'whether speaking or silent, active or still'** – in other words in anything and everything – **'there is nothing that is not profound clarity.'** This is the correct awareness. And that correct awareness – acting or not acting, doing or not doing – is not I-engendered. It comes from the true open awareness, without I. Perception without I, and in that perception, there is only profound clarity. Whatever is done is only in profound clarity.

Master Daie continues, **'And since you do not engage in wrong thinking, all is pure, whether it is thinking or not.'** We can also mention that whenever we come across 'pure' and 'purity' in Buddhist texts, it is better understood as 'empty'. So, when not engaged in wrong thinking' – because with I being out of the way there is no wrong thinking – then in that vast clarity 'all is empty and pure, whether there is thinking or not.' In other words, the thinking is also no longer warped by I-notions and is therefore clear, empty and pure. Two and two make four, not five, not three.

Master Daie continues, **'Once you have attained purity, when active you reveal the function of profound clarity.'** We have to look carefully at that 'reveal' in 'when active you reveal the function of profound clarity.' Perhaps it would be better to see it more neutrally as, 'when active, the profound clarity reveals itself in functioning.' It is not 'you reveal', because you are not there. The function is different from the essence. The function of profound clarity, when active – shall we say, when active the profound clarity is functioning in that activity. **'And when inactive, you return to the essence of profound clarity.'** The essence of profound clarity: this is the home ground. When activity is engaged, that is the function; and the function is the strength. If there was only essence, and nothing else, and that essence was not capable of functioning, what would be the use of it? This is the wisdom and power of the Tathagata that all beings are endowed with – this is the essence and the function as well. Just wisdom alone – if we can't function, it's not wisdom. And if it functions without wisdom, then it becomes the passions.

And so, 'when active you reveal the function of profound clarity; and when inactive you return to the essence of profound clarity.' There's something very clear about that: if that is truly there within that purity of emptiness, or that empty purity, then there is a particular feel about it that you can see and notice in a person: when functioning, not hurried but totally there; and when inactive, totally there. Totally sitting in the chair; totally sweeping out in the street. This totally, at-one-with, no longer separated by ideas and thoughts; all this is profound clarity.

Master Daie then says, to make quite sure that we do not mistake it, **'Though essence and function are distinguished'** – the essence and its function – **'the profound clarity is one: like when you cut up sandalwood, each and every piece is sandalwood.'** Essence and function are distinguished. The profound clarity itself is one. Depending on the circumstances it is both: quiescent – essence; and active – function. The profound clarity itself is one. The example given here is a very good one. 'Like when you cut up sandalwood, each and every piece is sandalwood.' You can't just have one piece of sandalwood and then the rest is something else; each and every piece is sandalwood. That is what we are headed for. And we start on this way for the function which is the full power of the Tathagata. If it is not the full power, it will fall down very quickly; it's too much of this or too much of that.

And in order to come to that, we need to start with meditation and Daily Life Practice; or actually, first Daily Life Practice and then meditation. If we really, truly give ourselves into our daily activities, we very soon find out that when it comes right down to it, we can't actually do it, because there are hundreds of moments in a day when we actually say, 'No.' We have long since learned to ignore that 'No', because it's neither here nor there. But if it has to be done, it has to be done, and it can be easily done, if it's only a little 'No'. But because of ignoring those little 'No's' most of the time, our strength peters out; and when it comes to a larger one, then it rebels and digs its hind legs in like a mule. So the strength to overcome that is not there. This is why along with the practice we also need to keep the form; and within the form adapt to what is. Immediately I rear up and say, 'Am I supposed to become an automaton, then? This is surely not the way of the Buddha!' Yet a new monk in the monastery is judged by two things. First of all, whether he keeps the form under all circumstances; that is expected of him. But he is also judged by how quickly he can completely adapt to the ways and the rules of the monastery. He's not told that; he's supposed to keep his eyes open, and to closely follow what he sees and to give himself into that. If he cannot adapt fairly quickly, he's not considered very suitable. And for this adaptation it is necessary to keep the form, because the form is the preserver of strength; and this preserver of strength is the important thing.

As I have already mentioned, when I first came to Japan, I used to ask Zen monks and lay practitioners, what made them interested in Zen training. And they all said, 'Strength!' I did not understand this. It took me quite some time until I realised that power of function, under all circumstances, good, bad or indifferent, which is so important, and which we can't do. When something goes right against us, we usually have very little power of functioning except by rebelling. We are the only creatures, the only sentient beings in that position because every other sentient being is perfectly capable of functioning. Whether an ant, elephant or tiger, they reliably act and function in conformity with the way of their nature. They do not indulge in thinking, they just reliably function as the specific sentient being they are. Only we, because of our thinking, do not function according to our nature as a human being. We only function according to how we think and with that we have lost most of the power. Since that completely hems us in, we are either totally inhibited, or we blindly throw ourselves about; but we certainly very rarely act as human beings. And acting as a human being, not only in our actions, but according to the Buddhist teachings also in speech and in thought: we are far from being human yet.

So, in our training, *sila* practice, the form and behaviour are strongly emphasised. It takes quite some time to cultivate that, but once it is forged, it goes into the body and then the body can contain an eruption of the emotions in quite a different and much easier way. The ability to keep the form makes it possible in all situations to behave in a decent human way.

So first of all, we need the form in order to come into the form of a human being. When that is there, then it can open up. And as a human being, with a human heart which is understanding of each other and in relationship with everything that is, that is when the Buddha Way then really ripens.

The Text

These days, there is a kind of phoney whose own standpoint is not genuine: they just teach people to control their minds and sit quietly, to sit at the point where the breath ceases. I call this lot pitiable. I am asking you to meditate in just this way, but though I instruct you like this, it's just that there is no other choice. If there really were something to work on in meditation this way, it would defile you. This mind has no real substance: how can you forcibly bring it under control? If you try to bring it under control, where do you put it? Since there is no place to put it, there are no times or seasons, no past or present, no ordinary people or sages, no gain or loss, no quiet or confusion. There is no name of profound clarity, and no essence of profound clarity, and no function of profound clarity, no one who speaks thus of profound clarity, and no one to hear such talk of profound clarity.

Ven. Myokyo-ni's Comments

This is Master Daie at his most direct. **'These days, there is a kind of phoney whose own standpoint** (insight) **is not genuine.'** They always have been there; they were there in Master Daie's time; they are also out there today; from one era to another. And we ourselves are also blinded by it. We often think that we get something from meditation; that one can meditate in order to get something. I know of one lot who meditate, for example, to get a red car.

So, there are phoneys who teach meditation, though lacking genuine insight. **'They teach people to control their minds and sit**

quietly; to sit at the point where the breath ceases.' Extinguishing themselves, deadening themselves to the point where there is hardly any life left. **'I call this lot pitiable. I am asking you to meditate in just this way; but though I instruct you like this, it's just that there is no other choice.'** When it really comes to meditation, speaking of it in the Buddhist way: it is just making the inner space empty, in order to become part of a vast inner roominess. And that means that the thoughts are not there. But to forcibly control and to suppress the thoughts, is only likely to, sooner or later, produce a blow-out.

But actually, when it comes down to it, meditation is our natural state. It is a quiet state of taking in what is, and going with what is. But since this is no longer possible for us human beings, in our delusion we have to learn it. We first learn it in our Daily Life Practice: giving ourselves into what we are doing rather than 'I doing'; and it's not 'I meditate' and it's not 'my meditation'. And it's not what method of meditation – it is just giving myself quietly into sitting quietly.

So, once we have begun to get the feel of Daily Life Practice a little bit, then this sitting quietly is one of the things that we have to cultivate. Again, it is not 'I count' or 'I follow the breath' but it is 'I give myself quietly into counting – one – two – .' The counting will help the quietening. No need to question the point where the breath ceases, nor is it a question of long or short breaths; just as it naturally goes. When it truly becomes quiet, and there is familiarity with that quietness, then, for example in *kinhin*, it is then taken out into movement. When it holds there too, then in the moving it remains quiet too.

In all Buddhist schools there are the two stages of meditation. First of all, there is the quietening meditation, *samatha*; and when that is truly established, then comes the practice of *vipassana*, the insight meditation. The Southern School goes directly on to that insight. In our case, that is when we are given a koan. To try to work on a koan before that quietness is established is merely an intellectual exercise that brings absolutely nothing, except that it makes us more deluded than we already are.

So, 'to sit to the point where the breath ceases,' etc., is all unnecessary. There is a very good Zen story for this. Master Matsu was one of the very great Zen masters. As a young monk, he was very devoted, and quite convinced that the only way to become enlightened was to meditate, meditate, meditate! Whenever he had a free moment, he would settle himself into a corner and meditate. His master realised that this young monk had good potential, but that he was obviously barking up the wrong tree. So, one day, as he was sitting in the corner of the yard meditating, the master came and sat himself down next to him and asked the young monk, 'What are you doing here?' And rather pleased to be noticed by the great master, he said, 'I'm trying to become a Buddha.' The master picked up a tile and began rubbing it on a stone. The young monk could not help but see what the master was doing, and could not stop himself from asking, 'And what are you doing, master?' 'I'm making a mirror,' he replied and went on rubbing. Absolutely baffled, the monk blurted out, 'But no amount of rubbing a tile will make a mirror out of it!' 'And no amount of meditation will make a Buddha out of a clod!' That was the end of the young Matsu trying to be holy.

To actually encourage controlling the mind and sitting to the point where the breath ceases, is truly pitiable, as Master Daie says. And though he also instructs in the *samatha* practice, he does not put it like that. There is no other choice, but to first of all begin with *samatha*, with the quietness, because as long as I hop around like dried peas on a hot shovel, there is not a chance of seeing anything. But as far as meditation is concerned, again it is the natural state, without I, when the delusion of I has fallen off.

Therefore, says Master Daie, **'If there really were something to** work on in meditation this way, it would defile you. This mind has no real substance.' We know that. Thought, this mind, our thoughts, the delusion of I, all have no real substance, and since it has no real substance, **'How can you forcibly bring it under control?'** You can suppress it, but you cannot bring it under control. How can you forcibly bring it under control? How can one forcibly bring under control something that is not?

Master Daie then says, **'Since there is no place to put it, there are no times or seasons, no past or present, no ordinary people or sages, no gain or loss, no quiet or confusion.'** In other words, when there is the realisation, the true realisation that there is no place to put it, because it doesn't exist, then the usual hubbub of the chattering mind, of the chattering monkey-mind, becomes quiet.

We cannot think without opposites. As long as we have opposites, we have options. When we have no options left, we are out of the thinking, and we can just go with the flow. That's why we have places like our temple, and need to have places like this or a monastery somewhere. Once through the gate, we have no options left. If we have places like this and come frequently enough, then sooner or later that carries over into our daily lives.

Quite few people who come here regularly for a few days or for longer periods have told me that as they come through the door, they can lay down everything, and all they need to do is to go with the way things are here. To respond to the clappers, to go with the timetable and so on. They do not need to worry about anything at all. It's a real letting-go and happy time for them. There is a quiet harmony with what is. Nothing can take hold.

And I know it myself from the cold winters when I lived in Japan, with bare feet in the monastery, no heating and sometimes even with the windows open. I dreaded leaving my little room and going down the hill to the monastery for the evening sitting. So in my tiny room I used to put on my little kerosene stove full blast, and I almost hugged it to the last minute, to really warm myself through and through, so that the warmth would stay with me a little bit. Then I had to run down the hill to be in time for the sitting – occasionally even being a little late. But miraculously, once I was through that gate, there was no more problem. That's just how it was. I just ran in, got my cushion out, sat myself down, and that was that. There was no more worry about cold, being late, this, that or the other. It was quite some time before I realised that on coming through that gate there was no more problem – well yes, it was cold, with bare feet on the floor, naturally it is cold – but once I was through that gate, I had no more option. That was that. Whilst I had the option, hugging the stove and wanting it warmer, and wanting to warm myself up, and not wanting to go, and frightened of going, and thinking I must go now, and just one minute longer – it was intense turmoil. But through that gate – in a flash, finished!

That is what we actually rob ourselves of, the joy of flowing with it, if we do not give in. Because it's not through meditation that I get warmer or closer to quietude or whatever it is. Master Daie says, 'If there were really something to work on in meditation in this way, it would defile you.' There is another story of meditation defiling you if you really try to suppress and suppress. It's again a story I've told many times, but it's a very important one.

An elderly monk on pilgrimage came to beg at the house of an elderly, well-to-do lady, with a lot of land. She thought, 'Well, if I asked the monk to stay, built him a hut up on the mountain there and sent him his food every day, he would stay here and do his practices, and we would all benefit by it.' So this is what she did, and the monk stayed.

After several years, she was curious to know what this monk was up to, how he was progressing in his practice. So she said to her granddaughter, a very nice-looking young girl, 'Today you take him his food up the mountain, and after you put it down on the table, go up to him and give him a big hug. Then run down to me and tell me how he reacted.

The young girl came back, visibly shaken, and said, 'I did exactly what you said and he pushed me away forcefully, saying, "For the last three years there has been no sap in this old trunk!"' And the old woman said, 'If I had known he was such a one! For years I have kept a block of wood' – and she ran up the mountain, drove the monk out and burned the hut down.

Now, if we really look at it, was the monk really free! He behaved correctly according to the rules, didn't he? So why did the old woman do that? It's not that he did not accept the advances of the young girl; but it was his response to the situation – the roughness with which he did it – which shows that he was terrified of his own passions, frightened of what might happen if he broke the rules and gave in. But if he had been a really mature old monk, settled, quiescent, he would have laughed with a friendly face, and said, 'Now, now, little girl, what do you think you are up to?' and perhaps given her a gentle pat on the shoulder and said, 'Go back home to your granny!'

You see? These are the things we can only too easily fall into, if we are not willing to keep giving in. So giving in we slowly become empty – not 'we' become empty, because we can't – but the heart becomes empty. With that empty heart, the *mushin* of which there is so much talk in Zen – with this, it is also seen that thoughts have no real substance. Yes, there is the relative and the absolute truth; but this again is only a concept. It is all just a shadow play, a dream. If you want to avoid the dream becoming a nightmare, then let it empty itself out. Realise there is no thing called mind that has any real substance. A thought – however much we are used to thoughts, however many thoughts run about in our head – how long can you keep hold of a thought? I think the only thought we can hang on to for most of the day is I. But otherwise, we are hopping about like a grasshopper. The chattering monkey-mind. It has no real substance. It has no place. How can you forcibly bring it under control? And even if you could, then, having got it under control, where do you put it? Where is a place to put it?

When it has become all quiet and spacious, with no hindrances and no obstructions, 'there are no times or seasons, no past or present, no ordinary people or sages.' All these opposites are in our thoughts, because we cannot think except in pairs of opposites. This is why in ancient Chinese what we call 'everything' is simply put as 'the two opposites'. 'No gain or loss, no quiet or confusion.' They have cancelled out, have vanished.

Master Daie concludes, **'There is no name of profound clarity, and no essence of profound clarity, and no function of profound clarity,'** and what's more, in this spacious roominess, **'there is no one who speaks thus of profound clarity, and no one to hear such talk of profound clarity.'** Such things are set up to help, but these kinds teachings are only like medicine to cure specific illnesses. This is the usual analogy. But when the illness is cured, do we then go on taking the medicine? If we did, it would poison us. So, what we now come down to once the medicine is taken away, is nothing but just the ordinary here and now. Master Rinzai said, 'Just be your ordinary selves. Do not give yourselves airs.'

Living in the past, longing for the future, our wants and passions – all this is actually missing the life here and now. If we realise the life here and now, there is just a unity of aliveness and a joyous participation in what is. In our case, as human beings, acting in a human way and responding to the changing situations as they arise; always in the here and now, not planning what I'm going to do tomorrow, or regretting what I have not done yesterday. All this is quite unnecessary. Functioning, fully and totally in that here and now: that is what actually rewards the heart and that is what the heart truly and sincerely is longing for. I, the fool, believe that if I can know things, then I will be satisfied. But the heart is totally disinterested in knowing anything. The heart wants to participate. And if it is hindered in this participation by my this and my that, then it is unhappy, dissatisfied, which is the state that the Buddha called *dukkha*, which is usually translated as suffering, but is the basic dissatisfaction of wanting something, yet not really knowing what. But the heart wants to be once more united with what is, and functioning in response to what is. The ordinary here and now.

Would you like to take that home from this weekend *sesshin* and ponder it, and keep it as a talisman? And when too much thought of I this, that and the other comes up, then think of this ordinary here and now and participation.

FURTHER READING

ON MASTER TA HUI (DAIE SOKO)

Cleary, Christopher, *Swampland Flowers: The Letters and Lectures of Zen Master Ta Hui*. [Selections from 瞿汝稷 Qu Ruji's (1548-1610) 指月錄; Zhiyue lu, *Records of Pointing at the Moon*, Vols. 31-32] New York, Grove Press, 1977, Shambhala Publications, 2006.

Broughton, Jeffrey, *The Letters of Chan Master Dahui Pujue*, edited and translated by Jeffrey L. Broughton and with Elise Yoko Watanabe, Oxford University Press, 2017.

Whitfield, Randolph S. *The Recorded Sayings of Chan Master Dahui Pujue: The Letters*, Translated by Randolph S. Whitfield, Norderstedt, BoD, 2023.

BOOKS BY VENERABLE MYOKYO-NI

Wisdom of the Zen Masters, New York, New Directions Books, 1976, (under her pre-ordination name Irmgard Schlögl).

– *The Zen Way*, London, Sheldon Press, 1977, Zen Centre, 1987, The Buddhist Society, 2021.

– *Gentling the Bull: The Ten Bull Pictures, a Spiritual Journey*, London, Zen Centre, 1988.

– *Living Buddhism*, Square One Publication on behalf of The Zen Centre, 2000.

– *The Daily Devotional Chants of the Zen Centre* (2008), reprinted as *The Great Wisdom Gone Beyond*, London, The Buddhist Society, 2021.

– *Look and See*, London, The Buddhist Society, 2017.

– *Yoka Daishi's Realizing the Way* (translation and commentary), London, The Buddhist Society, 2017.

– *Towards Wholeness*, London, The Buddhist Society, 2018.

TRANSLATIONS BY VEN. MYOKYO-NI

The Record of Rinzai, Berkeley, Shambala, 1976 (under her pre-ordination name Irmgard Schlögl) (Reprint), London, The Buddhist Society, 2021.

– *The Ceasing of Notions* with Comments by Soko Morinaga Roshi (1988), Reprint, Wisdom Publications (with Michelle Bromley), 2012.

– *The Discourse on The Inexhaustible Lamp of the Zen School* (with Yoko Okuda), London, Zen Centre, 1989.